Acknowledgments

IN THE CREATION OF THIS BOOK I am deeply indebted to Alan Beatts, for providing the crucial suggestion that brought the skyblades into focus; to Benito Cereno, for much needed Latin assistance; to Paul Cornell, whose excellent *British Summertime* helped suggest the structure of the present volume; to Lou Anders, for commissioning this monster when it was only a few bare paragraphs of synopsis and for accepting the final draft when it came in far more lengthy than estimated; and to my wife, Allison Baker, and our daughter, Georgia, for putting up with me during the months and years in which this story occupied so much of my attention.

End of the Century

Also by Chris Roberson

Novels

Voices of Thunder
Cybermancy Incorporated
Any Time at All
Here, There & Everywhere
Paragaea: A Planetary Romance
The Voyage of Night Shining White
X-Men: The Return
Set the Seas on Fire
The Dragon's Nine Sons
Iron Jaw and Hummingbird
Three Unbroken

Series

Shark Boy and Lava Girl Adventures: Book 1
Shark Boy and Lava Girl Adventures: Book 2

CHRIS ROBERSON

End ᴼᶠ ᵗʰᵉ Century

an imprint of **Prometheus Books**
Amherst, NY

Published 2009 by Pyr®, an imprint of Prometheus Books

Inquiries should be addressed to
Pyr
59 John Glenn Drive
Amherst, New York 14228–2119
VOICE: 716–691–0133, ext. 210
FAX: 716–691–0137
WWW.PYRSF.COM

13 12 11 10 09   5 4 3 2 1

Library of Congress Cataloging-in-Publication Data

Roberson, Chris.
    End of the century / Chris Roberson.
       p. cm.
    ISBN 978–1–59102–697–6 (pbk. : acid-free paper)
    1. London (England)—Fiction. 2. Time travel—Fiction. I. Title.

PS3618.O3165E63 2009
813'.6—dc22

                         2008046961

Printed in the United States on acid-free paper

for

Michael Moorcock,

Alan Moore,

and Kim Newman

CHAPTER ONE

Twilight

498 Anno Domini

IT WAS LATE MORNING when Galaad first caught sight of the city, looming in the east. The trip from Glevum should have taken six days, but with the winter's cold, it had taken him nearer ten. Ten days of icy bridges over sluggish streams, the ground hard and cold beneath his thin woolen blanket at night even when he went to the trouble of clearing away the snow, freezing rain sometimes falling from the unforgiving gray skies, and harsh winds blowing when it didn't. Had he ridden, he'd have made the journey in a fraction of the time, but he'd not been on a horse since the accident, and couldn't conscience doing so now.

Many of the hobnails from the soles of his *caligae* marching boots were missing, knocked loose and left along the roadside as signs of his passing, and those areas of his feet's skin not already thickened with calluses were now blistered, bloody, and tender. His left knee was swollen and sore from a fall two days before on an icy patch of road, but while the joint did not have a complete range of motion, it could support his full weight, though lances of pain shot up and down his leg when he did, so that he was able to continue, albeit with a pronounced limp.

The bundle on his back was lighter, if nothing else, now that he'd eaten nearly all the supplies of food he'd brought with him from his home in

Powys, though of course that meant that had he not reached his destination soon he'd have begun slowly to starve. But it was a point not worth dwelling upon, so Galaad pushed it from his thoughts.

Galaad had never before been this far from home. He'd been born in the municipality of Glevum in the kingdom of Powys, twenty-one years before, and had seldom strayed far from the banks of the river Sabrina. The western kingdoms had been largely spared the ravages of the Saeson invasion of Britannia, so that throughout most of his childhood, Galaad had known peace. By the time he was a full adult with a child of his own, the rest of the island knew peace as well, and had one man to thank for it. But the more Galaad's steps had brought him east, the more he saw upon the land the scars of the Saeson occupation.

In much of the west, the old order of the Romans had remained. The towns still survived, though their populations had diminished, tenants paid landlords, community farmlands were tended. But as Galaad had walked through regions where the war with the Saeson had been close at hand, it was clear that the public authority had collapsed. Towns stood abandoned, farms gone to seed and houses left to the elements. The remaining Roman nobility had fled across the channel to Gaul, ahead of the advancing Saeson hordes, while the peasantry had retreated to the rural areas of the west, watched over by former town magistrates who now styled themselves as landholders and kings.

But one man was bringing order back to the island, restoring authority and the rule of law. This was the same man who had driven the Saeson back to their huddled enclaves in the south and east, and established his court in the former Roman capital that lay between to hold the two groups of Saeson apart and to act as a bulwark against them for the rest of the island.

If any would know the meaning of Galaad's strange visions, the young man was convinced, it would be he. Perhaps then the phantom that haunted him could be laid to rest.

Limping, his feet blistered and bloody, his legs and back aching, Galaad approached the high city walls with a prayer in his heart. At the end of a long journey, he had finally reached Caer Llundain, home of the Count of Britannia and victor of Badon, the High King Artor.

Galaad, for his sins, did not know that his journey was only beginning.

Galaad's paternal grandfather had been to Caer Llundain, then still called
Londinium, before the Saeson revolt and the migrations of the nobility to
Gaul, when the city was still crowded with Roman citizens from all over the
empire. Ships had sailed up and down the river Tamesa, bringing trade and
traders from Gaul, Hibernia, and the Middle Sea, importing wine and textiles, exporting tin and silver. The capital's streets bustled not simply with
Romans and Britons, but were painted in the many hues of the Roman
empire—Germanics, Arabians, Syrians, Parthians, Africans, and more. Even
with the formal secession of Britannia from the empire more than a generation before, when the emperor Honorius had instructed the nation to look
after its own defense, some relations with Rome had been maintained, church
envoys sent to the island on rare occasion to root out the Pelagian and Arian
heresies, reports of the Vandals' sack of Rome carried back by traders. Londinium's brightest hours might have been behind it, its future uncertain, but
in those days the city still thrived.

But that had been in the time of the grandfathers. Galaad had grown up
hearing stories about the capital in the east, and had dreamt of seeing it at
the height of its powers, but that day was long past, the sun that had risen
over Londinium long since set. The city was now known as Caer Llundain, no
longer a Roman city, but a Britonnic one. And the empire to which it had
once been the furthest outpost was also no more, the last emperor Romulus
Augustus deposed by the Goths the year before Galaad was born. By the time
he had taken his first breath, the empire was only a memory.

Galaad was not sure what lay beyond the city walls that loomed before
him, but he knew it would not be the cosmopolitan metropolis of his grandfather's stories. For a young man from a relatively small municipality like
Glevum, though, the sheer scale of Caer Llundain was still intimidating. The
wall before him stood some eighteen feet high and ran right around the city,
constructed of gray ragstone hauled miles inland from Cantium. The bridge
he had to cross just to reach the western gatehouse spanned a ditch some six
feet deep and nine feet wide. And if the wall itself was not imposing enough,

then the foreboding bastions placed at intervals along the wall were sure to do the job. The bastions themselves, finally, looked like a child's playthings next to the gatehouse. Almost one hundred feet wide, side to side, the western gate was flanked on either side by square towers of gray stone, their red-tiled roofs towering far overhead, two or three times the height of the wall itself.

Londinium had never fallen to the Saeson, in all the long decades of the war, and looking at the city wall now, Galaad was sure that he understood why.

Two arches opened through the thick city walls, one for traffic leading into the city, one for traffic leading out, and a gatekeeper stood in each, leaning on long-bladed javelins, ridged helmets upon their heads. As the sun climbed to its zenith and the hour neared midday, Galaad stepped off the footbridge and onto the threshold of the gatehouse.

"Who approaches?" The gatekeeper's tone was bored, almost sleepy, his words slurred and near inaudible. It took Galaad a moment to parse the strangely accented Britonnic speech, and then he hastened to answer.

"Galaad." He paused, not sure what other information was needed. "From Glevum," he went on in Britonnic. "That's in Powys, in the west."

The two gatekeepers exchanged a look, and one rolled his eyes while the other returned his attention to Galaad. "And what's your business here, Galaad of Powys?"

"I come to see the High King Artor, Count of Britannia," Galaad said, in a rush. "You see, I am plagued with visions, and I'm sure that if I were able to relate them to the high king, then he might be able to . . ."

The gatekeeper who had spoken raised his hand, motioning Galaad to silence. "Do you bring craftwork to trade?" He spoke as if by rote, without emotion or passion.

Galaad considered this for a moment, and shook his head.

"Do you bear arms?"

Galaad began to shake his head, then thought better of it. He raised a finger, begging patience, and slung his bundle from his back. Slipping loose the knotted thong that held the bundle together, he pulled out a blade sheathed in cracked and greasy hide. "I have a sword," he said, proffering it.

The other gatekeepeer stepped forward, and holding his javelin in one hand took Galaad's sword in his other. Then, his javelin resting against the crook of his elbow, he tried to pull the blade from the scabbard, but only with repeated attempts and considerable effort would the blade come free. It was an ancient leaf-blade sword, the dulled blade black with rust, the leather wrapping of the hilt pulled and cracked with age.

"It belonged to my grandfather's grandfather," Galaad explained, helpfully.

"You must be so proud," the gatekeeper said, his tone affectless, and ramming the blade back into the scabbard, he returned it to Galaad, then nodded over his shoulder at his companion.

"Um, yes," Galaad agreed, somewhat confused. He tucked the sword back into his bundle and began retying the thongs.

"You are free to enter the city," the first gatekeeper said, returning to his script. "Know that the law of the High King is supreme here, as it is everywhere his rule extends, and that any infractions against his authority will be severely handled."

Galaad stood, slinging the bundle back on his back. "I understand," he said quickly.

The gatekeeper stepped aside, with a quick glance to his fellow, and then fixed Galaad with an amused stare. "In that case, welcome to Caer Llundain, man of Powys. And good fortune to you."

Galaad smiled and nodded.

"You're going to need it," the other gatekeeper added with a rough laugh, his voice low.

Galaad's smile froze on his face, but instead of answering he scurried ahead, entering the momentary darkness of the tunnel through the nine-foot-thick wall. A handful of limping steps later, he walked back out into the cold winter light, and found himself in the city of Caer Llundain, home of King Artor.

CHAPTER TWO

Jubilee

1897 AD

T HE LIGHT OF THE LATE MORNING SUN streamed through the open shutters of the sitting room, dust motes dancing in the beam, while the bones of the breakfast meal idled on the table. The lilting tones of a flute echoed from the paneled walls, an improvised air on the tune of one of Child's border ballads of Scotland, played by the man who leaned against the mantle, his eyes closed and his expression serene. The woman at the table, intent on the morning's penny papers, tapped her foot in time, unconscious of the action. It was early June, and outside the temperature already climbed, the Marylebone streets bustling with the morning's trade and traffic, but within the walls of Number 31, York Place, it was still relatively calm and cool. For the moment, at any rate.

There were some, even in this enlightened modern age, who might have considered it untoward that a man and a woman should pass the time together unchaperoned, which unmarried couples could not do without inviting comment, and which married couples seldom did at all. But this particular man and this singular woman rarely bothered themselves with what others might say about them, individually or collectively, and hardly gave the matter a moment's consideration.

"Blank?" the woman said, looking up from her papers and interrupting the impromptu recital.

"Yes, Miss Bonaventure?" The man called Sandford Blank lowered the flute from his lips, opening his eyes, and regarded his companion with a slight smile. "Something catch your interest in this morning's scandal sheets?"

"Not scandal," Roxanne Bonaventure answered, crossing her legs and turning in her chair to face Blank, folding a section of newspaper and laying it across her knee. "Or not precisely, rather. A bit of business that, were it to happen closer to home, I suspect you'd find of some interest."

Blank motioned with his flute. "Read on, Miss Bonaventure, read on."

Miss Bonaventure nodded and, smoothing the pulp paper against her knee, began to read aloud.

THE HISTORICAL HYDERABAD DIAMOND STOLEN.

CALCUTTA. It is reported from Hyderabad that the historical "Imperial" sold by Mr. Alexander Jacob, the dealer in jewels, to the Nizam has been stolen from the government Treasury of his Highness and replaced by a paste imitation. This has caused a great sensation. It is further reported that the Nizam intended to present the diamond to the Queen on the occasion of the Jubilee. The diamond in question formed the subject of a prolonged suit in India. Mr. Jacob, the original of the Mr. Isaacs of Mr. Marlon Crawford's novel, was charged in the High Court at Calcutta by the Nizam of Hyderabad with having criminally misappropriated the due of 25 lakhs, which had been deposited at a bank at Calcutta as earnest-money for the purchase of the diamond. The Nizam had in the first instance agreed to buy the stone, a gem of remarkable size and brilliance, for the sum of 46 lakhs of rupees, or nearly, and the sum of 25 lakhs was paid as security, pending the completion of the purchase, to Mr. Jacob, who was acting merely as a broker in the transaction. Eventually, owing to the intervention of the British resident, who objected to such lavish expenditures for an article of pure luxury, the Nizam declined to carry out the bargain, and, on Mr. Jacob making difficulties as to the return of the earnest, commenced a criminal suit, which terminated in the acquittal of the defendant.

"Stop there a moment, Miss Bonaventure, if you wouldn't mind."

Blank crossed to the shelves lining the far wall, and climbing up on the rolling ladder, pulled down the most recent *Whitaker's Almanac*. He consulted it for a brief moment, and then slapped the book shut with a satisfied air.

"Just as I suspected." Blank returned the book to its place on the shelf. "Miss Bonaventure, would you be so good as to wire the authorities in Hyderabad, at your earliest convenience, and ask them to take Mr. Jacob into custody? When they have done, they should check him for distinguishing marks, and when they discover the tattoo of a crown of thorns surrounding the initials 'J.A.,' they should send word to New Scotland Yard, whom I suspect will be very interested to hear the news."

Miss Bonaventure moved the paper to the table and crossed her arms over her chest, regarding Blank with a sly smile. "You've solved the case, I take it?"

Blank nodded, absently, busying himself with polishing his flute with a cloth.

"Just from listening to me reading a brief summary of the details in the morning's news?"

Blank gave her a look, quirking a smile, but didn't speak.

"And this man with the tattoo?" Miss Bonaventure went on. "He's the one who has stolen the diamond, then?"

"No," Blank said with a shake of his head, "but he's the guilty party, all the same." Returning his flute to its case, he crossed the floor and sat at the table across from Miss Bonaventure. He contemplating finishing his morning tea, but it had gone cold while he'd been playing, and he hadn't the will to continue with it. Glancing up, he took in Miss Bonaventure's perplexed expression, and explained. "It's quite simple, really. As you may not be aware, I have visited the government treasury of Hyderabad and was actually brought in to consult on the implementation of its security by the Nizam himself. And I can assure you that, under normal circumstances, the edifice is virtually impregnable. Knowing that there was the matter of twenty-five lakhs of rupees in the balance, and the Nizam's rupees at that, it is scarcely credible that the Nizam would not have ordered security heightened. The result being that a stronghold merely *virtually* impregnable would thereafter be *completely* impregnable, for all intents and purposes. There are, then, only two alternatives. One, that party or parties unknown succeeded in snatching a near-priceless gem from beneath the nose of the Nizam himself, substituting in its place a worthless paste imitation, or . . ."

Blank paused, looking to Miss Bonaventure to finish.

She smiled, nodding. "Or they didn't."

"Precisely," Blank answered casually, folding his hands in his lap. "There never *was* a Hyderabad Diamond. It was paste all along. And this Alexander Jacob, no doubt, had hoped to complete the transaction before the dubious quality of the gem was discovered."

Miss Bonaventure looked unconvinced. "Surely the Nizam had it appraised before making the offer?"

"Remember," Blank answered, pointing at finger at the newspaper article, "Jacob here claims to be acting merely as broker. Doubtless he would also have been in a position to secure the services of a suitable appraiser, or to influence the Nizam's choice of such, at the very least."

Miss Bonaventure arched an eyebrow. "Why did you consult the *Whitaker's?*"

"Oh," Blank answered, with an absent wave. "To confirm a suspicion. The name 'Alexander Jacob' is a commonly employed alias of a rouge and scoundrel named Jack Alasdair, with whom I have had some previous dealings. The man committed murder, but last year fled before he was apprehended, and remains at large. There *was* an Alexander Jacob, a dealer in gems, but as the obituary pages of *Whitaker's* confirm, he passed away in Portsmouth the year before. Jack Alasdair was no doubt surprised to see the obituary notice for one of his well-worn noms de guerre, and found it to his advantage to assume the dead man's identity abroad."

"Well," Miss Bonaventure said, with a sly smile, "perhaps you'll have another accolade and honor to add to your collection."

"Ppth," Blank sputtered, waving his hand dismissively. His feelings about such things were well known. Such piffle was more trouble than it was worth, by half, trinkets to clutter his already full lodgings. Blank's actions in Cyprus the previous year had earned him the recognition of the Sublime Porte and Number 10 Downing Street alike, but while the Turkish Sultan had presented him with the *Atiq Nishan-i-Iftikhar*, or Order of Glory, from Salisbury he'd received only a hearty handshake. The medal had already tarnished, and the green-trimmed red ribbon was grayed with dust, sitting on a high shelf. With Salisbury, Blank had merely to wash his hands, figuratively and literally, to be done with the whole affair.

There came a knock at the door. Blank lingered at the table for a long moment, before remembering that, with his valet Quong Ti temporarily called back to China on pressing family business, Blank was himself left without a manservant.

"Would you like me to answer that?" Miss Bonaventure asked with a faint smile.

Blank sighed. "No, I suppose I better had." Wearily he rose from the table, and crossed to the door.

From the sitting room, Blank walked into a narrow corridor and from there into the entry. Overhead hung a gilt Venetian lantern, in which burned three blue-flamed gas jets. His hat rested on an occasional table next to a vase of orchids, his silver-topped cane propped up against the wall beside it. To his right, through the high doorway, was the library, and beyond that Blank's own bedroom. How he longed to return to that octagonal chamber and to sleep; but he'd slept fitfully, if at all, these last nights.

Blank mused that it could be a sign, presaging some dirty business in the offing, this insipient insomnia. It had been some little while since he'd been called upon to do Omega's bidding, and it was only a matter of time before he would be again. He had never slept well in the days leading up to a summoning, and seldom did for a long period after.

Unlocking the door, Blank found a uniformed officer of the Metropolitan Police waiting on the threshold. After ascertaining Blank's identity, the constable related that he had instructions to escort Blank to Tower Bridge, but was either unable or unwilling to share any further particulars about the matter.

Blank pulled a silver hunter from his vest pocket, consulted the time, and shrugged. "I have no pressing business until midafternoon," he said to the constable, casually, and then glanced back over his shoulder, to see Miss Bonaventure lingering in the corridor. "Well, Miss Bonaventure, best get your coat and hat. It seems we are needed."

"Pooh," Miss Bonaventure said, with a moue of disappointment. "And I'd hoped to finish reading the papers."

CHAPTER THREE

Millennium

2000 CE

THE GUY BEHIND THE COUNTER wouldn't stop giving Alice the stink-eye.

"Name?"

"Alice Fell." Like it wasn't on her passport, right there in his grubby mitts.

"And how old are you, miss?"

"Eighteen." Again, like it wasn't there in black and white.

The guy pursed his lips and nodded, looking thoughtful. Alice got the impression he thought she was lying, but really, who would lie about being eighteen? Only a sixteen-year-old. If you were eighteen, and looked it, you'd lie about being twenty-one. At least you would in the States. But then again, the drinking age in England was eighteen, wasn't it? So maybe he had a point.

"And is this your luggage, miss? *All* of it?"

As if he found it difficult to accept that she'd just gotten off a transatlantic flight with no luggage but a ratty little nylon backpack with an anarchy symbol drawn on it in ballpoint pen. She nodded, trying not to giggle. She's just realized who his accent made him sound like, and found it funny to imagine Sporty Spice with a bristly mustache working the immigration and customs counter at Heathrow Airport.

"You've just arrived on Temple Air flight 214 from New York?"

Alice nodded.

"Anything to declare?"

Alice had to actively resist the temptation to say "Nothing but my genius," like Orson Welles or whoever it was had done. Oscar Wilde, maybe? But then, she wasn't really much of a genius, so maybe she'd have been better off saying "Nothing but my angst" or something equally self-aware and mopey. As it was, she managed to resist the impulse altogether, and just muttered "No" while she shook her head.

"May I look in your bag?" He said it like it was a question, but Alice knew that if she answered anything but "Yes," she'd be turned right back around and put on a plane back to the States. So she played along, and nodded.

Here was what the guy pulled out of her backpack, which presently represented everything Alice owned in the world:

A deck of playing cards, wrapped in duct tape.

A library bound copy of Lewis Carroll's *Alice's Adventures in Wonderland & Through the Loooking Glass*, stamped property of Grisham Middle School, Austin, TX. (She'd stolen the book from the school library when she was in the eighth grade, but she wasn't sure what the statute of limitation on library theft was, or what sort of extradition policy Austin ISD had with the United Kingdom, anyway, so she kept the fact that the book was stolen property to herself.)

A trade paperback edition of Mark Twain's *Personal Recollections of Joan of Arc*.

A copy of the 2000 edition of *Frommer's London From $85 a Day* (shoplifted from the Waldenbooks at Lakeline Mall which, again, Alice failed to mention).

Two T-shirts, one pair of denim jeans, three pairs of socks, and three pairs of undergarments.

Two packs of Camel Light cigarettes, one opened and one unopened.

An antique silver match holder, or "vesta case," engraved with the initials "J.D." and a stylized dragon's head, containing thirty-two wooden matches.

A wallet containing an American Express credit card, an ATM card, four hundred and fifty-two dollars in American bills, and seventy-two cents in American coins.

Sunglasses.

A Ziploc bag containing various toiletries, including toothbrush, toothpaste, and deodorant.

A half-dozen tampons.

A Diamond Rio 500 Portable mp3 player, with headphones.

Three spiral notebooks, one completely filled, one partially filled, one entirely empty.

Four Uni-ball Vision Micro roller pens, all with purple ink.

A vial containing 125 milligram doses of divalproex sodium, brand name Depakote, an anticonvulsant, prescribed to an Alice Jean Fell of Austin, Texas.

That, along with the clothes she had on—leather jacket, blue jeans, eight-hole Doc Martens, and black Ramones T-shirt—was all that Alice owned in the world. And her nose ring, she supposed, if someone wanted to get technical. And the ink in her three tattoos. And the platinum filling in her left rear molar.

"Reason for your visit to the United Kingdom, miss?"

Alice shifted her gaze away from the mustached Sporty Spice, trying to think of a convincing lie.

"Miss?"

The truth was, she was on a mission from God. Or she was completely batshit crazy. There wasn't much middle ground. But she was pretty sure that neither answer was likely what Sporty Spice wanted to hear, and that either answer would greatly diminish her chance of walking through the door and getting on with it.

Alice looked up from the counter, and with a smile, said, "Pleasure?"

Sporty Spice narrowed his eyes, pursing his lips again, making his bristly mustache stand out at all angles.

Alice was sure that the guy thought she was a drug mule or something like that. As if any drug mule worth their salt would show up to the airport with a nose ring and dyed-black hair, less luggage than most kids carried to a regular day at high school, stuffed into a backpack with the word "FUCK" scribbled in purple ink next to the carefully wrought anarchy symbol. Wouldn't she be better off wearing a sign around her neck that said, "Please give me the full body cavity search, I'm carrying drugs," and cut out the middle man?

An eternity later, the guy pulled out a little stamp, carefully laid Alice's passport on the counter, and after stamping it a couple of times handed it back to her.

"Enjoy your visit, miss."

Alice stuffed all of her junk into the backpack, slung it on her shoulder, and moved on before Sporty Spice had a chance to reconsider.

She breezed by all of the tourists and businessmen wrestling with their heavy luggage, or waiting around the carousels at baggage claim. She fished her sunglasses out, put them on, and stepped outside. It had been one hundred degrees outside and sunny when she left Austin the day before. Here, it was sixty degrees at most, about as cold as it got at night back home, this time of year, but just as sunny.

Alice pulled a cigarette from the half-empty pack and lit it with a match from the silver vesta case her grandmother had given her just months before. Months before, she'd been Alice Fell, the girl from that accident no one liked to talk about, finishing up her junior year at Westwood High School, watching her grandmother die by inches.

Now, she was all by herself in London, and she was on a mission.

That, or she was completely batshit crazy. The jury was still out . . .

CHAPTER FOUR

Twilight

GALAAD WAS LOST ALMOST IMMEDIATELY. Within moments of passing through the gate in the city wall, he had no earthly notion where he was or where he was going. Embarrassment and frustration rose red in his cheeks, and he struggled to seem anything but completely out of place.

It wasn't as if Galaad was a rustic, after all. Both of his grandfathers had been born Roman citizens of Britannia. He'd studied civics, geography, and history, and his first language had been Latin. He was a devout follower of Christ, duly baptized, and while the Church in Rome might reject Galaad's sect of Pelagianism as heresy, it made his belief no less sincere. And he'd spent his entire life within the city walls of Glevum, a former garrison town and home of the Twentieth Legion.

So why was it that he felt a complete bumpkin on the streets of Caer Llundain?

The streets thronged with men, women, and children from all over Britannia and beyond. Though Galaad knew that they must seem deserted compared with the time of his grandfather's visit, much less the capital's height of importance in the days of empire, to him it seemed a mad crush of people. Groups of ten, fifteen, twenty people clustered at intersections, haggling in makeshift markets over craft goods, livestock, textiles, wine, and grain, each word accompanied by a brief cloud of exhalation in the frigid air. Galaad was thankful for the cold, though, which served to dampen the stench of dung and urine from the cattle, sheep, horses, and dogs everywhere, some tethered or bound up in pens of wooden stakes and twine, others allowed to wander at will. Better that the animals' leaving should crunch icily underfoot than assault the senses on the wind.

Galaad, who had rarely seen more than a handful of strangers at once, and precious few altogether, was unsure how to address himself to them. His ears were met with a riot of languages and accents, everything from the refined Latin of the noble class to the gutter Latin of the streets, from the Britonnic of Galaad's countrymen to the clipped Gaelic tones of Hibernia. And though the weather was unwelcoming, there seemed a certain festive tang in the air, as though the city dwellers were anticipating some enjoyment to come. And one could hardly blame them. Midwinter was just days away, though whether any given citizen of Caer Llundain intended to celebrate the pagan solstice, the Roman festival of the unconquered sun, or the Christian observance of the birth of the Messias, it was impossible to say.

As he turned corners, one after another, quickly losing his way, Galaad slowly came to realize that for all its crowded intersections and rough market stalls, the city was far from full. Some of the buildings he passed were of Roman design, walls of fired brick roofed with interlocking red terra-cotta *tegulae* and *imbrices*, but where the tiles had slipped loose or broken, they had been left in disrepair, the gaps like missing teeth in a broken smile. And all of the Roman buildings were older structures, ancient when his grandfather had been a boy. All of the newer construction Galaad saw was of less ambitious design and of meaner materials, little more than wattle-and-daub structures with thatched roofs. Worse, many of both varieties, Roman and wattle, stood untenanted, empty and abandoned, the doors and windows like the eyes and mouth of bleached skulls through which the cold winds whistled.

Finally Galaad had no choice but to intrude on one of the conversations he passed, and beg for directions. He was desperate to find the home of the High King, to plead his case.

The pair of men he approached—a Gael with bright red hair and drooping mustache in plaid breeches and rough woolen tunic, a long sword hanging at his belt, and a Briton wearing a dull yellow cloak of thick wool bound at his shoulder with a bronze clasp—regarded him coolly when he inexpertly interrupted their exchange.

"Your pardon, friends," Galaad began in Latin, "but I am a stranger in your city, seeking the home of the High King."

The two men looked at each other, in evident confusion, and then back to him.

"I don't . . ." the Briton began in Britonnic, ending with a halfhearted shrug, while the Gael just regarded him with barely disguised contempt.

Galaad nodded, and then repeated in Britonnic. "I am a stranger here, and seek the High King's home."

"Can't help you there," the Briton said, with another shrug. "I'm not from here, myself."

"He's holed up in the old procurator's palace," the Gael said impatiently, waving a hand off towards the south and east, then turned his attention back to the Briton. "Now look, I won't be telling you again . . ."

"Um, your pardon again, friend," Galaad interrupted, reluctantly. "But where might I find the procurator's palace, in that case?"

The Gael sighed, dramatically. "On the east bank of the stream Gallus, near where it cuts under the wall and enters the Tamesa." He paused and took in Galaad's blank expression. "It's a palace. It's three stories high. You can't miss it."

The Gael turned back to the Briton, eager to conclude their business, but Galaad remained rooted to the spot, looking helplessly in the direction the Gael had indicated, his confusion evident.

"Um . . ." Galaad began, raising his hand.

The Gael sighed again, even louder, and shook his head. Without looking at Galaad, he said, "Let me guess. You've no earthly notion where to find the stream Gallus, have you?"

"Well, no," Galaad answered, "but what I meant to ask was . . ."

"Can you find your arse with both hands?" the Gael said, glancing sidelong at Galaad. "Assuming that someone drew a map for you and started you off right?"

Galaad blinked, unsure how to respond, cheeks burning with embarrassment.

"So I can assume you're *not* a complete imbecile, in that case?" the Gael continued.

"Come now, Lugh," the Briton said, looking with pity at Galaad.

"No, *you* come now, you great wrinkled teat," the Gael said to the Briton. "I'll not be chastised by a thief for failing to coddle and cocker some hapless rustic."

"Thief?!" the Briton sputtered, indignant.

"And why not?" The Gael sneered. "That price you quote is thievery, plain and simple."

"Now look, I have a reputation to protect . . ."

"Ach!" The Gael waved his hand in a dismissive gesture. "You can shove your reputation in your bung-hole. I'm through with you."

The Gael wheeled around and pointed a long finger at Galaad.

"You," he ordered. "Come with me."

With that, the Gael spun on his heel and stomped away, imperiously.

Galaad looked from the retreating Gael to the Briton, who stood eyes wide and red faced, mouth open but unspeaking. "Well . . . Here now . . . Wait!" the Briton said, shouting at the Gael's back.

When the Gael failed to turn, but continued up the road, Galaad shrugged and, hiking the thong of his bundle higher on his shoulder, hurried after him. The Briton, for his part, stood his ground, wearing an expression of helpless resignation.

The Gael's long strides carried him down the road at speed, and Galaad was out of breath by the time he caught up, limping on his swollen knee as quickly as he was able.

"He's still watching, isn't he?" the Gael said out of the corner of his mouth, just as Galaad came abreast of him.

Galaad glanced back over his shoulder and nodded. "Yes. Yes, he is."

The Gael chuckled and smoothed down his long mustache with thumb and forefinger. "Beauty."

Galaad felt completely out of his depth. "Um, friend? Where are we . . . ?"

"Relax, tadpole. I was on my way to Artor's place anyway, when I finished my business with that cheating bastard, so you've only provided the opportunity to stage a strategic retreat. He'll strike a fairer bargain when next I seem him, the fat bag of suet."

"Who?" Galaad knit his brow in confusion. "Artor?"

"What?" The Gael looked at him, lip curled. "No, *that* bastard." He jerked his thumb over his shoulder, then added with a chuckle, "Artor's parentage is none of my lookout."

They reached an intersection, and the Gael steered Galaad to the right, heading south towards the river Tamesa.

"If you'll forgive me, friend," Galaad said, timorously, "might I inquire after your name?"

"Lugh," the Gael said simply.

"Well met, Lugh. My name is Galaad. I come from Glevum, in Powys to the west."

"Sure," Lugh said, with evident disinterest.

"Do you wonder why I come to the court of the High King?"

Lugh shook his head. "Not really."

"You see," Galaad went on, undeterred, "I am plagued by visions, since this summer past, and I'm sure that if any were able to divine their meaning, it would be . . ."

"Honestly," Lugh interrupted with an impatient wave. "I'm not interested."

Galaad was crestfallen. "Oh," he said, hanging his head.

They continued on, winding their way through narrow cobblestone streets in silence. They passed a large timber building of recent vintage, in better repair than most Galaad had seen, and he'd have known it for a stable from the sound of wicker and bray from within, even if he hadn't caught the pungent aroma of horse dung on the wind. He got a better glimpse inside as they walked by, and Galaad could see that the animals within seemed to live better and more comfortably than many of the human denizens of the city.

Galaad could not suppress an involuntary shudder at the proximity of the stable. Ever since the accident he could not look at a horse without being reminded of that spring day, of that bright morning, of the sight of blood on stones before the darkness rose up to swallow him. It always came in quick flashes, brief glimpses, but the remembered pain was writ across his face, like the passage of dark clouds across a full moon.

He glanced at his companion, to see if his disquiet had been noted, and was surprised to see that Lugh's face was screwed up, as well.

"Stinking beasts," Lugh said with a sneer. "If it were my lookout, we'd have served their roasted flesh at table months ago, and I'd not be haggling with traders for scraps to feed the city."

"Whose horses are those?" Galaad asked.

"Whose do you think? The lot of them are Artor's in name, though in practice the possessions of his captains and cavalry."

Galaad's eyes widened slightly, and he glanced back at the stable with swelling admiration. Artor's cavalry that had been instrumental in the war, employed against an enemy with no horses, and no knowledge of their use had they possessed them. It had been five years since the final victory at Badon, when Artor, then just a war duke, had defeated the Saeson under the leadership of Octha Big Knife and Bödvar Bee Hunter. In honor of the victory, Artor had been raised to the position of High King and given dominion over all of the kingdoms of Britannia. Artor had gone on to reassert authority in the north and west, even beyond the wall of Hadrian, and again his cavalry had proved essential.

They continued on, until at last they came to a tall building on the east bank of a broad shallow stream, near where it entered the Tamesa. It was built of the same Cantium ragstone as the city walls, the roof red with imported Italian tile. It was an imposing structure, the high arch of the entrance, the serried ranks of the windows high overhead. And though its age was evident from the red tiles missing from the roof, the crumbling mortar of the walls, and the stained and dirtied stones, it was clear that the structure was sound. And with the guard that stood ready at the entrance, hand on the hilt of his sheathed sword, his eyes wary and watchful, it was likewise clear that it was a structure which could be well defended, if the need arose.

"This is it," Lugh said simply, pointing with his chin. They crossed a low bridge over the stream, and made for the entrance. "Used to be palace of the procurator, then fell to the keeping of a number of lesser municipal officers before Artor and his lot took it over."

"It's magnificent." Galaad was breathless. The palace was easily grander than the most lavish villas of Glevum.

Lugh shrugged. "It's drafty and damp, if you ask me. But then, no one does."

They reached the entrance, and the guard treated them to a wry smile. Galaad steeled himself to endure another barrage of mocking, but was surprised to find that he was not the object of the guard's derision this time.

"How goes it with you, Long Hand?" the guard japed. "Not troubled by your injuries, I hope?"

"They plagued me a little last night as I pleasured your mother," Lugh returned, "but I managed to do the job, still and all."

The guard's grin fell, and he tightened his fist around his sword's hilt.

"Draw your iron if you feel up to it," Lugh said, a slight smile curling the corners of his mouth as he laid his hand on the handle of his own blade. "But remind yourself that there is a reason you stand sentry outside Artor's door and I sit at his table."

The guard set his jaw, eyes narrowed, but relented, relaxing his grip on the hilt and letting his hand fall to his side.

"This one is with me." Lugh motioned to Galaad with a nod. "Keep watch out here, why don't you, and raise the alarum if the Saeson horde should swim up the Gallus." He then glanced over his shoulder at Galaad. "Come along, tadpole."

With that, Lugh disappeared through the entrance. Galaad glanced at the guard, who seemed to quiver with frustrated anger, and hastened after his guide.

As they made their way through the corridors of the palace, Galaad burned to ask Lugh why the sentry had called him "Long Hand," but the Gael's dark expression and the quickness of his pace suggested the question would not be welcome. Instead, he followed along, taking in the faded grandeur of the building and its fixtures. Sculptures stood atop pedestals in recessed alcoves, likenesses of long-dead emperors and forgotten gods. They passed outside into an enclosed garden, the hedges bare and leafless, the dead grasses underfoot rimed with hoarfrost. Then they reentered the building on the far side and came at last to a large reception hall, semicircular in shape, thronged with people, two dozen or more.

"Wait here," Lugh said, pointing along the wall, where a low bench sat. "Artor will be along presently, and then you can bore him with your strange tale yourself."

With that, Lugh turned and moved off into the room's center to join a knot of men talking closely, leaving Galaad on his own.

Galaad, eyes wide, sat on the stone bench and tried unsuccessfully not to look like a complete rustic. It wasn't as though he could help himself, though. These men gathered here, he knew, represented a larger sampling of humanity than he'd ever witnessed before. From their modes of dress and the varied accents and dialects Galaad could hear, he knew that they were representatives of the various client kingdoms of the island, from as far as beyond Hadrian's Wall in the north and the shores of Demetia in the west, and among them perhaps envoys from the Hibernian dynasts or the nations of Gaul beyond the channel.

The center of the audience chamber was dominated by *stibadium* dining couches surrounding a pair of semicircular *sigma* marble tables, placed with their straight sides facing one another so that the whole formed a large marble circle. At the head of the table was a heavy oaken chair, delicately gilt with hammered gold, which like the couches now stood empty.

The floor under Galaad's feet felt warm, no doubt with a Roman heating system hidden beneath, and was elaborately mosaiced. The mosaic was a disquieting mix of Christian and pagan imagery—representations of the Messias balanced by depictions of Bellerophon upon winged Pegasus slaying a monster, the Virgin Mother opposite Apollo and the seasons, cherubim vying with chimera, and at their center the Chi-Rho—suggesting that one of the previous tenants had practiced Gnostic heresies.

It was only midday, but with the warmth seeping from the floor into Galaad's tired feet and the long miles he'd already walked since dawn, he felt himself already growing torpid and weary. He was lulled by the susurration of voices of those gathered in the room, the crowd steadily growing as the moments passed. His lids were heavy over bleary eyes, and he found himself almost lulled to sleep sitting upright on the hard stone bench when the voices around him ceased, of a sudden.

Galaad's eyes opened wide, and he sat bolt upright, half convinced that he'd dozed and the room had emptied while he slumbered. But no, the room was even more crowded than before, though now silent. The reason for the sudden cessation of conversation was the figure which now stood at the entrance in the chamber's far fall. Having just entered, he paused, surveying the room.

This newcomer was tall, and though perhaps near the end of his fourth decade of life, carried himself with the ease and alertness of a much younger man. Draped over his back was a red cloak, so dark it was almost purple, clasped at the shoulder with a large bronze brooch. Beneath this he wore a linen tunic dyed a deep blue, bound at the waist with a broad leather belt, and a pair of white breeches, their bottoms stuffed into the tops of heavy cavalry boots. Around his neck was the torc of the High King, a thick woven braid of gold with the head of a dragon sculpted at either end. His beard and mustache were neatly trimmed, and his brown hair hung straight to the nape of his neck. Finally, at his belt hung a long sword, the spatha of a Roman cavalryman, but the simple soldier's hilt replaced with one of finely wrought gold and silver.

This was the man Galaad had come to see. This was Artor, High King, Count of Britannia.

At an unspoken signal from Artor, the knots of conversation dispersed, and everyone moved to find their accustomed place. A dozen men sat themselves on the couches, Lugh among them, leaning against the carved cusps of the table's edge. With a start, Galaad realized that these were the captains of Artor's cavalry, the elite of his fighting force that had driven the Saeson from Britannic lands. He looked with newfound admiration at his Gaelic guide.

As Artor took his place in the gilt chair at the head of the marble circle, his sword laid across his knees, the remainder of those gathered in the hall arranged themselves behind the couches, respectfully.

Galaad realized that he'd risen to his feet at some point, unknowingly, and sheepishly sat back down on the bench.

"God give you a good day, gentles," Artor said to the room, somewhat wearily. "What business have we today?"

In the hours that followed, it was not only Galaad that struggled to stay awake. Several others, Artor himself chief among them, seemed forced to shift themselves upon their seats constantly, blinking hard and forcing their eyes open, as the apparently endless parade of petty business was marched before them.

Galaad wasn't sure what he might have expected the day of a High King to be like, nor what type of industry he would have assumed a Count of Britannia would have turned his hand to, but he was certain that it would not have included the sort of trivial disputes and mean concerns which he heard aired that afternoon. This kingdom disputed the demarcation of borders with its neighbor, that tribe complained that those upstream polluted their shared waters in defiance of long-held custom, these farmers protested that the landlord to whom they were tenant refused the services for which their taxes made him liable. But the pleas were not limited to those under Artor's dominion. Merchants from the Middle Sea carried grievances that their trade agreements with the High King's government were not being honored, their monopoly on the export of tin infringed by business arrangements that Britannic sellers had made with their competitors. The envoy from a Gaulish king protested that Artor had not supplied the copper and grain which the treaty between their two nations demanded. And a Britannic missionary who worked to convert the subjects of the High King of Hibernia to the Roman religion carried word that the landholder of Alt Cult's soldiers once more raided the island and had again begun to take Christian converts as slaves, as they had in the days of the late Patricius.

One of the captains seated at the marble circle snored gently, head lolling, and Galaad began to suspect that for men who had been bound together on the field of battle, there were far more engaging pursuits than the dreary business of statecraft. Even Artor, who seemed better at hiding his thoughts than many of the others in the room, seemed far less than enthused.

Galaad busied himself identifying those he could from the stories he had heard. Artor was easiest, of course, but only slightly less easy to name was Artor's counselor, the man who called out the supplicants to address the High King and who silenced them when he felt they had spoken long enough.

Caradog, so the stories went, had once translated the Sais tongue to Britannic for the High King Vitalinus, long before Galaad was born. Later, he had fought against the Saeson at the side of Artor's father, Utor. It was said that Caradog had gained his strangely bent arm in battle, but that for all of its withered appearance it was stronger than the limbs of any other three men combined.

The afternoon wore on, and the hall gradually emptied, as supplicants stated their case before the High King, heard his judgement, and departed. Soon, the only ones in the room were Artor and his twelve captains seated about the marble circle, and Galaad sitting on the stone bench at the back of the hall.

"Is there any more business?" Artor asked, stifling a yawn.

"None that I know, majesty," Caradog answered, consulting the tablet laid on the table before him.

"In that case . . ."

Galaad began to panic. He felt sure he'd been forgotten, or else overlooked, and that his long journey to Caer Llundain would have been for nothing. With all the courage he could muster, he half rose from the bench into a standing position. He opened his mouth, intending to speak, but succeeded only in emitting a faint squeaking sound. He intended to try again, but never knew if his attempt would have succeeded, as in rising he jostled the bundled slung over his shoulder, causing it to slip far enough to one side that his grandfather's grandfather's sword slid loose from the bindings.

As the sword tumbled to the floor, Galaad grabbed for it, desperately, but even as he watched every inch of the fall, he felt as though he were moving through frigid water, so slowly did his limbs seem to move. So it was that he seemed to have moved but fractionally by the time the sword clattered to the mosaic floor. The deafening sound of metal on stone resounded on the hollow floor, coming back even louder.

Galaad looked up, horrified, and found that all thirteen pairs of eyes in the hall were directed at him.

"Ach, I forgot!" Lugh said, snapping his fingers. "This little tadpole has a story for you, Artor."

The High King glanced from the Gael captain to Galaad and raised an eyebrow. "Do you, now?"

Galaad opened his mouth once more, and discovered he'd forgotten entirely how to speak.

"My name is Galaad, and I come from Glevum, in Powys, in the west."

Galaad stood facing the gilt chair of the High King, his hands twisted into white-knuckled fists at his sides, trembling with nervous anxiety.

"I know where Glevum is," Artor said, his tone surprisingly gentle.

"Oh." Galaad blinked, and swallowed hard. "Of course. Well, as I say, my name is Glevum . . ."

"I thought your name was Galaad," Caradog said, glancing up from his tablet.

"Um, right, of course, my name is Galaad. And . . ." He broke off, his breath catching in his throat. He'd already forgotten his own name, so nervous was he, and now found that he'd forgotten what he meant to say. That is, he knew what he had in his head to say but could not for his life recall the words he needed to say it.

"Relax, friend," Artor soothed, folding his hands on the sheathed sword that lay across his lap. "There's no reason to be afraid."

"But I'm afraid there may be, majesty," Galaad said, eagerly. "That's just the problem. I don't know what the woman is showing me, but I think it could be something fearful indeed."

The High King narrowed his eyes and leaned forward in his chair. "What woman?"

Galaad took a ragged breath and tried to will himself to calm. "I'll try to start at the beginning. You see, two springs ago there was an accident, and I . . ." Galaad broke off, involuntarily reaching up and touching the scar that ran above his hairline, just above his right eye. "No," he said, resolute. "That's not the beginning. I'll start again. It was last summer that I first saw her."

"Saw who?" Lugh asked, his tone impatient.

"The White Lady," Galaad answered. "At least, that's what I call her. At first I thought she was the Holy Mother, but then I began to suspect that perhaps she was instead one of the goddesses of our grandfathers. Perhaps she was Ceridwen, who made the potion greal in her magic cauldron, on her island in the middle of a lake." He shook his head, lips pursed as though he'd just eaten something distasteful. As a follower of the precepts of Pelagianism, he knew there were many paths to the divine, but still the thought of pagan goddesses contacting him made Galaad uneasy. "But perhaps it doesn't matter who she is, only what she is showing me."

"So you see visions of a woman," Artor said, his tone slow and deliberate, like one speaking to a child or an imbecile. "And she shows you things." Galaad nodded, eagerly. "What things?"

Galaad closed his eyes for a moment, and he could see the vision before him, as clear and bright as if he saw it beneath the midday sun. The visions came at first only in his sleep, but in time had visited him in the waking hours of daylight, as well.

"It is a tower of glass," he said, opening his eyes. "It sits atop a smooth-sided mound, round on one end and pointed the other, which is itself upon an island in the middle of a lake or sea, connected to the mainland by a spit of land."

Artor nodded, his lips drawn into a line. "Go on."

"The White Lady is within the tower," Galaad continued. "I'm not sure how I know, but I do. And I feel that I must go there and help her, but I don't know why."

"Help her?" Caradog looked at him askance. "Why does she require help, this imaginary woman of yours?"

"I don't know," Galaad said. "I simply know that she requires help, and that I must give it to her." He paused and took in the hostile glances from around the table. "She doesn't speak to me in words, you see. Only images. Only feelings."

"I have a feeling," Lugh said with a smile, lacing his fingers behind his head and leaning back. "I feel like you're a lunatic."

Galaad's face burned with shame commingled with anger. He remembered others saying much the same thing, not long before. The townspeople of Glevum had whispered behind their hands as he passed, saying that his injury had done more than give him a scar, but cost him the use of his senses, as well. And his own wife, to whom he looked for support when everyone else had turned their backs, had looked away, saying she wanted nothing more to do with him.

As laughter rippled around the table, Artor steepled his fingers and regarded Galaad thoughtfully.

"This island you speak of," the High King said at last. "You say the hill is shaped like the bob on a mason's plumb line, yes? Round on one side and coming to a point on the other?"

Galaad nodded, dispirited, expecting some fresh mockery.

"I know of such a place."

All eyes turned to the High King, and Galaad's mouth hung open, his jaw slack.

"Have you ever been in Dumnonia?" Artor asked.

"No, majesty." Galaad shook his head.

"There is an island there just as you describe," the High King went on. "I saw it years ago, when I was in the area with the forces of Ambrosius."

"And was it then topped by a glass tower?" one of the captains asked.

"No," Artor said, either not noticing the captain's ironic tone or choosing not to acknowledge it. "But in every other particular it coincides with this man's tale. The island is linked to the Dumnonian coast by a thin sliver of land, just as he says."

"You're not suggesting that this man is telling the truth, are you?" Caradog asked, aghast.

Artor offered his counselor a smile. "Apparitions appearing to men of Powys? Towers of glass?" He shrugged. "It seems difficult to credit, to say the least." He paused, and then turned his attentions back to Galaad. "But I'd like to hear more about this, still and all. Galaad, was it?"

Galaad nodded, eagerly, when he realized the High King was awaiting a response.

"You will stay here in the palace tonight as my guest. Does that suit you?"

Galaad gaped, and then quickly nodded his assent. "Yes," he said. "Yes, majesty."

"Good." Artor rose to his feet and hung his sword once more at his belt. "Well, that's an end to it, gentles. I, for one, am starving."

With that, the High King turned on his heel and retreated from the audience chamber.

Galaad stood stock still, unsure what to do, his hands gripped tightly on his bundle. Fortunate for him, as the rest of the captains filed out of the room, one of them, a tall, fair-haired man with clean-shaven cheek and chin, came to his rescue.

"Come along, then," the man said in well-formed Latin. "Let's get you cleaned up."

CHAPTER FIVE

Jubilee

ONLY TWO WEEKS REMAINED until the observance of Queen Victoria's Diamond Jubilee, and London already swelled with well-wishers and dignitaries from all across the empire. Sandford Blank and Roxanne Bonaventure gazed idly out the windows as the four-wheeled "growler" cab rumbled through the thronged streets, while the police constable sat opposite them, stone-faced and unspeaking.

The participants in the Jubilee procession, the jewel in the celebration's crown, had been gathering for weeks. The Colonial contingent were mostly encamped at Chelsea, while the premiers of the eleven self-governing colonies had been put up at the Cecil, the largest hotel in Europe. There were no rooms to let anywhere in the greater London area, nor would there be for weeks, even months, following the Jubilee.

The city, never provincial, had taken on an even more cosmopolitan feel in recent weeks, with the parks and cafés, music halls and theaters crowded with a Babel of a hundred tongues, the more sedate tones of London attire enlivened by the introduction of the colorful silks and linens. Sikh businessmen rubbed elbows with Chinese diplomats, while Malay ladies exotic and serene fluttered their long lashes at Australian cattle ranchers, and West African policemen far from their usual rounds walked the streets ill at ease in the first boots they had ever worn.

Union Flags fluttered from streetlamps and posts, draped from window sills and awnings, and when the wind blew gave a sound like a flock of birds taking flight, the snapping flags closely approximating the flapping of wings. It had been ten years since the queen's Golden Jubilee, but if the preparations were any indication, this new celebration threatened to be even more ostentatious.

Blank remembered all too well the events of 1887, which seemed to him no more than a heartbeat before. He only hoped that the anniversary of the queen's sixtieth year on the throne cost him not as much, personally and professionally, as her fiftieth anniversary had done.

Finally, the Tower of London hove into view, its ever-present ravens starkly black against the morning sky, and the police constable called for the drive to stop.

As Blank helped Miss Bonaventure down from the cab, he noted that while the bascules of Tower Bridge were raised, the stairs leading to the elevated walkways overhead were closed to the public, blocked by one of their escort's brothers in arms. Blank could hardly imagine that it mattered, since in the short years since the bridge's opening virtually all of the foot traffic had remained on the ground while the bridge was raised, preferring to watch the bascules rise up and down to climbing the steps and crossing more quickly. But for whatever reason, the authorities did not want anyone to ascend, just now. He could only surmise that it had something to do with their summons from his house in York Place.

With that in mind, Blank did not wait for their escort to finish clambering down from the growler, but set off across the pavement towards the guarded steps with a will. Miss Bonaventure followed close behind, her heels dogged by the police constable as quickly as he was able. As it happened, their escort did not catch up with Blank until he'd reached the bridge, made his way through the crowd, and stopped just short of the steps leading to the elevated walkway.

"Sorry, sir," said the constable barring their way, "but there's no admittance to the stairs, just now."

"I shouldn't worry," Blank said, smiling. "I expect you'll find your masters are expecting me."

Just at that moment their escort huffed up, coming abreast of Blank and Miss Bonaventure, panting. "S'alright, Cogsgrove. This'n is Sandford Blank."

The constable's eyes widened, and he took in Blank's appearance—gray coat, waistcoat, and trousers, bowler hat, and silver-topped cane, an orchid in his buttonhole—before finally stepping to one side. "Go on up, guv. They're waiting for you."

Blank couldn't imagine what the constable had heard about him to elicit that sort of reaction, but he hoped it was down to the cases in which he'd been called to assist Her Majesty's Government, and not for the less savory aspects of his past which he hoped would remain hidden and forgot.

Miss Bonaventure in the lead, Blank following close behind, and their escort bringing up the rear, they mounted the stair.

The warm June wind whistled in their ears as they stepped out onto the western walkway, blowing through the white-painted girders of steel that formed the walls, a crisscrossed thatch of sturdy steel beams with large open spaces in between the intersections. To their left, a short distance off, was the eastern walkway. To their right snaked the River Thames, the Tower of London on one side, Southwark on the other. Ahead of them, under a tarp stained dark by the blood seeping through, was clearly the reason that they had been summoned.

Blank remembered another bridge, and other bodies. Watermen had loved "shooting the bridge," riding under the old London Bridge at high tide, when the water level on one side could be as much as six feet higher than the downstream side. But it had been a dangerous pastime, to say the least. "The bridge is for wise men to cross over, and for fools to go under," or so the popular saying of the day went. But old London Bridge had been pulled down long years ago, and Blank doubted that one in a hundred Londoners had ever heard that saying, or knew the stories behind it if they had.

Whatever had befallen the body under the bloodied tarp, Blank suspected it wasn't something likely to engender quaint and good-humored popular sayings, however quickly forgotten and lost to history.

There were two men standing just the other side of the body, one a stout, ruddy-faced Irishman with a full mustache, his hands folded behind his back, the other of a more delicate nature, holding a handkerchief over his nose and glancing with distaste at the bloodied tarp. Even if Blank hadn't recognized them at first glance, he would have known them in an instant as a policeman and a bureaucrat, respectively.

"Ah, Blank," said William Melville, superintendent of the Metropolitan Police's Special Branch. While he apparently was striving for lighthearted, he could not entirely hide the tone of disapproval in his voice, and his expression of distaste on seeing Blank was a close cousin to the bureaucrat's sour look. "About time you made an appearance."

"Sorry to keep you gentlemen waiting," Blank said, having to raise his voice slightly to be heard over the whistling wind. He fingered the orchid at his coat's lapel. "I had the deuce of a time finding the right flower for the day. I'd thought to go with a lily, but they so often seem to give an unnecessarily funereal look, don't they?" He paused and glanced at the body that lay on the floor of the walkway between them. "There again, perhaps funereal would have been more appropriate to the day, at that." He paused, and then tipped his bowler back on his head with the silver-chased top of his cane. "But where are my manners. You remember my associate, Miss Roxanne Bonaventure?"

Melville nodded in Miss Bonaventure's direction, dismissively. It was only after seeing Blank's gaze flicking meaningfully between himself and the bureaucrat at his side that Melville finally said, "Oh, yes, of course. Blank, this is Chalmers." He nodded to the thin man behind the handkerchief, as though that was sufficient.

"Lionel Chalmers," the thin man said, holding out a hand like a dead fish he was desperate to discard. Blank took the proffered hand. "I'm here representing the prime minister himself."

"Oh, Salisbury, is it?" Blank smiled. "And how is old Bobby, at that?"

Chalmers bristled, brow furrowed at hearing his lord and master being referenced so casually, but refrained from making any comment. Which, Blank quickly surmised, said a great deal about the circumstances in which he now found himself.

"What's this about, Melville?" Blank was suddenly all business, his mannered pose of indifference, for the moment, abandoned.

He and Melville had had run-ins before, having met the first time during their separate investigations of the Torso Murders. The case had dragged out from 1887 through to 1889, without clear resolution. Blank did not doubt that Melville felt the sting of leaving the case unsolved, especially considering that the headquarters of the Metropolitan Police, New Scotland Yard, was built on the site of the unsolved Whitehall Mystery itself. But if Melville felt a sting, then what Blank felt was more like a gaping wound. It haunted him that he was never able to solve the Torso Murders, in all the years since. He was sure that, had he not been distracted momentarily from his responsibilities, allowed for a brief moment to feel that he could live as a normal man and give in to his hidden passions, then the case would have been solved, and sooner, and the nameless victims of the Torso Killer would have remained unharmed. As it was, they were anonymous, unknown, bodies found with head, arms, or legs severed and missing, discarded in the street like yesterday's rubbish. Five vicious murders, and then they'd stopped as suddenly as they'd begun.

He'd assuaged himself a bit with the knowledge that he'd soon afterwards solved the Whitechapel Ripper case—though in circumstances that the public could never know—but it came as cold comfort, if any. He had pledged never again to allow his personal appetites to distract himself from his responsibilities, and to date never had.

"Look, Blank," Melville said, eyes narrowed, "it's not my decision that you be called in. If it were down to me, my boys'd take care of this business all on our own. But the P.M."—Melville rolled his eyes towards Chalmers—"doesn't quite agree, and here we find ourselves."

"As I'm sure we're all aware," Chalmers said, sounding breathless despite his Eton accent, "the Queen's Jubilee Procession is scant days away, and the remit of Special Branch in this instance is to ensure the safety of the Queen herself, not be mired in the trivial investigation of . . ." His expression of distaste deepened, and he finished, ". . . sordid *murders.*"

Blank could see his point. About the queen and her procession, at any rate, if not perhaps the trivial nature of murder investigation. It had been nearly ten years to the day since Melville had covered himself in glory by foiling a plan by Irish nationalists to blow up Westminster Abbey while Queen Victoria attended a service of thanksgiving there during her Golden Jubilee. If he'd not been Irish, there was every chance he'd have ended up winning his spurs, but instead of a knighthood, he saw his Special Irish Branch rechristened simply Special Branch, and his charter expanded from protecting crown and country against Fenians, republican dynamiters, and anarchists, to facing down all and sundry dangers to the empire. It had been four years since Melville was promoted to superintendent of Special Branch, raised up from the rank and file, and in that time he'd carried out his assigned office with vigor. It was a lofty height for the son of a baker and publican to reach, and Blank could see that Melville was ever mindful of his station and responsibilities.

"So it *is* murder, then?" Miss Bonaventure said, stifling a yawn. "I was beginning to wonder."

Blank flashed her a quick smile, then turned back to lock eyes with Melville. "Miss Bonaventure is quite right. Shall we see what we were brought here to see, or will you let us get about our business?"

Melville's expression darkened, but he motioned for the constable who'd escorted them to flip back the tarp.

It took a moment for the shapes and curves to resolve themselves into a unified image. It seemed to Blank as if his mind were refusing to process the visual information his eyes were providing, but while his thoughts recoiled, his exterior betrayed no turmoil.

It was a woman, or rather was the partial remains of what had once been a woman. Both hands had been severed, and the head cut off, and all three were missing, nowhere in evidence.

Blank remembered another Jubilee, other bodies, and suddenly even a practiced indifference was out of the question.

Blank examined the body more closely. The cuts were clean and precise, skin, muscle, and bone sheared off in an even plane.

"Given the amount of bleeding," he said, kneeling down, his cane laying across his knees, "I deduce that the hands were severed some time before the victim was decapitated."

Melville grunted in assent. "That's what we came up with, as well," he said, begrudgingly.

"I've never seen cuts like these," Blank said.

"And here I thought you had seen everything, Blank," Miss Bonaventure said, in a ill-advised attempt to mask her own squeamishness with levity. Blank shot her a hard look, and her weak smile grew even weaker. Subdued, and looking away from the bloody remains, she went on. "But no, I've never seen the like, either."

"I take it the head and hands have not been retrieved?"

"No." Melville shook his head. "No sign of them, same as . . ." He bit the words off, but Blank knew what he'd been about to say.

Same as last time.

"No sign of them," Melville repeated, his jaw set, his lips drawn tight. "It was a doxy reported it in this morning. Nobody else much comes up to the walkways, so the girls make pretty free use of them."

"Or are freely used, themselves," Blank said absently. "And not freely, at that." He scowled. "But at too dear a cost, oftentimes." He used the end of his cane to lift the hem of the dead woman's skirts. He examined her shoes, and then peered up her legs, at which Chalmers blushed, turning his eyes away from such indecorous probing.

Blank straightened up, tugging down the front of his waistcoat.

"Though you haven't said as much, Melville, I agree with your surmise that the victim was a streetwalker, given the state of her footwear, the condition of her clothing, and her evident poor health at the time of death. I find it unusual, given that she was dispatched in a place frequented by those of her profession, that she evidently was not engaged in the act of congress at the time of the murder, nor is there any indication that her body was misused in that fashion following her death. The nature of the wounds is indeed singular, and worthy of some study, but despite the superficial resemblance to a case with which we're both intimately familiar, I fail to see the case's significance. As a single murder, it is a matter for pity, but hardly worth the attention of Special Branch."

Melville narrowed his gaze, but didn't speak.

"Unless," Blank said, tapping the butt of his cane on the floor, "this is *not* a single murder."

Chalmers looked nervously at the superintendent, who quieted him with a rough wave of his hand.

"This is the third such body to be found," Melville answered in even tones. "The third in as many weeks."

Blank nodded. "But you've managed thus far to keep news of it out of the papers. That couldn't have been easy."

Melville blew air through his lips with an explosive noise and shook his head ruefully. "Pack of vultures, the lot of them."

"And both of the other bodies were in similar states?" Miss Bonaventure asked.

Melville locked eyes with Blank, and paused for a long moment. "Yes," he said at length, nodding. "All three cut up like that, all three with the same clean shears."

Blank found himself feeling an unexpected and unexplainable welling of sympathy for the superintendent. He knew how the Torso Murders must have eaten at Melville these last ten years, and it couldn't have been easy to be ordered to hand over the present investigation to another, knowing that there might be a connection between the two.

"Given the nature of the injuries," Chalmers put in, "there was some discussion at the highest levels that this might be a matter for the Strangers . . ."

"What?" Blank interrupted, flabbergasted. "Absalom Quince and his lot? *Them?*"

Melville shook his head, a scornful expression curling his lip. "That lot is worse than *you*, Blank."

Blank flashed him a tight smile. "Thanks for saying so, friend."

Melville sneered, while Chalmers struggled to gain control of the conversation.

"*As* I was saying, the question arose as to whether this should be a matter for the Strangers, who while not officially sanctioned by Her Majesty's Government, have nevertheless prove invaluable in a number of recent instances . . ."

"Lunatic ghost chasers," Blank muttered under his breath.

"*However*," Chalmers said, soldiering on, "given your own history, Mr. Blank, and your role in the speedy resolution of that unfortunate matter in Whitechapel, it was decided instead that you should be approached in this matter."

"Well," Blank said, doffing his hat in obvious mockery, "I thank you for this consideration."

Chalmers either failed to detect Blank's sarcasm or chose not to respond, instead turning his attentions to Melville.

"The prime minister has issued specific instructions that this matter will *not* be made available for public consumption. The newspapers are *not* to be informed of any aspect of the investigation or of the murders themselves until such time as the prime minister deems appropriate. With the Jubilee in the offing and the city already crowded with dignitaries, the last thing we need is another sensation such as the Whitechapel murders engendered. It might be good for the sales figures of the penny papers, gentlemen, but it will do Her Majesty's Government no good at all, and even less good for *you* all, should you allow it."

Chalmers glanced from Melville to Blank and Miss Bonaventure and to the constable who stood a few yards off, indicating that the prime minister's wrath would know no bounds of rank or privilege were news of these murders to be made public.

"I believe you mean 'worse' instead of 'less good,'" Blank said. "But I think we all take your meaning." He turned to Melville. "I'll solve this one, Melville. You have my word on it."

Melville drew his mouth into a tight line, but nodded. He evidently could not tell whether Blank had meant the words as a taunt or a reassurance; Blank did not really know himself.

"Now," he said, resting on his cane, his hands folded on its silver head, "if this is the third murder, I want to know *everything* that you have on the previous two."

CHAPTER SIX

Millennium

T HE BLACK CAB AT THE STAND looked like something out of an old
movie. Like you'd have to wear a fedora just to ride it in, or else hang
onto a sideboard with a Tommy gun in either hand. But the guy behind the
steering wheel didn't quite meet the dress code, in a ratty T-shirt and slacks.
Still, the steering wheel *was* on the wrong side of the car, so that had to count
for something.

Alice stood on the curb, while the guy leaned out the window and looked
her up and down. "Where you going, love?"

"London." The guy gave her a little smile and raised an eyebrow. Alice
felt a blush rise in her cheek. "The London Eye," she quickly added. "The one
near Westminster Bridge. The big Ferris wheel?"

The cab driver chuckled, and smiled, but gently. "Yeah, I know the one."
He stuck out his lower lip and rubbed it with a thick finger. "How much
money you got, love?"

Alice tightened her grip on her backpack's strap. "I've got enough."

The cab driver shook his head, still smiling. "Nah you don't, sweetie.
Here to there'll cost you forty pounds, easy."

Alice's eyebrows knit as she tried to do the conversion rate in her head.
That was something like sixty bucks, a significant percentage of all the cash
she had.

She didn't say anything, but evidently she didn't have to, her thoughts showing themselves on her face. "You don't want a black cab," the cab driver said, gently. "What you want is to take the tube. A one way ticket on the Underground'll cost you three quid forty."

Alice tried to look in control, and nodded like she'd known that all along. "That's definitely cheaper."

"Ennit?"

Alice's cheeks felt like they were on fire. She hadn't even gotten out of the damned airport and already she'd managed to look like a complete hayseed. She stammered thanks at the cabbie, who just waved merrily and went back to studying his racing form. Then she went off to look for the subway station. She'd gone two steps when she realized she could have just asked the cabbie, who was sure to have known, but having committed to turning around and walking away, she couldn't back out now.

Alice had only ever been on a subway once before, in Mexico City, on a school trip a few years before. Her mother hadn't wanted her to go, but Alice had pulled extra shifts after school at the family business, the postal contract unit on Anderson Mill, and saved up enough to cover almost all of the cost herself, and then successfully guilted her mother into picking up the tab for the rest. Alice didn't know much Spanish, and all that she got out of the trip was a suspension for getting caught drinking by one of the trip sponsors, a case of turista that she couldn't shake for a week, and the passport that she later used to get into the UK.

Alice had almost gotten lost on the subways in Mexico, neither her language nor her orienteering skills up to the task of deciphering the posted maps, but she figured she'd have an easier time of it in the London Underground, since a) the maps were in English, and b) the trains were full of people who could answer questions, if she got turned around.

As it was, she managed to get completely mixed up. She'd meant to end up at Waterloo Station, right next to the London Eye, but managed to get onto the Bakerloo line at Piccadilly Circus heading the wrong way and found herself instead in Paddington, a mile or two away.

Alice considered getting back on the train and heading back the other way, but that was another six bucks she really didn't have to spare, and according to the map in her *Frommer's* it didn't look like too far a walk, so she decided to hoof it instead and save the money.

Everything around her seemed disappointingly . . . *normal*.

When she'd traveled in Mexico, she'd never been able to forget for a second that she was in a foreign country—everyone was talking a different language, she had trouble reading all the signs, all of the brand names advertised on billboards and signs were strange.

Here, though, it was easy to forget she wasn't just in another part of the United States. Everything was written in English—though with the occasional extra 'u' tossed in for extra colo*u*r—and the bus stops all carried ads for the same movies and TV shows she watched back home. The people she passed on the street spoke with accents but were speaking English. And coming from Austin, which was not only a big college town with lots of foreign students but the hub of enough technology and dot-com business that there were always people from all different countries to be found in the stores and restaurants, accents were nothing new to her. At the barbeque joint where Alice used to go with her mother and grandmother, there were even times it seemed they were the only native English speakers in the place, between the Chinese and Japanese and Hindi being spoken at the tables around them and the Spanish being spoken behind the counter. The accountant who kept the books for Alice's mother was Irish, and their neighbors were German on one side and Korean on the other. So it was hardly culture shock to run into new accents in another country. That the majority of them were speaking English just meant it was even more familiar.

When Alice had been in Mexico, the punk rock white chick with the dyed-black hair and nose ring, Doc Martens and leather jacket, she'd gotten more than her fair share of stares. Here? Nobody gave her even a second glance.

Of course, what would they all say if they knew? If they knew that she was on a mission from God?

Technically speaking, Alice didn't know *who* she was on a mission for. She received visions, but for all she knew they could just as easily have come from the Queen of Faerie as from God, or space aliens, or another dimension, or a supercomputer at the end of time. All she knew for certain was that she was receiving visions, and that she had to *do* something about them.

They were, however, visions. Not just voices, not just hallucinations. That was for *crazy* people. And Alice wasn't crazy. At least, she was relatively sure she wasn't.

Her logic was that crazy people didn't know that they were crazy. They just woke up one day convinced that aliens from the Dog Star were communicating to them through the fillings in their back molars, or that the Virgin Mary appeared to them in their Pop Tarts, or that they were really the son of God or something. None of which applied to Alice. She, she wasn't crazy, because she knew for an absolute fact that she was mentally ill.

Alice had been diagnosed with Temporal Lobe Epilepsy and suffered from temporal lobe seizures. Electrical misfires in her brain made her see, hear, and experience strange things. And when she wasn't having an active seizure episode, she had a classic case of Geschwind's syndrome, in particular problems with her temper, hyposexual tendencies, hypergraphia, and hyperreligiosity.

And here was why Alice wasn't crazy. She knew for an absolute fact that the visions she experienced were caused by seizures in her temporal lobe. An EEG had proved it. What Alice also knew, though, was that her visions weren't *merely* the result of abnormal electrical activity in the temporal lobe, stimulating the visual and auditory centers of her brain. Instead, the seizures themselves were being *caused* by something outside herself, and the visions she received were messages intended for her alone.

So it could have been God giving her the seizures and making her see visions, or it could have been aliens, or Queen Titania of Fairyland, or a super-intelligent computer at the end of time, or any one of a thousand different things. All that Alice knew was that the visions were *real*, and that she had to do as she was told.

Which, so far as she'd been able to work out, involved coming to London and going up in the London Eye. There was something about ravens in there, as well, and some guy she'd never seen before. But after that it all got a little hazy.

Alice hoped that things looked clearer from the top of the Ferris wheel. Because even though she was in London, half a world away from home, things from the ground still looked more than a little indistinct.

It was when she almost got into a fistfight over the empty soda bottle that Alice realized that she was getting a bit tense. She'd had problems controlling her temper for years, ever since the first accident—not the *other* accident, the one that no one at school liked to talk about, but the earlier one, when the only ones Alice had managed to hurt were her own family—but being aware of the problem didn't make it any easier to handle. The doctors said that it was an aspect of her personality disorder, of her interictal behavior syndrome, which was a fancy way of saying that people with TLE had a tendency to be a mite off even when they weren't having seizures. All cases were different, but in Alice's, it meant that she had a tendency to fly off the handle with little provocation. And when she had major provocation? Well, watch out . . .

Alice had found a bank that was willing to swap her American dollars for British pounds, since so many of the shops refused to take her bills. After, that is, the first three banks refused. So a number of shops refusing her bills and then a number of banks refusing to change them, all in the attempt to get something to drink. Water, juice, soda, anything. She was desperate. She'd gone a few blocks from the Paddington Underground Station when she realized she'd had nothing but a couple of mouthfuls of water in the last few hours, and after smoking a cigarette at the airport and another couple while walking through the city, her mouth felt about as parched as a Texas highway in the middle of August.

With her nice American bills changed for strangely multicolored British currency that seemed like it belonged with a board game like Monopoly or something, she went into the nearest store and bought a bottle of Pepsi. She picked up a bag of potato chips while she was at it—*crisps*, the package said—since she'd not had much to eat, either. Then she wolfed down the chips as she continued walking, taking big gulps of the soda now and again.

The chips were good, but strange—*lamb & mint* flavor?—but the Pepsi tasted about like the ones back home. When she'd finished, Alice went looking for somewhere to throw the empty bag and bottle away. The bag was no big deal, she could just wad it up in her pocket, but the bottle was cumbersome and needed to be ditched.

She'd gone all the way through Paddington, and crossed Bayswater Road into Hyde Park. The *Frommer's* said she had to stop and check out the statue of Peter Pan in Kensington Gardens, which as near as Alice could tell was the other half of the same park, but the walk was already taking longer than she'd expected, and she was eager to get to the London Eye and get on with her destiny, whatever it was. Maybe when she got through with her mission from God or whatever she could work in a bit of sightseeing, but in the meantime it was strictly business.

Alice continued through Hyde Park, past people walking dogs and couples on bicycles and little kids with balloons. She crossed the street near a big memorial of some kind, an arch with a statue of a woman with wings riding a chariot pulled by four horses. Or maybe it was a man. It definitely had wings, though, which led Alice to wonder why it was riding the chariot in the first place, if it could fly. Either way, she couldn't find it on the *Frommer's* map, so it didn't seem to be all that important.

She was passing Buckingham Palace and still hadn't seen a trash can anywhere. Not a single one since she'd left the store with her Pepsi and chips. Looking at the map, she realized she'd walked the better part a mile and was still carrying the empty bottle.

For a normal person, this would have been a minor annoyance, at worst. And even Alice, on her better days, would likely have shrugged it off as no big deal. But she was tired, hungry, hadn't bathed in two days, and was on a mission from God, and was damned if she was going to haul an empty Pepsi bottle all over creation, just because the damned British couldn't seem to put trash cans in convenient places for people who needed them.

By the time Alice finally stopped and asked someone where the nearest trash can was, she'd worked herself into a searing white hot rage. There was a crowd around Buckingham Palace, the sort that only gathers in the States to see the president, or maybe Michael Jackson, so Alice figured one of the royal family must be at home. Or maybe Michael Jackson was visiting, instead.

Alice went up to a guy who looked like a local. For all she knew, he could have been from Texas.

"Hey, where can I find a goddamned trash can?" Alice voice hissed through her clenched teeth, and she brandished the empty Pepsi bottle like a club.

"A what, now?" The guy's accent put him somewhere closer to home than Texas, which was a step in the right direction.

"A trash can." Alice waved the bottle in front of his nose. "You know, for trash?"

"Ah, a rubbish bin?" The guy brightened. Then he shook his head. "Not many of those around, I'm afraid."

Alice seethed, and wondered how much damage she could do to the guy with an empty plastic bottle. Probably not much, she decided, but it might be satisfying to try. "Why. Not."

"Good question," the guy said, blinking. "IRA, I expect. Used to put bombs in them, you see. I suppose the authorities figured it was easier just to clear the bins out altogether instead of checking them for explosives at all hours."

"That . . . that's *crazy!*" Alice was full on yelling now. "And believe me, I *know* crazy!"

The guy seemed less than amused to find himself getting yelled at by a strange American girl in the street. "Now, see here . . ."

"No, *you* see here!" Alice reached out and shoved the guy in the shoulder, causing him to step back to keep his balance. Alice was shorter, just a hair over five foot two, but she packed a punch. "I'm tired of carrying this damned thing around, and *you* people aren't doing anything to help. Don't you get that I've got *things* to do?"

The guy's eyes narrowed for a moment, and Alice was sure he was about to start swinging at her, never mind the fact that she was a foot shorter, about a hundred pounds lighter, and a girl. Then his eyes widened, and his mouth opened in an "o" of surprise.

"What's all this, then?" came a voice from behind her.

Here's what Alice knew about the police in England: they wore funny hats, they didn't carry guns, and they were called "bobbies."

Here's what Alice noticed about the policeman in front of her: he wasn't wearing a funny hat, he was as big as a brick wall, and he didn't need a gun to get his point across. Whether he would answer to the name "bobby" or not, she wasn't sure, but she wasn't about to ask.

"Nothing, officer," Alice answered automatically, in her innocent-little-cute-girl voice. It was her reflex when dealing with cops, whatever the situation, after years of experience. "We were just talking, is all."

"She assaulted me!" The guy, who was about to throw a punch at a hundred pound girl a few seconds before, was now all of the sudden the aggrieved party. That he actually *was* did little to improve Alice's view of him.

"This little thing?" The policeman treated Alice to a toothy smile. "American, are you?"

Alice nodded. "From Texas."

"Texas?" The policeman got a strange look in his eyes for a moment, like he was seeing the lonesome prairie out there, somewhere in the middle distance. "Well, you run along, miss, and mind yourself." Then, he pushed the brim of his hat up with a fingertip, and in an atrocious imitation of a Texan accent, said, "Y'all be careful now, y'hear?"

Alice smiled sweetly, and failed to point out that "y'all" was a plural, only to be used when addressing a group, not when talking to a single person. "I sure will, sir. And thank you." Then she flounced away, holding tight to the empty Pepsi bottle and hoping to put as much distance between her and potential arrest as possible. For all she knew, her mother had put out some sort of international APB on her, and the last thing she needed was to get picked up taking a swing at a local before she had a chance to see what her destiny was all about.

Behind her, she could hear the guy talking to the policeman.

"But *she* hit *me*!"

"Shut it. One more word out of you and I'll run you in, you understand?"

Alice couldn't help but smile. She felt a little bad, having taken out her frustrations on a total stranger and then left him to deal with the mess. But she'd learned long before that batting her eyelashes, smiling sweetly, and trotting out the Disney Princess voice was enough to get her out of most problems, and if that meant that someone else was inconvenienced as a consequence, that was merely an unfortunate side effect.

Finally, overcoming the ingrained prohibition against littering that her mother had drilled into her since birth, she ditched the Pepsi bottle in the middle of the street when crossing in front of the houses of Parliament. If she'd just given herself up to littering before, she'd have saved everyone a load of trouble.

CHAPTER SEVEN
Twilight

THE FAIR-HAIRED CAPTAIN gave his name as Caius, and though he styled himself an *eques*, a member of the horsemen elite, he insisted that Galaad not stand on ceremony.

"I was on my way to my daily bath anyway," Caius explained, as they walked out the palace doors and headed across the Gallus to the northwest. "So it really isn't any trouble."

Caius, whose Italian accent sounded to Galaad's ears as something of an affectation, seemed perpetually to be smiling. Towering over Galaad, he was gregarious and welcoming, not at all like the Gael Lugh who had escorted Galaad through the city's streets. But for all of that, Galaad could not help but feel that there was a more sinister edge to some of the eques's words of which he should be wary. Galaad was reminded of something his late mother used to say, about not trusting the ready smile, and looking instead for the one hard won.

A short distance from the Gallus, in the lengthening shadow of the riverside wall, they came to a fired-brick building constructed along familiar lines. Even before they passed the threshold and into the warm air within, Galaad had recognized it as a *therma* public bath.

"Ohhh." Galaad sighed, shoulders slumping. "I've not had a proper bath in too long a time."

Caius grinned at him, and pinched his nose shut with thumb and forefinger. "I hadn't noticed," he said, his voice nasal and piping.

Galaad looked down at the filthy state of his clothes, the crescents of dirt packed into each fingernail, his hair hanging lank and matted, and could do nothing but shrug. "It is a long way from Glevum."

"Which is in Powys, I'm given to understand," Caius chided. "Come along, then. Let's get to it."

The baths were in reasonable repair, but not all of the rooms remained in use. They passed through the disused tepidarium and went straight to the caldarium.

The air within was steamy and warm, heated in the hypocaust beneath the floor and then fed through earthenware pipes in the wall, and the floor was so hot they had to wear wooden clogs to keep the soles of their feet from blistering. Galaad gratefully shucked off his breeches, boots, tunic, and undergarments and slid into the bath of hot water sunk into the floor. He breathed deeply as the dirt, sweat, and grime of his long days of travel streamed away from him into the steaming water, and closed his eyes, just luxuriating in the heat. Caius floated in the waters across from him, regarding him with amusement.

Once they'd rinsed off and wrapped clean linen towels around their waists, they moved onto the laconicum. The air was sweltering, even hotter than in the caldarium, and the sweat poured from their bodies as they lounged on benches.

"Your feet seem in a sorry state, friend," Caius said languidly.

Galaad looked down at his own bruised, bloodied, and blistered feet, and suppressed a shiver. Released from the confinement of his marching boots for the first time in nearly a dozen days, his feet seemed to throb and pulsate with a generalized pain, punctuated here and there by the more localized agony of individual blisters and abrasions.

"What did you do, *walk* from Powys?" Caius laughed.

Galaad answered with only a blank stare.

"What?" Caius's eyes widened. "Could you not arrange the loan of a wagon, or even just a horse?"

Galaad shook his head. "I prefer to walk," he said, struggling to keep his tone even.

Caius blew air through his lips. "Not me, friend. If I could stable my horses within the palace itself, I'd not even walk as far as the bath but ride everywhere instead. I'd take my meals in the saddle, at that, and roam from room to room on horseback. And when they came to inter me in the ground, when my hour comes around at last, they'd need to bury my horse first, that they'd have some place to rest me."

Galaad forced a smile on his lips, but the expression didn't reach his eyes, in which cold fires burned.

Later, after scraping the dead skin from their bodies with a strigil, they had a quick scrub and then a cool dip in the pool of the frigidarium. They dressed, Galaad having managed to get his clothing into a more respectable state by knocking the dirt loose against a pillar, and then, with Caius in the lead, returned to Artor's palace.

To Galaad's sincere relief, the subject did not turn again to horses, and he managed to go a short while without dwelling on the memories of that spring day.

A place had been made for Galaad at the palace. Formerly the room of a high-ranking slave or household servant, it had evidently stood unused for some time, if the dust lining the mantle and eaves was any indication. But it was dry and warmer than the outdoors, and for that Galaad was thankful.

When it came time for the evening meal, Galaad was made welcome in the kitchen while the High King and his captains dined in the audience hall. The meal was meaner than he might have expected in the home of the Count of Britannia, the stew more like a watery broth, but there was hard-crusted bread and watered-down wine, and the cook, maid, and scullions were pleasant company. One of the servants had skin the color of honey and a kink in her hair, suggesting something of Africa in her ancestry, and another had the olive complexion of a Scythian. Galaad was surprised to find that another had the coloration and accent of a Sais, though she insisted that she was not one of the Saeson but was from a place she called Geatland. Galaad was soothed by this, until the cook pointed out with a wry smile that the Saeson leader Bödvar Bee Hunter had himself been a Geat. After that, Galaad ate a bit more warily, keeping watch on his tablemates.

After dining, Galaad repaired to his chamber and prepared himself to sleep. By the light of an oil lamp he unpacked his bundle and arranged his effects on the mantel. He laid his leaf-bladed sword next to the simple tin cross that had once belonged to his father, and to his father's father before him. As a Pelagian, the tiny cross was merely symbolic, only a moral example instead of the atonement it represented for the followers of Augustine, but it comforted Galaad all the same.

Galaad sat down on the hard wooden sleeping pallet, his only bedding a thin woolen blanket, worked his way out of his tunic, and pulled off his boots. Then, just as he was about to douse the light and turn in, he heard footsteps on the far side of the door and the sound of someone knocking.

"Come in?" Galaad stood, the floor tiles cold beneath his bare feet. He thought perhaps one of the household servants had come on some errand. He even entertained the brief fantasy that one of the women had found him attractive enough to seek out the company of his bed. Then it occurred to him that the Geatish woman might be a hidden assassin after all, though even with his thoughts addled by lack of sleep he realized that he could hardly present much of a target for villainy.

When the High King himself stepped into the room, his purple-red cloak wrapped around him against the night's cold, Galaad wasn't sure whether to be relieved or even more worried.

"Do I disturb your slumbers?" the Count of Britannia asked, glancing around the small room.

"No, sir," Galaad said feebly, conscious of the fact that he stood dressed only in breeches and undergarments. "That is, I was about to sleep, but . . ." Galaad gestured to the still-lit lamp, his voice trailing off.

"Good." Artor nodded, satisfied. "I know the hour is late and that you have traveled far, but I would hear more about these visions of yours, if you will allow it."

"Of . . . of course!" Galaad stammered. Self-consciously he picked his tunic up off the pallet and pulled it on over his head. "What is it you wish to know?" he said, his voice muffled by the fabric as he struggled to work his head through the neck.

Artor crossed the room and sat on a stool set along the far wall. He was still dressed as he'd been earlier in the day, though had disposed of his sheathed spatha somewhere along the way. It seemed as though Artor's hands hungered for the sword, though, and they gripped his knees through the fabric of his cloak, unable to lie still at his sides. Galaad realized with a start that the High King seemed agitated in some way. Not nervous, precisely, but anxious like someone eager to begin a journey and forced to endure long delays.

"This woman you speak of?"

"The White Lady?" Galaad answered.

"Yes, the White Lady. Tell me about her. What does she say to you?"

Galaad blinked slowly, and when his eyes were closed it was as if he could see her standing before him, even now.

"She doesn't speak," Galaad replied. "Not in words, at any rate. But she conveys her intentions to me as pure emotion, as sensation. I *feel* her thoughts, rather than hearing them as utterances."

"What does she look like, this White Lady?" Artor regarded Galaad thoughtfully.

"I call her thus for her appearance. She wears clothing of the purest, blinding white, and her hair is the color of bleached bone. Lights seem to shine in her eyes, her teeth are straight and white, and her feet never touch the ground."

"Is she winged?" Artor said, skeptically. "Like some cherubim? Or part animal or bird, like the myths of the pagans?"

"No, no." Galaad shook his head. "In all particulars she has the likeness of a mortal woman, though of a flawless perfection that one could rarely find on earth."

"Hmm." Artor nodded, thoughtfully, then hummed again. "Hmm."

Galaad shuffled his feet, cold on the tiles, but then stopped. His nostrils caught a subtle tang on the air, and he breathed deeply, trying to identify it. Something floral?

"Majesty," he began, looking around the room, "do you smell . . . flowers?"

Even as he said the words, he realized what they portended, and in the following moment he was startled by a bright, flashing light. He squeezed his eyes shut, though it did nothing to diminish the glare, and then could hear a distant, high-pitched whine.

When he opened his eyes again, the room, and the pallet, and the High King upon the stool were all gone. In there place was the White Lady and the high hill, and upon it the tower of glass.

Galaad felt an overwhelming sense of bliss and comfort, as he always did in these visitations, such as he had rarely felt outside the throes of coitus. And though he could not name the reason for it, he always felt as though he were about to be entrusted some great secret, some special meaning. More frustrating, then, that this irrational certitude should always be followed by inevitable confusion at the vision's end, when he realized so little of what he had seen, felt, and heard made any sense.

Galaad wanted to speak, wanted to ask questions of the White Lady, wanted to pledge his devotion to whatever cause she held, to promise his undying affection if only this sense of well-being could continue into his waking life. But he could not speak. He could not ever speak, but only stood as mute witness, observer to the scenes the White Lady put before his eyes. He was there to receive and nothing more.

With a queasy sensation of movement in the pit of his stomach Galaad watched the perspective change, shifting until his attentions were on the tower of glass atop the smooth-sided mound.

Within.

Galaad felt the thought burning in his mind.

Trapped within.

Through what agency Galaad didn't know, the woman was placing feelings and concepts directly into his mind, without passing by route of his hearing.

Aid. Rescue. Release.

Galaad struggled to indicate some response, to communicate his confusion, but as always his attempts were in vain.

Here. Within. Trapped. Release.

The tower of glass and the smooth-sided mound fell away, and now Galaad's vision was dominated by the White Lady, and her alone. Her eyes seemed to glow with an inner light, like the full moon on a clear night, and her mouth moved soundlessly, wordlessly.

Aid me. Rescue me. Release me.

Galaad would have reached out to her, if he could, but wherever his limbs were, out of sight, he could not move them.

Come.

The last thought was urgent, but more an imperative than an entreaty. It was a command.

"Flowers?"

Galaad blinked, and the floral scent again pervaded his nostrils. And as quickly as it had come, the sense of bliss fled from him, and with it the sudden certitude. The woman was gone, as was the scent, and the bliss, and the certitude, leaving behind nothing but a cold, creeping confusion.

"Galaad?"

He felt strong hands on his shoulders, shaking him, and looked up into the face of Artor.

"Oh," Galaad said senselessly. "It's you."

And then he collapsed into a heap on the cold tile floor.

A short while later Galaad found himself before a hearth, the warmth of the flames licking at his bare feet. Artor had sent for wine, and poured strong undiluted cups for himself and for Galaad. Then the servants had been sent away once more, and the two men sat facing each other, made ruddy in the red light of the hearth's flame.

Galaad studied the cup in his hands, self-consciously. It was glass, and stamped with images of men in chariots driving horses and with the names of long-dead charioteers. A souvenir of some departed procurator's trip to Rome, perhaps, a prized possession for generations of his family, now all fled and gone. Galaad sipped the strong, heady wine and tried not to think of how easy it would be to smash the glass against the bronze of the hearth, and all those lingering memories of empire dashed into fragments.

Across from him, Artor drank from a simple clay cup. There was some irony in that, the man who was bringing order back to this farthest outpost of a dead empire drinking from a workman's vessel while Galaad drank from glass fired in the heart of empire itself.

"You have had a vision," Artor said at last, breaking the long silence. It was a statement, not a question, but Galaad could not help but answer.

"Yes, majesty," he said, his own voice sounding far away in his ear.

"But it happened between one moment and the next. You said something about smelling flowers, and then a glassy look came into your eye as you paused, and in the next moment you were talking again."

Galaad nodded, wincing. "Sometimes they last longer, I am told, but in the main they take no more time than that."

"What could you possibly have seen in so short a time?"

Galaad shivered, and tightened his fingers around the glass. "Time seems to run more slowly in my visions. Or with more speed. I'm not sure how best to say it."

"The duration seemed longer for you than it was in reality?" Artor suggested.

"Something like that," Galaad answered with a nod.

Artor leaned forward and regarded him through narrowed eyes. "And you say that you have never been to Dumnonia?"

"No, majesty. I've never been further south than Corinium, and then only briefly."

Artor leaned back in his chair and ran the tip of his finger around the rim of his clay cup, thoughtfully. A long silence stretched out between them, and Galaad was grateful to have the dancing flames of the hearth to watch, to give him something to occupy his attentions.

"You do not seem mad," Artor said at length.

"No?" Galaad could not help but smile. "I thank you for saying so, majesty." His smile wavered, and he struggled to keep it in place. He remembered the citizens of Glevum, and his own wife. "Though there are many who might take issue with that."

"Hmm." Artor nodded. "I don't doubt." He paused, reflecting. "I had a friend once who went mad. We fought together against the Saeson, when Ambrosius still lived and was Comes Britanniarium. When we were younger than you are now, our cohort suffered a terrible loss to the Saeson, and my friend and I were among the few who survived the retreat. I was shaken, having never before seen so many of my fellows fall before the enemy's iron, but my friend . . . It was as if he could not fit everything he had seen and heard inside of his head, and so had to force out things like reason and sense to make room. He seemed to dwell always in those short hours of battle, even when days and weeks had passed, fighting the skirmish over and over again in his thoughts. In the end, he threw himself from a high rampart, dashing his brains out against the flagstones, and that was an end to it." Artor took a sip of his wine, his eyes half-lidded. "Who knows? Perhaps he felt that was the only way to get the memories out of his head, to open up his skull and knock them loose."

Galaad tensed in his chair, trying not to see any parallels to his own situation, and failing. Like the High King's lost friend, Galaad too found himself living the same remembered incident again and again, and like him the memories threatened to drive out every other thought from his mind, if he would but let them.

"My friend was mad," Artor said. "I have seen the strange light which flickered in his eyes again, and again, over the long years since. But in your eyes . . ."

The High King trailed off, regarding Galaad.

"You see nothing in my eyes, majesty?" Galaad was reluctant to ask, afraid what the answer would be.

"It isn't that." Artor shook his head. "But it is a different look I see on your face. No, you are not mad. You are . . ." He paused, searching for the right word. "You are . . . haunted."

Galaad's breath caught in his throat, and he swallowed loudly.

"Yes, that is it," Artor said, nodding. "Haunted."

Galaad's sleep, when it finally came, was thankfully dreamless, and it was late in the morning before he woke. In the relative warm and proximate comfort of his small room, he found it nearly impossible to resist the temptation to remain abed and settled on lying for a short while longer beneath the thin wool blanket. He intended to rise momentarily, but despite his best intentions he drifted once more to sleep. This time, though, his slumber was not so dreamless.

Galaad dreamt that he was on horseback, riding across the Powys coun-tryside. It was a clear spring morning, the sun just pinking the sky to the east, and the rolling green hills were flocked with clover and cinquefoil, marigold and vetch, all flowering, all in bloom. In the hazy logic of dreams, Galaad realized that the flowers weren't on the hillsides, but were in his arms. He clutched a huge bunch of flowers. They were heavy and unwieldy in his arms, so that he had to shift on the saddle constantly and struggle to hold them to him. But for some reason, in the dream this unwieldy bunch of flowers were to him an endless source of joy and contentment, and he was happy just to have them near him.

He rode on, through the hills, laughing, spurring the horse to speed. But their course carried them away from the gently rolling hills and into an area pocked with rock outcroppings, the ground grown more rugged. And it became harder and harder to hold the flowers in his lap, though his laughter continued unabated. And just when he thought the horse could go no faster, and that he could laugh no louder, it all came to a crashing halt. The horse turned its ankle on a rock, cartwheeling forward and sending Galaad and the bunch of flowers flying through the air.

Galaad hit the ground headfirst, the pain setting off bursts of lightning behind his eyes, and he felt the side of his head go numb with pain. He reached up and his hand came away wet. He felt dizzy, nauseated, and only then did he think what had become of the flowers.

Gripped with sudden terror, he scrambled up onto his knees, looking around. And there, a short distance away, he saw the flowers scattered across the sharp rocks, the red clover bright in the morning sun against the gray stone.

And then he woke.

But the nightmare didn't end. It never did.

"Flora," Galaad said, his cheeks wet with tears.

It was only later, after the sobs that racked his body finally subsided a bit, that he was able to climb to his feet, dress, and meet the day.

The High King's council was gathering again in the audience chamber, and Galaad quietly found a place in the back, out of sight. He had been in the kitchen, breaking his fast with a simple meal of bread and thin stew, when a servant came with word that he was wanted in the audience chamber. Galaad wasn't sure why he'd been summoned but saw no reason to refuse.

Caius, the tall, fair-haired captain and self-styled eques, greeted Galaad with a smile from across the room, while on the opposite side of the marble table the Gael Lugh treated him to a raised eyebrow, no doubt as curious about the reasons for Galaad's presence as he was himself.

Galaad was eager to find out and didn't have long to wait. Shortly after he settled himself on the bench, the room fell silent as the Count of Brittania, High King Artor, strode into the rear of the hall.

"God give you a good day, gentles," Artor said, animatedly. He smiled as he sat in the gilt chair and drummed his fingers on the scabbarded sword he laid across his knees.

Caradog leaned forward, examining his tablet, on which were recorded the names of all the day's petitioners.

"Not today," Artor said, waving his chief counselor silent before he'd even had a chance to speak. "We have other business to attend, instead."

The captains seated around the marble circle glanced back and forth at one another in confusion, while around the room the various dignitaries, representatives, traders, and other plaintiffs grumbled their discontent.

"And what is this business, majesty?" Caradog asked, his tone perhaps a trifle too unctuous.

Artor smiled, seeming filled with a vigor that had been lacking the day before. "I come today to announce a new enterprise, gentles. A foray. An . . . expedition, if you will."

The murmurs rippling around the room increased in volume and intensity, and the looks of confusion deepened.

"An expedition, majesty?" Caius asked.

"Just so," Artor said with a nod. "To Dumnonia, by sea."

Scowls appeared on the faces of some of those around the room, amusement on others, while not a few cast glances in Galaad's direction, suspiciously.

Galaad couldn't help but remember Artor's repeated queries about Dumnonia, and whether he had ever been.

"Your pardon, majesty," Lugh said, waving a hand for attention, "but you don't suggest that you believe the tadpole's story, do you?"

Artor smiled, though Galaad noticed that the lines around his eyes deepened as he regarded the Gael. When he answered, it was in measured, even tones. "I cannot say, Long Hand. Or rather, I cannot say that I believe every jot and tittle. But neither can I escape the feeling that there is some truth to what he has described."

"And the purpose of this expedition would be . . . ?" asked another captain, short and compact, who spoke Britannic with a Demetian accent.

"To see the truth of it for ourselves, whatever truth there may be."

The grumbles from those gathered in the audience hall intensified in volume, and dark looks passed back and forth.

"Perhaps it would be best to adjourn the council for today," Caradog said quickly, seeking to sooth raising tempers. "To allow the High King time to . . . formulate how best to present his thoughts."

Artor's eyes flashed as he glared at his chief counselor, thin-lipped, but in a moment his white-knuckled fists relaxed on his knees and he drew several slow breaths, steadying himself. He opened his mouth as if to speak, then shut it again and contented himself with a curt nod.

"Thank you, gentles," Caradog said to the room at large, rising from the couch and taking up his tablet. "If you will all return tomorrow at midday, we will hear each of your complaints in due order."

As those gathered reluctantly shuffled from the audience hall, some shaking their heads in bewilderment, others muttering darkly in their discontent, Galaad rose from the bench, expecting to be ushered out with them. But he noted that none of the twelve captains had left their positions, except for Caradog who stood at the table's edge, and that the High King kept his seat. Galaad half turned to leave when Artor caught his eye and gave a quick shake of his head, his expression unreadable.

Glancing at the retreating backs of the plaintiffs, Galaad swallowed hard and sat back down on the bench.

When the room had cleared, the silence was finally broken.

"What madness is this, Artor?" Caradog fairly shouted, wheeling around and pointing a finger at the High King.

Artor sighed heavily, but didn't yet answer.

"Surely there is some jest in this, right?" Lugh asked, leaning back on the couch, chuckling. "Though I'll admit that the humor escapes me."

"Perhaps that says more about your faculties than about the jest," chided the captain with the Demetian accent, at which Artor cracked a slight smile.

From his privileged position at the rear of the otherwise empty room, Galaad noticed that, without an audience, the captains and their king comported themselves very differently. No longer the dignified ruler and his trusted counselors, they seemed now much more relaxed, much more a group of equals, though all still deferred to Artor to some degree. What he saw before him now, Galaad realized, was the easy camaraderie of the battlefield.

"Perhaps, Bedwyr," Lugh said to the Demetian captain, "you simply have a better vantage that I, what with your nose buried so far up Artor's arse."

Bedwyr flicked the end of his nose with his thumb and grinned. "Is *that* what that smell is? I thought for certain that it was the air wafting from that rotted maw you call a mouth."

"Will you two either fight or fornicate and be done with it?" said an auburn-haired captain who spoke Britannic with the accent of Gwent.

"Careful, Pryder," Lugh said with a leer. "You might give the impression that you'd like to join our coupling, and that would make your dear brother jealous."

Across the marble circle a captain, who except that his hair and beard was blond instead of auburn could have been Pryder's double, scowled and lay his hand on his sword hilt.

"Peace, Gwrol," Pryder said, raising a warning hand. "There's no need for that."

"You're all a pack of children!" Caradog barked, slamming his tablet onto the marble table and dropping loudly back onto the couch. "In case it has escaped your feeble attentions, there is a more serious matter before us." He glared at the other captains, then turned his attention to the High King. "Come now, Artor. What *is* all this about?"

Artor glanced around the marble circle at his captains and, shaking his head, let out a heavy sigh.

"Surely I'm not the only one bored senseless with this."

Caradog looked to the other captains, who seemed as confused as he. "With what, precisely, Artor?"

Artor waved his hand, though whether indicating the room, or the palace, or the city beyond, Galaad couldn't say. "With this. With all of this . . . this *officialism*."

The High King pushed his gilt chair back, scraping noisily against the floor, and climbed wearily to his feet, his scabbarded spatha in his hands.

"I don't know about you lot, but this isn't what I fought and bled for. My intention was to drive the Saeason from our lands and restore order. To make Britannia safe for our families, safe for our children and children's children. But I never intended this. Never intended . . ." He paused, and his lip twisted. "Grain levies." He pounded a fist on the marble table. "Or the boundaries of farm land. Or tin tariffs. Or preferential trade agreements."

More than a few heads around the marble circle began to nod.

"I had no intention to *rule*. Hell, I never even wanted to *lead*. But Ambrosius tapped me as his chief lieutenant, and when his hour came the sword of the Count of Britannia passed into my hands, and that was an end to it."

Artor held the spatha up, regarding the silver- and gold-worked hilt.

"But I might never have taken it up if I'd known it would all lead to *this*."

He threw the sword onto the marble table with a clatter of metal on stone.

"My heart scarcely seems to beat, these last few years, so sluggish does my blood course around my veins. I would have my pulse quicken again, if only once, before death takes me in my sleep or boredom at last reduces me to stone. And if that quickening comes at the cost of a fool's errand, of taking a stranger at his word and following a senseless vision to the ends of the earth, then so be it." He passed his gaze over those sitting before him. Then, with a shrug, he said, "And who knows, perhaps the boy does receive visitations from some angel or spirit or goddess, and there will be something waiting for us at our journey's end. But I can tell you one thing for certain. We'll never find it sitting here on our widening backsides, listening to the endless prattle of these petitioners."

A number of the captains seemed to find sense in Artor's words, while others were clearly unconvinced, Caradog chief among them.

"Listen to reason, Artor," Caradog said, his tone gentle. "I know that our present duties may lack the vigor of our younger days, but these are offices which must be fulfilled."

"Then leave others to fulfill them," Artor snapped. He calmed himself visibly, and took a deep breath. "I'm a soldier, friend, and a poor statesman. I'll not abandon my duties here, but if I'm not allowed to step away from them, if only briefly, I doubt my spirit could weather it."

"I'm with Artor," Bedwyr said, slapping the tabletop with his palm. "I'm tired of all of this statecraft, and could do with a bit of venturing."

Some of the other captains grumbled, shaking their heads.

"As much as it pains me to say, I agree with Bedwyr," Lugh said. "I feel myself suffocating within these city walls and would value the chance to roam."

"And I think you've all been at kegs that have gone bad," Caradog objected. "Artor was selected as High King by those he now rules, and he owes them his time and attention."

Other voices raised around the marble circle, some in support of the notion and some opposed.

"Enough," Artor said, his voice quiet but firm. "It's clear we won't be of one mind about this. Then let us be, for a moment, a democratia, such as the Athenians practiced. We shall put it to a vote, and each man shall decide his own course for himself. As for me, I know my own mind." He reached out a hand to the spatha that lay on the marble table, but stopped before his fingers touched the sheath. He paused, then drew his hand back, leaving the sword where it lay. "I'm for boarding White Aspect and sailing down the Tamesa with tomorrow's first light. Now, who is with me?"

CHAPTER EIGHT

Jubilee

SANDFORD BLANK AND ROXANNE BONAVENTURE reviewed the materials Melville had provided. The details were scant and raised more questions than they answered.

There had been a full coroner's inquest into the first murder, two weeks previous, though if it had been reported in the papers, it had escaped the notice of Miss Bonaventure and Blank, who habitually scanned the day's news for such stories. If they'd overlooked the story, they were hardly to be blamed. On the surface, it seemed just another anonymous murder, the sort that happened with an altogether depressing regularity in the city. The victim, evidently, had been a prostitute, or so the coroner concluded after hearing the testimony of the witnesses who had discovered the body and of the officers and physicians who had investigated the case.

It was to the credit of the city's police that they investigated the murder of those for whom society at large had such little regard, though admittedly with less vigor and tenacity than they would the slaying of a duchess. However, simply to label a woman, whether living or dead, as a "prostitute" was to paint a portrait with too broad a brush. In addition to the untold thousands of women for whom prostitution was their sole means of employment, there were countless more women engaged in the various menial and low-paying professions, seamstresses and the like, who were forced by circumstance to engage in more casual prostitution when needs must. There was little in the transcription of the inquest to suggest in which of these types of prostitution, career or casual, the victim had engaged. This was a point which Blank resolved to remember.

Of particular interest was the testimony of one Doctor Thomas Bond, a resident at Number 7, the Sanctuary, Westminster, and surgeon to the A Division of the Metropolitan Police. He had been the one to examine the remains of the first victim, which had been brought to New Scotland Yard, and who also visited the site where the body had been found, along the embankment. In addition to the transcript of his testimony at the inquest, Blank and Miss Bonaventure had been provided with the postmortem report that Bond had written and delivered to his superiors.

The portmortem was quite graphic in its descriptions, enough so that Miss Bonaventure, whose stomach for such unpleasantries was usually cast iron, was forced to turn away. The report dwelt on the appearance of the armless, headless torso, bloated white after some indeterminate amount of time spent in the Thames, with special attention given the condition of the wounds, which appeared to have been fodder for fish at some point after death. The inquest testimony was thankfully somewhat less descriptive, though even here there was enough to make Miss Bonaventure turn a bit green at the gills. Blank, who had seen far worse things in his time, was too overcome by a frisson of recognition to allow himself a moment of queasy unease.

He'd had dealings with Dr. Thomas Bond before. Bond had been one of the physicians to examine the remains of the Torso Killer's victims. The man was well regarded, both by his peers in the medical establishment and by the police authorities, but Blank had quickly deduced that the man was an unctuous buffoon. He seemed too eager to impress, too eager to please, and as a result he had a habit of rendering his verdicts sooner than was appropriate, preferring a ready answer that sounded clever and learned to spending the time necessary to root out the actual truth.

In the case of the Torso Killings, Bond had quickly determined that the bodies had been dissected by someone with anatomical knowledge, later amending the statement to say that the knowledge could have been that of a butcher, rather than a surgeon. However, based on his own examinations of the remains, Blank knew full well that the killer displayed little knowledge of anatomy whatsoever, having simply hacked at his victims like a poor woodsman with a dull axe, rather than carving them with the skilled precision of a surgeon or cleaving them into quarters with at least the workmanlike skill of a butcher.

If anything, Bond's assistant, a Dr. Charles Alfred Hibbert, was the more skilled of the two, and so it was with interest that Blank read the transcript of Hibbert's testimony to the inquest. It was Hibbert's contention that the cuts had not been made by an anatomist, given that the positioning of the cuts did not conform with the locations of the various joints. The cutting implement had simply been applied to the body and pressed straight through bone.

The body, when found, had been in the early stages of decomposition, having been dumped into the Thames somewhere further upstream and catching up on the embankment in Pimlico. As a result, the state of the wounds at the time of death was difficult to ascertain. However, both Bond and Hibbert made specific mention of the bones being sheared cleanly through, without hack or saw marks.

That was about all that could be learned about the first murder. Blank found it somewhat surprising that no one involved in the inquest had even raised the specter of there being some connection with the Torso Killings of the decade previous, when there were obvious parallels. He perhaps shouldn't have been surprised that Bond had failed to mention the possible connection, given the slapdash way with which the man conducted his business, but he could not help but feel some regret that Hibbert had not put up his hand, either.

Blank and Miss Bonaventure moved on to consider the evidence of the second murder. The body had been found on the grounds of the Blind Asylum in Lambeth by a police constable on patrol, who had reported it to his superiors before the locals were aware of the incident. The officer dispatched to investigate, one Inspector Marshall of the Criminal Investigation Department, immediately recognized a connection between this new case— a body found murdered, its head and one arm missing—and the body that had been found on the embankment in Pimlico the previous week. Knowing that there was potential for panic, to say nothing of the sensation should the papers catch wind of a new series killer, and having received orders on high that nothing was to be allowed to disrupt the smooth operation of the

Queen's Diamond Jubilee, the inspector had the remains quietly transported to New Scotland Yard and informed his superiors.

There was no publicly held inquest into the second murder, though there had been a full postmortem conducted by the Divisional Surgeon, Dr. Thomas Bond himself. Blank and Miss Bonaventure had been given a copy of Bond's report, to which were appended Dr. Hibbert's own working notes. The examination had quickly revealed that the victim had been dispatched no fewer than three hours earlier and no more than thirty-six, given the state of rigor in which the body had been found; further, given the fresh state of the wounds, lacking even the earliest stages of corruption or decomposition, it was determined that the body had been living less than twelve hours previous. Given that the scene made it evident that the murder had taken place at the Blind Asylum itself, rather than being conducted elsewhere and the body relocated after the fact, that meant that the PC had only missed stumbling upon the murderer by somewhere between three and twelve hours.

Again the postmortem made reference to the clean shearing of the bone, but in this instance there was the additional detail that the flesh had likewise been cut in a level plane. To all indications, the wounds had been administered in single blows, there being no indication that the cutting implement was removed and reapplied.

The postmortem was silent on the topic, but in his notes, Hibbert had ventured a supposition as to what sort of cutting implement might have been used. He advanced the notion that the killer might have employed a guillotine, which would have possessed the sharpness and force necessary to drive to skin, muscle, and bone in a single swipe. How the killer managed to maneuver a guillotine into the grounds of the Blind Asylum, without leaving any track or trace of it, Hibbert failed to speculate.

Blank knew at a glance that these were not wounds inflicted by a guillotine. He'd seen those kinds of cuts firsthand, and could not expunge the memory of them from his mind if he'd wanted to. Even Madame Guillotine had not been so precise in her cuts, the edges of flesh left ragged and torn, and on rare occasion the blades had even been caught by the bones of the spinal column, requiring the operator to wrench the blade free and pull it up for a second try. Whatever had been used by the killer had been even sharper, or used with greater force, or both.

That was virtually all that distinguished these new murders from those of a decade before. In all other particulars they could have been part of a single, unbroken series. Like the victims of the Torso Killer years before, these latest three had been prostitutes, though whether casual or career it was impossible to say. And like those, the three new victims remained anonymous. Of all the Torso Killer's victims, only one was ever given a name, and Blank questioned the means by which that identification was reached. Five anonymous victims before, and three more now . . . so far, at any rate. Even the players were the same—Doctors Bond and Hibbert, Superintendent Melville, Blank himself—and the locales—the Thames embankment, the Blind Asylum, Pimlico, and Lambeth.

The only difference between the two groups was that the latter was dispatched by some unknown, impossibly sharp implement, while the former had been done for with a blunter instrument. But Blank was committed that there be another difference between the two groups. This latest, he vowed, would not remain anonymous. And if it were within his power, he would see that it grew no larger.

Having learned all they could from the reports and transcripts Melville had provided, that afternoon Miss Bonaventure suggested that they visit the scenes of the crimes. They'd already seen the walkway on Tower Bridge where the third body had been found, and there seemed little to be gained from visiting Pimlico, since the first body has simply washed ashore there, the murder having taken place at some unknown location upstream. It seemed most sensible, then, to visit Lambeth, across the Thames, and the Blind Asylum where the body of the second victim had been found.

Leaving Blank's Marylebone home, the pair hired a hansom cab. At Miss Bonaventure's request they detoured to her own home in Bayswater, so that she might change into clothing more suitable to the climate and circumstance. The temperature had already risen precipitously since she set out that morning, and what had been a pleasantly warm spring morning was quickly becoming a beastly hot summer day.

The driver let them off in front of Number 9, Bark Place, and while Miss Bonaventure climbed the steps to her door, fishing in her reticule for the front door key, Blank paid the driver, enjoying the relative silence of the block. Bark Place was a short road just off Bayswater Road, near the Orme Square Gate of Kensington Garden, whose green leaves could be seen just the other side of Orme Court. With the serene quiet of Kensington on one side and the relatively sedate bustle of Moscow Road on the other, Bark Place was as a consequence inordinately quiet, even in contrast with the relative calm that hung like a heavy blanket over the whole of Bayswater. Blank had once remarked to Miss Bonaventure that it seemed hardly a fitting place of residence for a "New Woman" such as herself, who was as likely to go for a bicycling tour of the countryside as she was to stay at home knitting doilies, and was more skilled in arts martial than marital. He had difficulty imagining her in a typical domestic setting; but then, he had difficulty imagining a typical domestic setting, full stop, given his scant experience with them, so that was probably hardly surprising. In response, Miss Bonaventure had simply explained that the signal feature of Bayswater, and Bark Place in particular, was that it changed little with the passing years, being now virtually identical to the street it had been almost half a century before, and promised to remain unchanged for centuries to come.

Of course, Blank had known perfectly well that Miss Bonaventure had her own reasons for desiring that sort of immutable permanence in a residence, but he had no desire to queer their friendship and refrained from mentioning it. After all, who was he to begrudge someone their secrets?

Blank waited in Miss Bonaventure's study, on the first floor up, while she was upstairs in her bedroom, getting dressed. Mrs. Pool, the day maid, had sniffed audibly on seeing Blank accompanying her mistress, evidently disapproving of the notion that an unmarried woman should spend so much time in the company of an unmarried man, but had accompanied Miss Bonaventure upstairs without comment.

Blank passed the time scanning the spines of the books on Miss Bonaventure's shelves. Her collection was impressive, as catholic in its breadth as it was detailed in its depth. There also seemed to be, Blank noted with amusement, a small number of titles that had not, as yet, been published.

Blank's gaze was arrested at a copy of the Ward, Lock & Co. edition of *The Picture of Dorian Gray*. He reached out a hand, tempted to pull it down from the shelf and page through it, but resisted the urge. After all, he knew what it would contain. He moved on, taking down and flipping through other titles of less personal significance.

After some quarter of an hour had passed, Miss Bonaventure appeared at the door to the study, the heavier frock she'd worn that morning replaced by a silk walking dress, dark blue in color, the skirt straight and gored, tight around the waist, the hem a few inches from the ground. Over this was a matching double-breasted silk jacket. Her hair was gathered up under a straw boater, except for two strands that had defiantly worked their way loose and hung down on either side of her face like punctuation marks. The parasol in her bare hands was as much a concession to fashion as it was an item of practical use, but the only item of jewelry she wore was the wide bracelet which never left her wrist, the inset lenticular gem flashing in the sunlight through the open shade.

"Well?" Miss Bonaventure said, hand on her hip. "Are you ready to go, Blank, or aren't you?"

The driver steered his cab off Bayswater Road and south onto Park Lane, where the Marble Arch stood at the intersection of Oxford and Edgeware. Blank rested both hands on the silver-chased head of his cane, his eyes unfocused on the middle distance, already lost in thought. Miss Bonaventure, seated beside him, tucked her parasol to one side. She had pulled a copper coin from her reticule, which she now tossed in the air again and again; it glinted in the bright summer sun. Time and again she thumbed the coin flying into the air, spinning so fast it appeared a whirling copper sphere and then snatching it from midair before it fell.

By the time they passed Buckingham Palace and turned onto Vauxhall Bridge Road, Blank had still not spoken. Miss Bonaventure, evidently, had gotten her fill of silence.

"Penny for them," she said, snatching the coin from midair and nudging Blank with her elbow.

"Hmm?" Blank blinked, somewhat startled, as if he'd forgotten for a moment where he was.

"Your thoughts, Blank." Miss Bonaventure smiled. "Care to share them?"

He managed a weary smile in return. "Not really, if truth be told, but if you're hungry for entertainment, I'll do my level best."

In point of fact, Blank *had* very nearly forgotten where he was, for that brief span. His thoughts had been years and miles away. He'd begun to dwell on the defeats of ten years previous as they left Miss Bonaventure's Bark Place house, but by the time they'd gotten into the cab he'd followed a chain of association that led far away. Very far away, indeed. The Torso Killer to Oscar, and thence to William, and thence to Quexi, and to Michel, and to Roanoke, and finally to Omega. All roads led to Omega, in the end. At least, that was Omega's most cherished desire. And if that desire was manifest nowhere else, it most definitely held true in Blank's thoughts. Through a tangled skein of association, it seemed that every notion which entered Blank's mind inexorably led, through one means or another, to thoughts of Omega, and of what Blank himself had become, and had done, in Omega's name.

That was the nettle upon which Blank's thoughts had caught, and which Miss Bonaventure had offered coin in exchange for hearing. In response, though, he instead said, "There seem a great many soldiers abroad in the city's streets, don't you think?"

Miss Bonaventure raised an eyebrow, giving him a quizzical look. Then, with a somewhat amused air, laced through with suspicion, she nodded. "Yes, I imagine there are quite a lot of them about, at that."

She fell silent, her gaze lingering on Blank, while he turned to watch the buildings slip past the moving cab.

"Well," she said at last, holding out the coin, good naturedly. "Aren't you going to take it?"

Blank glanced back her way and shook his head. "No, thank you," he said, smiling.

Miss Bonaventure narrowed her eyes, suspiciously, and then resumed flipping the coin. "Suit yourself."

As he turned away, Blank's smile slipped from his face. Still, he couldn't in good conscience have accepted the payment. Not when he'd failed to meet his end of the bargain.

Crossing the Thames at Vauxhall Bridge, they turned back to the north and rumbled into Lambeth. As they made their way to the School for the Indigent Blind, in the shadow of the Obelisk in St. George's Circus, not far from Bedlam, they passed the entrance to Hercules Road.

"Blake used to live around these parts, didn't he?" Miss Bonaventure mused, glancing up the road.

Blank hummed his assent, and pointed with his chin up the road. "Number 13, Hercules Buildings."

"Thought so," Miss Bonaventure said, nodding. "Changed a bit since he lived here, though." She smiled, a sly look in her eye. "I imagine so, at any rate." She chuckled and tapped the foot of her parasol on the floorboard of the cab. "Mad old bugger, was Blake. Still, he was my favorite of the lot of them, much better than dour George Gordon, or strident Percy, or stuffy old Coleridge, heaven forefend."

Miss Bonaventure ran the fingers of her right hand over the jewel inset in the bracelet on her left wrist. Then, eyes closed, she recited aloud.

"To see a World in a grain of sand,
And a Heaven in a wild flower,
Hold Infinity in the palm of your hand,
And Eternity in an hour."

She opened her eyes, smiled, and glanced over at her companion.

"There are times when I'm convinced that he was completely dotty and other times when I'm sure he knew precisely what he was talking about."

"Mmm," Blank hummed thoughtfully, moving his hands back and forth, palm to palm around the cane, spinning it like a caveman attempting to start a fire. "I wonder what he'd have made of all this martial finery, though, all

this talk of celebrating a great dominion upon which the sun shall never set."
He suddenly stopped the spinning of his cane, wrapping a fist around the
silver-chased handle. "You can have your auguries of innocence," he said,
glancing over at Miss Bonaventure, "and leave for me his more fiery polemic."
He sighed. "But if once the king of England looked westward at America and
trembled at the vision, I'm sorry to admit that his successor Victoria can cast
her gaze where'er she will and suffer not the slightest twitch. In its prime the
Roman Empire comprised perhaps one hundred twenty million people in an
area a few million square miles in extent; today, Victoria holds dominion over
some three hundred seventy million people spread across eleven million
square miles, more than ninety times the size of these small islands. That's
some quarter of the globe."

Miss Bonaventure gave him an unreadable look. "It won't last, of course."

"It's a comforting thought," Blank said, "but how many years has it been
since poor old mad William prophesied empire's end?" He took a deep
breath, his eyes half-lidded.

"The Sun has left his blackness, and has found a fresher morning,
And the fair Moon rejoices in the clear and cloudless night;
For Empire is no more, and now the Lion and Wolf shall cease."

He opened his eyes and smiled sadly at Miss Bonaventure.

"More than a century since, and I'm sorry to say that far from ceasing,
the lion and wolf are very much still at it. And empire, as we've seen, has
weathered the years quite nicely."

Miss Bonaventure quirked a smile, her expression soft, and reached out
to pat Blank's knee, consolingly. "Cheer up a bit, Blank. It's not all bad, you
know. Look at all the positives empire brings."

Blank cocked an eyebrow.

"Don't give me that look," Miss Bonaventure scolded. "I'm quite serious.
Just fifty years ago, a letter traveling from here to the farthest outposts of the
empire took months, even years. Now, post from London can reach Australia
in no more than four weeks, India in little more than two weeks, and Ottawa
in scarcely more than a week. And if that's not quick enough, a telegraph

message can now be sent anywhere in the civilized world in just a matter of minutes."

"And in future, these times will just diminish, and the distances themselves will seem to shrink, is that it?"

Miss Bonaventure smiled, knowingly. "Naturally. Though prices might fluctuate a bit, admittedly. Seventeen days and fifty pounds can get you to India, but I shouldn't be surprised if that time drops precipitously as the cost rises in inverse proportion."

"As the steam engines' speed is improved, no doubt. No, let me guess. As they are gradually replaced with electrically powered engines, no doubt, cables snaking from London to Bombay."

"Of course not," Miss Bonaventure answered. "That would be ridiculous. No, by air, naturally."

"Airships, is it, now?" Blank rolled his eyes. "My dear Miss Bonaventure, if nature had meant us to fly, it would not have put the sky so high up off the ground, now would it?"

Miss Bonaventure chuckled. "And what do you suppose mad old Bill Blake would have made of air travel, at that?"

Blank smiled. "Well, he was never one for convention. I suppose if there was some scandal to be had in an airship, William might well have been induced to fly. Not that he was a scandal monger, but seemed constitutionally incapable of escaping it. I remember the time that a Mr. Thomas Butts interrupted William and Catherine in the summer house at the end of the garden in Hercules Buildings, freed from 'those troublesome disguises' that have prevailed since the Fall, and reciting passages from *Paradise Lost*. As Butts fled, blushing at the sight of so much naked flesh, Blake called out, 'Come in! It's only Adam and Eve, you know!'"

Miss Bonaventure shuddered, squirming on the bench. "I quite prefer my Milton fully dressed, thank you. If at all, come to that."

"I found old John a crashing bore, myself," Blake said. "But enough of that." He tilted his bowler back on his head with the top of his cane, as the hansom came to a halt. "The School for the Indigent Blind awaits, my dear."

Once, long before, an inn had stood here, under the sign of the Dog and Duck. The patrons could drink at their leisure while watching a duck put into the water and a dog set to hunt for it. Sometimes the duck dove, and the dog went under after it. It hardly seemed deserving of the name "entertainment," and Blank had never quite understood the appeal, but there it was.

It had been nearly ten years since Blank was last on the grounds of Lambeth's asylum for the blind. The arm of a woman had been found there, apparently the mate to another arm found floating in the Thames at Pimlico two weeks before, and both apparently the property of the limbless torso discovered on the building site of the New Scotland Yard two weeks further on. It had been the Torso Killer's second victim, and the killer had gone to special lengths to scatter the puzzle pieces far and wide.

Now, nearly a decade later, the School for the Indigent Blind was once again the site of a gruesome discovery, but this time, instead of a lonely arm, it had been an entire torso, albeit one limbless and headless.

Blank and Miss Bonaventure were met at the school gate by an attendant who, unlike his charges, was quite definitely sighted. And on seeing the approach of two strangers, however well turned out they may have been, so soon after the unpleasant discoveries of the previous week, the attendant seemed in no eager mood to allow them admittance.

Blank smiled easily, as the large man blocked their path.

"And what do *you* lot want?" the man grumbled. He had the large hands and thick neck of a laborer, and though his hair had gone to gray, his whiskers very nearly white, Blank could tell that the man had worked for a living before securing his present employment. Had he been drawn to this vocation for family reasons, perhaps, finding himself the father of a blind child or perhaps having been the child of a blind parent himself? What road led a man who seemed more suited to work by the strength of his hands and the sweat of his back to oversee an asylum devoted to the care and comfort of the indigent blind? It was a mystery, and Blank had an insatiable appetite for solving such, but he also knew that he had more pressing matters to attend, and that the question of the overseer's provenance would likely have to remain unsolved.

"We're here about the recent . . . unpleasantness," Blank said, his expression open and inviting. He pulled a calling card from his pocket, completely white and featureless front and back, and presented it for the attendant's inspection. As the attendant leaned forward for a closer look, a hum thrummed deep in Blank's throat, a subharmonic just below the range of human hearing. Then he spoke, mindful of the cadence and pitch of his words, the thrumming persisting as an undercurrent, the two vocalizations interweaving like the threaded tones of a Tuvan throat singer. "If we could just trouble you for a few moments of your time, to show us where the . . . remains . . . were found, we can look after ourselves from there."

The overseer's face, which had been closed and guarded, softened by inches. "Well, the police have already come and gone, and they said not to talk about it with any . . ."

"We're not with the Yard, but I assure you that we are completely within their confidence." Blank gave an easy smile, and the barely audible hum shifted in tone.

By now, the overseer's guarded expression had completely melted and been replaced by one of trust. "It's right this way," the overseer said, absently handing the calling card back to Blank, who pocketed it. "It's just a blessing that none of our patients were awake when the PC found the thing. I can't imagine the state of them, had they seen it."

Miss Bonaventure stifled a chuckle, which the overseer failed to notice but which Blank did not. He cast her a quick glance over his shoulder, warning her silent. She smiled, sheepishly, and gave a helpless shrug. Then, despite his warning, she said, "I expect your patients wouldn't have *seen* anything of the sort before, would they?"

The overseer looked back at her, wearing a queer expression. "They'll not have seen anything t'all, miss," he said simply. "They're blind, you see."

Her witticism left to whither in the wind, Miss Bonaventure scowled and twirled her parasol over her shoulder, defiantly.

"Here it is," the overseer said, coming to a halt. They stood before a sheltering oak in a courtyard, the ground underfoot hard packed dirt, punctuated here and there with little scattered wisps of dried brown grass. It was a garden sore in need of attention, but Blake could see that the *appearance* of the place was a low priority for an asylum of sightless patients.

"Here?" Blank asked, and the overseer pointed to a spot a few yards from the base of the wide-boled trunk. Following his gaze, Blank could see that there was still visual evidence of the discovery, the dirt discolored in a wide circle, bits of dust dried into dark balls. "Here," Blank said, nodding.

They were a short distance from the open gate. As they'd passed through, Blank had seen that, while the iron of the gate itself was rusted with age, the lock that hung opened from the hook was shiny and new.

"You've had to replace the lock, I take it?" Miss Bonaventure asked, evidently having noticed the same.

"Why, yes," the overseer said, startled somewhat by the question. "Was the strangest thing, too. The morning the police came and hauled the body away, I found the lock in two pieces just inside the gate. Cut clean through, like butter cut with a hot knife, it was."

Blank nodded, thoughtfully. He looked up at the windows of the surrounding walls, which were dark and grimed but unshuttered. "It was early morning that the constable found the body, I believe?"

The overseer nodded. "Mike does his rounds starting just before dawn, and most mornings comes by to have breakfast with me and the missus." He smiled, somewhat sheepishly. "And he may linger a bit for a pipe of my best shag, and a cup of tea with a bit of spice to it, if you get my meaning." The overseer tugged a small flask from his vest pocket, which glinted dully in the afternoon sun. "It's a dreadful habit, is gin, but it can certainly improve the outlook of a day, taken in moderation."

"I'm sure," Blank said with a smile. "Now, on this particular morning, when entering the gate, the constable happened to spy something lying on the ground here beneath the oak. Is that correct?"

"Yes, just so. He thought I'd been up early, finding the gate already unlocked, and reckoned I might have breakfast laid out sooner rather than later. As it happened, none of us got to eat that morning, more's the pity."

"Though I expect you didn't neglect your *other* appetites." Miss Bonaventure smiled sweetly and indicated the flask in the overseer's pocket with her parasol.

The overseer blushed, and looked away.

"I don't think we need to keep you any longer," Blank said, clapping his hands together. "I'm sure that you've much more important things to do than play nursemaid to us." He gave the overseer a broad smile.

The overseer looked a little lost for a moment, then nodded, absently. "Yes, of course." He glanced from one side to the other, as though not sure which way to turn.

"In your office, perhaps?" Blank suggested, an almost silent thrum beneath his words.

"In my office," the overseer repeated. "Yes." He straightened up, blinking several times, and looked from Blank to Miss Bonaventure and back again. "You'll excuse me, but I've some important business to attend in my office. You'll see yourselves out, I trust?"

Miss Bonaventure nodded, while Blank reached out and patted the overseer on the arm. "I'm sure we can manage," he said. "Thank you for all your assistance."

With that, the overseer turned on his heel and walked away, rounding a corner and disappearing through the front doors of the building.

"I'll never understand just how you do that, Blank," Miss Bonaventure said, admiringly.

"It only works on particularly susceptible minds," Blank said, turning his attention back to the stained dirt at their feet, "and not always then. But I find it smoothes over so many of the rough edges of social interaction in circumstances such as these."

Blank tested the soil, tapping it with the foot of his cane. It was a thick layer of dried earth beneath a thin blanket of dust and covering the moister soil underneath. Footprints were difficult to discern in the dust, which was blown hither and fro with the winds that circulated around the courtyard like a turbine. In another hour at most, all signs of his and Miss Bonaventure's passage through the yard would be obscured. Tightening his grip on the cane, he brought its foot down hard on the ground, puncturing the mantle of dried earth and sending cracks creeping a few inches in every direction. Digging in and levering up with the cane, he knocked loose a clump of earth about the size of his palm.

"Correct me if I'm mistaken," he said aloud, "but it's not rained in at least a fortnight, has it?"

Miss Bonaventure nodded. With a crooked finger she tugged at the collar of her jacket, a glow of perspiration on her cheek. "If not more, sadly."

"Given that the overseer hardly seems the sort to concern himself with watering the garden, then, we can safely assume that the only moisture the ground here has seen in the last week was the spilled blood of the victim."

Miss Bonaventure pointed to the blood-stained earth with the tip of her parasol. "Still very much in evidence."

"Yes," Blank said with a nod. "And the state of the ground is such that, even *if* someone were by some means to wrestle a guillotine or similar into the yard, the soil would still be broken and cracked beneath its weight."

"Thereby dismissing Hibbert's already dubious suggestion."

"Fairly conclusively, I would say. So whatever cutting implement was employed, it was not heavy enough to leave an impression on the ground."

"Though clearly it was sufficient to leave an impression on this poor girl." Miss Bonaventure knelt down and ran her finger along the rust-colored ground. "And sharp enough to cut an iron padlock in two, at that."

"So it would seem." Blank swung his cane up, resting it on his shoulder, and spun on his heel in a slow circle, regarding the windows which overlooked the courtyard. "If the postmortem is any indicator, the murder took place between three and twelve hours before the body was discovered. By the overseer's testimony, the discovery came sometime just around dawn. Sunrise would have been sometime just short of a quarter hour before five o'clock, putting the murder somewhere between five o'clock the previous afternoon and two o'clock in the morning. My guess is that the deed was done in the latter part of that window, sometime past midnight. The overseer and his wife, who presumably live here on the grounds, would doubtless have been abed by that hour."

"And any witnesses who happened to be awake," Miss Bonaventure said, indicating the windows overhead, "were not in a position to *witness* much of anything. So long as the killer prevented the victim from making much in the way of noise, the whole thing would have passed completely unnoticed beneath the sightless eyes of the asylum."

"Just so." Blank nodded. "Which tells us . . . ?" He trailed off and looked to Miss Bonaventure.

"Very little, I would think. Except that the killer had the presence of mind to choose a secluded locale for his business and was in possession of some unknown implement capable of cutting iron as easily as muscle and bone."

"That's not quite all, my dear."

Miss Bonaventure cocked an eyebrow.

"It tells us that the killer shows very little concern for whether the remains are found, since the overseer could not have failed to notice them on waking. As borne out by the discovery of the third body in the Tower Bridge walkway. The killer desires uninterrupted solitude during the commission of the crime, but has no compunction against leaving the body in plain view when the task is done."   ·

"Except for the missing limbs and heads," Miss Bonaventure said, her voice low. Then, after a pause, she looked at Blank, an expression of disquieted horror creeping across her features. "What do you suppose he does with them?"

"Or 'she,' Miss Bonaventure," Blank corrected. "Let's not unfairly dismiss your own sex as possibly including our killer in its number. There has been no evidence as yet to suggest that the murderer could not have been a woman." His slight smile faded, and more seriously he added, "But I'm afraid that I don't even have an informed guess for you on that count, my dear. And I confess that I shrink from contemplating the possibilities."

"Blank, if you *shrink*, then I positively *vanish*." She laid a hand over her stomach, the blue silk of her jacket crinkling under her touch. "I feel . . . ugh." She shook her head in distaste.   ·

"Are you sure, Miss Bonaventure, that the sensation you detect in your innards is not the early twinges of hunger pangs?" Blank came and stood beside her, brightening. "I believe we've learned all we can here, at least for the moment, and as for myself I am ravenously hungry. If memory serves, there is a serviceable chop house not three blocks from here, and if we hurry, we just might beat the dinner rush."

Miss Bonaventure smiled, somewhat soothed, and threaded her arm through his. "I shouldn't wonder, Blank, if you don't at times use a bit of your mesmerism on me, as well."

"Miss Bonaventure!" Blank opened his mouth in a wide "o" of outrage. "I'm shocked that you'd suggest such a thing." Leading her back through the courtyard towards the gate, he patted her hand and smiled. "Which is not to say that I haven't *tried*, on innumerable occasions, but you seem to be too obstinately strong-willed to succumb, I'm sorry to say."

Miss Bonaventure's smile widened, and her eyes twinkled. "Why, Mr. Blank, but you do say the most flattering things."

CHAPTER NINE
Millennium

WHEN ALICE STEPPED ONTO WESTMINSTER BRIDGE, she got her first look at the London Eye. It was just like she'd seen on television the week before. But she'd been seeing it for a lot longer than that.

It was an enormous Ferris wheel and looked for all the world like a gigantic bicycle wheel, spokes radiating out from the hub to the rim, but in the place of a tire were little pillbug-shaped pods of glass and steel spaced at regular intervals. It stood right on the banks of the Thames River, across from the Houses of Parliament and up a bit. According to *Frommer's*, it was an "observation wheel," whatever that was, but was the tallest one in the world, so Alice supposed that made it the tallest Ferris wheel in the world, too. She'd been up in the Texas Star at the State Fair, which was supposed to be the biggest one in North America or the Western Hemisphere or something-or-other, but if it was half as tall as the London Eye, Alice would have been surprised.

Luckily, Alice wasn't scared of heights. Not really. She was scared of *falling*, but not from heights. She was scared of falling off of anything, tall or short.

So the idea of falling from the top of a four-hundred-foot-tall Ferris wheel wasn't any more scary than that of falling from the top of a flight of stairs. And she'd done that once and survived, hadn't she? More or less, that is.

But when Alice saw the London Eye, she didn't just see a giant Ferris wheel. Or an enormous bicycle wheel surrounded by metal pillbugs. She saw an eye, looking out over a city. You had to squint a little to see it as an eye, but it was there, all the same. And it was this image, the eye looking out over the city, that had brought her here.

She'd been seeing that eye and that city since she was seven and a half years old, since a few months after the accident, the first one, not the one that no one at school liked to talk about. The eye above the city had been the central image of her very first "episode," as her grandmother called them, or "temporal lobe seizure," as the doctors later called it. Of course, her grandmother Naomi had been going through a Catholic phase at the time and had been convinced that the episodes were evidence of demonic possession and had taken her down to the church and insisted that the priest give her an exorcism. The priest had refused, and Alice's grandmother had to continue to look further and further afield until she was able to find a clergyman willing to administer the rites. Of course, she also took Alice to a curandera, who shaved her head just in case she had lice; a palm reader, who smelled of mentholated cough drops and stale tobacco; and a hairdresser who dabbled in the occult, who couldn't bring herself to sacrifice a live chicken and so instead performed a few cleansing rituals with a frozen turkey her grandmother brought from the supermarket. Alice's mother had been busy with the postal contract unit, pulling double shifts after the death of Alice's father a few months before, and didn't know how much school Alice was missing until the school sent around a truant officer. Then the trips to the crazy-eyed hairdressers and disreputable priests stopped, and when Alice's mother found out about the episodes, all of those weeks later, she rushed her to the doctor, who hooked her up to an EEG and diagnosed her with Temporal Lobe Epilepsy.

As soon as Alice started taking the anticonvulsants the doctor prescribed, she stopped having her episodes. For a while, at least.

Here is what Alice saw during her episodes:

An eye over a city. (What city, she didn't know.)

A jewel or diamond or crystal that seemed to shine with an inner light.

Large black birds. Lots of them. (Originally Alice thought they were crows, or maybe even oversized grackles, but when she saw a nature documentary a while later, she knew she'd been wrong. They were ravens.)

A small body of water, a pond or lake, the surface motionless as glass, smooth and featureless as a mirror's face.

A man she didn't know whose eyes were ice-chip blue.

Alice had missed so much school that she was held back a year, and when all of the other kids moved on to the third grade, she stayed back in the second. She didn't have any more episodes, not until she was almost sixteen and a freshman in high school. But the images she'd seen in those weeks stuck with her, and she was forever doodling them in the margins of her schoolwork or drawing them in art classes. In particular the eye above the city. The eye was giant, Alice had remembered that, but there hadn't been a face, or another eye, or even an eyebrow and lashes. More a giant eyeball floating in midair. And the city was indistinct, more the abstract suggestion of a city than an actual place.

Alice started keeping a diary around the time she was nine years old, and by the time she was eleven had graduated to spiral notebooks that she carried everywhere. Like most girls that age, she was paranoid about people reading her innermost thoughts but couldn't afford a diary with a lock and key, especially not considering the fact that she filled up a new one every few weeks, no matter what the days and dates preprinted on the pages. So she had to devise another way to keep her thoughts secure, and started writing backwards. Right to left, mirror-image style. The idea at first was that she would hold the pages up to a mirror to read them, but after a little while she found it as easy to read backwards as it had become to write that way, and so she didn't bother. That she wrote almost exclusively in purple ink was just a question of aesthetics.

It wasn't until later that she discovered that Leonardo da Vinci had written backwards in his own journals, for much the same reason. And later still before Mr. Saenz told her all about how Lewis Carroll had been a temporal lobe epileptic, too, and that he'd written backwards in his notebooks, as well. When Saenz told her that Carroll had used only purple ink, it seemed like it must have been fate.

In any event, in the pages of her mirror-written, purple-inked notebooks, Alice frequently sketched the image of the eye over the city, along with her compulsive lists of television shows she hated, books she'd read, kids at her school who ignored her, and all of the places she would go if she were ever able to leave home. London was usually on this last list, but as an afterthought, far down the pecking order, somewhere after Disney World but before Six Flags Over Texas.

It wasn't until she'd seen a news story about tourist attractions in England, the night after her grandmother's funeral, that Alice knew anything about the London Eye, but as soon as she'd seen it on screen, she'd recognized it as the image from her episodes. Of course, by this point, she'd started thinking of them as *visions*, instead, but all the same. There was the giant eye above the city, just as she'd seen when she was seven and a half, and like she saw again her freshman year. And suddenly, Alice knew what one part of her vision, at least, was trying to tell her. She had to go to London. She had to go to the London Eye. And there, she hoped, she would find out what the rest of the vision meant. It was the only thing that made any sense at all.

Alice's arrival at the London Eye was something of an anticlimax. If she'd been expecting the heavens to open up and a host of angels to descend, she'd have been disappointed. Not that she had, of course. But still, something a little dramatic would have been nice.

Instead, she'd stood in one line to purchase her ticket—seven pounds, or about eleven dollars American—and then gone to stand in another line to wait her turn. And waited. And waited. And waited.

It was some hours before her turn came around at last, hours of shuffling forward slowly, with a pair of German tourists in hiking boots and brightly colored T-shirts in front of her, bandanas tied jauntily around their necks, and a group of London schoolchildren behind her, kept in line and more or less in control only by the sheer force of will of the teachers who were with them, one at either end of the group, merrily carrying on a conversation at the top of their lungs over the shouting of the kids, pausing occasionally to bark reprimands at this kid or that for cutting up or for stealing each other's action figures or whatnot. Finally, she mounted the ramp that zigzagged back and forth, carefully watched over by a guy in a uniform, but Alice couldn't tell if he was a cop or a security guard, not that it mattered. Then she and the German tourists and half of the school kids, accompanied by one of the teachers, were ushered into one of the glass and steel pods. They looked less like pillbugs up close, and more like some impossibly large lozenge. But more distressing was the fact that the things *didn't stop moving*. The wheel kept on turning, slowly but inexorably, and as the pods slid by the deck, the doors opened, the people on board jumped off, the people waiting on the deck jumped on, the doors closed, and the pod climbed back up into the sky.

Now Alice started to worry about falling. There was maybe an inch of daylight visible between the edge of the deck and the pod, so it wasn't likely that she could fall through, but if anyone could manage to do, it was Alice. Maybe she'd suddenly shrink down to the size of the action figure between one step and the next, and find herself plummeting through the gap and out of sight. She'd fall into the green-gray waters of the Thames, and that would be that.

But she didn't shrink to the size of an action figure, and she didn't fall through the gap but jumped on board the pod, and when the door slid shut behind her, she finally started breathing again, and her pulse started to slow, if gradually.

Then the wheel turned, and the pod climbed into the sky.

Alice thought about pictures she'd seen in books of medieval engravings of the wheel of fate, which never stopped turning. In the pictures there was always a king sitting at the top, thinking that he would never fall, and some poor bastard being crushed underneath. But the pictures also showed that some schemer was on the side of the wheel heading up, and some unfortunate soul was on the other side heading down. The lesson of the wheel was that it kept on turning, no matter what, and that today's king could be tomorrow's poor bastard crushed underneath. Which meant, by analogy, that Alice was on the way up, right? So what happened when she reached the top of the wheel? And, more worrying, what happened when she started to come down again?

As it happened, she needn't have worried. *Nothing* happened, not going up, not at the top, not coming back down. It took half an hour for the wheel to make a complete revolution and the pod door to slide back open again at the deck, but in all that time, all Alice could see was the city of London. And the German tourists and the half complement of school kids with their teacher. But mostly London.

No choir of angels. No pink light striking her forehead and imparting holy wisdom. No flock of ravens and no gem and no mysterious guy with the ice-chip blue eyes. No fate, no destiny, no message, no meaning.

The German tourists were first off the pod, eager to soldier on to some other tourist destination, and the teacher had to struggle to herd all of her charges off the pod. Alice was the last on board, standing at the edge of the pod, watching the deck slip slowly by. The people running the Eye kept shouting at her to step off and onto the deck, pointing urgently at all of the passengers waiting on the other side of the deck to get on, but Alice found herself frozen, unable to move.

Was she not on a mission? Not for God, or the Queen of Faerie, or space aliens, or future super computers? What if she didn't have some special destiny, but was only a mixed up eighteen-year-old runaway who was off her meds, confused and alone in a foreign country?

In the end, two of the attendants stepped into the pod, gently but firmly took hold of Alice's arms, and dragged her off onto the deck, just in time for the rest of the passengers to get on board. The attendants told Alice not to worry, as they ushered her back to the ground, saying that it happens from time to time, that people get a bit locked up trying to get off the wheel. But Alice knew better. She wanted to tell them that just as the wheel of fate never stopped spinning, no one could ever get off, not really. No one got off alive. But she was pretty sure that they wouldn't understand.

Alice had a few hundred bucks in cash, converted into British monopoly money. Assuming that her mother hadn't cut off her AmEx and her ATM, she could always use plastic, but even if the accounts were still active there was a chance that her mother could use the transactions to trace her whereabouts and send the police after her, so Alice didn't want to try the cards unless it was absolutely necessary.

Alice figured she probably had enough to stay in a hostel somewhere for a while. Her *Frommer's* didn't list any, just hotels and beds & breakfasts and the like, presumably because a hostel would be beneath the dignity of anyone traveling London on eighty-five dollars a day, but Alice was reasonably sure she could find an affordable one, if she looked. Then again, the drinking age in England *was* eighteen, and she could just as easily spend her remaining money on drinks at a bar. She hadn't had a drink since she was almost sixteen, not since the accident, the one that no one at school liked to talk about.

Maybe it was time to start drinking again.

Alice was on her third drink at the pub, but it really wasn't helping matters any.

She'd had to stop drinking after the accident, for obvious reasons, but also because she went back on her meds. She'd stopped taking her medication originally when she was almost fifteen and about to start high school because she'd started drinking, and alcohol interfered with the medication and made her sick all the time. She'd be trucking along, having a few drinks with her new friends, and all of a sudden she'd feel dizzy, her stomach upset, and then she'd vomit everywhere. Nancy and the others had all just assumed she couldn't hold her liquor and teased her mercilessly. She hadn't told them about her episodes, of course, or about the accident—the first once, since Nancy was still alive and the second one hadn't happened yet—or about the medication. She'd just tried to grin as she cleaned the vomit off her chin and clothes, and decided then and there to stop taking the little salmon-colored pills altogether. When, a few weeks later, she still hadn't had any more seizures, she figured she'd been cured. She even joked to herself, in purple-inked mirror-writing, that it was the wine coolers and lite beer and rum that had cured her.

Then, of course, there'd been another episode, another seizure, and that had caused the accident, and with Nancy gone suddenly the other kids didn't feel like hanging out with her anymore, and no one else at the school much wanted to talk to her either, not that they ever had, and so Alice had been pretty much on her own. She'd stopped drinking, started going to counseling and group sessions, gone back on her medications, and that was that. She concentrated on her schoolwork, started getting A's and high B's in her Latin and math and science classes, spent her nights and weekends watching movies and old TV shows instead of socializing, did mazes and crossword puzzles, and basically turned into a geek.

Then her grandmother had gotten sick and told her that she'd been wrong all those years before and that her episodes weren't demonic possession but messages from God. And then her grandmother had died, and the London Eye was on television, and that was that. They were messages, and visions, and Alice had packed up her backpack and emptied her bank account and run away. Technically, she was sure, she wasn't really a runaway, since she was eighteen and legally able to make decisions for herself. But she was still in high school, and now technically truant from summer school—to make up for the days she missed sitting with her grandmother, this last spring—so she was sure her mother could make a convincing case to the authorities, if need be.

She hoped that drinking might help. It wasn't as if she was going to be driving again any time soon. Not only were the steering wheels all on the wrong sides of the cars and the cars on the wrong sides of the roads, but Alice didn't have a driver's license, not even an American one. The Department of Public Safety apparently frowned on handing out licenses to kids who'd been involved in vehicular manslaughter before they even took a driver's education class, so it didn't seem likely she'd be getting one any time soon.

So Alice sat at the bar and ordered a drink, and when she finished that one, she ordered another, and another. It wasn't a bar, as near as she could tell, but a "pub," at least according to *Frommer's*, but Alice was hard pressed to tell the difference. Maybe it was the fact that the place sold fried fish with fries on greasy wax paper, inexplicably served with frozen peas, which she'd never heard of any *bar* doing.

Alice wasn't sure what she was drinking. She hadn't exactly been a connoisseur when she was a drinker. Nancy and the others were more interested in being drunk than drinking, per se, and anything that worked was fine with them. Cheap wine coolers, warm cans of lite beer, bottles of fortified wine, rum mixed with generic colas, whatever they could get their hands on. Whatever the bartender was serving—or *publican*, she supposed—wasn't anything she'd had before. She'd started by ordering the same as the person just before her in line, and ended up with something the color of hot chocolate with a frothy white head. It was a little heavy for her tastes, though her lips were pleasantly numb by the time she finished. Then she saw a woman order something a little lighter in color, and tried that, instead. It was a bit more her speed. Then she ordered something called a lager, which just looked like beer, to her, and tasted about like it looked.

There was a television in the pub, over the bar, and while Alice tried to drink her way to numb oblivion, she watched it. She didn't have any particular interest in what was on, but televisions screens are like magnets for eyes, and when one is turned on in your field of vision, it's hard to look away. It was all sports of some kind, soccer or, as they called it over here, football. Alice didn't care much for sports, not for American football or the kind the rest of the world played. The game wrapped up, and there was a brief news story about a music festival going on in some place called Glastonbury. There were a couple of quick-edited shots of hippies setting up tents and crowds of people with their shirts off, dancing in mud, bands on stage, and so on. It looked like Lollapalooza turned up to eleven.

The Glastonbury story sparked some controversy in the pub. Alice was sitting at the end of the bar, minding her own business, and there were a group of guys sitting in a booth a short distance away. The place had been pretty empty when Alice came in, sometime just past noon, but as the afternoon wore on it had filled up slowly. There were four guys sitting at the booth, between the ages of maybe twenty years old and fifty, and they looked like regular office workers, just like guys in polo shirts and khaki pants Alice used to see all over Austin. It was Friday afternoon, and it looked like the guys had taken off work early and had been quickly making up for lost time. They'd come in while Alice was on her second drink and had already finished off their fourth rounds.

One of the office guys, who looked to be about twenty-five and who wore a bright orange shirt and blue tie, said that he had originally planned to go to the Glastonbury Festival but that it had just gotten too commercial since the New Age Travellers were kicked out, and so he'd decided not to go. Another, who seemed about the same age, expressed his disappointment that he wasn't going to be going, since he'd always wanted to see David Bowie, who was supposed to be performing on Sunday. Another said that he'd been the year before and been so out of his head on ecstasy that he didn't remember a thing, but that he'd have stayed straight for a chance to see Bowie play live. Then the oldest of the group, who was maybe fifty, said that the other three didn't know what they were talking about. He said that he'd been there in 1971 when Bowie played the festival the first time round, and that he could take Bowie or leave him. The one *he'd* really like to see on stage again was Iain Temple.

At which the other three pounced on him, verbally and metaphorically. Iain Temple? they said. The guy who owns the airline? And the music stores? And the line of clothing and men's fragrances and software and frozen gourmet entrees? *That* Iain Temple?

At which the older guy got his back up and started in on the younger guys' fashion choices, and poor work ethic, and such like. From the way they talked, Alice assumed the guy had a position of some minor authority at whatever office employed them, the way he lorded it over the other three in the pub.

Then the television started showing an ad for something called *Queer as Folk*, and the conversation drifted on to other topics.

Alice was just starting her fourth drink, another lager, when it happened. One minute she was staring absent-mindedly up at the television screen, feeling miserable and sorry for herself, when she started smelling something burning. She'd just stubbed out a cigarette and thought for a second that it was still smoldering in the ashtray. But when the edges of her vision started to go white, she knew what was happening. She was having an episode. A vision. Whatever.

It was almost tiresome, really. She'd been off her meds for a week, ever since her grandmother's funeral, and though it had been several years since she'd last had a seizure, nothing much had changed. First came the olfactory hallucination, a smell like something burning. Then the white light. Then Alice felt like she was falling. Or in free fall, perhaps. Weightless, mainly, but never hitting the ground. She heard indistinct voices that she almost but never quite was able to recognize, whispering things she could never manage to understand.

Then there it was again, the same cavalcade of images, the mix-and-match jumble of symbols that had featured in nearly every vision she'd had since she was seven and a half years old. The eye over the city. A flock of black birds in flight. The man with the ice-chip blue eyes, and the mirror-still water of the lake or pond. And the jewel.

And then, an eternity later, a moment later, the vision passed, and the world returned to her. Just not as she'd left it.

It took her a minute to work out what had changed. Her right hand was still wrapped around her pint glass, her left hand was on her stomach, and she caught herself licking her lips, like always. There was a weight across her shoulders and a warm presence on her right.

She turned her head, feeling a little crick in her neck, and there was the office guy in the orange shirt and blue tie sitting next to her, about to stick his tongue in her ear, his arm around her shoulders.

"The fuck?!" Alice lurched to the left as she swung her right arm back. She'd meant to push the guy away with her right hand, forgetting that it was presently holding her lager, and so as she launched off the stool her drink ended up all over the guy.

Alice fell off to the ground gracelessly, and as she lay sprawled on the grimy floor, the guy jumped up, knocking over his own stool, looking with horror at the sopping ruin of his already questionable shirt.

"What, are you mental?" the guy spat, red-faced. "You were gagging for it a second ago!"

Alice wasn't sure how long she'd been out, but it was bound to have been a couple of minutes at least. What had gone on while she'd been in crazy-land? She climbed to her feet.

"Look," she said, stabbing a finger at the guy, "whatever else went on, I'm *positive* I didn't tell you it was okay to stick your tongue in my god-damned ear."

Now two of the guys friends were at his sides, the younger ones. Alice wasn't sure where the older guy had got off to.

"What, is she Canadian or something?" one of the guys said.

"American," Alice said. "Got a problem with that?"

The other guy nodded appreciatively, and leered. "I feel a bit peckish for American, myself. Sometimes you feel like a curry, and sometimes like a burger, am I right?"

"Like you'd ever have a chance with an Asian bird, you wanker," the first guy said.

"Hey, I was only saying," said the leering guy, his feelings clearly bruised.

"Shut it, you two," said orange-shirt-blue-tie, sopping wet. "Now look, this shirt cost me fifty quid, you dozy cow, and it's dry-clean only. So you'll be buying me a new one, I think." He held out his hand, palm up, and glowered at her.

"Hey," Alice held up her hands, defensively, "I don't remember inviting you to come grope me, all right? Besides, any moron who pays that much for such a godawful ugly shirt deserves whatever he gets."

The guy's two friends chuckled at that, but orange-shirt-blue-tie wasn't so amused. "You bitch!" he said, and launched himself at her, his hands out and grasping. Apparently he took his wardrobe very seriously. Or didn't like being called a moron. Or both, for that matter.

Alice had been in three fights before: once with Nancy, who had been seventeen to her fifteen; once with a Latina girl her own age outside a nightclub in East Austin; and once with an boy a year or two younger than her in the parking lot of a 7-Eleven. All of them had been when Alice was between the ages of fourteen and fifteen, when she hung out with Nancy and her friends. The fight with Nancy had ended up a draw, and they'd just had another rum and generic cola and laughed about it; the fight with the Latina girl had ended with the girl pulling a knife and Alice turning and running away as fast as her legs would carry her; and the fight with the kid in the parking lot of the 7-Eleven had ended in a resounding victory for Alice, but only because the kid tripped over his own skateboard and sprained his ankle. Still, that's what he got for calling Alice crazy and Nancy a slut; whether either was a true statement or not was beside the point.

Therefore, Alice didn't have a terrific track record when it came to physical altercations. She had one loss, one win, and one tie. And considering that her one win had been against a pimply kid four inches shorter and thirty pounds lighter than her, Alice wasn't liking her chances against orange-shirt-blue-tie, who towered over her and easily outweighed her by eighty pounds. She'd have turned and run, but she had her back to the wall and didn't see any way out.

Then, just before the guy closed the distance between them, a woman appeared out of nowhere. She was wearing a black leather jacket, black skirt over tights, and boots, with her blonde hair in a bob. As the guy plummeted forward, she handily took hold of his left arm in both her hands, shifted her weight to one side while turning, and then sent the guy flipping over her back in some sort of judo move, to land headfirst on the floor a few feet off with an audible thump.

"Right," the woman said, dusting her hands and turning to face the two other guys. "How's about you pick up your friend there before he gets himself hurt, and you lot go and find someone else to bother for the rest of the night, eh?"

The two guys exchanged uneasy glances, shrugged, and then helped their moaning friend to his feet. For a second it looked like they were going to start more trouble, but the woman just gave them a withering smile, and they were on their way out the door.

The woman turned around and faced Alice. "You all right, girl?"

Alice nodded but wasn't sure.

"How about I buy you a drink and you can tell me all about it?" The woman slid onto the stool that orange-shirt-blue-tie had just vacated. "Don't worry, sweetie, I'm not trying to pick you up. Just being friendly."

Alice was always a little out of it after one of her visions, but she was usually back in her right mind after this much time had passed. Still, as near as she could tell, the woman had just appeared out of nowhere.

"What's your name?" the woman asked, as Alice climbed back onto the stool.

"Alice."

The woman grinned and stuck out her hand. "My name's Roxanne."

CHAPTER TEN
Twilight

I N THE END, five of the captains elected to accompany Artor on his journey. Lugh the Gael, called Long Hand; Bedwyr of Demetia; tall Caius; and the brothers Pryder and Gwrol, who Galaad learned were in fact the twins they appeared.

With Artor and Galaad, whom the High King insisted accompany them, they were seven in all. As the captains disbanded, Caradog given the task of governing in Artor's absence, the seven set about preparing themselves for their imminent departure.

Galaad, who had carried on his back from Powys all of his earthly possessions, spent the remainder of the day and night in his rooms, trying to recover some of the rest which he had missed in the long days of his recent journey. That evening he ate a hearty meal with the servants in the kitchen, while from the main dining room the sounds of Artor and his captains were much subdued since the previous night. Galaad repaired to his room early and slept somewhat fitfully, though thankfully free of nightmare or vision, and in the morning rose before dawn and dressed himself.

As the sun was just rising in the east, Galaad found Artor and his captains down on the quayside, loading their provisions onto a boat. It was a captured Saeson longship, a Snekke measuring some fifty feet from stem to stern, eight feet from port to starboard, outfitted with both sails and oars. At its prow was a carved dragon's head.

"How do you like it?" Caius asked in Latin, as Galaad drew near, his breath fogging white in the chill morning air. "Artor calls it Pryd Gwyn. On account of the sails."

"White Aspect," Galaad repeated, nodding. It seemed a good omen, considering that the boat was to carry them to find another white form.

"These are the last of the supplies," Caius explained, indicating the bundles stacked on the quay, "and with them loaded we'll be ready to depart."

Galaad looked over the assembled gear, which included clothing, victuals, supplies, saddles, and tack, and self-consciously tightened his hold on the meager bundle in his arms.

"By midday we'll reach the mouth of the Tamesa River, and then we'll be at sea and gone." Caius seemed excited, eager to be on their way. He was one of the first to nod his ascent to Artor's words the day before and seemed genuine in his desire to pursue an adventure. Still, with his too-easy smile, Galaad found himself reluctant to trust him unreservedly.

"Ach, I'd forgotten what it was like to wake up to your damned sunny disposition," Lugh said, coming up the quay, a pack slung on his back. He shivered in the cold. "Ten years that grinning visage greeted me every dawn," he explained to Galaad, "and every day of those ten years I was tempted to wipe that smile off with the back of my hand."

"You could always try, friend," Caius said, still grinning, "but you should remember that teeth don't only smile. They also bite." To punctuate his words, Caius snapped his jaws together, with an audible click, like a dog snapping at a fleeing hare.

Lugh made a disagreeable sound, somewhere between a grunt and a moan, and then vaulted the side of the longship. On board, he dropped his pack unceremoniously onto the deck, stretched out upon the planks with the pack serving as head pillow, and, crossing his arms over his chest, closed his eyes. "Wake me when we get somewhere interesting," he said, and then fell silent. Within moments, he was snoring gently.

"He's a noisome creature with breath that could stun an ox," Caius said, "but he has a true heart, and a specialized attack that few swordsmen can withstand. You'd do well to keep in his good graces."

Galaad nodded, looking from Caius to the now sleeping Gael.

"Have you a sword, by the by?" Caius asked.

"Well, I . . ." Galaad shifted the bundle in his arms, his grandfather's grandfather's leaf blade tucked safely inside. Having seen *proper* swords at the sides of Artor and his captains, Galaad was self-conscious of the shabby state of his own blade. "That is . . ."

Before Galaad could say more, the brothers from Gwent appeared on the scene, arguing loudly. Auburn-haired Pryder apparently took issue with the decisions that blond-haired Gwrol had made regarding their provisions, from the sound of it.

"What if we run aground?" Pryder asked, pressing the point. "In some remote stone promontory, unable to return to land. Do you honestly expect to survive on wine alone?"

"I get thirsty," Gwrol answered with a shrug. "I thought it better to bring a few more skins of wine along, instead of sacks of grain which will only swell with water and weigh us down needlessly."

"Weigh us down . . . needlessly?!" Pryder sputtered, disbelieving. "And if we run out of bread, what will you say then about 'need' and 'needless'?"

Gwrol hoisted the string of wine skins higher on his shoulder. "In that case, brother, I think I'll just have another drink."

Caius chuckled, and leaning over to Galaad whispered behind his hand. "Their parents judged well when they christened Pryder, whose name means 'Care.'"

"Yes," Gwrol said proudly, overhearing, "and they were right to name me 'Courage.'"

"If by that," Pryder put in, "you mean the type of courage found in the grape, then yes. Oh wait." He slapped his forehead, miming sudden realization. "Perhaps they better ought to have named you 'Consumptive.'"

Gwrol scowled, but in good humor, and the brothers shifted their gear on board.

"They fight like a cat and dog," Caius said, "their temperaments as different as their faces are alike. But woe betide anyone who criticizes one of them in the hearing of the other. They attack each other endlessly but will meet any attack from the outside with iron in their fists."

Galaad helped Caius move what remained of the gear onto the boat, though he trembled when he regarded the saddle and tack. He considered it an unexpected stroke of fortune that Artor had chosen to travel to Dumnonia by boat, and not overland, for fear that he'd be left behind when he refused to once more go on horseback.

If Caius noticed that Galaad was loathe to lay hands on any of the horse tack, he made no mention of it, but hoisted each item up and into the boat, where the brothers from Gwent helped secure them on board.

The quay was nearly cleared when Artor arrived, with him Caradog and Bedwyr. The High King wore his red cloak flung back over his shoulder, his hand resting lightly on the pommel of his spatha at his side, his step easy and light. A faint smile played around the corners of Artor's mouth, which was echoed on Bedwyr's face but which found no semblance on that of the chief counselor.

"I still oppose this fool's notion with my every fiber," Caradog said, as the trio drew near.

"Of course you do," Artor said with a smile. "That's why you're my chief counsel, and that's why I'm leaving the island in your charge."

Caradog snorted, an undignified sound. "Better for me that I was less reliable, then."

"It's your curse, I'm afraid," Artor said, clapping him on the back. "Be well, old friend. And don't worry, we'll be back soon."

Caradog made a noncommittal sound, but managed a weak smile. Still, there was something in his look that suggested mourning, and it occurred to Galaad that Caradog had the look of someone saying a final farewell over a gravesite, not one wishing a departing traveler well.

Artor vaulted on board handily, with little seeming effort.

"Well, farewell," Bedwyr said, offering Caradog his hand. "I'm sorry you'll not be with us."

Caradog took the Demetian's proffered hand and held onto it. He pulled Bedwyr close, and in a voice pitched low enough that Galaad could barely hear, said, "You watch out for him, do you hear me? I have black thoughts that he won't be sailing back this way again."

Bedwyr blanched and breathed out a cloud of white into the cold morning air, unspeaking. Then he tugged his hand back and forced a smile. "You worry too much, old man," he said, his words coated with a thin veneer of humor. Then his smile slowly began to fade. "Don't worry. I'll be at his back, whatever comes."

The old chief counselor considered the Demetian's words and slowly nodded. "Be well, Bedwyr."

With that, Caradog gave a curt wave to those already on board, turned on his heel, and walked back up the quay.

"Come along," Caius called to Galaad, hoisting the last of the bundles of victuals on board and then jumping over the railing. "Let's be off, or would you rather stay behind?"

Casting a last glance back at Caer Llundain, the city he'd dreamt of all of his life and only just glimpsed in these last two days, Galaad tossed his small bundle up to Caius, and then climbed aboard.

Bedwyr untied the longship from its moorings, and then the seven were under way, their journey begun.

By midday, they'd reached the mouth of the Tamesa, with Bedwyr and Caius pulling on the oars on the port side, Gwrol and Pryder pulling on the starboard, and once they were past the estuary and into the open waters of the channel, the sails were unfurled, the oars shipped, and the longship steered to the south and east.

Galaad had never been to sea before. He'd never been near a body of water larger than a lake, for that matter. And so the fact that he could see nothing to north but water and more water was more than a little unsettling. He found himself sitting more often on the starboard side, watching the rocky shore drift slowly by. It seemed to tether him, to give him some sense of perspective, though it did nothing to calm his roiling stomach, or to tamp down the bile that kept rising in his throat.

"That's Cantium," Lugh said, pointing to the land. "Keep an eye out for Saeson ships, if you've a mind to. They live on the island under Artor's sufferance, but there's nothing to say they wouldn't take the chance to test their mettle if they spotted the High King sailing by on a winter's day."

"S-Saeson?" Galaad's eyes widened.

"Aye." Lugh glanced at Artor, and then back to the shore. "We couldn't manage to push the whoresons off the island entire and had to leave clumps of them stuck to the shores in the south and east like balls of dung on the hairs of your arse."

Galaad nodded. He knew that two kingdoms of Saeson remained, held separate by Artor's forces at Caer Llundain. While not client kings as such, the rulers of the Saeson had agreed to a treaty that allowed them to remain, in exchange for withdrawing from the rest of Briton-held lands. And so in the former lands of the Icenii in the east, and in the region of Cantium to the south, the former invaders and oppressors of the island remained, in a wary state of truce with their erstwhile enemies.

Still, knowing a thing and being confronted with it face to face were quite different propositions, and finding himself now a potential target of Saeson aggression on the open waters, where their seamanship would serve them as well as the Britons' horsemanship had served on land, was an unappealing prospect.

"Damn Vortigern's soul for ever inviting the bastards in," Bedwyr said, coming to stand beside them. "If there is any justice, in his next life he'll be born a maggot."

Galaad raised his eyebrow. "Excuse me, friend," he said to the Demetian, tentatively, "but do I take your meaning correctly, that you believe in the transmigration of souls?"

Bedwyr gripped the railing more tightly and looked guardedly at Galaad. "Why would you know? What is it to you?"

"Oh, I mean no offense," Galaad said in a rush. He already felt queasy, and the fear of having offended one of the great captains only worsened his condition. "It is just that I have never met someone who still practiced the beliefs of our grandfathers."

Bedwyr nodded slowly, giving Galaad an appraising glance. "Yes," he said at last, "I follow the ancient Derwydd faith. There are a few of us, though fewer with each year, it would seem."

"Tree-lovers," Lugh scoffed. "Feckless bastards, the lot of you."

Bedwyr's eyes flashed, and Galaad got the impression this was a familiar disagreement between the two.

"And you, friend Lugh," Galaad said quickly, trying to avoid a confrontation. "What beliefs do you hold?"

"Me?" Lugh rubbed his chin, thoughtfully. "I believe in iron." He patted the sword at his hip, which he'd refused to take off when the others stowed their weaponry with the gear. "As for gods and goddesses, spirits and saints, I was raised to believe the ancient lore of Eriu, but damned if I've seen any sign of the truth of it in my lifetime. If the great gods of wind and wave want to present themselves and give me a knock, I suppose I'd consider saying a few prayers, but otherwise they can all kiss my arse."

To punctuate his words, Lugh hacked, and then spit a huge glob of phlegm overboard, where it spattered into the dark channel waters.

"Keep quiet!" Caius shouted from the far side of the boat, making the sign of the cross. "I don't believe in spirits of the waters, either, but there's no need to go around offending them, is there?"

Lugh looked at him, struck dumb for a moment, and then threw his head back in laughter. Caius reddened, considered his words, and then joined in, slapping his knee. In short order, the laughter rippled throughout the boat, except at the helm, where Artor stood alone, hand on the tiller, watching the far horizon.

The winds picked up as the day wore on, so that as the sun was setting, the white cliffs of Portus Dubris loomed off the starboard bow. The skies ahead were painted in yellows and reds, while behind it was already full night, the stars twinkling above in their countless numbers.

Bedwyr faced the setting sun and began to chant some sort of prayer under his breath. He had produced a spring of mistletoe from somewhere on his person, which he clutched in his hands at chest level. Galaad could not make out any of the words but couldn't help but notice the devotion that seemed to transfix the Demetian, the strange ecstasy that gripped him, his eyes half-lidded. Was this how he looked himself, when in the throes of one of his visions?

Artor came from the stern to stand beside him, smiling at Bedwyr's back. "It's midwinter," he explained to Galaad in a low voice. "The shortest day and longest night. Bedwyr says the prayer of the Derwydd that the light will not fade, but be born again with the dawn."

Galaad nodded. He'd always found it strange that each of the island's faiths observed the occasion, each in its own way. There were still those who celebrated the festival of the unconquered sun, brought to the island by the Romans, just as there were still pagans like Bedwyr who prayed for the reborn light of the winter solstice. Galaad himself observed the birth of the Messias, though the occasion did not hold for him the meaning it did for an Augustinian, since to a Pelagians the whole human race neither died through Adam's sin or death, nor rose again through the resurrection of Christ, but each man worked his own salvation through his words and deeds.

Galaad shivered in the mounting cold. As frigid as the streets of Caer Llundain had been, out on the open waters of the channel it was even colder. He had his simple wool cloak over his shoulders, and hugged it tight around his chest, for all the good it did him.

Beside him, Artor seemed hardly to notice the cold at all, though his breath frosted on the wind just as Galaad's did, and frost rimed the corners of his mouth where he'd inadvertently spilled water from a drinking flask onto his beard and not bothered to wipe it dry.

The curve of the sun at last slipped below the horizon, its final glow still burning a minute arc of the western sky, the rest given over to night.

"The light fades," Galaad said, suddenly uncomfortable in the silence and eager to fill it.

Artor turned and looked at him, an unreadable expression on his face.

"Yes," the High King said, his voice sounding far away. "But it has not gone out. Not yet."

Then Artor turned away, leaving Galaad alone, Bedwyr lost to his prayers.

Galaad shivered again, but this time not merely because of the cold.

When it was full dark, the seven gathered near the mast and had their evening meal. It was rough, simple fare, hard bread and dried meats, but

Gwrol had opened a wineskin and was generous in filling everyone's cups, and in short order the men were warmed from within, increasingly heedless of the cold. They fell to talking, aimlessly, drifting off to sleep where they were when the mood struck, drinking and talking more when it didn't. Even out at sea, in the frigid air, the men seemed more relaxed, more at ease than they had in the city, and Galaad realized that these six men must have spent countless late nights like this together during their war on the Saeson. He was an interloper, of sorts, but their leader had welcomed him into their circle, and that seemed good enough for the others. As it was, though, Galaad kept quiet, listening to the stories the men told, somewhat overawed to be in their presence at all, much less privy to so many personal tales.

And so they passed the long watches of the night, taking turns at the tiller, steering always in the direction of the setting sun, now long gone below the horizon. If any in that long night wondered whether the sun might not be rising in the morning, after all, they kept their peace and said nothing.

The days on board ship passed slowly, with the coast to their starboard rising and falling, rocky outcrops becoming low gray beach becoming the hay-colored hills of dead grasslands becoming rocky outcrops again, while to their port there was nothing but endless gray waves, as far as the eye could see. The awe that Galaad felt at first finding himself among Artor and his captains had begun to recede, while not vanishing entirely, as he came to know the six warriors somewhat better, privy to their conversations and discontents.

There was a strange skein of relationships between the six men, difficult to see at first but which gradually became more apparent with the passing days. These men who had fought and bled side by side for so many years were as close as brothers, it seemed, but like family often failed to see eye to eye, and many of the arguments Galaad overheard were clearly merely the latest skirmishes in long-standing disagreements.

If Caius had a too-easy smile, and seemed overly gregarious no matter the circumstance or cause, Bedwyr seemed an eternal optimist, at least in one significant regard.

"And I tell you," Bedwyr said, on their third day at sail, as the sun was westering towards the horizon, "that the day of Rome has ended, and will not come again, but that a new empire might wait for us past tomorrow's horizon."

"I'll grant you that we've had little news of the Empire these last years," Caius said, "and that since the Vandals of Geiseric sacked Rome the prospects for her continuance might seem bleak, but Rome civilized the known world and will not quickly fade from the pages of history."

"But Artor may well accomplish what Rome in her glory never could," Bedwyr replied, fervently. "Already he has improved relations with the High King of Hibernia and extended his dominion beyond Hadrian's Wall. He may well go on to unite all the various kingdoms of both islands under his banner, and then who can say what may come? Perhaps he may one day find common cause with the Gauls across the channel and in so doing bring them to heel and forge a new empire to eclipse that of the Romans."

"Feh." Lugh spat, his phlegm slapping noisily onto the deck. "Bugger the Romans, Caius, and bugger your talk of empire, Bedwyr. Unity with my cousins in the dynasts of Eriu? Have you forgotten that my grandfathers were brought to Britannia to act as foederati in Demetia, to keep the western shores clear of Eriu raiders? That's generations of blood spilled on water, stone, and sand, which you think to wash away with pretty words of empire and a bright tomorrow. Are you mad or merely simple?"

Galaad had remained silent, as he had so much of the journey, but a thought occurred to him, and he spoke it before his better judgment stilled his tongue.

"Artor was victorious over the Saeson," he said. "Could he not win a similar victory against the Hibernians if the need arose?"

The three captains looked from Galaad to one another, their reactions mixed. Lugh merely grinned darkly, while Caius's smile seemed to flag. Bedwyr, whose position Galaad championed, opened his mouth as if to speak, but paused.

"Well," Bedwyr finally said, tilting his head to one side, shoulder raised to his ear and hand held palm up, a gesture of equivocation. "I grant that it's *possible* . . ."

"No, it isn't," came the voice of Artor from the tiller.

The High King motioned for Pryder to take the helm, and then came forward to join the conversation. His brows were knit, and his mouth was drawn into a thin line.

"What my captains are reluctant to say, at least in company, is that there was no victory."

Galaad looked up at the High King, confused. "But . . . but what of Badon, and . . ."

Artor held up a hand, silencing him. "Oh, we may have been victorious on isolated occasions, winning the day at this battle or that. But the war?" He shook his head. "There was no victory there. At best, what we achieved was merely stalemate."

Galaad looked from Artor to his captains, who each averted his gaze, finding something of interest to look at in the grain of the wood beneath their feet, or the swell of the gray waves on the horizon, or in the dreary skies overhead.

"The Saeson were not driven from the land, no matter what the bards might say in song. The enemy remains on the island as part of our accommodation, as everyone well knows."

"Yes," Galaad objected, eagerly, "but they *were* driven out of the rest of Britannia."

Artor sighed, wearily. "True. And there is nothing to say that they will remain forever content behind their new borders. Some day, and perhaps soon, they will seek once more to take the rest of Britannia by force. In which case what we have accomplished is not the end of the war, but merely an interval."

He turned and caught the eye of the three captains.

"And as much as it makes me sick at heart to admit it, you are all correct in one regard or another. Caius is correct that Rome has been, for all of her faults, the light of civilization for long generations. Bedwyr is right to say that Rome's day is ended. And Lugh speaks the truth when he says that there will never be a unity formed between Britannia and Hibernia, much less with Gaul, at least not in our lifetimes or those of our grandchildren's grandchildren."

Artor turned away, looking towards the prow and the sun that dipped towards the western horizon.

"Between the light of day and the dark of night comes a gray period of transition, the twilight which is neither fully one thing or the other. After the end of one kind of world, but before the beginning of another. I wonder often if that is where we are now, these years, in the twilight. Rome has retreated within its own walls, its empire gone and fled. Here, on the world's edge, we have kept the light of civilization burning and pushed back the Saeson, but how long until that fire burns out at last and the Saeson overrun us all? Through our lifetimes? Through that of our sons? And our son's sons? It seems clear to me that it is not a question of whether, but when."

Artor turned back and faced the others, not only Galaad and the three captains, but Pryder and his brother at the tiller as well.

"What unity we have been able to forge is, I fear, a tenuous one. When my hour comes, will my successor be able to maintain those ties, or will they wither and fade?" He paused and shook his head, sadly. "No man can know the future, but I fear that the answer is a sad one." He took a deep breath, straightening, and looked to starboard, at the coast of Britannia sliding by. "But our concern is today, not tomorrow. Our duty is to survive and to protect those who cannot protect themselves, and let the future worry after its own."

It was morning, and Galaad was breaking his fast with a simple meal of dried meats and stale crusts of bread. Pryder and Gwrol sat with him, while Lugh worked the tiller and the others slept.

Pryder and Gwrol had eaten quickly, each complaining about the portions the other had taken, and then had retrieved their swords from their packs. Now, with whetstones and cloths, they tended to their blades, which flashed in the morning sunlight like lightning.

"Why do you sharpen your weapons, friends?" Galaad asked around a mouthful of stale bread.

The brothers exchanged glances and shrugged.

"Because . . ." Gwrol began, and then his words trailed off, as though Galaad had just asked him why they felt the need to breathe. "Because . . ."

Pryder shook his head at his brother, blowing air through his lips noisily.

"Because, because, because," he parroted. He turned to Galaad. "We sharpen our blades because they needs must be sharp."

"Oh." Galaad nodded, thoughtfully. Then, after a pause, he said, "But why?"

Pryder sighed. "Why what?"

"Why must they be sharp?" With a sharp intake of breath, his eyes opened wide. "Do you fear an attack by Saeson?"

Gwrol chuckled, and Pryder treated him to a friendly, if somewhat patronizing smile.

"There are more things to fear in this world than the Saeson, my young friend," Pryder said.

"Not that we fear the Saeson," Gwrol added quickly, chest puffed with pride.

"No, indeed." Pryder nodded. "Still and all, our potential enemies are many, and not all fight under the same banner."

Galaad was confused, as his expression made evident.

Pryder set his whetstone down on the deck and sighted along his blade. "Tomorrow, if the winds hold, we should reach Llongborth, home of Geraint, king of half Dumnonia."

"Or should that be 'half-king' of Dumnonia?" Gwrol said, snickering.

Pryder shot him a sharp glance. "Do you mind stilling that babbling tongue of yours, if only for a moment? The boy and I are trying to have a conversation here."

Gwrol pulled a face, but kept silent.

"In any event," Pryder went on, "tomorrow we reach Llongborth. Now, Geraint is some distant relation to Artor, as I understand it, and is subject to the crown of the High King. But a study of history will show that client kings have not always shown obeisance to their masters, nor subjects to their kings. A warrior should always be on his guard, especially when abroad in some strange land . . ."

"And Dumnonia is stranger than most, if the boy's visions are to be believed, however unlikely," Gwrol put in.

Pryder took a deep breath through his nostrils, closing his eyes momentarily. "Will you shut your hole?" Then he opened his eyes and continued speaking to Galaad as though no interruption had occurred. "A warrior's blade should be as ready for combat as the warrior himself, and a blunted sword could mean the difference between life and death." He held up his sword, a simple spatha with a pattern-welded blade and a bronze pommel. The sword's edge was notched here and there, scars of past battles, but was in otherwise excellent condition. "I don't say that I expect some treachery from our hosts. Or rather, that I always expect the possibility of treachery and gird myself appropriately. If it comes, I will be ready for it."

Gwrol ran a whetstone down the edge of his own blade, with the hiss of stone on metal. "And you, boy? Have you no blade of your own?"

Galaad began to shake his head, then quickly scrambled to his feet. "Just a moment," he said, and hurried to the place where they'd stored their effects. He rummaged around until he laid hands on his own bundle, then fumbled with the twine bindings until he'd got it opened. He pulled out his antique leaf-bladed sword and returned to where the brothers from Gwent sat.

"This is my sword," Galaad said proudly, displaying the sheathed blade. "It belong to my grandfather's grandfather and has been passed from father to son since those days, finally coming into my keeping."

Gwrol and Pryder exchanged glances, suppressing smiles.

"Do you mind?" Pryder said, sheathing his own blade and reaching out to Galaad. "Might I have a look?"

Galaad nodded, and handed the sword over.

"Well, now." Pryder accepted the sword, glancing at Gwrol, his eye twinkling. "Your grandfather's grandfather, you say?"

Pryder examined the sheath, the leather aged and greasy.

"Buried with him, was it?" Gwrol said, grinning.

"Oh, no," Galaad answered quickly, shaking his head, before he realized the Gwentian was jesting with him. "No," he added, his tone firm, his lips thin, "it was not."

"It is a . . . well-traveled sheath," Pryder observed. Then, with considerable effort, he tugged the blade free and held it aloft.

Seen so soon after the flashing brightness of Pryder's spatha, Galaad's sword seemed in even poorer repair than ever. The leaf blade was black with rust and pitted with age, the leather wrapping on the hilt frayed and loose.

"Oh, no, no, no," Pryder said, shaking his head sadly, his expression like that of someone witnessing an unfortunate accident or an untimely death. "That's . . . that's just . . ."

"That's criminal, is what that is," Gwrol said.

"Yes." Pryder nodded in rare agreement with his brother. "This isn't a sword, boy. This is a relic."

"Perhaps it should better have been buried with your grandsire after all, eh?" Gwrol reached out and, heedless of any danger, ran his finger down the length of the blade's edge. He held up his fingertip, unscathed. "It's as blunt as a baby's ass."

"That's 'smooth as a baby's ass,' imbecile," Pryder said, scornfully. "But my brother is right," he said to Galaad, and held the sword out to him. "No disrespect to your honored dead, but this thing is useless. Worse than useless, come to that, and you'd be better served swinging a stout length of wood than this crumbling antique." Galaad took the sword by the hilt, and Pryder reached out and flicked a large flake of rust from the blade with his thumbnail. "The best use that this thing would be in a fight would be to serve as a distraction, since no opponent could bring themselves to accept the possibility that you were seriously wielding it in earnest and would likely double with laughter at the thought."

"This is a real blade," Gwrol said, presenting his own sword to Galaad, hilt first.

Galaad laid his leaf blade on the deck beside him and gingerly accepted Gwrol's spatha, fittingly a twin to Pryder's.

"Feel the weight of it," Gwrol went on.

Galaad hefted the blade, which was so perfectly balanced that its apparent weight in his grip was only a fraction of what it actually weighed. He reached out a finger to touch the flat of the blade and found it surprisingly warm in the chill air, realizing only after a minute that it still bore the heat of the whetstone's friction.

"The blade should be an extension of your arm," Pryder put in. He looked with scorn at the rusted leaf blade on the deck. "Not stand out from your hand like an overgrown scab waiting to be picked."

Galaad's cheeks flushed red with anger and shame, and his fingers were white-knuckled around the spatha's haft.

"All joking aside, boy," Gwrol said, "you should bury that thing with honors, and get yourself a proper sword."

Gwrol reached out, and Galaad returned the spatha to his keeping. Giving the blade a final careful wiping with his cloth, Gwrol resheathed the blade and laid it across his lap.

"Don't worry," Pryder said, smiling encouragingly. "When we reach Llongborth, we'll procure you a blade of your own."

Galaad gamely tried to smile, fighting the lingering sense of humiliation. "But what if the Dumnonians prove treacherous, as you'd thought?"

"Well, then," Gwrol said, grinning. "In that case, swords will be even easier to come by, as they'll be lying at our feet once we send their bearers off to meet God."

Galaad found himself plagued by visions only once in the course of their journey, the scent of flowers filling his nostrils, the gloom of the night replaced by a flash of light, and then the world fell away from him and before his eyes was the White Lady and the tower of glass. Again he felt the thoughts embed themselves in his mind, the call for assistance, the plea for rescue. And washing over him, the inexorable, inexplicable sense of bliss and comfort.

And then it was gone again, as suddenly as it came. Caius at the tiller seemed not to have noticed any change in Galaad's mien or manner, and the rest of the seven were deep in their slumber, and so the vision went unremarked. But Galaad would not find sleep that night, and lay shivering in his thin blanket on the deck throughout the long cold watches of the early morning, trying desperately not to remember and proving unsuccessful.

CHAPTER ELEVEN
Jubilee

THAT NIGHT, RETURNING TO MARYLEBONE, Blank and Miss Bonaventure enjoyed a bottle of syrah in his sitting room and recounted to one another the events of the day. It had been only a scant handful of hours since the police constable had arrived at Blank's front step and summoned them to Tower Bridge. As much as he hated to end a day with a mystery left unsolved, Blank feared it would be some time before a solution was within reach. But he would lay hands on a solution, eventually. That, he most fervently believed.

A cab was summoned and idled at the curb, waiting to carry Miss Bonaventure back to Bark Place and her own bed. Blank saw her to the door.

"And tomorrow, Miss Bonaventure?" he said, taking her hand. "Can I expect to see you in the morning, as usual?"

Miss Bonaventure's eyes fluttered. "Well, it isn't as if you could be expected to work this case all on your lonesome, is it?"

Blank quirked a smile. "I suppose not, at that."

Miss Bonaventure tightened her fingers around his. "Blank, I'll never know just how you survived before meeting me."

A haunted expression flitted across Blank's face, only briefly, like a dark cloud slipping in front of a full moon, only to be blown clear by winds. "That is a mystery you may never be able to solve, my dear."

"Oh?" Miss Bonaventure's gaze darted to the stairs which led up from the foyer. "Along with the secret of what you keep locked behind the door at the top of the stair, I take it?"

Blank's eyes narrowed, and while his smile remained on his lips, it became hollow and thin, a mask without humor behind it. "Perhaps," he said at length, his voice strained. "Perhaps."

Miss Bonaventure gave him a queer look but visibly resisted the temptation to look up the stairs, at the door just visible beyond the first-floor landing. Then she gave Blank's hand a shake, wished him a good night, and went out to the hansom cab waiting at the curb. As the driver helped her into the seat, Blank lingered in the open door for a moment, and then as the cab rattled away down York Place, he closed the door on the night, retreating inside, all alone with his secrets and mysteries.

That night, he received a summons from Omega. He was loath to communicate but unable to refuse. He slept little afterwards, and what little sleep he had was fitful, plagued with strange dreams and ancient memories which could not be forgot.

In the morning, the only sign of his recent distress the faint circles beneath his eyes, he drew himself a bath. As he soaked in the water, heated suitably within the gas-fired cistern in the basement, he counted the days until Quong Ti returned from China and he could return to the proper indolence of a gentleman.

After seeing to his toilet and dressing himself in his customary gray, he set out to see to the business Omega had communicated to him and was returned to his lodgings in time to greet Miss Bonaventure on her arrival, the morning's penny papers under her arm.

"I do hope I'll be able to finish the papers today, Blank. I've felt at loose ends since yesterday morning, having been forced to abandon the news of the day. Who is to say what I might have missed?"

Blank smiled and ushered her inside.

"I'm afraid your quest for knowledge in the printed page might be stymied again today, my dear." Then, at her raised brow, he said, "I thought we might do a bit of exploring today, in the perhaps less fashionable quarters of the city."

Miss Bonaventure collapsed into a chair, the papers in her lap.

"Oh, no," she said gloomily, "you want to go incognito again. Well, you can count me *out*. The last time I had to pass a few idle hours dressed as a gin-soaked vagrant for the purposes of surveillance, it took me *days* to wash the smell from my hair."

"All right, all right," Blank conceded, holding up his hands defensively. "I'll play the part of the vagrant this time round, if need be. But surely you can't object to the guise of a music hall performer?"

A slow smile crept across Miss Bonaventure's face, and she laid a hand on her neck, her fingers on one side, her thumb the other, as though sizing her throat. "Well, I *do* have a pleasing singing voice . . ."

The days that followed passed quickly. In various guises and disguises, Blank and Miss Bonaventure haunted the streets of London, the music halls and coffeehouses, the gin houses and rookeries, ferreting out any information about missing women. Of course, women went missing with alarming regularity in certain quarters, though only marginally more so than the men of their station and slightly less so than the children, and so it was disappointing but hardly surprising that, while the pair was able to produce a mountain of information, they derived from it very little in the way of intelligence.

The city, already congested, became even more tightly packed as the days wore on, and more and more people streamed into London in anticipation of Victoria's Jubilee. In the meaner sections of the city through which Blank and Miss Bonaventure moved, there was a noticeable deficit of patriotic fervor, though the police were much more in evidence than was typical.

Blank had communicated very little with New Scotland Yard since accepting the case, disregarding the urgent telegrams he received on a daily basis from Chalmers requesting updates on the status of his investigation. But while it was clear that news of the series of murders had not yet reached the fourth estate, the penny papers and their more respectable brethren likewise lacking any sensationalist headlines about the case, it was just as clear that the rank and file of the Metropolitan Police had been made well aware of the circumstances. Or, even if they lacked sufficient details, at least the constables had been informed that *something* was afoot, and that it was on their shoulders to see that it didn't interfere with the Jubilee celebrations. This was evident in the diligence with which the constables carried out their duties, scouring the streets, ever vigilant, arresting people on the mere suspicion of malfeasance, the actual commission of a crime for the moment not necessary to invite the attendant punishment.

Blank and Miss Bonaventure made their way back to Marylebone shortly before dawn, having passed the day and night in Whitechapel, hunting for news of any disappearances which might correspond with the appearance of the as yet anonymous murder victims. As had become a pattern in their investigations, they had found ample evidence of foul play in any number of disappearances, but sadly none that conformed to the details of the case at hand. They made their way through the still-dark morning, forced to walk since, given the state of their adopted clothing and the early hour, they'd have been hard pressed to convince a driver to accept their custom. As they walked, Miss Bonaventure expressed the desire to solve all of the evident crimes the evidence for which they'd stumbled upon in the days previous, if they had only the time and resources to do so, and Blank allowed that there were times when it seemed too grave an injustice to bear that he had to pass over so many crimes committed against those least able to protect themselves in pursuing the interests of those with power and prestige at their command. Many were the times that, singly or in concert, Blank and Miss Bonaventure had taken up the interests of the city's less fortunate souls, but it always seemed that, like Sisyphus and his rock, no matter how hard or how long they pushed, the rock simply kept coming crashing back down.

Finally, they rounded the corner of York Place and approached Blank's home. There, in the street before his door, they saw positioned a laundry van, a pair of well-traveled sway-backed nags between the traces. A quartet of Orientals, Chinese by their look, was wrestling a pair of wicker baskets to the door of the type used to transport soiled laundry away and to return cleaned and pressed clothing and linens, two men to each basket.

Blank and Miss Bonaventure paused at the corner, as yet unseen in the dim predawn twilight.

"I didn't know that you employed a Chinese launderer, Blank."

"I don't," Blank answered, evenly. "And if I did, I can scarcely imagine generating that amount of work for him." He allowed himself a sly smile. "Let us see how this plays out, shall we?"

Blank offered Miss Bonaventure his elbow, and then with her arm linked through his they continued up the street towards his door. As the pair approached, the quartet of laundrymen did not pause in their labors, giving every appearance of struggling under heavy loads, not speaking and not raising their eyes. Despite their best efforts, though, in the time it took Blank and Bonaventure to walk the length of the street to the steps to Number 31 York Place, the laundrymen had succeeded in shifting their burdens only a short distance.

Finally, Blank and Miss Bonaventure were only a few short steps from his door, and the trap that they had been expecting was finally sprung, to the surprise of neither.

The laundrymen flung their burdens to either side, the wicker baskets rebounding off the pavement lightly enough to make evident that their supposed weight had been only a sham. Then, in deadly silence, they launched themselves at Blank and Miss Bonaventure, arms and legs lashing out in meticulously precise movements.

Miss Bonaventure met the attack with relish. With an easy smile on her lips, she dodged the punch thrown by one of the laundrymen and snapped out with a high kick to the side at another, catching him in the jaw. As the kicked man went sprawling to the ground, spitting teeth, another of the laundrymen rushed forward, arms wide, apparently with the intent to encircle Miss Bonaventure and pin her own arms to her side. She allowed him to take her in a crushing bear hug, but just as his arms clamped vicelike around her, she bent backwards, knees bending and back arching, pulling the laundryman from his feet. Then, as the laundryman kicked his legs in the air, Miss Bonaventure strained upwards with her arms, having the dual effect of breaking the laundryman's hold on her and of shifting his weight forward and down so that he slid headfirst into the pavement, landing with a sickening thud.

The other two laundrymen had not been idle, but had converged on Blank. For his part, though, Blank stood still, his arms relaxed at his sides, an almost bored expression on his face. He let Miss Bonaventure have her fun for a moment, a brief bit of exercise to get the blood flowing, and then just as his two attackers rushed him, he held up a hand.

"Peace, gentlemen, in the name of the Ghost Fox," he said in fluent Cantonese. "We will accompany you to see your mistress without need for any further conflict."

The two laundrymen stopped in their tracks and exchanged confused glances.

"Miss Bonaventure," Blank called out, as she wheeled around to face his attackers, her own pair lying moaning on the ground. "If you would, please desist from your exertions."

Miss Bonaventure was brought up short, and cocked her head to one side, giving Blank a quizzical look. "What's that, again?" she said, only slightly out of breath.

"These gentlemen represent the Ghost Fox Triad," he explained casually. "I have informed them that we will come along with them without further incident." He paused, examining the frayed cuff of his vagabond disguise with a moue of distaste, and then in Cantonese addressed the laundrymen. "We would honor your mistress in not appearing before her in these rags. May we go within and change into more appropriate dress?"

The laundrymen exchanged uneasy glances. Clearly, this abduction was not going according to plan. One of them looked to the empty wicker basket lying nearby in the street.

"Oh, and we won't be traveling in *those*, thank you very much," Miss Bonaventure said, her Cantonese carrying a slight accent, dusting her hands on the rough fabric of her skirt. "I've been forced in a basket a time or two, and I'd much rather take a cab, if it's all the same to you."

Blank looked at his companion with an easy smile. "Miss Bonaventure, you never cease to surprise me."

To the laundrymen's continued dismay, the abduction persisted in failing to follow the accepted script. The four Chinese gentlemen, one rubbing an aching jaw and another a sore pate, lingered in the foyer of the York Place house while Blank repaired to his octagonal bedroom, bathed, and dressed. Miss Bonaventure, for her part, hired a cab and rode home to do the same.

Three quarters of an hour later, Miss Bonaventure returned, to find Blank in the library having a cup of coffee and a cigarette, and trying unsuccessfully to engage their would-be abductors in conversation.

"I suggested that we might all have breakfast before going on," Blank said, brightly, "but they'd have none of it."

Miss Bonaventure shrugged. "I'll confess I grabbed a quick bite of the meal Mrs. Pool had prepared for me, so I'll survive until lunch, I think."

"Splendid!" Blank clapped his hands and strode to the foyer, where he retrieved his bowler hat and cane from the table. Then, carefully selecting an orchid from the vase, he affixed it to his buttonhole and turned to smile at the laundrymen. "We're ready when you are, gentlemen."

The quartet of laundrymen, exchanging dark glances, shuffled out through the foyer, eyeing Miss Bonaventure warily.

As Miss Bonaventure had suggested, transportation within the wicker baskets, as the laundrymen originally intended, was simply out of the question. And there seemed little point in going to the expense of a carriage when the laundrymen had their van ready at hand. So it was that Blank and Miss Bonaventure sat up front with the driver, while the other three jostled in the rear of the van, and as the sun was rising over the city, they drove out in the direction of the dawn.

Turning left off Baker Street onto Oxford Street, entering the increasing flow of morning traffic, Miss Bonaventure leaned over and, with her lips brushing Blank's ears, spoke in a voice scarcely above a whisper. "And how did you recognize the allegiance of these gentlemen, Blank? And what's your connection to the triad of the Ghost Fox?"

Blank gave her a weary smile, and with an abbreviated nod of his head indicated the black tattoo inked on the back of the driver's left hand. It was a pair of boxy Chinese ideograms.

"*Zì yóu*," Miss Bonaventure whispered.

Blank nodded. "'The cause of the self,'" he translated. "Or more simply, 'Freedom.' It is the emblem of the Ghost Fox Triad, and one I have not seen for some long time."

Miss Bonaventure opened her mouth to speak, but the driver had caught snippets of their brief exchange and fixed them with a hard look. Blank motioned her to silence, and she grudgingly obliged.

They continued on past Tottenham Court, onto High Holborn, and from there past Skinner and Newgate, along Cheapside and Cornhille, until they passed Aldgate in the east. The City of London proper behind them, they were once more in the East End. Whitechapel seemed scarcely to have gone to bed before it was up and bustling. It was a truism that the East End tended to rise earlier than the rest of the city, being the home of the working poor, and as the rising sun still pinked the eastern sky, the area had already become a great plain of smoking chimneys.

The driver turned off Whitechapel Road and onto Commercial Road, following it east towards the docks. Already, at this early hour, the first of the public houses were opening and would remain in business until half past midnight. The inhabitants of the East End provided the bulk of the manual labor which kept London running and perforce worked at all hours and spent what little leisure time allotted them, day or night, and the littler still coin left in their pockets, at the sundry lodging houses and brothels, public houses and beer-shops which dotted the narrow winding streets of the docklands.

Finally, Commercial Road ended where the East End Dock Road began, and they came in view of the Limehouse Basin, where the murky waters of the Regent's Canal met the waters of the Limehouse Cut, made urinous in appearance and smell by a match factory upon the banks of the River Lea, the two streams commingling in swirls of sickly yellow and greenish gray.

Now, they were in the Limehouse and might well have stepped into some other world. While Victoria ruled the rest of London, the rest of the Empire, here the Ghost Fox held dominion.

The last census had showed only a few hundred Chinese in London, of which fewer than a hundred were resident within the Limehouse. Far fewer than the hundred thousand Jewish immigrants who crowded in Whitechapel and Spitalfields, much nearer the scattered number of Malay sailors who drifted in and out of port. But the recorded numbers of the Chinese population were far from accurate. The queen's census takers had been baffled by the warren of narrow, winding streets which had grown up like kudzu around the Limehouse Dock, and had walked away with little clear understanding of how many Chinese really dwelt within and even less understanding of what sort of society these immigrants from the East had fashioned for themselves.

Blank knew too well. He had been in the east during the Opium Wars and seen firsthand the dark underbelly of Western imperialism. He had seen up close the toll demanded by empire.

The driver brought the van to a halt out front of a humble-seeming laundry and ordered Blank and Miss Bonaventure to step down. By the time the pair had climbed down to the cobblestones, the other three laundrymen had come around from the rear of the van and taken up positions behind and to either side of them.

"Come along, then," Blank said amiably in Cantonese. "I'm sure your mistress awaits."

The three laundrymen, now joined by the fourth, glowered at him but stayed their hands. With a sharp motion of his hand, one impatiently signaled for the rest to follow and strode through the laundry's front door. Blank bowed slightly to Miss Bonaventure and said, "After you." She inclined her head with a smile, rested her parasol on her shoulder, and sauntered after the laundryman.

In through the cramped confines of the laundry, thick with the alkaline smell of lye, they came to a narrow door behind a counter. The lead laundryman pushed his way through a thick curtain and the other three urged Blank and Miss Bonaventure on from behind. With a shrug, the pair elbowed their way past the curtain and found themselves in a labyrinth-like winding corridor from which innumerable chambers opened. These were heavy hung with a floral scent, sickly sweet like rotting fruit. Miss Bonaventure arched an eyebrow at Blank, and he nodded in ascent to her unspoken observation. It was a secret opium den, the rooms littered with the insensate bodies of the patrons stretched on couches and divans, or else sprawled unceremoniously on the floor. Blank noted that the vast majority of the patrons were Occidentals, the few sons of the Orient in evidence those employees of the establishment who tended to the needs of the lolling patrons.

At the rear of the opium den, they came to a sturdy, barred door. This the laundryman swung open, after first beating a staccato rhythm on the wood, and on the other side appeared a burly figure, his forehead shaven in the Manchurian fashion, his hair hanging in a heavy plait down his back. He wore loose-fitting black silk garments, shirt and trousers, with a golden circle stitched to the front, upon which were embroidered the ideograms for Freedom.

The black-clad gatekeeper did not exchange more than a glance and a nod with the laundryman, but without speaking to Blank and Miss Bonaventure, escorted them deeper into the labyrinthine bowels of the building. Beyond the heavy door was a steep stairway leading down, which jogged at a landing, then again, zigzagging back and forth every few dozen feet. The walls of the stair were close on either side, unadorned wood paneling which seemed black as pitch in the dim lighting.

Finally, they reached the bottom of the stair and another door, but while the door above had been rough-hewn oak, this was more elaborate, lacquered red with a gold fox rampant in bas relief on its surface. In the place of a knob was a heavy brass ring, large enough to be worked around the neck as a torque, and this the gatekeeper turned. The red-lacquered door swung open easily, noiselessly on well-oiled hinges, and Blank and Miss Bonaventure stepped out of the darkened stair into the bright light of a throne room.

It was a massive chamber, substantially underground it would seem, lit by rows of massive lanterns that depended from iron stanchions on the walls, with polished marble underfoot. The chamber was dominated by an immense golden statue of a fox which was raised on a dais at the far side of the floor. The fox held two jade disks, one in either paw, one engraved with the symbol "$z\grave{\imath}$," the other with "$y\acute{o}u$," which together comprised the ideogram for "freedom." Standing in ordered rows along the walls to either side of the door were guards dressed in traditional Chinese armor, swords at their belts and long halberds in their hands, staring forward dispassionately.

Seated before the dais, on a simple and unadorned wooden chair, sat an ancient Chinese woman in a simple dress of green and black silk embroidered with gold thread. She seemed almost like a child's doll, given her diminutive size. Her eyes, staring out from a face like a nest of wrinkles, were the color of violets, her fingers thick jointed and gnarled, while her skin and hair were a uniform shade of alabaster, the color of bleached bone.

In one sense it had been only days since Blank had seen her, but in every other way that mattered it had been a lifetime.

"Miss Bonaventure," Blank said, taking his companion's hand and leading her forward into the chamber. "Allow me to introduce Madame Quexi, better known as the Ghost Fox."

"It has been a long time, Kongbai," the ancient woman said. She motioned with one hand, the white nails on her fingertips impossibly long. "Come closer that I might see you better. These eyes of mine . . ." The albino trailed off, indicating her violet eyes with a long-nailed finger.

"You never could see very well, could you?" Blank said, meaningfully. "But that was your problem all along, wasn't it?" He took a step closer, but Miss Bonaventure hung back. "Come along, my dear," he said to his companion, reassuringly.

Miss Bonaventure shrugged and swung her parasol up onto her shoulder.

"It *has* been a long time, Quexi," Blank said, somewhat sadly, stopping a few dozen feet from the dais. "I must say that you're looking . . . well?"

The Ghost Fox made an angry gesture, and the guards on either side of the room rippled into motion, raising their halberds menacingly. Then the ancient albino moved her bone white hands in a soothing gesture and leaned back in her chair, sighing heavily. "At least have the good graces to lie more convincingly, Kongbai. I know very well that I am hideous with age."

"Are you?" Blank raised an eyebrow. "I hadn't really noticed."

"Bah!" The Ghost Fox curled her white lip in disgust.

"Blank?" Miss Bonaventure said in a low voice, leaning close. "Just who *is* this woman, anyway?"

"Have I never mentioned her?" Miss Bonaventure shook her head, and Blank gave a playful scowl. "Oh, I was sure that I had. Well, in any case. The Ghost Fox"—he mimed an abbreviated bow in the direction of the ancient woman—"controls the lion's share of all criminal activity conducted in China and throughout Asia."

"Crime?" the Ghost Fox sneered, tapping her long white fingernails on her chair's arm. "Crime, is it? A great empire seizes an entire nation and calls it expansion. A small band of men and women take back what little they can, and it is called theft. If that is your notion of justice, Kongbai, you can keep it. But we are not relegated to the Eastern Hemisphere any longer. These last years, the reach of the Ghost Fox Triad has extended, first to Australia, then India, and now as far as your beloved London itself. There is no 'crime' committed within the boundaries of the Limehouse without my permission, and no crime committed elsewhere by Limehouse's inhabitants but that they pay a percentage in tribute to our cause."

"My, my," Blank said, nodding admiringly. "You *have* been busy, haven't you?"

"Blank, you do have the most *interesting* friends," Miss Bonaventure said, spinning the parasol on her shoulder. "I admit I'm often forced to wonder what your life was like before that day six years ago when we met."

Blank looked at her and smiled. "Bleak and lonesome, my dear. Bleak and lonesome."

"Enough of this prattle!" the Ghost Fox snapped.

Blank turned back to the ancient woman, shaking his head disapprovingly, clucking his tongue. "Such manners, Quexi. What would Michel Void say, if he were to see you now, hmm?"

The Ghost Fox exploded out of her chair, jumping to her feet with a loud curse. From all sides came the clang of steel on steel as the armored guards took a step forward, brandishing their halberds, eyes narrowed at Blank and Miss Bonaventure.

"If you wanted to kill me, Quexi, you'd have tried it long, *long* before now," Blank said with a slight smile, inclining his head.

The ancient albino breathed heavily, violet eyes flashing menacingly, but by inches relaxed, bringing her emotions once more under control.

"You bring out the worst in me, Kongbai, and always did." Then she gently eased her ancient bones back onto the chair and addressed the guards to either side. "You may leave us," she said, a subtle thrumming sound humming beneath her words at the very edge of hearing. "You will be called if needed."

The thrumming continued for a long moment and then stopped, at which point the guards turned as one and filed out of the chamber in an orderly fashion. The last to leave closed the large red-lacquered door behind them, and Blank and Miss Bonaventure were left alone with the ancient Chinese albino.

"It's your fault I've become as I am now, you know," the old woman said in a quieter voice, sighing. "I could have lived a long life of service, not thinking to ask the questions that couldn't be answered. And then you had to teach me to segment my thoughts, to hide myself away from Omega, and now look what's become of me."

"I am looking, Quexi," Blank answered, tenderly.

"Youth lost, beauty faded," the ancient albino said. "But worth it in the pursuit of the cause."

Blank scoffed. "What cause is that?"

"You know full well! I fight against empire, Kongbai!" The Ghost Fox's voice rose now, with a pleading tone. "Just as you always said. And like you said, I pay whatever price necessary."

"But . . ." Blank began, shocked. "I never meant . . ." He shook his head. "We've had this conversation a thousand times before, child. There's little to be gained from another performance. As I told you when last we spoke, all those years ago, I work for the end of the empire, and against the interests of Omega, but not at the cost of civilization itself. There is a balance to be struck."

"Balance? Ha!" The ancient albino waved her long-nailed fingers in a dismissive gesture. "You sell yourself short, *lacuna*, if you think you don't still serve the interests of Omega and empire alike. You protect a system which facilitates the domination of one people by another. Or did you fail to notice the white men lounging on the couches in the opium den upstairs? Or the poor who crowded the streets through which you came to this building?"

Blank shook his head. "It is unfortunate, but I am forced to take a longer view."

The Ghost Fox exploded with anger, leaping out of the chair. Her bone white hair streaming behind her like a nimbus, she rushed towards Blank, long-nailed fingers out like claws. Miss Bonaventure moved to block a blow, but Blank waved her away at the last instant and stood still as the old woman came to a halt just short of him, her talonlike nails stopping bare inches from either cheek.

"Ask the innocents if they should take a longer view. Ask the men, women, and children who were ground underfoot in the Opium Wars. Ask them!"

Blank closed his eyes for a moment, a pained expression on his face, the memories of those dark times rising unbidden from the depths of his mind.

"I didn't come here to argue," Blank said at length, opening his eyes and meeting the violet gaze of the ancient albino. "And I'm sure you didn't bring me here to replay old discussions. What is it you want of me?"

The anger slowly bled from her, and the white-haired, white-skinned dervish who had leapt from the chair seemed to diminish, reduced once more to an elderly Chinese woman of short stature, her hands small and frail, her bones thin. She looked up at him, standing no taller than Blank's chest, and for a brief moment he could see in her the girl she'd once been, the daughter he'd never had, the child who'd been lost to him forever.

"Kongbai," she said in a quiet voice, her violet eyes glistening. She reached out her hand to him again, but tenderly this time, not in anger.

"Child," he said, his voice cracking, and reached out his own hand.

Their hands drew nearer, nearly touching, but the years had driven a gulf between them that could never be breached, and there were things they had done and said which could never be taken back. With bare inches of empty space separating them, the old woman snatched her hand back and turned away. They stood frozen for a moment in tableau, the man reaching out, the old woman turned away, hand clutched to her chest. And then the moment was gone, passed as quickly as it had come, and they were no longer a man and the child he'd lost, but a consulting detective and the mistress of crime, staring at one another across an impassable gulf.

The Ghost Fox returned to her chair and with a groan eased her tired bones back down. She drew a ragged breath and let out a sigh. Then she turned her violet eyes back on Blank and Miss Bonaventure.

"The police hunt the streets of my Limehouse for a killer," the Ghost Fox intoned, regal and aloof. "They seek to protect the interests of their bitch queen and of the coddled masses who live above the bridges. This interferes with my business and with the operations of the Triad, and I would have it stopped."

"You would, would you?" Miss Bonaventure said, hands on her hip. She'd followed little of what had gone on between Blank and the ancient albino, but she clearly recognized a puffed-up piece of self-importance when she saw it.

The Ghost Fox ignored the jibe, focusing her attention on Blank. "I want this killer caught and this harassment stopped, detective. I know you have been engaged in this matter, but it is not for *their* sake that you must catch this killer, but for ours. The Triad must be free to pursue its cause unimpeded."

Blank nodded, thoughtfully. "The matter already has my every attention," he said. "But if I were to have the assistance of, say, a large network of resources, I might find a solution that much sooner."

The Ghost Fox narrowed her violet eyes. "Go on."

"Will you cooperate?" Blank asked, flatly. "If I call for your assistance, will you give it?"

The Ghost Fox regarded him for a long moment, unspeaking. Then she folded her thin arms across her chest, wrapping her long-nailed fingers around her upper arms. "In this one regard," she said, closing her violet eyes, "yes."

A long silence stretched out between them. Miss Bonaventure shifted uneasily, glancing from side to side. Finally, Blank broke the silence. "Quexi, I . . ."

The Ghost Fox interrupted with a quick shake of her head, her eyes still squeezed shut. Then, taking a deep breath, she said simply, "You may go."

The ancient albino fell silent and would not be induced to speak again. Their audience with the Ghost Fox had come to an end.

CHAPTER TWELVE
Millennium

B Y THE TIME THE PLACE REALLY STARTED TO FILL UP, when all the banks and shops closed down for the day, Alice and Roxanne had moved over to the booth vacated by orange-shirt-blue-tie and company and become fast friends.

Roxanne had explained that she lived not far from here, in Bayswater, but that she traveled a great deal. She stopped in at the pub when she was in town, but since most of her friends lived elsewhere, or "kept different schedules" as she put it, she was most often alone. And since she hated drinking alone, she usually struck up conversations with strangers, a favorite hobby of hers, and passed the time getting to know them.

She'd been on the other side of the pub when orange-shirt-blue-tie had tried to put the moves on Alice, as it were, and had seen the whole thing.

"Oh, God," Alice said, feeling a blush rise in her cheeks. "Was I rubbing my stomach and licking my lips like a hungry cartoon character?" Roxanne nodded. "Jesus."

Roxanne raised one of her dark eyebrows, quizzically. Her eyebrows were one of the first things Alice had noticed about her. That, and the fact that she knew how to use judo or kung fu or whatever on big drunk guys in ugly shirts and ties, which was a habit that certainly must have come in handy. Roxanne had really striking eyebrows and looked to Alice like an older, taller, blonder Natalie Portman or someone like that. She was maybe thirty years old, but didn't show any signs of slowing down.

Before Roxanne had a chance to say anything, Alice went on. "Anyway, I thought the guy was gay when I saw him earlier. I mean, that shirt? Really?"

Roxanne laughed. "No, not gay, just English. But sometimes it's hard to tell the difference." Then she narrowed her eyes and studied Alice closely. "Is this something you do often, though? Zone out and make like a cartoon thinking about something good to eat?"

Alice shook her head, sheepishly. She hesitated for a moment, and then figured, why the hell not? It wasn't as if she was going to be seeing this woman again, right? She reached into the backpack on the ground by her feet and pulled out a little orange plastic bottle with a bright white childproof cap. She popped the top, effortlessly, and then shook out a single tablet onto the table between them. It was tiny and salmon pink, with a little symbol and a couple of letters stamped on it in black.

"What's that?"

"That's 125 milligrams of Depakote," Alice said. "Divalproex sodium. If I take that, then all of my problems go away." She chuckled ruefully. "At least, that's what my doctors and my mother think."

Roxanne reached across the table to pick the tablet up, and as she stretched out her arm her leather jacket rode up enough to expose the bracelet on her wrist, a wide silver band with a big round gem inset, like the face of a watch. She put the tablet on the palm of her hand and held it up for inspection. "It's an anticonvulsant, right? Used for seizures and the like?"

Alice raised her eyebrow. Impressive. She nodded.

Roxanne looked up from the tablet and met Alice's eyes. "You epileptic, then?"

Impressive, once more. Alice nodded again. "Not the grand mal kind, though. No frothing at the mouth and writhing on the floor. Just the kind where you hear and see things that aren't there."

Roxanne hummed, thoughtfully. "The god spot."

"The what now?"

"A scientist name Michael Persinger did some experiments back in the eighties, where he stimulated the temporal lobes of patients with electromagnetic fields. He found that he was able to generate something very much like temporal lobe seizures, and that in many cases the subjects reported a feeling of a presence in the room with them, and some even had visual or auditory hallucinations. Some said it was God, some said it was angels, or aliens, or demons, but some just thought it was indistinct presences. It's called the 'god spot' because some people think that's where all religious experiences come from."

Alice remembered what Mr. Saenz had said, about Lewis Carroll and van Gogh and Tennyson all having TLE, and all of them taking their seizure experiences and turning them into art.

"Do you believe in God, Roxanne?"

Roxanne cocked an eyebrow and quirked a smile. "I thought that politics and religion were topics never to be discussed in the pub. Or was that the dinner table?" She chuckled. "But it depends on what you mean. If you mean a guy with a beard sitting up in the sky, lording it over us, then no. If you mean something more like the universe itself as a living mind, and us as its thoughts . . . then maybe. I've seen a great many strange things, Alice, and while I've more questions than answers at this stage, I'm still very much interested in the asking." She tapped the bracelet on her wrist, thoughtfully.

"My grandmother believes . . . believed . . . in everything," Alice said. "My mother doesn't believe in anything. I believe in something, but I'm not sure what it is. Something bigger than me, bigger both in space and in time. I've caught glimpses of it during my seizures, my episodes, my visions, whatever they are, but I just can't put it into words." She thought of the hundreds of spiral notebooks she'd filled over the years. "No matter how hard I try."

"It isn't just eldritch horrors that are indescribable, you know."

Alice caught the Lovecraft reference, but let it slide. "I wonder sometimes about religion, you know. They think that Joan of Arc and Ellen G. White were probably epileptics who thought their seizures were messages from God. And they think maybe even Moses and Saint Paul were, too. So what if all religions, everywhere, are started by people whose neurons keep misfiring, experiencing hallucinations while they drool on themselves or tap their feet . . ."

"Or lick their lips while rubbing their tummies like hungry cartoons?"

"Exactly."

Roxanne thought for a moment. "So if God exists, then no one has ever heard from him."

"Oh, I'm not saying that just because they're epileptic they're not hearing God." Alice shook her head. "What if *all* of them *were*?"

Alice was lighting a cigarette, striking a match on the ridged bottom of the vesta case.

"That's nice," Roxanne said, leaning in for a closer look. "Victorian, isn't it?"

Alice exhaled twin streams of smoke from her nostrils and looked down at the silver case. She shrugged. "I guess."

Roxanne reached out. "May I?"

Alice handed the thing over and took a long drag of her cigarette, then followed it with the last of her beer. "My grandmother gave it to me."

"'J.D.'" Roxanne looked up from the case. "Are those her initials?"

Alice shook her head. "Her name was Naomi Vance. She didn't know what the D stood for, but said the J was for 'Jack.'"

"A friend of hers?" Roxanne gave a sly grin as she handed it back.

"Something like that."

Naomi Vance had been on her deathbed. It was the cigarettes that killed her, in the end, but not cancer. That would have been too quick. Instead it was all manner of unpleasantness. Emphysema, uterine prolapse, ulcerative colitis, you name it.

Alice was a junior at Westwood High School when her grandmother went to bed for the last time. She missed so many classes, sitting by her grandmother's bedside, that she'd have to go to summer school to keep from being held back a year. And having already *done* that once, when she was seven, she wasn't in any hurry to do it again. The fact that she was older than all of her classmates, and the only ones she really got along with were the other kids who had been held back, too, reprobates like Nancy and company, was what had gotten her into trouble in the first place.

So Naomi lay in bed, for all those weeks, waiting to die. They wouldn't let her smoke anymore, which Naomi considered incredibly rude, but she liked to make Alice lean in close when she got back from smoking cigarettes out in the parking lot, so she could smell the scent of tobacco smoke and out-side breezes that clung to her granddaughter's clothes and hair. Alice had started smoking when she first met Nancy, back when she was almost fifteen and starting high school, and kept smoking even after the accident that no one at school liked to talk about.

Naomi was tired all of the time, which was understandable. Dying took a lot out of you. So Alice spent a lot of time reading to her grandmother, when the crappy daytime talk shows and soap operas and game shows on the TV bolted high up on the wall got to be too much to take. Alice read newspapers and magazines and books, but most often she read to her grandmother from the copy of Lewis Carroll's *Alice's Adventures in Wonderland & Through the Looking Glass* that she'd stolen from the Grisham Middle School library years before. Alice's father, James Fell, had read Carroll's stories to his daughter over and over again when she was a little girl, right up until the first accident. Later, when her mother, Samantha, had gotten rid of all of her husband's things in that crazy week when she decided that she just couldn't stand to look at them any longer, just couldn't bear the memories one day more, one of the things to go had been James Fell's copy of Lewis Carroll's collected works. The next month, Samantha had come to her senses and tried to buy everything back, but one of the few things that they were never able to relocate was James's copy of Lewis Carroll, which had been bought off the shelves of Half Price Books in the inter-vening days. It was years before Alice had another copy, when she'd stuffed the library bound edition into her back pocket at the Grisham school library, at Nancy's prompting, and walked right out the door with it.

Alice had just gotten to the part about the Red King's dream, with the television bolted high up on the wall muted and silent, when Naomi had another one of her coughing fits, and by the time it had died down, she was ready to tell her granddaughter her last secret, the one she'd held for so long.

Naomi waved her hand, fluttering like a dying bird's wing, and motioned for the television remote, which was over on the rolling table, just past the plastic tray holding the day's lunch, untouched. Alice, taking a moment to realize that her grandmother wasn't asking for the lime JELL-O, grabbed the remote and handed it over. Naomi stabbed the buttons until the sound came up and waved Alice silent.

The television was tuned to a twenty-four-hour news station that was running a story about a volcano erupting in Iceland. Mount Hekla, it was called. The volcano had started erupting the week before, on February twenty-sixth, and had just subsided that morning, seven days later.

The news anchor started talking about something to do with computers, and Naomi shut off the television. Alice had come to distrust computers deeply, after Y2K ended up being such a disappointment. If you couldn't count on computers to bring on the apocalypse, what good were they, anyway?

Alice looked to her grandmother and was surprised to see tears streaming down her cheeks. She asked Naomi what was wrong, not sure she wanted to know the answer.

Naomi's husband had died when Alice was just a few years old, and she had only the dimmest memories of the man. In Alice's vague recollections, her grandfather was a mountain covered in a wool suit that smelled of Aqua Velva aftershave, who always had pieces of hard candy in his pockets for her.

Tearfully, Naomi explained that her husband hadn't been Alice's grandfather at all, not really. Another man had been the father of Alice's mother, Samantha. And all because of that damned volcano.

Back when she was only a few years older than Alice was now, Naomi, then Naomi Ward, had been a flight attendant. They called them "stewardesses" in those days, but it amounted to the same thing. Young Naomi had worked for American Overseas airlines, flying back and forth from Paris to New York.

Alice had known this since she was little. She'd always known the story about how her grandmother had worked in an airplane, until something bad happened, she lost her job, got married, and gave birth to her only child, Alice's mother.

Only, that wasn't what happened. Not really.

Naomi explained. The plane she worked on, all those years before, had been a Douglas DC-4 airliner. In those days, planes couldn't make it all the way across the Atlantic in one hop but had to stop for refueling along the way. They'd take off from Paris, then land in Shannon, Ireland, then Keflavik, Iceland, then Narsarsuaq, Greenland, then Frobisher Bay, Canada, and then finally New York, America, where they'd empty out, rest up, and do the whole thing all over again.

In 1947, when Naomi's plane was refueling in Keflavik, a goddamned volcano had erupted, blanketing the skies with smoke and ash, blotting out the sun. They'd been grounded for days, waiting for the air to clear enough for them to navigate at takeoff. The passengers and crew waited in the town, crammed into the few available rooms to let, drinking with the civilian employees of Keflavik Airport, all of whom were Americans, either employed by American Overseas or by Lockhead Aircraft Overseas Service. They hardly saw any Icelanders at all the whole time they were in town. But there were a few other foreigners in the mix, including a trio of Brits. One of them was named Jack.

Naomi never did learn his last name, but she fell in love with him all the same. They spent three days together in a cramped little hotel room, hardly even leaving to eat or drink, wrapped around each other. Jack was older than Naomi, maybe even fifty, but Naomi didn't mind. He was in terrific shape, and had stamina to beat the band, and they even smoked the same brand of cigarettes. When the smoke cleared, and the plane was ready to take off, Jack was already gone, along with his two friends, off on some business or other elsewhere on the island. All he'd left Naomi were a few days' worth of pleasant memories, a soreness that meant she walked funny for days, his engraved silver match case, and the child growing in her belly.

Naomi was reasonably sure he hadn't meant to leave his match case behind and was positive that he hadn't meant to leave a child, but there it was.

Naomi didn't know about the baby until weeks later, of course, and by then there was nothing that could be done about it. Even if she'd been married, her employers would have fired her on the spot, but at least then they might have been a bit more forgiving. But unwed? They booted her out the door in New York with her last paycheck, and that was that.

Naomi ended up marrying the first man she found, a Texan, and when he moved back home to Austin to be nearer his family, she went with him. It wasn't the greatest marriage—how could it have been, since Naomi had just married the first guy she found—but if George Vance knew that his daughter Samantha hadn't been born premature at all, he didn't let on.

There in the hospital room, the television once more silent, the lime JELL-O slowly melting away, Naomi asked Alice to bring over her purse from the side table. From its fusty interior, she pulled out the silver match case. Alice had no idea how many times she'd seen her grandmother light cigarettes with matches from that case. Hundreds of thousands? Millions? Enough to kill her, at any rate, which was plenty.

Naomi started crying again, but with a different expression on her face. She wasn't feeling sorry for herself. She was feeling guilty.

She told Alice that she felt horrible about the exorcisms and everything else she'd put her through, all those years before. She said that maybe, just maybe, it wasn't the devil that Alice was hearing at all. Maybe it was really the voice of God, instead. Maybe by silencing those voices, they'd really prevented Alice from doing something really amazing.

Then Naomi had given the silver match case to Alice. As a gift? As a token of apology? Alice was never sure. But when she went out into the parking lot next to smoke, she tossed her disposable lighter in the trash, took out one of the wooden matches from the case, and sheltering from the unseasonably cold March wind, lit another cigarette. She knew the things would kill her, too, if she let them. But then, Alice doubted she'd live long enough for them to have a chance.

And then, a few months later, Alice's grandmother died. Naomi Vance had been a part of Alice's life every day since she was seven and a half. After James Fell had his heart attack and Alice fell, Naomi had moved in with her daughter and granddaughter to help run the family business on Anderson Mill and to help raise Alice.

Alice had watched her grandmother move through stages of belief like a farmer rotating crops, Buddhism one week, nature worship the next, crystals the week after that. The only constant in Naomi Vance's system of beliefs was the unwavering conviction that there was meaning in the universe and that everyone and everything had a destiny to fulfill. Samantha Fell had given up on the idea of meaning and destiny when her husband had a heart attack and died, all while she was out working in the garden. Alice knew that her mother didn't blame her for falling, but in some strange way Samantha blamed herself for not being there to catch her.

Now, Naomi Vance was dead, and Alice felt that she'd fallen farther away from her mother than ever.

"So what happens if you don't go back on your meds?"

Alice looked up at Roxanne and thought about how truthfully to answer. Again, what the hell? It wasn't as if they'd ever see each other again.

"If I stay off long enough, and have enough seizures, I've got a fifteen percent chance of psychosis. Not quite schizophrenia, but close enough to count, if you ask me. If I stay on the meds, I don't have visions, but I'll still have all the symptoms of Geschwind's." She paused, and then cocked her head to one side. "Do you have any kids, Roxanne? Or want any?"

Roxanne thought for a moment. "No, and I'm not sure, in that order. I have trouble enough keeping relationships with adults working, you know? I'm not sure how successful I'd be establishing any kind of connection to a child."

A good answer. "Well, if I take the meds, I can't get pregnant, unless I want to have a kid with all kinds of birth defects. My TLE means I'd have a hard time getting pregnant, even if I wanted to, since a messed-up temporal lobe means reduced fertility. But since I exhibit what the doctors call 'hyposexual tendencies,' it's not as if I'm much interested in sex, anyway."

Roxanne nodded, wearing a sympathetic look.

An awkward silence stretched between them.

"Another round?" Roxanne finally asked. "My shout."

Alice wasn't sure what she was shouting about, but it seemed a good idea to her.

Roxanne knew what time it was without checking a clock. It was time for her to go.

"I've got to meet my dad for dinner," she explained, shouldering back into her leather jacket, which had lain across the back of the bench. "You sure you're going to be all right?"

Alice nodded again, and for the twelfth time lied and said she'd be fine.

"And you've got somewhere to stay, with these friends of yours?"

Alice tried to remember the names she'd given her imaginary friends with the apartment not far from here and managed a fairly convincing smile.

Roxanne gave her a close look, suspiciously, but didn't call her on it. "You have something to write on? And with?"

Alice thought a moment, and then fished her partially full notebook from her backpack, along with one of her pens.

Roxanne flipped open to the first blank page and wrote her name and number. Then she cursed herself under her breath, crossed out the number, and wrote another below it. "They just changed all the dialing codes in April, and I can never remember whether I'm before the change or after. This is June, so this is the 0207 number. Call me if you need any help. Okay? You promise?"

Alice made a show of looking at the number. She nodded. "I promise."

Roxanne stood by the side of the table, chewing her lower lip. "I don't know. Maybe you should just come to dinner with me. I'm sure my dad would love to meet you."

Alice shook her head, still smiling. "No. Go on. I'll be fine." She waved a hand at the notebook, merrily. "Look, I've got your number right here. I'll call you if I run into any trouble. I promise."

Roxanne continued chewing her lower lip, still looking unconvinced, but finally shrugged with defeat. "Okay, then." She reached out and put a hand on Alice's shoulder "You take care of yourself, you understand?"

Alice smiled, blinked, and nodded.

When Roxanne was gone, Alice scowled at the number on the page, the purple ink looking black in the poorly lit booth, and shoved notebook and pen back into her backpack.

As if she could face someone who knew her secrets. Not all of them, of course, but enough.

The next little while passed in a blur.

Here's what Alice later remembered:

Alice was hungry, and so had an order of the fish and fries, though steered well clear of the frozen peas.

She drank some more.

She smoked all the cigarettes in the pack and started on the next.

She fended off all manner of losers and creeps who tried to hit on her.

There was only one other incident that stuck out in memory. One of the creeps who tried to hit on her had adopted, at least, a novel approach. When he saw that Alice was reading Lewis Carroll—but she wasn't reading it, not really, just finding comfort in flipping through the pages, looking at the familiar images and well-worn clusters of words—he started talking about mathematics, and physics, and fractals. He said he was an amateur mathematician himself, and had read a book all about a mathematician named Kurt Gödel, and that the book had used characters and stories from Carroll's Alice stories to illustrate its points. He talked about Carroll's mathematical paradoxes, the word games she remembered from her father's book. And he talked about how Gödel had espoused all kinds of strange notions, including the idea that if the universe were revolving, then it would be possible to travel backwards and forward in time just by moving far enough through space.

Hadn't Roxanne mentioned something about time travel, too? Alice couldn't remember.

The amateur mathematician had moved on, getting bored of his unsuccessful attempts to dazzle Alice with his erudition and trying the tactics on a pair of clerical workers further along the bar.

Then it was last call, and the bartender or publican or whatever was telling everyone that they didn't have to go home, but they couldn't stay there.

Alice couldn't go home if she wanted to. She'd only bought a one-way ticket and couldn't afford to get back. She doubted there was room on her credit card to cover the cost and knew there wasn't enough in the bank. She was stuck.

Alice slid off the stool. She'd moved from the booth after Roxanne left and hadn't stood up in hours. Now, it seemed like the universe *was* revolving after all, the way the walls spun around her.

She lit a cigarette, to cover her disorientation, and then followed the burning coal at the cigarette's end like a lighthouse beacon, managing to get outside and onto the sidewalk without falling down. Barely.

It must have taken her longer to stand up and walk out then she thought. As soon as she was outside, the lights behind her turned off, the bartender or publican or whatever locked the door, and Alice was alone on the sidewalk. Where had everyone else gone? Home or somewhere else, she supposed. Just not here.

Alice started walking up the road. She didn't know where she was going, just that she was moving. Then she heard the sound of fluttering and looked down.

There, blocking her path, was a large black bird. At first she thought it was a crow, or a grackle. Then she realized. No, it was a raven.

A raven, and it wasn't alone.

It wasn't just one raven, blocking Alice's path. There were several. No, a half dozen. More. Seven, altogether.

There were three on the sidewalk, moving in little hops, two more ruffling their feathers atop the streetlights, and two at the edge of the awning over a nearby shop window. Seven ravens. It was like a scene from that old Hitchcock movie.

None of the birds made a sound. They just looked at her with their cold, ink black eyes. Dead black eyes like the loveless, joyless eyes of a shark.

Alice drew the last of her cigarette into her lungs, then dropped the butt to the pavement. She tried to grind it under her heel, missed, but felt the attempt was enough.

"Leave me alone," she said, slurring her words. "I don't want any special destiny, you get me?"

Then she turned around, spinning on her heel, almost but not quite losing her balance, almost but not quite getting dizzy again and throwing up all over her shirt. She kept her fish and fries and alcohol down, though, thank you very much the ghost of Nancy, and took a step away from the ravens.

"Alice. Wait." The voice was squeaky and high, but ragged, like someone with laryngitis had just sucked down a balloon's worth of helium and tried out their best monster voice. "Unworld. Waits. Soon."

Alice stopped and sighed. Was it one of the creeps from the bar, come back to try his luck again? Maybe the amateur mathematician?

It was only when she was turning around that Alice realized she hadn't told any of the creeps her name.

"Alice. Unworld. Waits."

Alice narrowed her eyes. There was no one but the birds, on the ground and overhead.

"Who's there?" Alice asked. She knew already, but couldn't admit it, didn't really want to know.

One of the ravens hopped forward.

It opened its black beak.

"Disk. Memory. Within. Save. Alice. Unworld. Waits. Alice."

There was the high squeaky laryngitis-helium voice she'd heard. Coming out of the raven's mouth. Just like she'd known it would.

"No." Alice shook her head. "No, no, no." She put her hands over her ears. "Not for me."

If she'd smelled smoke, or seen the flashing light, she'd have thought she was having an episode. But this didn't have the same sense of meaning suffused through everything, the feeling that something important was happening. She was just drunk on a sidewalk in London, being accosted by a flock of ravens. Or was that a murder of ravens? She could never keep that straight.

"Alice. Memory. Save. Disk. Unworld. Waits."

She could still hear the high-pitched, growly-squeaky voice even with her ears covered.

"I've changed my mind, okay?" Alice said, lowering her hands, pleading with the ravens. "I went up in the Ferris wheel like you said, then nothing happened, and now I just want to go home again. Is that okay? Can't you find someone else?"

The raven hopped forward another few inches, tilted its head to one side, and studied Alice intently through one ink black eye.

"Alice. Save."

She'd had enough. Alice turned and took to her heels.

Alice ran as fast as she could, but given how drunk she was, it probably wasn't very fast. She wasn't sure where she was going, didn't even know what she was running from, just that she had to get away.

She rounded the corner at the end of the street and plowed right into somebody.

Whoever it was that Alice had run into was surer on their feet than she was, since they were still standing when she rebounded and fell sprawled on the pavement.

"Hey, watch it!"

Alice looked up from the pavement, breathless. There was an old man standing over her. Old as in fifty, not one hundred.

"You okay, love?"

The guy looked like Michael Caine in *Dirty Rotten Scoundrels* without the mustache, but talked like Michael Caine in *The Italian Job*. Naomi had always had a thing for the actor, and Alice must have seen every one of his movies growing up.

The guy reached out a hand to help Alice to her feet and she couldn't help but think he looked familiar somehow, beyond the resemblance to her grandmother's favorite actor.

Alice looked at his proffered hand like it was a dead fish.

He chuckled. "Don't worry, love, I won't bite. Trust me, you're not my type."

The guy pulled Alice to her feet, and she got a better look at him. He looked a little less like Michael Caine than she'd thought. He was wearing a gray suit that had seen better days, his shirt open at the collar with no tie, and over this a ratty-looking trench coat. Blond hair gone to gray, a week's worth of beard on his chin. But his eyes. His eyes, they were the color of the iceberg in the nighttime shots of *Titanic*, ice-chip blue.

Ice-chip blue eyes.

"Still waters," Alice said, scarcely above a whisper.

The guy narrowed his eyes and regarded her with surprise and suspicion. "Yeah, my name's Stillman Waters. Who told you that?"

So that was the eye over the city, and the ravens, and the mirror-still water, and the man with the ice-chip blue eyes. Alice almost had a complete set. Where was the jewel?

"Look, love," the man called Stillman Waters said, releasing his hold on her arm. "Much as I'd love to stay and chat, I really don't want to stay and chat, so if you'll excuse me I think I'll be on my way."

There was a noise from behind her, and Alice looked to see a raven alighting on a red cast-iron mailbox. In seconds, its six friends flapped into view, settling on lampposts and awnings.

"Alice," said the squeaky-growly voice of the raven. "Run."

Stillman Waters looked from the raven to Alice. "Friend of yours, is it, love?"

Then, before introductions could be made, the dogs crashed the party.

There were five of them, so the ravens outnumbered the dogs by two, but what the dogs lacked in numerical superiority, they more than made up in terrifying hostility.

They had white coats, except for their ears, which were tipped with swathes of red, and when they curled back their lips Alice could see that their fangs, like their claws, had been dyed red.

"Bugger!" Stillman Waters spat, and his hand dove into the pocket of his ratty trench coat. When it came out again, there was a weird-looking pistol in his fist.

Alice opened her mouth to ask what was going on, but never had the chance to speak.

"Come along," Stillman said, and grabbed hold of her arm. "We need to go. Now!"

CHAPTER THIRTEEN

Twilight

INALLY CAME THE HOUR when the land to their starboard fell away. They'd sailed the breadth of the island, and it was time to steer the longship again to the north. In short order they were sailing back in the direction of the rising sun. The winds were sluggish for a time, requiring the captains to pull on the oars while Artor worked the tiller, but fortune was with them when the winds picked up from the west, driving them steadily towards their destination. Within less than a day more at sail, they came at last to Llongborth, the port of the warships.

Having traveled so far from Glevum by foot, and then again by sea for days more, Galaad knew that if they continued up the coast to the north and east they would make landfall not far from his home. But knowing that he was so near the lands where he'd spent all his years did little to make this area seem any less unfamiliar. A matter of hours at sail from Glevum, Llongborth was like nothing he'd seen before.

The port of the warships was well named. The harbor bristled with the masts of sailing vessels of all varieties, even more than could be seen at anchor in the river Tamesa. Captured Saeson longships like Artor's White Aspect, merchant ships from the Middle Sea, ancient Roman triremes and biremes, scattered dromons and liburnas.

Artor had explained to Galaad that they would make landfall at Llongborth, replenish their supplies, and head overland to the island of Galaad's vision. The waters approaching this length of the Dumnonian coast were shallow, little more than marshy fen in some areas, and even with as shallow a draw as the White Aspect boasted, there would be too great a risk of running aground.

Llongborth was the home of Geraint, king of half Dumnonia. Geraint, or more properly Geraint ab Erbin ab Custennin, had fought with Artor at Badon, and later returned to Dumnonia after the death of his father to take the throne rather than taking his place among the captains around Artor's marble circle. However, Geraint ruled only half of Dumnonia, while his cousin Mark ab Meirchion ab Custennin ruled the other half.

The connections between High King and ruler of half Dumnonia were stronger still than those forged in battle, but were instead bound in blood. Artor's mother was the daughter of Custennin and a sister to Geraint's father Erbin, making Artor and Geraint cousins. And though Artor and Mark were, by extension, cousins as well, if it came to a struggle between the Dumnonian kings for control of the kingdom, it was clear which of the two had Artor's allegiance.

With sails furled, the longship was maneuvered towards the dock, though it soon became easier to use the oars like a ferryman's punt pole, as they moved into waters too shallow for the larger vessels anchored further out in the harbor. The longship moored to the dock, the oars were shipped and the captains made ready to disembark.

They had not been able to send word ahead of their arrival, having traveled from Caer Llundain by sea faster than any could make the journey by land in this icy season, and so came to Llongborth unannounced. It did not take long, as the captains unloaded their gear from the longship, for the White Aspect to be recognized, and in short order her master the High King as well, so that by the time their provisions, saddles, tack, and weapons were arranged on the dock, an envoy had been sent from the court of Geraint to greet them.

"You are welcome to Llongborth, High King and Count of Britannia," said the page, bowing low. He was a thin man with a misshapen nose that had long ago been broken and healed crooked, but he spoke clear and precise, albeit with a distinct Dumnonian accent. "King Geraint sends you greetings and asks that you join him in his court at your earliest convenience."

The page half turned and indicated the large wooden structure that dominated the small clutch of buildings perched at the water's edge. Of recent vintage, constructed of stout wood and mortar, it rose some three dozen feet above the ground, and half again as many wide, and though not as imposing as Artor's palace in Caer Llundain, in context it was a striking sight.

"Relay my thanks to your king for this kindness," Artor said, "along with our glad acceptance. We have only to see to the disposition of our things and we will be along presently."

"Oh, these?" The page indicated the gear stacked on the deck, around which the five captains and Galaad stood, stretching their legs and arms, grateful once more to be on solid ground. "The king instructs me that our porters shall see to your every need, and if you wish shall transport your things to rooms in his palace, where accommodations are being prepared for you."

Galaad noticed that Pryder and Gwrol tensed, no doubt sensing treachery, but reasoned that they must be habitually paranoid, since neither Artor nor any of the other captains exhibited any undue concern.

"It would be impolite to refuse, I should think," Artor said.

"Well, thank bugger for that," Lugh said in a whisper loud enough for everyone in a hundred feet radius to hear. "I was afraid we'd have to lug that dung around on our backs forever."

Artor cast him a quick glance, not entirely without amusement, and then returned his gaze to the page. "So we'll be coming with you, it would appear."

"Yes," the page said, nodding eagerly, as a trio of burly porters approached up the quay, ready to haul their gear after them. "The king waits your coming eagerly."

"Then lead on," Artor said with a smile.

With the bent-nosed page scurrying in the lead and Artor following close behind, the seven made their way through the narrow streets of Llongborth.

Galaad couldn't help but feel a moment's concern that they'd left their goods and gear unattended with virtual strangers in an unknown city. Pryder seemed to read Galaad's thoughts in his expression and laid a comradely hand on his shoulder.

"Don't worry," he said, patting the sword hilt at his belt. "We've got with us all the luggage we need, if push should come to shove."

"Thank you," Galaad said, feeling not a bit reassured.

The streets of Llongborth were just hard-packed dirt, not cobbled like those
of Caer Llundain, and even after the frigid air on the open waters, the breezes
which wafted through chilled to the bone. The buildings were all of wood
and mortar, with only a few outfitted with tile roofs, the rest with thatch, and
leaned one into another, seeming like old women huddling together to escape
the cold. So far did some of the buildings overhang the narrow streets that it
seemed at times that the seven were passing through tunnels, not through
thoroughfares.

When they reached the court of Geraint, they were relieved to find it
sturdily built and, more important, well warmed by numerous hearth fires.
The air within, though smoky and thick with the scent of unwashed bodies,
was warm and inviting, and Galaad luxuriated in the heat. His fingers and
toes, warming for the first time in days, sent pinpricks shooting up his arms
and legs, unaccustomed to anything but the icy winds of the sea.

Though the harbor was crowded with ships, the streets through which
they'd passed had seemed virtually deserted, and Galaad had heard more than
one of the captains wonder aloud where the townspeople could have fled.
From the din within the walls of Geraint's rude palace, to say nothing of the
sights which met the newcomers' eyes, it was clear that they had found their
answer. The building was longer than it was wide and dominated by a single
large room, which ran nearly the entire length of the structure, with smaller
rooms divided off by walls on either end. This central room served the Dumnonian king as his court, as the chairs upon the dais at the far end suggested,
but in the winter months it evidently served dual purpose as the center of
public life. Men, women, and children, of all ages, were gathered together in
the smoky room, which pealed with their laughter and rang with their
shouts, engaged in all manner of industry and entertainment. Here a cadre of
aged widows and mothers sewed and embroidered, here musicians played a
merry tune for dancers, here young men tested their mettle and honed their
abilities in wrestling matches or fenced with blunt wooden swords. A pair of
old campaigners played a game of gwyddbwyll, maneuvering the pegs across

the checkered board, princes defending their king against the raiders. In a secluded area along the long wall a group of young men even gauged their strength by hurling iron bars as far as they were able, which seemed to Galaad a somewhat dangerous and foolhardy sport in such close quarters, but none of the Dumnonians seemed to mind the potential danger.

When Galaad and the others entered the hall, the chairs upon the far dais were unoccupied, but as the heavy doors were closed and latched behind them, a man and woman appeared from the rooms at the hall's far end and mounted the dais steps. The man looked to be about the age of Artor, near forty summers, and though his dark hair was streaked with gray and his beard more white than not, he had an easy smile and only scant lines at the corners of his eyes. The woman at his side, his wife, or so Galaad assumed, carried an infant in her arms, swaddled tightly.

"Artor, dear cousin!" The man shouted, raising both his arms in greeting. "This is an unexpected pleasure, but no less pleasing for all of that. You are welcome in my home."

The High King grinned broadly and crossed the floor to stand before the dais. "You are most kind, cousin Geraint."

Galaad and the other captains trailed behind at a distance, just able to hear the exchange over the general hubbub of the crowded hall.

"Come here, you," Geraint said, jumping down from the dais and wrapping his arms around Artor, taking him in a firm embrace. He pounded the High King on the back, vigorously, then pushed away and held him at arm's length.

Artor laughed. "And I am glad to see that the burdens of rule have not driven *all* of the joy from you."

Geraint glanced at his wife, an expression of lust fleeting across his features, and then with a softer emotion at the babe in her arms. "In fact, the advancing years bring even more joys with them." He stepped back up onto the dais and put his arm around her.

Artor looked at the infant, and then back at his cousin. "Is this your progeny then, Geraint?"

The Dumnonian king nodded, proudly. "Cadwr is still too young to head my royal bodyguard, I'm sorry to report, so he's yet to earn his keep. But as

soon as he can swing a blade we'll be quick to put him to work, have no
doubt."

Artor nodded but seemed to Galaad to be at something of a loss for
words. He struggled to find some proper response, before finally saying,
"Cadwr. It is a . . . strong name."

Geraint gave his cousin a queer look and shrugged. "I suppose so." He
leered. "And how about you? Have you any family yet, or do you still share
your bed only with that sword of yours?" He indicated the silver and gold
hilted spatha at Artor's hip.

"No," Artor said, perhaps too quickly, shaking his head. "No. I have no
family, I'm afraid. No wife or child."

Galaad began to realize that Artor was uncomfortable in some regard
when discussing families, either his cousin's or his own lack of one. That
accounted for his seeming nervousness on the subject of Geraint's son. Artor
seemed not quite to know what to say about, or to, a child. And he flustered
at the mention of a romantic relationship much like a beardless youth first
catching sight of the curve of a woman's back.

The thought of wives, though, and of children, reminded Galaad of that
which he couldn't forget, and he tightened his hands into fists, his throat con-
stricting and his tongue feeling thick and useless in his mouth.

Clearly seeing the discomfort evident in his cousin's expression, Geraint
hurried to change the subject. "But you haven't traveled all this distance to
return to such old topics of conversation. Come, sit by me and tell me the
reason for your journey."

Geraint motioned to one of his servants, calling for a chair to be brought
forth and placed beside his on the dais. Artor nodded and mounted the dais,
and the three were seated, Geraint in the middle, his wife on one side and
Artor on the other.

Galaad and the others had slowly made their way from the hall's entrance as
the two kings spoke, and Geraint now turned his gaze upon them. "And what
reprobates have you brought with you on your travels?" the Dumnonian king
said, waving the captains forward. "Ah, dour Lugh and grinning Caius, obedient
Bedwyr and the ever bickering twins, light and dark. Welcome, friends, welcome." He paused, wistful. "I have often found myself fondly remembering our

days together and the rough fellowship of the battlefield. Home and hearth are things to cherish, but still and all I prize the memory of those younger days and sometimes wish for their return." He shook his head, as though knocking loose the clinging memories, returning to the present moment. "But as I say, you are most welcome to Llongborth, my friends. Most welcome."

Geraint's gaze drifted past Galaad, and he paused, raising an eyebrow.

Galaad swallowed hard, uncomfortable in the lengthening silence and squirming under the king's gaze. "My name is Galaad," he quickly said, voice quavering, "from Glevum, in Powys in the west." He paused, and then quickly added, "That is, Powys to the north of here, and somewhat to the east I suppose . . ." He was babbling in his nervousness, but unable to stop himself.

Beside him, Lugh covered his eyes, muttering under his breath. Caius, a little more charitably, reached forward and laid a hand on Galaad's shoulder, and in a quiet voice said, "I imagine that the Dumnonian king knows where Glevum is, friend."

A deep red blush rose in Galaad's cheek, and he began to stammer his apologies.

"The youth travels with us," Artor said, rescuing him, "and is in fact the reason for our journey."

"Ah," Geraint said, nodding. "In which case, you are likewise welcome, man of Powys, as would be any traveling companion of Artor." He looked from the captains and Galaad before him to his wife, and then quickly to Artor. "But I have been terribly derelict," he said, admonishing himself. "Your majesty, brave captains, please allow me to present my wife, the lovely Enid ferch Ynywl."

The woman at his side, handsome and sturdy, nodded graciously to the High King, and then inclined her head to the standing captains.

"And this is our son," Enid said, "Cadwr ab Geraint ab Erbin."

"A proud lineage." Artor's disquiet on the topic of children had not left him, and he fidgeted in his seat, regarding the infant.

"Yes." Geraint beamed, his gaze lingering on his wife and babe-in-arms. Then, seeming to snap from this brief reverie, he clapped his hands together, brightening. "But you must be famished from your long journey, and in much need of refreshment."

"A fair drop of the liquid variety," Lugh said with a sly smile, "would not go far astray, majesty."

"And you shall have it!" Geraint snapped his fingers, motioning for his pages. "Bring tables and chairs for our friends. And trenchers of meat and vegetable, loaves of bread, and wine enough for each man to drink his fill."

"Now he's talking my language," Gwrol said in a loud whisper. Pryder punched his brother in the arm to silence him, but Galaad did not fail to notice the smile playing on Pryder's own lips.

Not that Galaad could blame them. He could use a fair drop of the stuff himself.

The day wore on, as Galaad and the others surfeited themselves on the Dumnonian king's generosity. The sky outside, glimpsed when the hall's great doors were infrequently opened and quickly closed, grew increasingly dark as sunset rapidly approached.

The more time they spent within the hall, in the company of Geraint and his people, the more Galaad began to notice a strange undercurrent to everything that went on around him. A tension permeated the room, an almost palpable sense of dread, or even fear, that underlay even the most boisterous song, dance, or wrestling bout. At first, he wasn't sure if he'd just been blind to it initially, but as the hours slipped past he came to realize that in fact the tension was growing. As nightfall drew closer, the smiles on the faces around them became less easy, less wide, the laughter more infrequent and more forced.

Too, Galaad noticed that the number of people within the hall increased as sunset approached, more and more entering from the cold, and few abandoning the warmth within to venture back outside. In time, it began to seem as if the entire population of Llongborth must have gathered within the walls, and none showed any indication of leaving any time soon.

Galaad saw that he wasn't the only one to have detected the shift in the hall's tenor. The captains seated around the rude wooden tables spoke in low voices, glancing around the room with narrowed eyes. Even Artor, seated upon the dais next to the king and his wife, the bones of their meal lying on the long table that had been set before them, clearly had sensed the tension.

"Cousin," Artor finally said, curiosity evidently getting the better of him, "I cannot help but note the crowded state of your hall, these last hours. Nor less the fact that so many of your people glance to the opening doors with expressions of apparent dread. Wherefore this disquiet?"

Geraint's jaw tightened, and he glanced to his wife, who had blanched immediately at Artor's words.

"The Huntsman," Enid whispered, drawing her son close to her bosom.

Artor raised an eyebrow, but when Geraint turned back to face him, it was with an unconvincing smile painted on his face.

"An unpleasant topic, and one I'd sooner not discuss at present," Geraint hastened to say. "But what of yourself, Artor?" He reached over and patted the High King's knee. "You've not yet explained the reason for your journey, nor what business brings you here to Dumnonia." He glanced in Galaad's direction. "You mention it has something to do with this young man from Powys?"

Artor nodded, eyes narrowed, clearly still somewhat suspicious about the tenor of the hall. "It does indeed," he said at length, and then motioned to Galaad. "Come forward, if you will, and relate to our host the tale you first told me in Caer Llundain."

Galaad swallowed noisily and, pushing back from the rough-hewn table, stood on shaky legs. He glanced to the captains, as though for encouragement, but was greeted instead by shrugs of indifference, with Caius's too easy smile the only friendly sign. Wiping his sweaty palms on the fabric of his linen tunic, nervously, he tentatively approached the dais.

"M-majesties," he stuttered, managing a bow.

Geraint waved his hand in a regal gesture, lounging in his chair.

"As I have said, my name is Galaad, and I am from Glevum"—he bit back the desire to place the city geographically—"and since the summer last I have been visited by visions of a White Lady. She shows me the image of a smooth-sided mound atop an island, and atop the mound a tower of glass. The island is surrounded on all sides by waters but is connected to the mainland by a spit of land."

Finishing, Galaad bit his lip, expecting the Dumnonian king's reaction to be laughter, or scorn, or dismissal. But to his surprise, Geraint instead narrowed his eyes and regarded Galaad thoughtfully, his expression unreadable.

"Go on," Artor instructed, nodding to Galaad. "Tell the rest."

"Well," Galaad said, uneasily, "As I told the High King these days past, I do not know whether the woman in the vision is Ceridwen, or the Holy Mother, or some other spirit or saint. She is dressed all in white, with hair the color of snow and straight white teeth. All I really do know is that the White Lady sends for assistance, and that she requires rescuing, imprisoned somehow in the glass tower she shows me."

"The tower which is atop the island with the smooth-sided mound, rounded on one end and sharp on the other, connected by a narrow bridge of land to the shore," Artor said.

"Exactly so." Galaad nodded.

Artor turned to Geraint. "Now, tell me, cousin. Does not the island which the youth describes confirm in all particulars to that which lies just to the north of Llongborth, further up the Dumnonian coast? On hearing the boy's tale, I was immediately minded of the time I wintered here with the forces of Ambrosius, when we two were but boys ourselves, and spied that island through the mists."

A brief smile tugged up the corners of Geraint's mouth. "But those were good times, weren't they? The Saeson aside, they were good days." For a brief moment his eyes seemed to settle on the middle distance, as his thoughts drifted back. "But that was twenty years ago, or more," he finally said, snapping back to the present. "Another time."

"But do I err, or is that not the island which the boy describes?"

Geraint nodded, seeming reluctant. "Yes," he said after a lengthy pause. "But it has been some years since I, or any of my people come to that, have laid eyes on that island of happier memory."

"What?!" Artor was taken aback. "But it cannot be more than a few hours leisurely ride from here. What bars your way?"

"More that something obscures our vision," Geraint explained, cryptically. "At least initially. Though now indeed something does bar our free travel, preventing even the approach."

Artor glanced at his captains, seeking some explanation, but saw that they were just as confused as he, and Galaad even more so.

"What do you mean, cousin?" Artor's tone grew more grave, his expression serious.

Geraint drew a ragged sigh, and his wife reached over and put her hand in his, comfortingly. When he spoke again, his voice sounded distant, lifeless, funereal. "The hedge and the Huntsman." He shut his eyes, some remembered pain lining his features. "That is the cause of our distress, and our sorry state of dread and woe. The hedge and the Huntsman."

"It was some years ago, ten or more, that the hedge of mist first caught our notice," Geraint explained, while Galaad and the others listened intently. "In those early days, it seemed to cling to the top of the mound you mention, atop that small island to the north. We thought little of it, save that it was strange than on otherwise bright and warm days that so thick a white cloud of fog should remained so localized, so persistent. But as time went on, the cloud expanded, growing slowly but inexorably larger, never wavering in the fiercest winds or in the brightest sunshine. In time, it hugged the whole of the small island you remember, cousin, until the island itself could not be seen, only a dome of white mist hanging over where the island had been." He paused and shook his head. "There was no tower, of wood, stone, or glass, on the island in those days, but who can say what the years since have wrought?"

Artor mulled over Geraint's words, thoughtfully tugging at the fringe of his beard with thumb and forefinger, but his captains were more vocal in reaction.

Lugh was the first. "Do you mean that none of your people have had the stones to walk a few steps through a bit of mist to see for themselves?"

Bedwyr, looking alarm, rushed to add, "I'm sure that my comrade means no disrespect, your majesty."

"Well," Gwrol said, sloshing the wine in his cup, his words somewhat slurred, "if it comes to it, I've no fear of walking through mist or fog or such like. Let me at it, and I'll show you."

Pryder didn't speak, just clicked his tongue disapprovingly and shook his head.

For his part, Geraint responded with a dark look, eyes flashing, but then seemed to soften gradually, sighing. "If you were to brave the mists, you'd not be the first. Many were the men from my court who sought the mysteries of the mist."

"And with what intelligence did they return?" Caius asked.

Geraint drew his mouth into a tight line. "None who went through the hedge was ever seen again."

"Still," Bedwyr said, affecting a casual indifference he clearly did not feel, "if it is just a mist atop an uninhabited island, what is the concern?"

"Perhaps," Geraint said, his tone level, "if the mist had confined itself to that unnamed isle. But it has not. In all of the months and years since first it was sighted, the hedge has expanded, growing always wider, always higher. Now, it covers an area many miles in circumference, reaching up into the sky almost further than the eye can see. And there is no sign of its abating, no indication its steady increase will not continue indefinitely."

Galaad shivered, feeling despite the warm air that ice crept up his spine, freezing him by inches.

"But that is not the worst of it, my brothers." Geraint's face had taken on a haunted look, and his gaze darted to the door of the hall. "Not the worst by far. For the mist, in its slow march across the coast, can at least be avoided, at least at this point. But that which comes from the mist . . ." His jaw tightened, and his hands gripped the arms of his chair in white-knuckled fists. "What comes from the mist must be *fled*."

Artor leaned forward, wearing a wary expression. "What comes from the mist, cousin? What is it?"

Geraint looked away, as if afraid to meet the High King's gaze, but Enid sat upright with a sudden intake of breath, and said, "The Huntsman. It is the *Huntsman*."

The Dumnonian king looked to his wife, and nodded gravely. "Aye. It is the Huntsman."

All around them came the susurration of whispers as those gathered in the hall heard the words of their king and queen. Some made the sign of the cross, while others moved their fingers in ancient pagan sigils meant to ward off unkind spirits. Fear was evident on every face, young and old, man and woman. Fear of this Huntsman.

"You mentioned such earlier," Artor said. "What kind of man is this hunter to inspire such fear?"

"Not a man at all, some would say," Enid replied, arms wrapped tight around her infant son.

Geraint nodded. "Or if he were a man, at some point, that hour has passed. Mayhap he was tossed up from the grave, or else from beneath the waves. He is said to have the coloration of corpse flesh, hairless, and with dead-seeming red eyes, and does not speak, but lets the barking of his spectral hounds instead give voice to his wrath."

"It is said . . . ?" Artor repeated, suspicious. "Have you not seen him yourself, then?"

"Only from a distance," Geraint answered, with evident gratitude. "But some of our people have been fortunate enough to flee his presence and carry back to us more detailed descriptions than long sightings would allow." He shook his head, ruefully. "Those that have stood their ground and faced the Huntsman's red sword . . ." He trailed off, eyes shut.

"What?" Bedwyr asked, mouth hanging open, eyes wide. "What happened?"

Geraint took a deep breath and let out a ragged sigh. "The Huntsman carries a sword whose blade is the red of the hellfire with which it sometimes seems to glow. And when this blade meets flesh or iron or wood . . ."

He paused, turning his head away, as if he could escape the sight of the memories that sprang before his mind's eye.

"We have found the Huntsman's victims in the following mornings, or rather what is left of them. This red sword of his cuts through anything like a hot knife sliding through warm butter, severing heads from shoulders in a single clean sweep, or hands from arms, or feet from legs. Not hacked and chopped, like a woodsman and his axe, but single strokes, clean through." He shuddered at the memory.

"You mentioned something about dogs?"

Geraint nodded. "A pack of dogs. They are ever close at his heels, always with their horrible baying."

"Artor and I know well to fear dogs," Caius put in. "The Pictii use specially trained war-dogs, which we had to face two springs past, when going north to meet with the kings of the Scotii in Caledonia." He shivered. "Foul creatures, all teeth and claws, always in motion."

"No, my friend." Geraint shook his head, sadly. "These are like no dogs used by the Picts, or raised by any man alive. They are the same corpse-flesh white as their master, with red on the tips of their ears and tails, and fangs and claws the incarnadine hue of fresh spilt blood. And their baying, strange as it may seem, sounds more like the calls of wild birds in flight than any dog you or I might ever have raised from a pup."

Artor glanced around the hall, which had grown quiet and still while the Dumnonian king had spoken. Anxious dread was etched on each face, and often eyes glanced to the barred doors of the hall, with horrible anticipation.

"And it's in fear of this Huntsman that your people gather here in the hall, I take it?" the High King asked.

"Just so," Geraint said with a beleaguered sigh.

Artor regarded him, thoughtfully. "It is a difficult story to credit, cousin," he said at length. "And were I to hear it from any lips but yours, I'd scarcely believe it. But I have known you too long, and can hear the timber of truth in your words." He paused. "How often is this strange figure seen?"

"Not every night, but often, and then always when the sun is gone and the stars shine overhead. We don't know if he fears the day, but light seems somehow to hold him at bay, as he is never seen in close quarter with a well-fed fire. In these last years, though, he has come more and more often, and always venturing farther afield, so that once he was only seen out in the hills and vales by night, but now he can be found roaming the streets of Llongborth herself."

Geraint paused and look from the High King to his captains and back again.

"You must not think me a coward, brothers," Geraint went on, shame-faced, "for sheltering inside stout walls while this monster roams the streets of my city unchallenged. In the early days, as I say, many of my bravest stood against him and his spectral hounds, in my name, and not one was ever seen alive again." His hands began to shake, and a tremor crept into his voice.

"They stood in my name, and not one of them survived." He tightened his hand into a fist and pounded it onto the arm of his chair. "What choice did I have?!"

"There now, cousin," Artor soothed, laying a strong hand on Geraint's shoulder. "From the sound of it, you did what any of us would do in trying circumstances, and there is no shame to be found there." Artor paused, thoughtfully, and glanced towards the door. "But I have a mind to see this Huntsman and his red sword for myself, if just to quell my own mounting curiosity."

"As would I," called Pryder, proudly.

"Oh, blessed Jesus," Gwrol moaned. "No one asked you, did they?"

Artor ignored the two with good humor, keeping his eyes on Geraint. "With your leave, I'd like to pass the hours of the night out of doors, in the hopes of catching a glimpse of this Huntsman with my own eyes."

"As will we all," Bedwyr quickly put in.

"Bugger," Lugh spat. "And here I was looking forward to a warm bed for the first time in days."

Geraint looked from Artor to the captains and smiled, his chest swelling. "And I will come along with you, brothers," he said, brightening. "We can stand together, side by side, and relive our days of battle."

"It is cold, husband," Enid said gently, laying her hand over Geraint's.

"Ah, it was colder still in those days, am I right?" He clapped a hand on Artor's back, comradely. "But we weathered it well enough, as I recall."

"That we did," Artor agreed.

"And what of you, man of Powys," Geraint called to Galaad. "Will you stand with us through the cold watches of the night, watchful for the coming of the corpse-fleshed Huntsman and his damned hounds?"

Galaad swallowed and raised his hands in a shrug. "Yes?" he said feebly.

"Splendid!" Geraint leapt to his feet, as though filled with a new vitality. "Then we're agreed."

He jumped down from the dais and strode across the hall.

"Open the door! Tonight these brothers of battle will face the monster!"

In the end, Geraint remained outdoors with Artor and the captains only as long as the sun remained in the sky. As night fell, and the last light of the sun faded in the west, Geraint had a sudden change of heart.

"My apologies, brothers," the Dumnonian king said, his gaze darting nervously back and forth, his hand in a death grip on his sword's hilt. "But I find I've not the stomach for this after all." He looked to Artor, his expression commingling fear and regret. "I've seen the bugger myself, after all, if only from a distance. And perhaps my days of battle are too far behind me, for all of that. But I . . . I just can't . . ."

Artor nodded. "It's all right, cousin. Go inside to your wife and child and leave us fools to our foolish errand."

Geraint nodded, eagerly, and then pounded on the barred door of the hall.

"Open up!" he called out, his voice ragged. "Let me in, damn your eyes!"

The door opened, the Dumnonian king hustled inside, and then the door was shut and barred again, leaving the seven outside alone.

"Well, Artor," Bedwyr said, appraisingly, "I think that he's put on a bit of weight, don't you?"

At Galaad's side hung his new sword, its hilt cold under his hand. At Artor's request, Geraint had found the blade for him to replace the antique that the captains insisted he could not wear in good conscience. It was of Saeson manufacture, captured during the late war, with some indecipherable runic inscriptions on the crossbar and pommel. If these runes were meant to curry good favor from the Saeson's pagan gods, they clearly had not served the sword's previous owner well, so Galaad put little stock in their efficacy.

Still, Galaad could not help but feel a little bolstered by the sturdy weight of the iron at his hip, which made him feel less out of place amongst the captains, at least in some small measure. And bolstering he needed, indeed, considering the frozen lump of dread that sat in the pit of his stomach, seeping cold fear in his veins like ice. He had been deeply disquieted by Geraint's story of an inhuman Huntsman and his spectral hounds and in no eager hurry to see them for himself. But when Geraint had invited him along on Artor's little expedition, Galaad had been afraid to refuse for fear of losing what little respect he might yet have garnered with the High King and his men.

And now the Dumnonian king himself had retreated indoors, leaving Galaad shivering in the icy cold outside. If only Geraint had discovered his lack of courage earlier, he might have spared them both the trouble, but as it was Galaad had no option but to remain where he was, however reluctantly. He considered the thought that one of the captains might decide to retreat inside, in which case he would easily find grounds to accompany them. But considering the shaking heads and scornful looks that had been exchanged by the captains when Geraint had left them, Galaad knew that any retreat on his part alone would likely be met with even greater reprobation.

It was clear that many of the captains doubted the truth of Geraint's story altogether, come to that. And Galaad couldn't blame them. Having seen what he had in his visions, though, Galaad had come to believe that there was more to the world than that which immediately met the eye and was willing to give the Dumnonian king the benefit of the doubt. But if Geraint's story were true, what did it suggest about a connection between this strange mist hedge and the tower of glass Galaad saw in his vision? If Artor continued with his stated plans and the company continued on to the island, what would they find if they tried to pass beyond that misty veil?

Galaad could scarcely say. If the Dumnonian king's story were true, though, he had much more pressing concerns to consider. Specifically, that he was outside freezing by inches, losing all feeling in his fingers and toes, in the almost certain knowledge that he might soon be faced by a sword-wielding nightmare come to life.

They had lit a fire on first stepping out of doors, which had served to keep the cold from seeping too far into their bones. But when after some hours the Huntsman failed to appear, Artor had insisted that the fire be doused, saying that the strange figure might be kept at bay by the flame's light and heat, as Geraint's story suggested. With considerable grumbling, Pryder and Gwrol had scattered the burning logs and kicked dirt on the embers. As the fire died, the cold returned, with a vengeance.

When another hour had passed, though, the captains drowsing on their feet, the Huntsman had still failed to make an appearance, and so Artor suggested that he might be put off by the slight warmth radiating from the thick walls of the hall, or the light which peeked through chinks in the mortar between plank and log. With that in mind, Artor ventured that they might best be served by walking abroad themselves, out into the dark and unlit areas of Llongborth, left all but deserted as the denizens retreated within the comforting walls of Geraint's hall earlier in the day.

So it was with palpable reluctance that the seven walked away from the hall, their boots crunching on the icy ground underfoot, the steam of their breath only barely visible in the faint light of the moon. They carried no torch or tinder, but moved through the monochrome chiaroscuro of the darkened streets tentatively, hands on sword hilts, voices stilled. Even those that gave no credit to Geraint's tale found themselves disquieted by the silence of the dark streets, or so it seemed to Galaad.

Feet numb in his marching boots, blowing on his fingers to keep them warm, Galaad found it impossible to say how much time had passed, but it seemed to him that it must have been an hour or more since they had begun snaking their way through the city streets. Llongborth was relatively small, at least compared to Caer Llundain, and perhaps not even as large as Glevum, but the only landmark Galaad could discern was Geraint's hall, and as it appeared again and again in his field of vision, first on one side and then the other, now ahead of them and now behind, he realized that their course must have twisted and turned back on itself several times, moving around the city in a spiral pattern, like the shape of a nautilus.

No longer entirely silent, the captains has begun once more to give voice to their discontent, at least in some small measure, grumbling now and again, complaining of fatigue, the dark, and the cold, and even in Gwrol's case his thirst for more of the grape.

Finally Artor came to a halt, and it seemed that he was on the verge of announcing a retreat indoors, when something moved in the corner of Galaad's field of vision. A flash of white that for an instant Galaad was sure presaged the onset of another vision. But his nostrils were filled only with the sharp tang of the freezing night air, not the customary scent of flowers, and the white flash was too quick, too localized.

Galaad turned his head, and there, at the end of a long street, he saw it.

Bathed in the light of the moon, stark white against the dark street and buildings, it was the figure of a man. It stood some considerable distance away, at the city's edge, and so Galaad was hard pressed to discern any details, but from this vantage the figure seemed to be male, hairless, and dressed in some dark fabric whose color appeared simply black in the low light but might have been any hue. Only his neck and head were bare, and these were shocking white, but for the eyes that weakly reflected back the light of the moon, glinting red.

"A-Artor," Galaad stammered, keeping his voice low.

The High King looked, and followed Galaad's gaze.

"Well, I will be damned," Pryder cursed beneath his breath.

Artor's sword was already in his fist, and in a sudden chorus of metal on leather the other captains all drew their own blades.

As if in answer, the spectral figure at the far end of the street reached to one side and drew a blade of his own. Or seemed to do so, at least, though when he straightened, it initially appeared that his hand was empty. Then he turned, but fractionally, and a sword appeared in his hand, as if by magic, its blade seeming to glow faintly red in the moonlight.

From the near distance, Galaad heard a sound like wild geese in flight, and from behind the spectral figure there appeared fleeting white shapes, coursing across the cold ground.

His red sword in hand, the Huntsman advanced on the seven, the voice of his wrath baying at his heels.

CHAPTER FOURTEEN

Jubilee

BY THE TIME BLANK AND MISS BONAVENTURE had climbed back up from the Ghost Fox's underground audience chamber, made their way back through the sickly sweet corridors of the opium den, and were out into the Limehouse streets, it was already near time for luncheon. They agreed it was high time for a bite to eat and set about finding a suitable locale.

They settled on a public house in the shadow of St. Mary-le-Bow off Cheapside. The fare was rough but filling, and given the relatively early hour they had a few tables to themselves. Miss Bonaventure had picked up some penny papers on their way west from Limehouse, and once they'd finished with eating, she spread them across the tabletop, sipping at a cup of tea from time to time while Blank nursed a pint of bitter, his manner withdrawn.

Miss Bonaventure had ventured to ask Blank about his history with the mistress of Chinese crime, but after a few tentative attempts to draw him out, it had become clear that he was not yet in a mood to discuss the matter. Instead, she busied herself with her customary scour of the day's news, leaving Blank alone with his thoughts.

"You were right about the soldiers," Miss Bonaventure said at length, the silence evidently proving too much for her. "It says here that there are some fifty thousand troops in London for the procession, the largest military force ever assembled in the city."

Blank hummed absently in assent and nodded. Miss Bonaventure shrugged, returning to her papers.

A short while later, the silence was broken again. "Oh, dear," Miss Bonaventure said, eyes widening. "Well, *that's* not likely to help matters much, is it?"

When Blank failed to respond, Miss Bonaventure sighed dramatically, and shook the papers in her hands, making a loud rustling noise, like one would make to scare off a flock of birds.

"Blank? Hello? I know that you're enjoying your sulk and pout in there, but I think that *this* might be of some interest."

Blinking, as though just coming out of a nap, Blank looked up at Miss Bonaventure. "Yes?"

She shook her head good-naturedly. "You're hopeless." Then she slid the paper across the table to him. There, above the fold, was the banner headline:

JUBILEE KILLER STRIKES.
POLICE MAINTAIN SECRECY ON THREE PRIOR VICTIMS.

"You're right," he said, ruefully. "I imagine that's not likely to help matters at *all*."

The article recounted that a police constable had discovered the body of a man lying in the thoroughfare at the junction of Abingdon and Great College streets, practically in the shadow of Parliament itself. The man had been respectably dressed and in apparent good health at the time of death, leaving aside the fact that he appeared to have been cut nearly in half and effectively disemboweled. The postmortem had indicated that he had been cut across the small of the back while fleeing from his attacker, the blow neatly slicing through the spine and muscles of the lower back. Internal pressures had forced internal organs and viscera out through the gaping wound, and if having his spinal column severed had not killed the victim in short order, he would have died quickly from loss of blood.

The body had been discovered two nights previous, apparently some short time after the murder had occurred, and an inquest held the following night, while Blank and Miss Bonaventure had scoured Whitechapel for any clue as to the identities of the three unknown victims of the series killer. The victim had been identified as one Xenophon Brade, twenty-seven years of age. As the victim had no living relations the coroner could locate, his body had been identified by his neighbors.

Several of the penny papers, it transpired, carried reports and transcriptions of the inquest, but only one suggested any connection to the decapitated body that had washed ashore in Pimlico two weeks before. A reporter with *Lloyd's Weekly*, who had reported on the earlier inquest, noted a correspondence between the manner in which the decapitated woman's wounds were said to be clean shears, showing no indication of hacking or chopping, and the way in which Xenophon Brade's fatal wound appeared to be a single cut that drove straight through flesh, muscle, and bone. With some persistence, he had wormed from a particularly garrulous constable the information that there had been two other decapitated and limbless bodies found, which New Scotland Yard had kept secret.

So, while the authorities had not yet begun to suspect that the murder of Xenophon Brade was anything but mundane homicide, though a particularly brutal one taking place so close to the corridors of power, the *Lloyd's Weekly* reporter had laid out a skein of supposition that connected the dead man with the three previous victims, and given the hypothesized series murderer a name: The Jubilee Killer.

Though fatigued, having slept not at all in nearly thirty-six hours, Sandford Blank and Miss Bonaventure hadn't the inclination to sleep, the news having presented to them a new piece for the puzzle that had harried them these last days. The first order of business was to contact the authorities and arrange for a viewing of the body of Xenophon Brade to add the evidence of their own senses to the testimony recorded in the inquest's transcriptions. They thought to find a telephone and ring New Scotland Yard but were hard pressed to find an establishment on the wire, and instead of spending the time of sending a telegraph across town, resorted to the expedient of simply hauling their bodies the distance and presenting themselves in person.

So it was that, in early afternoon, they arrived at New Scotland Yard to find that they had come too late. The body of the late Mr. Brade, having already been examined, had been sent off to the mortician. Worse, when contacted, the mortuary informed Blank and Miss Bonaventure that the departed, lacking any living relatives, had written a last will and testament, and was now being interred in accordance with his recorded wishes.

The mortician had already sent Brade's remains by hearse to the Necropolis terminus just outside Waterloo Station, to be borne by rail to Brookwood Cemetery.

"Come along, Miss Bonaventure!" Blank said, racing from the mortuary. "We might still catch it!"

It was a mad dash through the streets, into a cab and across Westminster Bridge. By the time the pair reached the terminus, in the shadow of Waterloo Station, smoke already curled from the stacks of the Necropolis line's engine, preparing at any moment to steam out of the station.

Blank vaulted from the cab, rushing across the pavement towards the station, hopped a rail, and grabbed the stationmaster on the platform by the lapels.

"You must stop that train," Blank said, thrumming.

"On whose say-so?" the stationmaster demanded, flustered.

Blank stuck a featureless white calling card under the man's nose and hummed. "On mine," he said simply, jaw set.

The stationmaster concurred, immediately, and blew the whistle that hung on a lanyard around his neck. "Stop the train!" he called out, waving his arms to catch the conductor's eye. "Stop the train!"

As Miss Bonaventure leisurely strolled up the platform, Blank straightened his coat and shot his cuffs. "That was an unanticipated touch of melodrama, Blank," she said with a smile. "Couldn't we simply have ridden on the next train down to Brookwood if we missed this one?"

Blank made a disagreeable face and shook his head in distaste. "Oh, no, my dear. I never go to the suburbs if I can help it."

They found the body of the late Xenophon Brade in a simple unvarnished wooden casket. A label at the casket's head indicated that the body was bound for the Noncomformist section of the Brookwood Cemetery rather than the more fashionable Anglican areas. That suggested something of the character of the man inside, whose background they would investigate after viewing his remains.

Also suggestive was the fact that the dead man rode to his reward in the second-class section. Just as on the trains of living passengers that departed from nearby Waterloo with clockwork regularity, on the Necropolis line there were provisions for first-, second-, and third-class travel, not only for the dead but for their mourners as well. No one, it seemed, accompanied the body of Brade to his final rest, his bank having followed the instructions in his last will and testament and paid for the travel and final accommodations. Here was a man who, on the face of it, had gathered few associations in life and who now joined a select company in death—the victims of the newly christened Jubilee Killer. But it occurred to Blank that Brade might well have had other acquaintances and friends who had elected not to appear beside him at the time of his interment. This was another matter to investigate.

The conductor, who had escorted the pair to the second-class compartment, raised an objection when Blank asked Miss Bonaventure to open the casket, but the judicious application of some subvocal harmonics and suggestive words had been sufficient to quiet the conductor's complaints. Blank had not even been forced to draw one of his calling cards from his pocket.

So it was, then, that in short order the lid to the plain wooden box had been pried away and the body within lay revealed. Lying on his back, he might just have been slumbering, his arms crossed over his chest, his eyes heavy lidded, but for the fact that his skin was lifeless and gray. The dead man had an unruly shag of hair atop a long, high-cheekboned face. His nose was patrician and his fingers at the ends of his long hands were thin and delicate. To all appearances he had been dressed in the same clothes in which he had died following the postmortem, there being new vents and cuts scissored into the fabric of his jacket, shirt, and trousers, then hastily restitched by the mortician while preparing him for the grave.

The body exposed, there remained the gruesome task of rolling it over to expose the wound on the dead man's back. Miss Bonaventure, wiping the palms of her hands on the fabric of her skirt, dusty from the exertion of prizing the coffin lid open, shook her head, resolute. "Don't look at me," she said, holding up her hands, protectively. "You want to see his back, *you* turn him over."

It was unfortunate that Blank's form of mesmerism could not induce anyone to do something they would not otherwise be willing to do, and while the conductor worked all day surrounded by the dead, it was quickly evident that no amount of thrumming or persuasion would be sufficient to convince him to lay hands on a corpse. It fell to Blank, then, to do the dirty work himself.

The smell of corruption already rose from the corpse, now two days dead. Removing his jacket and rolling his shirt sleeves up past the elbow, Blank closed his mouth shut tight and leaned in, working his hands beneath the body, one beneath the thigh and one beneath the shoulder, and as gently as he was able rolled the body up and onto its side. Immediately the smell of putrefaction and decay worsened, as the gore-soaked tatters at the back of the man's shirt, vest, and jacket were displayed. The fabric was stained black with dried blood, obscuring some details, but it was evident that something sharp had sliced through all of the layers of clothing laterally, cutting cleanly from one side of the man's abdomen to the other.

Continuing to work the corpse's bulk forward, Blank managed to roll it further over, until the dead man was now lying face down. His right arm had worked itself loose and now folded indecorously behind his back, but Blank was able to tuck it up under the body, giving him an unobstructed view of the back. He was relatively sure the dead man wouldn't mind.

With the tip of a penknife, Blank peeled back the neatly sheared edge of the fabric and peered at the rent flesh beneath. It was as if a new, impossibly wide mouth had grown in the man's back, a smile that ran straight across the back and seemed to curve up as the sides sloped down and away. This was a trick of perspective, and when seen level, it was perfectly, inexorably straight. In the course of the postmortem, and later under the mortician's care, the body had been cleaned, so that the bulk of the blood and viscera had been cleaned away. What remained was gray, lifeless flesh and the darker meat of viscera within. The white of bone glinted where the vertebrae had been neatly severed in twain.

Blank moved from the man's back to investigate the rest of the body. He checked the soles of his shoes, checked the fingertips and palms, looked in his mouth, and peered into his ears. He made as thorough an examination as the circumstances allowed, while Miss Bonaventure perched atop a nearby coffin and watched, only half interested. The conductor had quickly excused himself and left them to their own devices.

"Well?" Miss Bonaventure said, when Blank straightened up and wiped his hands as clean as possible on his handkerchief. "What have you found?"

"The only detail of immediate relevancy that presents itself is the fact that this man was most definitely dispatched with the same sort of cutting implement that felled the three previous murder victims and that which was used to severe the lock at the blind asylum. Beyond that?" He held his hands out to either side in a shrug. "Who can say? There are perhaps more questions than answers to be found here. Why was this victim a male while the others had been female, and why was this one killed in the apparent act of fleeing, and out in the open no less, while the others had been dispatched in secret places and on much more intimate terms?"

"There is one question I'd very much like to have answered, myself," Miss Bonaventure said, kicking her heels against the sides of the wooden casket.

"And that is?"

"Just who was this Xenophon Brade, anyway?"

Blank fixed her with a smile. "Miss Bonaventure, I believe you've been reading my thoughts. That was precisely the next question on my list."

Blank bathed, washing the smell of corruption from his hands and arms, while Miss Bonaventure availed herself of the opportunity to catch a brief catnap on the divan in the library. When he had seen to his toilet and dressed, Blank joined her in the library, and while she still slumbered pulled down editions of *Whitaker's* from the shelf and consulted social registers, *Who's Who*, and an encyclopedia of reference. By the time Miss Bonaventure awoke, feeling at least marginally rested and refreshed, Blank had compiled a précis on the late Mr. Xenophon Brade.

"Xenophon Brade," Blank intoned, only occasionally forced to consult his notes, "born the son of a solicitor in Wolverhampton, 13 March, 1870. His father later moved the family to London, where young Xenophon attended school. Mrs. Brade died due to complications in childbirth when Xenophon was a boy, leaving his father a widower and he himself an only child. The elder Brade himself passed on while young Xenophon was still in school, bequeathing the boy a small sum. Xenophon left school and found work in the Clerkenwell District Surveyor's office. His passion, however, was for art, and he devoted his free time to acquiring the skills necessary to earn a living in the arts. He used what little remained of his inheritance to attend classes at Hubert Herkomer's private art school in Bushey. He became well known in Holywell Street, where the stalls of honest booksellers that line the thoroughfare obscure the discreet unmarked doors of the pornographers and publishers of *curiosa*. It was in one of these bookshops that he met a publisher who commissioned Xenophon to illustrate a book of salacious poems in translation, which he would publish in a limited edition. The book, and its illustration, met with the approval of the buying public, though the opprobrium of the authorities, and Xenophon and the publisher embarked on a series of projects, to varying degrees of success. I have here in my library, should you care to see it, a collection of myths and legends of the French province of Varadeaux with accompanying illustrations by Brade, which is why the name seemed so persistently familiar, while I could never place it. In any event, as his work found an increasing audience, Xenophone himself found entrée into society. By the time he had his first gallery show at the Grosvenor, he had taken rooms at the Albany off Piccadilly and joined a number of clubs and organizations, most notably"—and here Blank was forced to consult his notes—"the Fabian Society, the Society for Psychical Research, and the League of the Round Table. The reviews indicate that after a prolific period of years early in the decade, he has been much less productive in recent years, with only a handful of commissions seeing print and no new gallery shows to speak of. Whether his attentions were elsewhere is unknown, but it has been speculated in some quarters that he has instead been working on a large project, the nature and scope of which Xenophon refused to discuss, or the existence of which he would not confirm."

Blank left off, leaning against a desk, his arms folded across his chest.

"And that's it?" Miss Bonaventure asked.

Blank nodded.

"A pretty piece of information gathering," Miss Bonaventure said, admiringly. "Just how long *was* I asleep, anyway?" She sipped a steaming cup of tea. "Now, I know the Fabian Society. Socialists. Bernard Shaw, H. G. Wells, Annie Besant, that lot. But I've never heard of the other two clubs. The Society of . . . *Psychical* Research, was it?"

Blank confirmed with his notes. "Yes. And the League of the Round Table."

"I've not heard of either of those, I'm afraid."

Blank nodded. "The Round Table bunch is new to me, as well, but I've run across the Psychical Research crew before. They're a group that believes it's possible to send messages directly to people's minds, without recourse to speaking or written communication."

"Telepathy?" Miss Bonaventure scoffed. "Bunkum. Doesn't exist."

Blank smiled knowingly for a moment, as if laughing inwardly at some private joke, and then nodded, slowly. "Naturally," he said, amused. "But nevertheless, the rolls of their membership include Lord Tennyson, Lewis Carroll, Mark Twain, and the film maker George Albert Smith." Blank picked up the most recent edition of *Whitaker's* from the desk, flipping it open to a marked page. "Presently, the society is headquartered at 14 Dean's Yard, Westminster, the personal residence of Frank Podmore, an address about which there are two points of interest, one trivial and one potentially less so. First, that same residence had at one time been the first official head-quarters of the Fabian Society."

Miss Bonaventure raised an eyebrow. "Suggesting that socialists are more likely to believe in thought transmission?"

"Possibly," Blank said with a smile, "or indicative of the fact that Mr. Podmore might have an affinity for hopeless causes. The other point of note, possibly much less trivial in nature, is that Dean's Yard is only a short distance away from the intersection of Abingdon and Great College streets."

Now both of Miss Bonaventure's eyebrows lifted, and she leaned forward in her chair. "The intersection where Xenophon's body was found."

"Got it in one, Miss Bonaventure." Blank slapped the book shut. "Would you care to accompany me in paying Mr. Podmore an early evening visit?"

Miss Bonaventure jumped from her chair, eyes flashing with the thrill of the hunt. "Why, Blank, I would be delighted!"

A hansom cab carried them through the late afternoon traffic, as clerks and shopkeepers completed their day's work and scurried off to see to their various needs before sleep overtook them. South past Trafalgar, through Charing Cross and Whitehall, past Downing Street, and into the lengthening shadow of the houses of Parliament. They turned off Broad Sanctuary and south towards Dean's Yard.

They passed the Westminster Column, erected to the memory of pupils of Westminster School who had died in the Russian and Indian wars some forty years before, and passed under the arch into Dean's Yard itself. It was near time for dinner, though sunset was still hours away, and students lounged in the warm sunshine on the green, or sheltered in the shade of the larger trees, the London planes, the red horse-chestnut, the maple, the sycamore.

Dean's Yard was bordered on the south side by the Church House, on the north by the archway to the Great Sanctuary, and by the collegiate buildings of Westminster, school and abbey, on the east and west. In amongst the buildings of Westminster were a number of private residences. It was here that Henry Purcell had died, shortly after composing his anthem for Queen Mary's funeral, and was buried a short distance away, under the organ at Westminster Abbey. And it was here that they found Number 14, Dean's Yard, the residence of one Mr. Frank Podmore.

When he answered his door, Podmore looked as if he might have been weeping, his eyes red-rimmed, his cheeks flushed. He was dressed in a brocade waistcoat and shirt sleeves, his cravat all askew, and his neatly trimmed hair seemed tussled and unkempt. He had a full dark beard and mustache, well groomed but so bushy that his mouth was almost completely obscured, with only a hint of his lower lip visible as he voiced certain consonant sounds.

"Yes?" Podmore asked, standing in the doorway. "What is it you want?"

Blank produced one of his featureless calling cards and made their introductions, and in short order the three of them, Blank, Miss Bonaventure, and Podmore, were seated in his library, having tea.

Podmore was some forty years old, an official at the post office in St. Martin's Lane, but there was little in his residence that suggested the dry and dusty life of a dedicated civil servant. On a Florentine table beside a well-stuffed chair were spread back issues of *The Idler* and *The Savoy*, and a neat stack of cloth-bound volumes of *The Yellow Book* of recent vintage, suggesting distinctly modern tastes. On the wall, between two towering and crowded bookshelves, was a framed certificate, indicating that Podmore had graduated first in his class in Science, at Pembroke College, Oxford. And in a place of prominence, on the opposite wall, was a pen-and-ink drawing in a gilt frame behind glass.

The drawing caught Blank's eye on entering. It seemed to depict Podmore in the role of Merlin, bushy beard and flowing robes, in a style reminiscent of the medievalism found in the work of Morris and Burne-Jones blended with the Orientalism of Beardsley. At first glance, Blank had taken it to be the work of Aubrey Beardsley himself, but on closer examination it was evident that it was the work of another hand, instead. Seating himself in the overstuffed chair while Podmore fetched them tea, he happened to notice that the copies of *The Idler* and *The Savoy* in evidence shared in common cover illustrations that appeared to be done by the same hand. Blank picked up the volume of *The Yellow Book* from the top of the stack and leafed through the pages, not surprised to discover several full-page and spot illustrations by the same artist. A glance at the indicia identified the artist as one Xenophon Brade.

So it was that Blank and Miss Bonaventure sat over cooling cups of tea, facing the clearly distraught Podmore.

"I read your *Apparitions and Thought-Transference*," Blank began, without preamble, referring to a recent work on the topic of telepathy. He'd made it a habit to follow the examinations and findings of those who researched topics that touched on his dealings with Omega. He'd been disappointed, but not surprised, to find that Podmore's work had seemed to offer no insight.

Podmore seemed to brighten, if fractionally, at the mention of his book, eye's widening with surprise. "You . . . you did?"

Miss Bonaventure, too, regarded Blank with some surprise, giving him a sly look. Blank knew that she wondered about him and about his provenance. One day, and perhaps soon, he would have to tell her the truth.

"I'm afraid, if you'll excuse my being frank with you, no pun intended, I shared the view put forth by the reviewer in the *American Journal of Psychology*, and sadly not that found in the review for *Mind*." Blank shrugged apologetically, while Podmore seemed to deflate. "That said, I've found your writings on Mesmerism and Animal Magnetism to be quite insightful."

Podmore sat a little straighter, hearing that, and lifted his teacup as if in salute. "Well," he said, nodding to the nearby desk, thickly carpeted with handwritten notes and folders, "perhaps you'll find my forthcoming *Studies in Psychical Research* more to your liking."

Blank fixed him with a smile. "I shall certainly endeavor to try." He sipped his tea, and then indicated the drawing of Podmore as Merlin on the wall. "That's quite an interesting piece, if you don't mind me saying, Mr. Podmore."

Podmore turned to look at the framed picture, and a sudden look of pain stabbed across his face. Squinting in apparent agony, he turned away, but when he once more looked up to meet Blank's gaze he'd brought his features under control, and looked only somewhat distressed, as he'd done before, and not abjectly tortured.

"It's by Xenophon Brade, unless I'm mistaken," Blank said, a question in the form of a statement.

Podmore nodded, his gaze vacant.

"I'm sure you're aware that Mr. Brade met with an unfortunate . . . accident, the night before last," Miss Bonaventure said, setting her cup down on the table and folding her hands over her crossed knee. "And not far from here, it would appear."

Podmore's first answer was only a sharp intake of breath, and then an absent nod of his head. "Y-yes," he said at last, his voice sounding as though it were coming from far off. "I . . . I believe I read that . . . somewhere."

Blank narrowed his eyes, studying Podmore's reaction. He got the impression that Podmore was well practiced at concealing his feelings and reactions but that something in his present circumstances was taxing his best efforts at concealment.

"You were acquainted with the young man, I take it?" Miss Bonaventure asked.

Behind his bushy mustache and beard, Podmore caught his lower lip between his teeth but a brief moment, as if biting back his initial impulse to respond. Then, marshalling his reserve, he said, "Yes, in a vague way. He was a member of the Fabian Society, and had attended some meetings of the SPR. And . . ."

He trailed off, and Blank leaned forward. "And?"

Podmore met Blank's gaze, and the detective saw something familiar in the other man's eyes. "And I believe I'd seen him once or twice in the town," Podmore finally answered, his tone level and firm. "We spoke, on rare occasion, as I recall."

Blank stood and crossed the floor to stand before the illustration of Podmore in the guise of Merlin, a flowing robe across his shoulders, a crooked staff in his hand. His face was seen in profile, nose prominent, beard bushy, while over his shoulder a sliver of moon lit the night sky.

"It's a bit like the work of Beardsley, wouldn't you say?" Blank said to Miss Bonaventure. She pursed her lips and shrugged in response. Blank nodded and looked back at the picture. "Yes, I can definitely see the influence of Beardsley."

From behind him came the startling crash of china hitting china, as Podmore slammed his cup back onto the saucer. Blank turned to see Podmore regarding him with flashing eyes. He'd clearly hit a nerve, as he'd suspected he might. He'd a collection of *The Yellow Book* in his own library and knew that the name Xenophon Brade had not appeared in the indicia until after Beardsley's own name had disappeared altogether. That, and the similarities of style, was highly suggestive of a rivalry of some kind on one side or the other.

"Xenophon hated Beardsley," Podmore finally said, in his quiet, far-away voice. "Though he was several years Beardsley's senior, Xenophon always felt that his career was the one less developed, the one that lagged behind. He'd been incensed that Dent had hired Beardsley to illustrate his *Morte Darthur* and had jumped at the chance to begin illustrating *The Yellow Book* when Beardsley was dismissed." Blank remembered the time well. When Oscar had been arrested, two years before, he'd been seen clutching a book with a yellow cover, or so the newspapers reported. It was assumed to be a volume of *The Yellow Book*, and in the resulting furor, Beardsley had been sacked. He resisted the urge to lose himself in memory and concentrated on Podmore's words. "Xenophon was sure that this latest project of his would be the one to cement his popularity and finally bring him out of Beardsley's shadow and into the light, but then. . . ." He glanced towards the door, and Blank realized that the intersection where Brade had been slain lay in the same direction. Podmore trailed off and lifted his shoulders in a helpless shrug.

"What project was that?" Miss Bonaventure said, as Blank walked back across the room and leaned against the back of his empty chair.

Podmore shook his head. "I don't know, he'd never say. Only that it had suggested the idea for that"—he indicated the portrait of himself on the wall in Merlin's robe—"and nothing more."

Blank laced the fingers of his hands together and carefully chose his next words. "You and Brade were friends, I take it." He paused, and then said, "More, perhaps, than mere casual acquaintances?"

Podmore opened his mouth as if to speak, and then closed it, his lips disappearing entirely behind his thick mustache.

Blank nodded, knowingly. It had only been a matter of short weeks since Oscar had been released from prison, having spent two years in Reading gaol for the crime of giving himself in to the love that dared not speak its name. The word from Berlin was that the newly founded Scientific-Humanitarian Committee had begun to campaign for the abolition of legal penalties for homosexuals, but Blank did not allow himself the illusion of optimism.

"When did you see him last, Mr. Podmore?" Miss Bonaventure asked.

Podmore shifted his gaze from Blank to Miss Bonaventure. "Two days ago," he finally answered, after a lengthy pause. "The morning before . . . the morning before he died. We were to dine together that night, here in my rooms, but . . ." His voice choked off, and when he continued, his words were strained. "But he never arrived."

Miss Bonaventure leaned forward, evidently intent on asking another question, but Blank stayed her with a quick wave of his hand. "Thank you, Mr. Podmore," he said, inclining his head to Podmore and offering his hand to Miss Bonaventure. She gave him a quizzical look, but took his hand and rose to her feet. "I think we've troubled you enough for one evening. I thank you for your hospitality and for your fine tea."

With Miss Bonaventure on his elbow, Blank made his way to the door. Podmore, lost in his own thoughts, followed after, absently.

At the door, Blank paused and glanced from Podmore to the framed pen-and-ink drawing on the wall. "It really is a good likeness, Mr. Podmore, and the work of a clear talent. You should be honored to have it."

Podmore seemed to brighten fractionally, and something like a smile twitched beneath his full mustache, though his eyes remained pained and half-lidded. "Thank you," he said, and then Blank and Miss Bonaventure left him with his pictures and books, his pains and his memories.

As Blank and Miss Bonaventure made their way back to York Place, she regarded him curiously. "You know, Blank, I think we might have discovered something if you'd let me question Podmore a bit more."

Blank took a deep breath and sighed, before turning to face her. "No," he said sadly, shaking his head. "We wouldn't have. Or rather, we would, but what we would have uncovered would not be germane to our investigations, I suspect. That Podmore was keeping something concealed, I have no doubt, but to expose him wouldn't benefit anyone."

Miss Bonaventure cocked her eyebrow at him, quizzically.

"What we *did* learn from Podmore, and what *is* germane," he continued, "is that Brade was on his way to Podmore's rooms that evening and never arrived. Whatever else he is keeping hidden, I am convinced that Podmore is sincere when he says that he did not see Brade that evening. The most likely conclusion, then, giving the proximity of the murder to Podmore's rooms, is that the murderer interrupted Brade en route."

With a slight nod, Miss Bonaventure said, "Fair enough. So we shall eliminate further questioning of Podmore from our agenda." She paused, thoughtfully. "Still, I find myself curious about this mystery project of Brade's that Podmore mentions. Could that have any bearing on the case, do you suppose?"

Blank considered it. "It certainly seems possible. Shall we dig a little deeper into the matter in the morning?"

"Certainly," Miss Bonaventure said, stifling a yawn with her hand. "But in the meantime, I could use a meal, a bath, and a bed, in that order."

"I can stand you to dinner," Blank said, "but for the rest of your list, I'm afraid you're on your own."

Miss Bonaventure said with a smile, "Don't worry, Blank. I know that in your bath, as well as in your bed, there's only room for one."

Blank managed a game smile in response. Since they'd known one another, Miss Bonaventure was quite right to point out that he'd been consistently and exclusively solitary in his habits, bordering on the monastic, at least as regarded matters domestic. That he'd had a life before they met, and a long one at that, was a factor that she seemed not to consider, and Blank was in no mood, at the moment, to disabuse her misconceptions.

CHAPTER FIFTEEN

Millennium

IN MOVIES AND BOOKS, Alice had always come across characters who went from stinking drunk to stone-cold sober in a matter of moments when faced with life-threatening crises. That kind of thing might happen, she supposed, but only if they weren't really that drunk to start with. For her part, having twice found herself in serious peril while three sheets to the wind, she didn't find that she got sober any faster. It just made being drunk that much more of a pain in the ass.

Stillman Waters was dragging Alice through the streets of London with the white dogs following close behind. They didn't bark like regular dogs, Alice noticed, but sounded instead like a bunch of migrating birds. But their fangs, dyed red or not, still looked damned sharp. And they seemed to have a serious mad on for Alice and the old man.

"Where are we going?" Alice panted, breathless.

They rounded a corner, and Stillman stopped to point his weird-looking pistol back the way they'd come, leaning against the wall and sighting along the barrel. He pulled the trigger and instead of a bang there was a little popping sound, like a paintball gun firing or a damp firework petering out, and something shot out of the barrel and struck the foreleg of the nearest of the dogs.

The dog was trying to dislodge the raven that had sunk its claws into its back and was now busily engaged in attempting—unsuccessfully, as luck would have it—to peck the dog's eyes out with its beak. The other four dogs were surging forward, each fending off a raven or two of its own.

Stillman fired his strange pistol again, and this next shot kicked up little bits of shrapnel from the pavement just in front of another dog's paws. Whatever the gun was firing wasn't bullets, but it was getting the job done.

"What *is* that?"

"Webley Hotspur fletcher," Stillman said, matter-of-factly. "Flechette pistol." He reached into his pocket and pulled out a slender sliverlike dart. "Not exactly standard issue, you understand."

Alice took the dart out of his hand and looked at it. It looked something like an overfed sewing needle with little ridges on one end.

"Oh, for the love of . . ." Stillman pulled back around the corner, slamming up flat against the wall.

Alice peeked around, to see what had given Stillman such a stricken look.

There was a tall, slender figure approaching, following the dogs. He was more than a block away, and in the faint light of the streetlamps it was hard to make out too much in the way of detail, but the guy looked to be completely bald and wore big wraparound sunglasses.

"Friend of *yours*?" Alice asked, pulling her head back around the corner.

"I don't know who you are or what your game is, love," Stillman said, his mouth drawn into a tight, thin line. "But I'll not leave anyone to *his* tender mercies." With a minute jerk of his head, he indicated the guy approaching around the corner. "So come along; you're coming with me."

Stillman grabbed Alice's hand and took off running.

Alice kept up as best she could, tugged along behind like a skier fallen behind a boat and skipping across the water, arms and legs flailing.

"What are those things, anyway?" Alice asked.

"Gabriel Hounds," Stillman answered, then he shook his head. "Doesn't matter." He stood at the intersection, looking left and right.

"Looking for something?"

"We could use a big bunch of water. Slows them down a bit."

Alice pointed through the nearest buildings, at the dark ribbon of the Thames. "Isn't that enough for you?"

Stillman shook his head. "It slows them down. It doesn't stop them. They'd still catch up." He looked around again, looking like someone who'd already realized what the correct answer was, but was still afraid to admit it.

Stillman looked at Alice and narrowed his ice-chip eyes.

"Listen, love, can you keep a secret?"

Alice was still for a long moment before it occurred to her to answer. She heard the migrating-birds baying of the dogs growing closer. Then she nodded, vigorously. "Yes. Yes. Yes, I can keep a secret."

Stillman bit his lower lip, resisting the answer still.

"All right," he said, and started moving again, dragging Alice behind. "You're coming home with me, then. But listen. Don't touch *anything*. Got it?"

The Tower of London was just up ahead. Alice and Stillman were across the street and a short way up. The dogs were out of sight but couldn't be far behind them. In the middle of the sidewalk was an old metal railing, surrounding what appeared to be steps leading underground. There was a rusted iron chain strung across the gate.

Stillman lifted the chain and hustled Alice beneath, then followed.

"Come on, in here."

It was dark as the pit down there, and smelled twice as bad. "What *is* this?"

"Victorian public convenience," Stillman said, and hurried deeper into the narrow room. There were stalls along the left wall, a kind of trough along the other. Stillman kicked one of the stalls open. It took Alice a second to recognize the blackened stump of porcelain within. This was a men's room.

Stillman dragged her into the stall behind him.

"Um, seriously?" Alice sneered. "The dogs are bad enough, but if it means getting groped in a grungy old toilet, I'd just as soon take my chances."

Stillman flashed her a smile that glinted in the moonlight filtering through the grates overhead. "I already told you, love. You're just not my type."

With that, Stillman slammed the stall door shut and lashed out his foot, kicking at a brick above the toilet. With a rusty groan, the whole section of wall swung inwards, toilet and all.

As gloomy and dark as it was in the underground restroom, seemingly abandoned for decades, it was pitch black in the space beyond the wall. Alice found herself dragged bodily through the gap, and then, when the wall swung back into place, was surrounded by an inky darkness.

Alice wasn't sure if her eyes were growing accustomed to the gloom, or if lights were coming on somewhere in the distance. But the ink black darkness was slowly tinged with gray, and shapes and forms gradually resolved out of the shadows.

"What . . . ?" Alice began, but found herself silenced when Stillman slapped a hand over her mouth.

"Shhh," he hissed. In the gray twilight she could see him point at his ear. "Listen."

Somewhere above them the sound of migrating birds grew louder, and louder, and louder. Then, just when it seemed that they could grow no louder, the sounds began to fade, gradually at first and then faster and faster. It was like some slow motion Doppler effect, like an ambulance driving by very, very slowly.

"I think we shook them," Stillman said, lowering his hand from her mouth. "If the dogs didn't enter the loo, then *he* probably didn't either. Which means we're safe. For now."

"Where are we?" Alice said in a harsh whisper. "Who are you? What's going on?"

Stillman smiled.

"You said you could keep a secret, right?"

The space behind the wall turned out to be a landing at the top of a long flight of steps. At the bottom of the steps was a door. And behind the door?

"My home," Stillman said, hitting the Frankenstein's lab switch on the wall, turning on the lights.

They had to be hundreds of feet underground.

Stillman tucked the Hostpur pistol into the pocket of his slacks, and then shucked off his trench coat and suit jacket.

"I'd offer you something to drink, but you look like you've had enough, love."

The walls and ceiling were an unbroken curve, with the floor flat, the large space like a long cylinder with one side cut off. It was just like the Underground stations Alice had gone through. Had it only been that morning?

"This is a subway station, isn't it?"

Stillman nodded. "For a few minutes, at least. On the Metropolitan Line. Opened in 1882, and closed two years after that." He pointed over Alice's head, and she looked up to see the sign.

TOWER OF LONDON.

"They built Mark Lane, later Tower Hill, just a little ways off, and shut this one down. It was just an empty hole until the Second World War. Lots of the old stations got used for the effort. Churchill and his War Time Cabinet used Down Street Station in a pinch, when they couldn't use the War Rooms in Whitehall and Paddock was still being built. The SOE used this one for sensitive records storage. Then after the war, it ended up MI8's patch, and that was that."

Alice was sure she must look as confused as she felt. "What?"

Stillman quirked her a smile. "Can you keep a secret, love?" He winked. "I'm a *spy*."

Stillman's home was a kind of H shape, two long tunnels connected by a narrow hallway. The first tunnel, the one behind the door at the bottom of the stairs, was like some kind of insane subterranean yard sale, all sorts of furniture and filing cabinets and desks and chairs strewn across the floor in no discernible order. In one corner was an elephants' graveyard of ancient computers, typewriters, telex machines, and telephones. There was a world map on the right-hand wall, enormous, like something from a NASA control room, or maybe a mad scientist's lair, only partially obscured by the towers of junk before it. The map was decades out of date, as near as Alice could tell, with pushpins marking positions in the USSR and other nations forgotten to history.

Opposite the map was some kind of crest, a black raven atop a castle tower, that on second glance looked more like a chess piece, with the initials S.I.D. and a Latin motto in a scroll. *PERICULA OCCULTA, DEFENSOR ARCANUS.* Something like "hidden dangers, secret defender."

"S.I.D.?" Alice read aloud.

"Signals Intelligence Directorate, originally." Stillman had his jacket and trench coat draped over his arm. "Special Intelligence Directorate, eventually." He smiled. "Don't know what they call it, nowadays, but it hardly matters. It was always MI8 when anyone came calling."

The man started toward the narrow hallway that opened off of the middle of the tunnel. Alice didn't know where the tunnel went yet and wasn't sure she wanted to.

"Come along, girl. Let's get some coffee in you, sober you up a bit. Then maybe you can tell me why the Huntsman and his Gabriel Hounds are after you."

Huntsman? Alice nodded absently and followed along behind.

On the other end of the hallway was another tunnel, which must have originally been the same size and shape as the first—and both of them, she realized, must have had trains running through at some point, the tracks buried somewhere under the floor—but where the first tunnel had been a big unbroken space, this second tunnel had been sectioned up into smaller rooms. The center section was probably the largest, with carpet on the floor, a large sofa flanked by recliners on either side, an ancient television atop a stand, and a big coffee table. On the wall was a smaller version of the crest from the other room, with the raven atop the tower and the Latin motto scrolling beneath. Opening off this large room was a kitchen, and opposite it a bathroom. Doors on either wall, one to the left of the kitchen and one to the right of the bathroom, led to a narrow hallway that seemed to run the length of the tunnel. At one end, Alice would later learn, was a bedroom, at the other a library.

Stillman left Alice on the couch, her backpack in her lap, and returned a short while later with a steaming pot of coffee and a pair of mugs. Alice wasn't much of a coffee drinker, but she was glad for something to wash the taste of stale smoke and beer from her mouth, and accepted the proffered mug with thanks.

"So, wait," Alice said, trying to get her bearings. "Why'd you say you're a spy? What's *that* about?"

"Well." Stillman shrugged. "I suppose it's because I *am* a spy." He chuckled. "Or was, at any rate."

Alice tugged the pack of cigarettes from her jacket pocket. She had one of the butts between her lips before she thought to ask, "Mind if I smoke in here?"

"Those things'll kill you, you know." Stillman smiled. "But I'll allow it if you'll spare one for me. It's been too many years since I indulged."

Alice shook a cigarette out of the pack for him and handed it over.

"Might I trouble you for a light?" Stillman asked.

It took a moment, but Alice managed to fish the match case from her pocket.

"Mmm." Stillman studied the case, his brows knit. "How *oddly* familiar." Then he shook his head, struck a match, and held it up, first for Alice, then himself. Then, coffee and cigarettes in hand, the two of them settled back onto the couch.

"So you're a spy," Alice said, a statement and not a question. "Like James Bond?"

"I hope not." Stillman sneered. "No, we were of a different sort, I suppose you'd say. Didn't do all the regular sort of cloak-and-dagger cat-and-mouse like the lads and ladies of Five and Six—that's the Security Service and Secret Intelligence Service, if you want to be pedantic, but everyone always called them MI5 and MI6. Just like our lot was the Special Intelligence Directorate, but everyone called us MI8. We'd picked the name up during the war, back when Eight was just signals intelligence for the Special Operations Executive. MI8, or Military Intelligence Section 8, in charge of signals intelligence and cryptography. That's how we got in this business, you understand. See, the Y Services of the armed forces, along with the SID, began to intercept German wireless traffic encrypted with some new code. Ultimately, the SID and Alan Turing and the rest of the cryptographers at Bletchley Park were able to decode these transmissions, which turned out to be information about top-secret investigations carried out by the SS Ahnenerbe."

"The what?" Alice wasn't sure if it was the residual drunk, or if he was really just talking nonsense.

"The Ahnenerbe. Supposedly some sort of cultural heritage group set up by Himmler and his goons, but they were much dirtier than that. The Nazis believed all sorts of crazy things—that the world was hollow and we lived on the inside, that the ancient Egyptians had nuclear power, that Atlantis was real and was where flying saucers came from, you name it—but the job of the Ahnenerbe was to go out and prove this malarkey. Well, these transmissions we'd picked up said that the mad buggers were attempting to establish communications with intelligences in another plane of existence. Another universe altogether."

"Another *universe*?" Alice wasn't sure they even had long-distance *telephone* calls back then, much less person-to-person in another universe.

Stillman nodded. "It was all immediately classified Above Top Secret and put on a strictly need-to-know basis. And since we in the SID, along with Turing and the gang at Bletchley, already knew, it was quickly decided that no one else needed to know anything. Operatives of the SOE were dispatched to interfere with the Ahnenerbe's plans, and from that point on the SID was in the occult business."

Alice didn't believe a word of it. She was trapped in a hole, deep below the street, with a crazy man. Who, unless she was mistaken, was very definitely gay. So what did he want with *her*?

On the other hand, she *had* recognized this guy from her visions, and even knew his name, kinda-sorta, though in a rebus-in-*Highlights*-magazine sort of way. A lake's still waters for Stillman Waters. So what did she know?

There were three options, as she saw it. Either she was crazy, or he was crazy, or neither of them were crazy and everything he was saying was the truth.

"So let me get this straight. Not only are there ghosts and ghouls and monsters and such, but there are secret agents who keep tabs on them?"

"Well, not precisely, love, but that's the general gist of it, I suppose."

"And the secret agents got their start eavesdropping on Nazis' *phone* calls?"

Stillman laughed and took a sip of his coffee. "You think that's bad, you Yanks have your own bunch who muck about in the dark corners, but they were originally part of the post office!" He set his coffee cup down and took a long drag of his cigarette. "My hand to God, if you believe that sort of thing. The offices of Bureau Zero are still under the old Post Office Building in Washington. And the French Cabinet Noir, come to that, got their start snooping in people's mail, so were postal, too, of a sort."

Seeing Alice's expression, Stillman crushed out his cigarette in the ashtray he'd dug up, and continued, somewhat more seriously.

"Look, don't get me wrong. I'm not talking about fantasy here. What I'm saying is that there is often a verifiable phenomenon behind supposed supernatural occurrences. If you dig deep enough into myths and fairy tales and legends, like as not you'll come up with something really going on back there that doesn't fit with the everyday view of things. And it *is* supernatural, but only in the dictionary definition of a realm or system higher than nature. There are worlds beyond this one, love, other planes of existence that sometimes intersect with our own. And it's guys like me who see that those intersections don't mean curtains for the rest of you."

"And it was the Nazis that discovered this, I take it?" Alice was sobering by the minute, but finding this no easier to swallow.

"Well, no. That is, they did, but others already knew. See, there's always been guys like me, standing at the borders. Back in Queen Elizabeth's day there was the School of Night, John Dee and that crowd, that had worked it out from first principles. They had their own agents, Lord Strange's Men, who came to be known as the Strangers further down the line. There's your Bureau Zero over in Washington, who've been knocking about since the early 1800s. The Soviets had a mob of them, as did the Japanese in the old days. As did the Chinese. There've never been too many, you understand, on-the-job mortality being pretty high in this business, but we've always been around."

"So why don't people know about this stuff?"

"Well, it was my job to see that they didn't, wannit? Which isn't to say that stories don't leak out, here and there. But most people just believe what they want to believe, so it's pretty easy to pass off a projection from a faster universe as swamp gas, or a probe from another continuum as a weather balloon, if need be."

Alice narrowed her eyes. "So what's this Huntsman about, then? Is he one of you guys?"

"See, perfect example!" Stillman snapped his fingers. "Near as we can figure, he's a regular human who was affected by exposure to a reality incursion, long time ago." He took in Alice's confused expression. "By a little bit of another universe impinging on our own. Happens from time to time. Scientists are starting to talk about it in the open, nowadays. About quantum interactions between different universes. Happens all the time but we hardly notice, since most of the encounters are with universes too small to make a difference. But if our universe were to collide with a much bigger one, we could all find ourselves living in a world where the boiling point of water had dropped to zero, or gravity was the strongest force, or some such." He mused. "Course, when I was D and in charge of MI8, we'd put a stop to scientists publishing talk like that. Hell, when I was a Rook the old D authorized sanctions, a time or two, on just such an occasion. But after I put myself out to pasture, years ago, they moved the shop across the river, and I guess they're using a different playbook nowadays."

He grew silent for a moment and glanced around the room. Alice felt her lids growing heavy. She hadn't had a good night's sleep in days, and instead of perking her up the coffee was just counteracting the effects of the drunk enough to make her aware of just how tired she was, really.

Stillman took a deep breath and shook his head, as if dislodging memories stuck to the sides of his skull.

"Anyway, the Huntsman, right? He was a human affected by a reality incursion, like I said, who subsequently gave rise to legends about the Wild Hunt. A rational event become a myth. He's been around for years, but has to spend half a century hibernating for every couple of years he's awake. When last he was abroad . . ." He fell silent for a moment, and a cloud passed over his face. He closed his eyes tightly for a moment, as if remembering some old pain. Then he opened his eyes and continued. "His dogs, on the other hand? The Gabriel Hounds, as legend remembers them? They can stay awake and active all the time, more's the pity. Usually they stick near where the Huntsman sleeps, though, which is far enough away not to bother the rest of us. They're damned hard to kill, they are. I saw one of them put down back in the forties, but I'd not want to try that again myself any time soon."

Alice's head dipped, her chin touching her chest, and she jerked her head back up, trying to make it look like a nod. It felt like her brain was sloshing around in her skull, and she felt dizzy as her eyes rolled.

Stillman's gaze was on the crest on the far wall, his thoughts somewhere far away.

"What about the raven?" Alice said, slurring.

"It's a rook," Stillman said, still looking at the crest. "As is the tower, if you get right down to it. The legend goes that the continued existence of England depends on the presence of at least seven ravens in the Tower of London. I suppose that's where they got the idea for calling MI8 field operatives 'Rooks,' what with our headquarters being here beneath the Tower and all." He turned and took in her bewildered expression. "Oh, you meant the ravens on the road, didn't you?" He shook his head. "Can't help you there, love. Don't have a clue what that was about."

Alice tried unsuccessfully to stifle a yawn, and with her voice rising and falling with the yawn, said, "If this is so secret, why are you telling me?"

"What's that?" Stillman cupped his hand to his ear. "Couldn't quite make that out."

Alice shook her head and, as clearly as she could manage, said, "Why are you telling me all of this, if it's so secret?"

Stillman smiled, sadly. "I'm tired of secrets and mysteries, love. I gave all that up a long time ago. But why I'm telling you? Well, you're something of a mystery yourself, aren't you? Like how you knew my name when I've been careful to be off the books and out of sight for a long, long time. And just what the Huntsman and his dogs want with you, anyway."

Alice opened her mouth to answer, to say she had no idea, but only yawned again.

"That's enough for one night, I think," Stillman said, standing up and taking the half-empty mug from Alice's hand and the smoldering cigarette from between her fingers. "Get some rest, all right, and maybe tomorrow we can find some answers together."

Alice woke early, as she always did after a night of heavy drinking. It never seemed fair that just when her body most needed the rest, it just couldn't seem to get it. She'd fallen asleep on the couch, right where Stillman had left her. The lights were all off, except for those under the cabinets on the walls of the kitchen, streaming dimly into the living space.

Alice's stomach churned. She felt like she needed to eat, or to vomit, or both. Best to try some food and hope for the best.

In the kitchen, she found what looked like some kind of cinnamon roll in the fridge, and the remains of a pot of tea on the stove. The tea probably belonged down the drain, but while it smelled a little bitter, it tasted all right poured over ice with a few generous spoonfuls of sugar.

With the pastry and iced tea in her, Alice felt marginally better. She turned on a lamp near the sofa, and by its light fished her toiletries out of her backpack. A short while after she emerged from the bathroom, freshly showered, teeth brushed, and dressed in a clean white T-shirt, jeans, and fresh bra and panties. From the looks of the bathroom, there must be another shower in the place, since this one clearly hadn't been used in some time. Probably behind the closed door at the end of the hallway, behind which Stillman was presumably still asleep.

The whole place had a makeshift look to it, as though spaces intended for other uses had been repurposed. The furniture in the living room, for example, must have been the height of fashion in the sixties or seventies, and was still in good enough repair that with the rug underneath it was cozy enough, but on closer examination it was clear that the room had originally been some sort of work space. The kitchen had the look of a filing room into which someone had just added a sink, stove, and refrigerator.

The door to the right of the bathroom was open and led to a narrow hallway. Padding quietly on her bare feet, Alice ventured into the gloom, curious.

At the end of the hallway was another room, and when Alice flipped on the light switch, she saw it was nearly as large as the living space. Aside from a door in the far wall, the rest of the room was covered in shelves, crammed full of leather-bound books and piles of loose-leaf paper and folders, or framed pictures and paintings.

One painting in particular had a place of prominence, on the left-hand wall. It was hung high with a pair of small spotlights trained on it. It was a portrait of a man in Victorian evening dress, with a red orchid in his lapel. He had an unreadable expression on his face, at once wistful and sad and strange. Alice thought he looked something like Jeremy Irons in *Brideshead Revisited*, which her mother had insisted that they watch every time it was replayed. Where Naomi Vance had a weakness for Michael Caine, for Samatha Fell it was all Jeremy Irons, all the time. Alice, of course, thought they were both crazy; as if any actor could be better than Johnny Depp.

Below the portrait, in a display case, was a silver chalice of some kind. It had a large bowl with letters or runes engraved around the rim, sitting on top of a conically shaped foot, with a round bulb where the bowl met the base.

"Quite the liberty taker, aren't you, love?"

Alice whirled around, her heart in her throat.

In the open door stood Stillman Waters, wearing a silk dressing gown, leaning casually against the jamb. His hair was out-of-the-shower damp, and his face was clean shaven.

"Helped yourself to the last of my Chelsea buns, I see. And used the shower in the bargain."

"The knob for the cold water sticks in the shower."

Stillman smiled. "That's why I never use that one, myself. Put it in for visitors, didn't I? But doesn't do much good if no one ever visits, which they don't."

Alice turned and looked up at the portrait. "Who is that?"

Stillman came to stand beside her. It was a long moment before he spoke. "A . . . friend . . . of mine. He died in Iceland, a long time ago."

"Ah." Alice nodded. She could tell by the way he'd said it that "friend" really mean "more than a friend."

"Ah?" Stillman looked at her with an eyebrow cocked.

"Sorry," Alice said, flustered. "I mean . . . I just wasn't sure, you know?"

She shoved her hands into the pockets of her jeans, her elbows tucked in tight. "I apparently have difficulty telling the difference between English and gay."

Stillman smiled. "Well, I don't make it any easier on you being both, do I?" He looked up at the portrait. "But *he* wasn't even English. Was one of the original Americans, I suppose you might say."

Alice looked back at the young Jeremy Irons with the strange, far-off look and the red orchid in his lapel. "He doesn't *look* much like a Native American."

"Oh, not a Red Indian, love. I meant . . ." He shook his head. "Oh, never mind."

Alice shrugged and drifted on down the wall. Next to the portrait in its place of prominence was a black-and-white photograph in a gold frame. There were two men and a woman in the picture. One of the men was clearly the same as the one in the portrait, but Jeremy Irons a few years on, *Lolita*, maybe, or even older. The other seemed to be a younger Stillman Waters, a Michael Caine somewhere between *Alfie* and *The Ipcress File*. And the woman?

"Hey!" Alice leaned in close. Sure enough. "That looks just like the chick I met last night in the bar. Her name was Roxanne . . . Roxanne Something-or-other." She turned to Stillman. "A few years older, though. And it couldn't be the same woman, of course. Maybe her mother? Or grandmother even?"

Stillman looked from the photo to Alice, head tilted to one side. "Roxanne, you say?" He glanced back at the picture. "Interesting." He seemed lost in thought for a moment, puzzling something out. He moved to stand before the chalice and squinted at the figures engraved around its rim.

"What's it say?" Alice asked.

"Never could make heads or tails of it. It's Old Norse, but nonsense." He leaned closer, raising his eyebrows, and began to read aloud, "*Vetki, tveir, vetki, sjau* . . ." He left off, straightened, and turned to look at Alice. "'Nothing, two, nothing, seven . . .' Just goes on like that. If it's a poem, it's an exceedingly poor one. It was a gift from a friend a long time ago. But . . ." He trailed off and glanced at the portrait. Then he clapped his hands and brightened. "But enough of these moldering memories. Come on, let me fix us a proper breakfast."

Alice sat on the couch with a fresh mug of coffee, watching television while
Stillman stood over the stove, a frying pan's handle in one hand, a spatula in the
other. The room filled with the smell of toasting bread and bacon and made
Alice's mouth water. The cinnamon roll—or Chelsea bun, as Stillman called it—
had staved off the worst of the hunger pangs, but she was still absolutely starving.

Lighting a cigarette, Alice moved the ashtray onto the cushion next to
her, propped her feet up on the coffee table, and flipped through the channels
with the remote. On one channel there was something called *Blue Peter*,
which seemed to be about a group of extremely friendly people who couldn't
stop smiling, their pets, and crafts. Another channel was showing American
cartoons. Another was running some sort of newsmagazine. Another sports
highlights. And so on. Alice settled on the newsmagazine.

She'd flipped over midway through a story about the Glastonbury Festival, the same outdoor concert she'd seen on television the day before. This
one was a bit more in depth, and kept showing clips from previous festivals,
apparently dating back to the late sixties or early seventies, from the looks of
them. There was David Bowie, in his long-haired hippie days. And here was
David Rapapport backstage, whom Alice recognized as the little person from
Time Bandits. And here was Iain Temple, made up to look like an alien in a
silver jumpsuit, head and brows completely shaved, and eyes hidden behind
opalescent contacts. The host of the news show came on and informed younger
viewers that, Yes, the alien on screen was indeed the founder and CEO of
Temple Enterprises in his more carefree days. Cut to a more recent bit of file
footage, and a more normal-looking Iain Temple dressed in a collarless shirt
and vest, being interviewed on the occasion of the grand opening of his
London headquarters, Glasshouse in Canary Wharf; Temple responded to old
accusations that Bowie had stolen his entire look for *The Man Who Fell to
Earth*, which had fueled rumors that the idea of Ziggy Stardust, too, had been
inspired by Iain Temple's opal-eyed "Visitor from a Broken Earth" persona.

Then the story shifted, talking about the origins of the Glastonbury Festival, about how it had supposedly been inspired in part by *The View over*

Atlantis, John Michell's 1969 book that proposed that nearby Glastonbury was part of the hidden landscape of England, one of a number of nexuses of power where ley lines met, an ancient holy sanctuary.

"You about ready, love?"

Alice turned down the television. "Sure." She began to stand. "Say, is something burning . . . ?"

Then the world went white before her eyes in a flash, and Alice fell.

Alice fell for what seemed an eternity. No sense of time or place, only an awareness of presences around her, and the unshakable sense that there was some meaning behind it all.

Indistinct voices called at the edge of hearing.

Over the city, the eye turned.

A flock of black birds blotted out the sky.

A mirror-still pool of water and the man with the ice-chip eyes.

And at the center of it all, the jewel.

". . . okay, love?"

Stillman had his hands on her shoulders, holding her steady. Her lips felt rubbed and chapped, and her left hand was describing circles on her belly.

"Y-yeah," she said, blinking rapidly, shaking her head minutely from side to side. "Yeah, I'm fine."

Stillman leaned in close, his eyes narrowed, and Alice could smell the mix of aftershave and bacon on his skin. "You don't look all right, you'll excuse me saying."

He steered her into the kitchen and sat her at one of the chairs at the low table, the Formica of its surface scratched and stained with age.

"You saw something." Stillman sat in the other chair, facing her with his hands on his knees. "I know you did."

Reluctantly, Alice nodded. "I . . . I have Temporal Lobe . . ."

"Epilepsy," Stillman said, interrupting. "I know; I saw the Depakote in your bag when you got the cigarettes out last night." He looked at her, thoughtfully. "Tell me, does the name 'Omega' mean anything to you?"

Alice shook her head before even thinking about it, but then said, "No, I don't think so. Last letter of the Greek alphabet, I think. And maybe a kind of watch? I don't know. What's Omega?"

Stillman breathed in through his nostrils, deeply, and sighed. "I suppose you could say that once upon a time I served two masters and now serve none."

"You were . . . What? A double agent?"

Stillman smiled slightly. "Something like that." He reached out and placed his hand over Alice's on the table. "Tell me, what do you see when you experience a seizure?"

Alice shifted, uneasy under his close gaze. "Well, I call them 'visions,' actually. Promise you won't laugh. Anyway, it's always the same elements, in differing combinations. An eye over a city. A body of water. A man." She paused, looking at him for any sign of reaction. "Ravens. And a jewel."

"Hmmm." Stillman took back his hand, got up, and walked into the living room. When he returned, he had one of Alice's spiral notebooks in hand.

"Hey, that's mine!"

"Of course it is, love." Stillman smiled. "But I wasn't just going to leave a mystery like you snoring on my couch without doing a bit of snooping. I mean, come now, I'm a spy, after all. It's what I *do*." Stillman sat down and flipped the notebook open on the table before him. "Whose phone number, by the way? This the same Roxanne you mentioned?"

Alice nodded, eyes narrowed and glaring.

"Mmm." Stillman hummed and nodded thoughtfully. Then he read aloud, unfazed by the mirror-writing, occasionally pointing to images sketched in the margins. "So you believe that you're receiving messages. You're not sure from whom, precisely, but you think that God's the one reversing the charges. The problem is, you can't work out what the message *means*. Now, the eye over the city is the London Eye, you surmise. And the 'still water' and man both refer, I assume you've decided, to me." He paused and looked up at her. "Tell me," he said with a smile, "are my eyes really 'ice-chip blue?'" He chuckled. "The ravens are, so far as I can tell, just ravens. Sometimes a cigar, and so on. But this?" He stabbed a finger at the image of the smooth-surfaced gem, carefully rendered in purple ink. "That's the jewel you mention?"

Alice nodded.

Stillman replied with a nod of his own. Then he picked up the spiral in one hand and took her hand with his other, and led her back to the living room. He pointed to the television. "Is it something like *that?*"

There, on the screen, was a smooth-surfaced gem, like a glass teardrop falling in midair, just like she'd seen in countless visions, just like she'd sketched in her notebooks.

"Yeah," Alice said, her voice low. "Something like that."

Authorities were reporting the discovery that morning of the theft of the so-called Vanishing Gem.

Only a few weeks before the jewel had been discovered in the basement of the museum, forgotten to history, with no record of it in the museum's holdings. The museum's director had commissioned a routine examination of the gem, to identify its makeup and hopefully pinpoint its origin, when it was discovered that the gem appeared to be *shrinking*. Looking like highly reflective glass, almost like a small spherical mirror, the gem apparently resisted any attempts to peer within, either by electron microscope or fluoroscope or functional magnetic resonance. However, a pair of simple measurements on highly calibrated scales showed an all-but-imperceptible, though measurable, reduction in mass over time. And given enough time between measurements, a slight reduction in size could also be detected.

The museum had dubbed it the "Vanishing Gem" and issued a press release to the public, outlining the facts as then understood. Plans were announced to put the jewel on display within the British Museum itself, and investigations were launched in the hope of discovering its provenance.

The hope came to an end that morning, Saturday the twenty-fourth of June, when it was revealed that the gem currently under lock and key in the British Museum was a fake, a simple forgery of glass. The discovery had apparently been made on Thursday morning, when researchers arrived to make another set of measurements, but not revealed to the press and the public for another three days while authorities investigated the apparent robbery. Now, they were alerting the public and soliciting any information that might lead to the recovery of the gem.

"Curiouser and curiouser," Stillman said, switching off the television.

Alice was sitting on the couch, trying to work out what it all meant. Now she'd found everything from her visions but was no closer to understanding what any of it meant. And worse, in meeting Stillman with his crazy stories about occult spies and other universes, she'd only ended up with even more questions.

"I've got to find that gem," Alice finally said, staring at the floor. "That's all there is to it. If I find the gem and hold it in my hand, then maybe I'll understand. No, I *will* understand."

Alice heard Stillman sigh, heavily, and looked up to see him smiling wistfully.

"Come on, man," Alice said, jumping to her feet. "You've got to help me. You believe me, don't you?"

"That you're receiving messages from some unknown source?" He chuckled. "Believe me, love, that's the easiest part of your story *to* believe."

"Then you've got to believe that you're mixed up in it, too!"

Stillman shook his head. "Not necessarily. And even if you *are* receiving messages, which I'm not saying you're not, then who's to say that they're telling the *truth*?" He sighed again, and shook his head. "But no, you're right. For good or ill, I'm mixed up in it, whatever it is." He glanced around at the living room, at the kitchen behind them, at the library down the hall. "I've been hiding down here in this hole for more than a decade, getting older, waiting for death to come for me, hiding from the past and the future alike." He smiled. "Maybe it's time to get back in harness again, after all."

CHAPTER SIXTEEN

Twilight

GALAAD WAS SURPRISED to find he'd drawn his Saeson sword, its point wavering uncertainly before him. His pulse pounded in his ears, almost drowning out the sound of the spectral white hounds loping towards them.

The Huntsman advanced, slow but steady, his sword like a red brand on his hand, while his dog pack coursed ahead, bearing towards the seven, their teeth and claws glinting red in the moonlight.

Artor and his captains said not a word but sprang immediately into action, fanning out across the street, preparing to meet the charge.

The dogs reached their quarry far in advance of their master, their unearthly baying like the calls of birds in flight, half a dozen in number. As if guided by some uncanny intelligence, each of the hounds chose a prey, snapping and clawing at the High King and his captains. Seen close to, it was apparent that they were not like true hounds, but longer in the body, with shorter legs, and completely white but for the splashes of bright red on the ends of their long ears. Still, their claws and teeth were no less sharp, for all of that.

Artor slashed with his long spatha at the hound which harried him, the silver and gold hilt of his sword glinting, the long blade flashing like lightning in the gloom. The force of his blow swept the hound to one side, its bite failing to find its mark, but the hound landed on its feet and immediately resumed the charge, bounding back toward him.

Lugh lay about him with his own sword, howling imprecations at the white hound which dogged his heels, while Caius used his own blade as a club, battering the head of his tormenter, but though the sword battered again and again at the hound, it failed to draw blood, doing little but annoying the seemingly indestructible beast.

Galaad counted himself lucky that he had himself been so far unmolested, until he looked back and saw the Huntsman heading straight towards him, his red blade held high. The spectral figure's advance was slow, but inexorable.

Tightening his grip on his Saeson sword, Galaad raised the blade's tip. He'd never wielded a sword in combat, never even struck a blow in anger, and he quavered at the thought of facing such an imposing opponent. But the others were all engaged in their own struggles with the strange beasts, and even had he wanted to cry for help, he found his throat constricted with fear, his voice choked off.

At the last instant, just as the Huntsman bore down on him, Galaad tensed, anticipating the blow that would end his life. But instead he felt himself being struck from the side, knocked off his feet and sent sprawling onto the icy ground.

The moments that followed were a confusion of images.

Pryder stood where once Galaad had, having knocked him from his feet and taken his place, the hound that had worried at him only moments before kicked some distance to the side.

The Huntsman's sword had already begun its descent, but Pryder handily parried the blow, his own spatha catching the flat of the red blade and batting it aside.

The Huntsman immediately recovered and renewed his attack, reversing his blade in a backhand motion, sweeping back towards Pryder.

Pryder leaned back, raising his blade to block the Huntsman's blow, but the Huntsman's sword sliced into the spatha edge on.

The tip of Pryder's spatha clattered to the icy ground, Pryder left holding the hilt in a two-handed grip, the blade sliced clean through.

Galaad may have shouted out, but in the aftermath he wasn't sure if he had, or what he'd said if so. He could only watch with horror as the Huntsman raised his blade a final time, Pryder helpless before him, the gelded stub of the spatha in his hands. In the instant before the red blade fell, the Huntsman locked eyes with Pryder and seemed to hesitate.

The blow never fell, but the Huntsman backed away, and while his face was still frozen like a death mask, the corpse-white flesh immobile, his eyes seemed in that moment to burn brighter, flashing red.

Pryder scrambled back, for the moment not questioning this unexpected reprieve, holding his sheared-off sword before him like a club.

The Huntsman stood still for a moment, regarding Pryder, and then lowered his red blade, its point to the icy ground. He opened his mouth, as if to speak. Instead of words, though, a strange series of noises emerged, each distinct utterance something between a click and a whistle, that taken together sounded to Galaad's ears like, "Tekel lili."

All around them, the melee came to a sudden halt, as the white hounds froze in place and turned their baleful red eyes towards their master.

"Tekel lili, tekel lili," the Huntsman repeated, and in a fluid movement raised his red sword. As the blade turned, it seemed to disappear from view. Then the blade reappeared as the Huntsman sheathed the sword and lowered his hands to his sides.

In the next instant, the hounds again exploded into motion, only this time instead of renewing their attack on the captains, they bounded away, back up the darkened street. The Huntsman closed his mouth and took a last look, his fiery gaze passing over the assembled captains, and then took to his heels after the hounds. He ran back up the street, his gait strange but impossibly fast, seeming to outpace even a horse at gallop, and within an instant the Huntsman and his hounds had rounded a far corner, disappearing back into the black night.

If Artor and his captains had harbored any doubts about the veracity of Geraint's story before, such had been entirely dispelled. The cuts they bore on hands, arms, and legs, inflicted by the scarlet claws of the strange white hounds, were evidence enough. And convinced as they were of the concrete nature of the pack, had they any question as to the truth of the stories about their master, the Huntsman, they had only to regard Pryder's severed blade. The two pieces had been cleft one from the other so cleanly that, had they not known otherwise, the captains would never have believed they were originally whole.

Following the Huntsman's retreat, Artor and the others had given chase, though admittedly halfheartedly, and when they failed to discover any sign of the spectral figure or his unearthly hounds, they were scarcely crestfallen. Some of the captains made appropriately disappointed noises, but these were empty gestures for the sake of form.

Galaad, for his part, knew that should he never again come face to face with the lifeless-seeming visage of the Huntsman, never again peer into those baleful red eyes in that face of corpse-flesh white, then it would still be too soon.

Their cursory pursuit of the Huntsman performed, the captains were quick to suggest to their sovereign that they should retreat indoors, both to carry news of the encounter to their host and his people, and to seek the warmth and safety of the hall. Artor seemed reluctant to give up the hunt, the only one for whom the chase was anything but perfunctory, but a quick survey of his captains' faces was enough to convince him. There were wounds to tend, as he said, and frozen limbs to warm by the fire.

So it was that in short order the seven were pounding on the door to Geraint's hall, demanding admittance, and only a brief while after were sitting in places of honor before a large hearth, light and heat radiating out from the iron.

Of their wounds, the most serious was a bite that Lugh had scored on his right hand. The red teeth of the hound had bitten nearly clean through the smallest two fingers, and taken a considerable hunk of flesh from the middle one, but with the frigid air the bleeding had been sluggish, and so it did not appear that he'd lost an incapacitating amount of blood. Still, as the bitten fingers were cleaned and dressed, Lugh hurled imprecations at the attending physic that were just as foul and vicious as those he'd shouted at the beast who'd bitten him, if not more. Liberal application of undiluted wine, though, taken by mouth, had a gradual softening effect.

As for the others, their injuries were principally confined to cuts and abrasions. Galaad was embarrassed to admit that the severest injury he sustained in the encounter was a large bruise to his backside when Pryder pushed him to the icy ground, and so instead of announcing his infirmity resigned himself to rubbing his throbbing posterior and refraining from sitting down as much as was practicable.

Galaad could not help but wonder about the Huntsman. Though disquieting, his strangely immobile face had been hauntingly familiar, though Galaad could not isolate the familiarity. And what of his relationship to the unearthly hounds who obeyed his whim, stark white but for the scarlet fringe of their ears and the bloodred hue of their teeth and claws? Seeming fierce, wild beasts, they had been instantly brought to heel when the Huntsman had uttered his eerie call. Thinking back on it, the sound now brought to Galaad's mind the scriptures, which told of the words that the prophet Daniel found written upon the palace walls of Belshazzar, king of Babylon. One of them had been *tekel*, which the holy writ said carried the meaning, "you have been weighed on the scales and found wanting."

Was that why the Huntsman had called off his hounds' attack and stayed his hand against Pryder? Had those red eyes appraised the captains in some wise, and found them wanting? Or, instead, had they seen in Pryder or the others something it found of value, something that should not be cleaved with its unearthly blade?

Much of the discussion around the hearth, on their return to the hall, had been centered on the Huntsman's red blade, the shards of Pryder's spatha passed from hand to hand for inspection.

"I have never seen the like," Caius intoned, holding the sheered edge of the neutered blade up to his eyes, squinting at it closely. "The cut is entirely clean, completely smooth." He lowered the blade and looked around the red glow of the hearth at his fellows. "I'd go so far as to say I'd never seen so smooth an edge, ever. The frozen surface of a lake, perhaps? A pane of glass? But even those have bubbles and imperfections, none of which can be discerned here."

Pryder shook his head, ruefully. "The blow didn't even jar my hands as the red sword passed through mine. It was as if my blade wasn't even there, and the Huntsman's swing carried only through empty air."

"But you parried his earlier blow," Galaad said, from his position standing behind the circle of chairs. He couldn't help but have noticed that the captains had instinctively arranged their chairs in a near perfect circle around the fire, and wondered whether any of them were conscious of the fact that they had seated themselves in precisely the positions he had seen them adopt around Artor's marble circle in Caer Llundain.

"That I did." Pryder nodded, thoughtfully. "And when my blade met his, both felt solid enough. I fair felt the impact in my teeth, so much force did the parry require."

"That makes not a bit of sense," Gwrol said, stone sober despite the number of cups of wine he'd quaffed on their return. He sat on the edge of his seat, tensed, as though he'd not yet calmed from the rush and quickened pulse of their encounter. "Either the swords were solid or they were air, it can't be both."

Pryder shrugged, seeming to lack both the energy and the will to spar with his brother.

"Those hounds," Bedwyr said, hands gripping the arms of his chair, staring into the red glow of the hearth intently, open faced, as though he saw some secret meaning writ there. "What were those hounds?"

Lugh, who may have had thoughts of his own about the beasts, snored loudly in his sleep, finally rendered insensible by the prodigious amounts of wine he'd drunk to quell the throbbing pain of his bitten hand. As it stood, the loud snort had an undeniably dismissive quality to it, in keeping with the Gael's spoken responses to Bedwyr's repeated litany of "those hounds, those hounds, what were those hounds" before losing consciousness.

Artor sat silent at the head of the ring of chairs, at his side Geraint, who had taken around the hearth the place he could not accept at the marble circle in the High King's court. Geraint's wife, Enid, had repaired to their private chambers, nursing their infant son away from the press of sleeping bodies close packed in the hall, enjoying some momentary measure of privacy. Both High King and Dumnonian ruler had kept their own counsel while the captains reviewed the details of the encounter, Geraint wearing a look that made evident his sense of embarrassment and shame at having proved unable to stand beside his erstwhile companions, and Artor thoughtful with an unreadable expression.

Finally, when the conversation of the captains reached a lull, the High King broke his silence to speak.

"Whatever the beasts were, whatever manner of man this Huntsman may be, they were real enough. Real enough to bite and tear, real enough to swing a blade." He paused, thoughtfully tugging at his beard, and then turned his gaze to Galaad. "Had you seen in your visions any creatures such as we encountered tonight, or such men as their master?"

Galaad shook his head, suppressing a shiver. "No, majesty. Not that I recall."

"How could you forget such a thing?" Bedwyr said, lifting his staring eyes to meet Galaad's.

"No one could," Artor answered for him. "Still, I can't but think now that they are linked in some way with the White Lady and glass tower of Galaad's visions, though what whole these parts together make is beyond my reasoning."

Caius gingerly laid the severed halves of Pryder's sword on the flagstones at his feet. "So you're still for piercing this hedge of mist, I take it?"

Artor gave a determined nod. "Aye. And for piercing the veil of mysteries surrounding these events."

Pryder gave a snort. "Assuming, that is, that these mysteries do not pierce us first."

The captains' laughter was rueful, but it was better than none.

It was near dawn before Galaad was able to get any sleep, and soon after he'd drifted off to an uneasy slumber, curled uncomfortably on the flagstones of the hall's dusty floor, wrapped in a thin woolen blanket, the rest of the sleepers in the hall rose to begin their day, and he perforce was obliged to rise with them, unable to remain asleep with the mounting hubbub.

With the arrival of the sun, which gave more light than warmth, the people of Llongborth were again emboldened to venture out of doors and about their daily tasks.

As Galaad stood uneasily on weary legs, his neck and back aching, he counted himself lucky that Artor had decided that they would abide in Geraint's hall for a short while longer before continuing on to the hedge of mist and the island beyond. The swelling in Galaad's knee had only begun to subside in the days at sail, but now with one buttock covered with a stinging bruise that had already begun to yellow, it seemed as if the pain had only migrated up his body, not lessened. What sleep he had gotten on board the White Aspect had hardly been refreshing, and the few moments of slumber he'd caught on the floor of Geraint's hall had only served to make him more weary, not less. The prospect of a day to warm before the hearthfires, and a night in the warmth to rest, was an appealing one.

Galaad was trying to work the kinks from his neck when Pryder came to stand beside him. The auburn-haired Gwentian carried in his hands a borrowed sword, another of Saeson manufacture from Geraint's plunder, replacement for his unmanned spatha.

"That showed considerable fortitude, what you did yesterday," Pryder said, testing the heft of the sword in his grip. "Foolishness, as well, but fortitude all the same."

"What?" Galaad craned his head from side to side, hearing audible pops as the bones of his neck ground together.

"Standing your ground against the Huntsman." Pryder sliced through the air with the sword and nodded approvingly.

Galaad was confused. "But I'd have been cut to ribbons if you hadn't pushed me aside."

"Perhaps," Pryder said with a shrug. "My point is that you didn't quail and flee but remained steadfast."

Galaad hung his head, averting his eyes. "If so, it was only because I was immobilized with fear."

"There's no shame in feeling fear, boy," Pryder said with a sly grin. "It's all a matter of what you do with it. Do you let the fear take you over, or do you control it and use it to your advantage?"

"Use it?" Galaad wore a disbelieving expression.

"Look, fear is simply your body's way of telling you that you stand in some peril. It is an indicator, nothing more. By mastering your feelings, you can monitor your reactions to situations, use them like a copper miner uses a finch to gauge the quality of his air. If you feel afraid, it may well be because there is something to fear; therefore you should be wary and move with caution. But it should not debilitate or incapacitate you." Pryder scratched at his beard and gave Galaad an appraising look. "And despite what you say, when that . . . creature attacked, you stood your ground and held your sword's point high. So perhaps you don't have so far to go in conquering your fears as you might think."

Galaad nodded, unconvinced. "Perhaps," he allowed. "But if I held my sword in battle, it isn't as if I have any notion at all what to *do* with it."

Pryder did an experimental thrust, testing the reach of the blade on empty air, and then righted himself, glancing at Galaad. "Well, we've got you a proper sword, which is the first step. Perhaps now it's time to teach you how to use it."

When Galaad recalled that he'd started the morning expecting a leisurely day of relaxation before a warming fire, he had to suppress a laugh. The day may have been warm, but it was not due to a fire, and had nothing at all to do with leisure.

Galaad sweated through the rough fabric of his linen tunic, the Saeson sword in his hand feeling like a lead weight. It had been hours now, but seemed like days, since Pryder had cleared a space for them at the rear of the hall, now vacated as the natives had gone about their daily business, and begun training Galaad in the rudiments of the blade.

The first thing that Galaad learned was that he was holding the sword all wrong. That was fairly easily addressed. Then he was told that his posture and stance was completely incorrect, which proved somewhat more involved to make right. When he was standing correctly, with his arms and legs appropriately positioned and the sword gripped properly in hand, he'd expected the next thing Pryder to teach him would have something to do with a thrust or cut, a parry or block.

Instead, Pryder had insisted that he stand immobile in that posture for as long as possible. It was essential, Pryder explained, that the appropriate stance become instinctual to Galaad, and the best first step in accomplishing that was to accustom his muscles to the feeling.

Finally, when it seemed to Galaad as if he couldn't remain in that position for a moment longer, the sword held at the ready, Pryder had shown him how to take a step forward. Galaad joked that he'd been taking steps forward almost since he was a babe-in-arms, and knew well how to perambulate, but Pryder explained that it was important that he knew how to advance and retreat without losing his sure footing, to remain balanced while stepping forward and back, of course keeping otherwise in his ready stance with his sword held at the proper angle.

And so Galaad stepped forward. Then Pryder demonstrated how to step back, and he did. And forward again, and back, and forward and back, again and again, each time with Pryder pointing out where he had gone wrong and where his movements could be corrected, until Galaad felt for certain that he had worn a groove with his steps in the flagstones.

The nearest fire blazed some distance off, but though its heat failed to reach across the expanse of the hall, Galaad felt no chill, warmed from within by his constant exertions.

"Taking as many steps as this," Galaad said breathlessly, when Pryder at last allowed him a break, "I feel that I ought to have been getting somewhere."

Pryder chuckled and slapped Galaad on the back between his shoulder blades in good humor. "Ah, but I think you *are* making some progress, at that. Your advance and retreat are considerably more assured than they were just a short while ago."

Some of the other captains now lounged on chairs by the fireside, some distance off, watching the lesson with expressions of amusement.

"Perhaps," Galaad said, unconvinced. "But to speak of progress, I thought when you'd promised to teach me the uses of the sword that I'd learn . . . well, how to use the sword." He leaned on his sword, its point on the ground. "So far all I've learned is how to hold the blasted thing."

Pryder swept out with a kick, the side of his foot smacking into the flat of Galaad's blade, knocking it to one side, the point sending up sparks as it ground against the hard stones underfoot. Galaad, off balance, stumbled and nearly fell, only barely managing to right himself and remain on his feet.

"The next thing you should learn is to treat your blade with a little respect," Pryder said sternly, his eyes narrowed. "One does not lean on his sword like a farmer leaning on his hoe." He shook his head, disbelieving. "You should cherish your blade, even revere it."

The color rose in Galaad's cheek, and he averted his eyes.

"Still," Pryder said, his tone soothing, "I can understand your frustration. When I was a child, and first learning the art of the blade, I felt that it would be forever before I acquired any skill of practical use. The old campaigner who taught my brother and me had insisted on a solid grounding in the fundamentals before we ever crossed swords, blunt and wooden or no." He sighed, seeming to look back on fondness to those days. "And while you've many long hours to go before you're ready for anything but the most basic of fundamentals, perhaps a brief demonstration of a more advanced technique would not be completely out of order."

Pryder turned to address the captains lounging some distance away.

"Lugh?" he called. "A moment of your time, if you please."

With a scowl and grumble, the Gael reluctantly pushed off his seat and ambled across the floor to where they stood. "What?" Lugh asked, his voice only somewhat slurred by the heroic amounts of wine he'd already drunk by midday to deaden the still-lingering pain of his bitten hand.

"I was wondering if you would assist me in demonstrating your signature attack for our young friend here."

Lugh cocked an eyebrow, his hand drifting almost unconsciously to the sword hilt ever present on his hip. "What, my 'answer'? You want me to poke a hole in him, then?"

Pryder laughed when he saw Galaad's widened eyes and horrified expression.

"No," Pryder explained, smiling in his beard, "I think shadow fencing with air should prove sufficient for our purposes."

Lugh shrugged. "Have it your way."

As the Gael drew his blade, Galaad could see his gratitude at not having been bitten on his sword hand. Then, Lugh took up a position in the empty space before them, standing much as Pryder had been teaching Galaad to do, but with his dominant left foot forward instead and with considerable more ease than Galaad had been able to muster.

"So, you've got to picture some bugger standing here, right? Making a nuisance of himself." Lugh held his sword in his left hand with the point towards the ground, his right hand behind him, looking over his left shoulder at some imagined opponent.

Galaad nodded when Lugh glanced his way, in affirmation.

"So it's attack and block, attack and block, that sort of dung, right?" Lugh moved the point of his sword in a tiny wave, halfheartedly miming the exchange. "He takes a swing at you, you knock it aside and take a swing at him, on and on." He sighed, wearily. "That kind of nonsense gets old, let me tell you."

Galaad glanced to Pryder, who was standing to one side, his arms folded, a faint smile visible behind his beard.

"So when you think you've had enough," Lugh went on, "then you've just got to wait for your moment, and then . . ."

Lugh seemed to explode into motion, all at once. He extended his left arm to its full extension, the blade held straight out, point first, while at the same time kicking his left leg forward, his heel barely skimming the floor, and straightening his right leg out, throwing his right arm behind him. The combined effect of these movements was to push his body forward in a single, fluid motion, as powerfully as an arrow leaving a bow.

The heel of his left foot struck the flagstones, and as his foot rocked forward his leg bent and absorbed his forward momentum, his shoulders, hips, right arm, and left thigh held parallel to the ground.

". . . strike," Lugh said casually, completing his thought.

The move had increased the reach of Lugh's thrust remarkably and had allowed him to cover a considerable amount of ground in a lightning-fast strike.

"What the devil was *that*?" Galaad's mouth hung open.

"That," Pryder said admiringly, "is why they call him 'Long Hand.'"

Lugh straightened with a shrug. "It's just something I worked out some years back. I call it my 'answer.' But it's a move that's held me in good stead a time or two, I can tell you."

Galaad nodded, eyes wide. "I can well imagine." He tightened his grip on his own sword, playing back the move in his mind. "Please, if you don't mind, sir . . . ?"

"Yes?" Lugh asked. "What is it?"

"Could you do it again?" Galaad asked, a hungry look in his eyes.

A watch was posted the second night that the seven were in Llongborth, out-side the doors of the hall, vigilant for any sign of the Huntsman or his hounds. But the night passed without any appearance by the spectral visitors, and those within the hall were allowed to slumber uninterrupted.

Galaad was among them, wedged into a narrow space and bordered on every side by bodies, but while the hall reverberated gently with the rustling and snoring of the many sleepers, Galaad himself was unable to find solace in sleep. He'd had another of his visions during the evening meal, the smell of the hearty stewpot before them replaced by the scent of flowers and the cozy red glow of the hearthfire forgotten in the blinding white flash. The images had been the same as always, as had the emotional content of the message, but for the first time, beneath the sudden and pervasive sense of bliss that he felt, Galaad detected a tiny glimmer of fear, a minor but persistent irritant.

Whether this fear was his own, or else part of the feelings engendered in him by the vision, Galaad couldn't say. But knowing that there was some connection between the tower of glass, the White Lady imprisoned within, and the haunting figure of the Huntsman gave new meaning to the vision. The White Lady had always called for assistance, for rescue, but until now it had never occurred to Galaad to wonder, rescue from *what*?

The Huntsman was part of the equation, that much was certain. Was he the power which held the White Lady prisoner, or instead some agent of that power? And if he were only agent, and not the power in himself, then what did that suggest about the nature of the Huntsman's master?

When Galaad's vision ended, and his senses returned to him, he found that no one had noticed his momentary fugue, the dining continuing unabated around him. He returned to his meal, though as the scent of flowers faded in his nostrils, he found that the food tasted only of ashes in his mouth.

CHAPTER SEVENTEEN

Jubilee

T HE NEXT MORNING, Blank was awoken from a much needed and pro-
tracted slumber by someone ringing his front doorbell. Pulling on a
Japanese dressing gown of black silk embroidered with red and gold, making
it the most colorful item of clothing in his current wardrobe, Blank left his
sleeping chamber, crossed the library, and entered the foyer. Opening the
door, he found a telegraph boy at the threshold, in a crisp brown uniform and
matching cap, a leather satchel over his shoulder. The slip of paper the boy
presented was from Superintendent Melville and in abbreviated words indicated that there had been a discovery in the early morning hours behind the
Tivoli Music Hall that Blank was certain to find of interest.

Blank tipped the boy, shut the door, and returned to his bedchamber to
bathe and dress. Melville had been circumspect in the details of his commu-
niqué, but it was clear from reading between the lines that the so-called
Jubilee Killer had likely struck again.

Without calling ahead to warn her, Blank knocked on the door of
Number 9, Bark Place. When Mrs. Pool answered the door, a barely concealed scowl of disapproval at finding him standing on the step, he said,
"Kindly give these to your mistress," and handed her the bouquet of long-
stemmed white roses he'd purchased on the way. Tucked in between the
stems, speared on one of the longer thorns, was a card.

Mrs. Pool left Blank standing in the entryway, and in moments Miss

Bonaventure was standing at the top of the stairs in a nightgown, the roses in one hand, the card in the other. "*Miss Bonaventure, we are needed,*'" she read aloud. She smiled. "Blank, why do I get the impression that your gift of flowers arrives with some strings attached?"

Mrs. Pool, scandalized at her employer appearing before a gentleman caller in such a state of undress—practically *naked*—stuck her head out from around the corner and glared at them, before ducking back out of sight.

"Well, Miss Bonaventure, I'm afraid that I must interrupt your much deserved rest. It appears that our friend the Jubilee Killer has been busy."

A short while later, Blank and Miss Bonaventure arrived at the front door of the Tivoli. It was on the south side of the Strand, across from the Adelphi and next door to the Savoy.

"It's been just ages since we've been to the theater, Blank," Miss Bonaventure said, stepping down from the hansom cab that had carried them. "When was the last we saw together? Was it *The Importance of Being Earnest* at St. James's?"

Blank tugged down the front of his waistcoat, which had ridden up in the cab, and scowled unconsciously. "No," he said with a shake of his head. With his silver-topped cane he pointed up the street at the Lyceum. "It was *King Arthur.*"

"Ah!" Miss Bonaventure clapped her hands. "Of course. With Arthur Sullivan's incidental score, and Henry Irving as that other Arthur, the one with the sword."

"Don't forget Ellen Terry's Guenevere," Blank said, helpfully.

"Forget it? I wish I *could*. Ghastly."

Blank shrugged. "I liked the scenery and costumes well enough, but then you never can go too far wrong with Burne-Jones. Bram Stoker was wise to bring him in on the production."

"Bram Stoker, the writer?" Miss Bonaventure asked.

"Bram Stoker, the theater manager," Blank answered. "Though I understand that both writer and manager receive their mail at the same address and are married to the same woman."

"We shall have to go to the theater again together soon, you and I," Miss Bonaventure said, threading her arm through his.

"I expect we shall momentarily," Blank said, guiding her towards the door, "but I doubt it will be quite the experience you're looking for."

Miss Bonaventure smiled at him. "Well, if the experience is worse than that of Carr's *King Arthur*, I shall be very much surprised."

As it happened, the body had been discovered not in the Tivoli Music Hall itself, but in a studio built behind it. The woman had been identified as one Miss Cecilia Villers, and her body had been discovered first thing that morning by William Kennedy-Laurie Dickson, an employee of the Mutoscope and Biograph Company that leased the studio from the Tivoli.

Kennedy-Laurie Dickson, it appeared, had briefly left the studio to conduct some business in the city, but was expected back momentarily. While they waited, Blank and Miss Bonaventure questioned the other employees on hand to learn what they could. What they discovered amounted to very little: that the principal address of the Mutoscope and Biograph Company was 2 to 4 Cecil Court, Westminster; that their films included "Pelicans at the Zoo," "The Home Life of a Hungarian Family," "Elephants at the Zoo," and "The Coldstream Guard"; that the "Biograph" was a projector using wide-gauge sixty-eight-millimeter film, and the "Mutoscope" was a viewing device utilizing bromide prints in a "flick-book" principle; and that the cameras used in the studio were manufactured by Perihelion, Unlimited Company of London. All of which was perhaps interesting, if marginally, in the way that weather reports from other countries might be of trivial interest but hardly have any bearing on one's own daily plans. The only information of any relevance which Blank and Miss Bonaventure were able to procure was the fact that Miss Villers, a photographer of some small talent, had been these past weeks employed as a camera operator by the Mutoscope and Biograph Company, who were so desperate for material to meet the growing demand for moving pictures that they were willing to overlook the fact that she was a woman. That her films seemed to be several cuts above the lackluster record of animals in cages which accounted for a significant percentage of the company's output, it seemed, had no doubt argued somewhat in her favor.

Miss Bonaventure recalled having seen some of Miss Villers photographic work on exhibition in a small gallery. On the evidence of those pictures alone, Miss Villers had obviously been influenced by the work of the late Julia Margaret Cameron.

Blank was somewhat surprised, as he often was, at Miss Bonaventure's seemingly encyclopedic knowledge of women who excelled in the arts and sciences. Though to his certain knowledge Miss Bonaventure had not met many if any of the women in question personally, when their names were mentioned she was invariably able to recall some salient details from their personal and professional biographies. It was as though Miss Bonaventure had made a study of successful women, though through the use of what resources Blank was unable to guess.

"I knew she didn't do any more photography," Miss Bonaventure had said, absently, staring off into empty space, "but I'd just assumed she married, or . . ." She trailed off, and caught Blank looking at her. "I'm sorry," she said, bringing her features under control. "We'd never met, but having seen her work, I felt that I knew her, somehow."

So far as Blank had been able to discover, Miss Villers had once done a single gallery show, and that one at a small and seldom-visited gallery of little repute. He wondered how many photos might have been displayed for Miss Bonaventure to come to know her so well.

Finally, William Kennedy-Laurie Dickson arrived. He wore a Homburg and a neatly trimmed little mustache, and spoke English with an American accent, with the slightest traces of France creeping around the edges of some words. He explained that he had immigrated to England the month before to take up an appointment as technical manager and cameraman for the newly formed Mutoscope and Biograph Company. Then, without prompting, he explained that he had until 1895 been a senior associate to Thomas Alva Edison, whom he described as a "rat bastard," their association having ended when Edison discovered that Dickson had been sharing trade secrets with his competitors, the Lathams.

"Well, thank you for agreeing to answer our questions," Blank said, having to work to keep his slight smile from erupting into full laughter. He'd not had to ply Dickson with one of his calling cards, or employ his mesmerism in the slightest. The cameraman was clearly *born* to talk and needed only the slightest provocation to let out a torrent of words, on whatever topic.

Dickson continued, unabated, talking about the KMCD group he'd set up with three friends, Koopman, Marvin, and Casler, still more "rat bastards," who had failed to offer him a senior management position when the initial development work for the company had ended. He'd spent the previous year and the early part of 1897 as a traveling cameraman, filming in various parts of the United States, living out of hotels and roadside inns, and his roaming finally ended when he accepted the Mutoscope and Biograph Company's offer and moved to London. Only after accepting the offer and relocating, though, was he informed by his new employers, whom he refrained from calling "rat bastards," but only just, that he would be expected to travel widely throughout Britain and Europe, providing the company with a steady stream of filmed product.

"You're right, that hardly seems fair," Blank said, his manner consoling. "Now, about the matter of the dead woman. . . ."

Dickson blustered on, hardly pausing for breath, segueing from the topic of his new employers to the other employees with whom he'd been forced to work. Including the aforementioned Miss Cecilia Villers, who if it had escaped everyone's notice, was a *woman*. That he was expected every morning to restore the damage done in the night to the camera and its settings by the second-shift crew was bad enough, but that the inept camera operator in question was of the distaff variety simply added insult to injury.

"So she was not an accomplished photographer?" Miss Bonaventure asked.

Dickson allowed that Miss Villers had produced a few very watchable films, though perturbed to be questioned by a woman, but went on to say that anyone could fall off a building and hit a bucket of water, but that it didn't make them marksmen, which analogy seemed to escape Blank and Miss Bonaventure. That Miss Viller's work was evidently skillful, it appeared, was not evidence of her skill.

"What can you tell us about the scene this morning?" Blank asked.

Here, Dickson seemed to soften, remembering the sight that had greeted him on first arriving at the studio a few short hours ago. He recounted that he had arrived early, not long after dawn, having not yet accustomed his sleeping schedule to the early London sunrise. He had gone to unlock the studio, as was his habit, and been surprised to find the door standing open. Dickson had entered to investigate, and almost collided with another man on his way out. This stranger had been tall, dressed in a shabby suit, and completely bald. His skin, that of his hands and on his head and neck, was chalky white, almost cadaverous in coloring. There was something strange, too, about the man's eyes, but Dickson had only caught a glimpse of them and could not put into words just what it was that had struck him odd.

"So the man rushed past you and out of the building, and that's when you found the body?" Blank glanced to Miss Bonaventure, and then back to Dickson.

Dickson allowed that he was correct.

Miss Bonaventure leaned in close to Blank. She'd had the chance to talk with the constable who'd first arrived on the scene, in response to Dickson's urgent call for help. According to the constable, Miss Bonaventure said, in a voice pitched so low only Blank was close enough to hear, the victim had been dead some little while before Dickson supposedly found her.

Dickson shared rooms with two of the other employees, temporarily he assured Blank and Miss Bonaventure, and when these employees arrived at the studio, they were able to corroborate parts of Dickson's story, namely, that he had left their rooms shortly after dawn, making enough noise to wake them in the process.

"Did you notice anything in his hands," Miss Bonaventure asked, "this man you encountered at the door? Any sort of tool or weapon?"

Dickson shook his head and said that he'd taken careful note of the man's hands as a matter of course. He'd seen that they were both empty. He'd had nothing under his arm or across his back, come to that. The man might well have secreted something in his pockets, but Dickson was reluctant to guess, not having seen anything to suggest it.

"Thank you," Blank said, taking Miss Bonaventure's arm and backing away from Dickson. "I think we have the information we need."

Dickson, seeing his audience slipping away, but with a good head of steam built up, continuing his harangue, simply shifting targets, and without missing a beat turned to one of the laborers standing nearby and started castigating him for the poor quality of the painted set at the opposite side of the studio.

Counting themselves lucky to have extricated themselves from Dickson, Blank and Miss Bonaventure walked out of the studio into the London morning.

Based on the evidence at hand, the woman would have been murdered some-time shortly after Dickson had woken but long before he'd have been able to reach the studio, eliminating him as a suspect. The natural assumption was that the hairless, chalky-skinned man whom Dickson had glimpsed fleeing the scene was the Jubilee Killer, but Blank wasn't so sure.

"Remember," he said, as he and Miss Bonaventure made their way to New Scotland Yard, "that the constable thought the woman had been dead for some time when Dickson discovered her. But if that is the case, why would the killer have lingered so long beside the body?"

Miss Bonaventure nodded. "And, as Dickson reports, he saw no weapon or cutting implement in the man's hand, and the constable who arrived on the scene saw no indication of one having been left behind."

"True." Blank narrowed his eyes, thoughtfully. "Well, perhaps something can be learned from viewing the poor woman's remains."

Unfortunately, as it happened, all that was learned from their viewing was that seeing so much blood in recent days had not inured them to the sight of more, and that Miss Villers appeared to have been dispatched with the same implement used on the three women and Mr. Brade before her. Unlike the three women, though, Miss Villers had not been decapitated or had her limbs severed, and unlike Mr. Brade she had not died with her back to her attacker. She had sustained grievous wounds on her torso and her upper legs, and had lost several fingers on her left hand, perhaps when raising it to ward off a blow. The cuts were clean and straight, as all the others had been, the cutting implement seeming to have passed unimpeded through skin, muscle, and bone.

In death, it was easy to see that Miss Villers had been a handsome woman in life, if perhaps with coarser features than society would deem aesthetic. Her clothes were well tailored if not fashionable, and beneath her skirts she had worn well-cobbled walking boots. In all, Miss Villers appeared to be a respectable unmarried woman of the middle classes, free from disease or other impairment. The postmortem had been conducted by Dr. Thomas Bond, and when he studied it, Blank for the first time felt no inclination to throttle the man. Bond's summary of the woman's condition at death and the nature of her wounds were essentially in line with his own thinking.

Blank and Miss Bonaventure thanked the constable who had, on Melville's orders, shown them to the body, and then went to visit the flat which the police had found registered in her name. It was a stolidly middle-class residence in Islington, not far from the Agricultural Hall, off Theberton Street.

Miss Villers had been in the early years of her third decade, the daughter of a trader, and had been fairly well set up by her family. Despite the respectable address, though, and the relative good quality of the furnishings, Miss Viller's flat was fairly small, one might even say cozy, with something of a threadbare feel to it. Aside from a wardrobe and dresser, a sideboard, bed, and nightstand, there was little in the room to indicate it was even inhabited. And aside from a framed print over the mantle, nothing to suggest the character of the woman who had lived there.

Blank stepped close to the print and read aloud, "*For I'm to be Queen o' the May, Mother, I'm to be Queen o' the May.*"

"What's that?" Miss Bonaventure asked, setting a handheld looking glass back on the dresser and coming to stand beside him.

"It's from Tennyson," Blank said. "One of his *Idylls of the King*, if I'm not mistaken."

It was a photographic print, depicting a woman holding a wreath of flowers in one hand, her head tilted slightly to one side. She had a broad-brimmed hat on, pushed back, looking almost like a halo, and was wearing a white dress, with her long wavy hair falling past her shoulders. Written beneath the print was the inscription Blank had recited.

"If that's Miss Villers's work," Blank went on, "then she was quite talented, indeed."

"She may well have been," Miss Bonaventure said, "but you'll need to look elsewhere for evidence of it." She pointed a finger at the photograph. "This one is by another dead woman, actually. Julia Margaret Cameron."

Blank glanced at her, and then looked back to the photograph, appraisingly.

Miss Bonaventure drifted off and went to the sideboard along the wall. There was unopened mail lying in a heap, all of recent vintage.

"Here," she said, opening the first and holding the contents aloft for Blank to see. "A cheque, made payable to Miss Cecilia Villers, and drawn on an account with the name 'LRT.'"

"Long Range Transportation?" Blank ventured.

"Little Red Train?" Miss Bonaventure countered.

"Less Redemptive Taxidermy?" Blank chuckled slightly, and came to take the cheque from her hands. "What else is there?"

"Just a letter," she said, holding it up. "From a W.B. Taylor, addressed to Miss Cecilia Villers." She read aloud.

Dearest Miss Villers,

I am in receipt of the photographs you've sent, those which depict an early passage from "The Raid on the Unworld." I can hardly express my first responses in words, which seemed instead a tumult of emotions. Coupled with Mr. B's scenery and costumes, I think your photographs have precisely captured the feeling I had hoped to evoke, the frisson I felt when first reading Lady P's account. I can't tell you how grateful you've made this country boy by taking on the project, and I know that I speak for Lord A and the rest of the league when I say that we're proud to have you on the team.

(When next we meet, I have some notes for you about how you might approach the next stage of the project, which I'll refrain from outlining here, for fear of sullying these well-wishes with criticism.)

Sincerely,
W.B. Taylor

"League?" Blank raised an eyebrow. He glanced at the cheque, and then at the framed print on the wall. "LRT?"

Miss Bonaventure caught his meaning, and gave a slight smile. "League of the Round Table, perhaps?"

"The same which counted the late Xenophon Brade among its members?"

"Could he be the letter's 'Mr. B,' perhaps?" Miss Bonaventure asked.

"I think," Blank said, putting his bowler hat back on his head, "a visit to this 'W.B. Taylor' might be in order."

Blank and Miss Bonaventure found themselves a short while later standing before the return address listed on the envelope for W.B. Taylor, which was revealed to be a modest residence in Paddington. Ringing the bell, they were greeted at the door by Taylor himself.

If Blank had formed an impression of the man based on hearing a few lines of correspondence read aloud, his impression had struck far of the mark. The man who stood before them, towering some inches above himself and Miss Bonaventure, looked like he'd just stepped from the pages of a penny dreadful about the wild American west. Broad-shouldered, with large, long-fingered hands, he had a long drooping mustache and a small pointed beard on his chin, his hair worn brushing the collar of his starched white shirt. Judging by the gray which shot through his hair, and the wrinkles which ran from the corners of his eyes, which made him look as if he were perpetually squinting in the sun's glare, he looked to be about fifty years of age, though in evident excellent health. He wore a brocade waistcoat over his shirtsleeves, a string tie was knotted at his neck, and on his feet were western-style boots.

"Mr. Taylor?" Blank began.

"Look," barked the man in the doorway in a brusque American accent, "if you've come on Cody's say-so, you can go hang, and to thunder with Cody!"

Blank smiled. "You're American."

"Hell, no!" Taylor snapped. "I'm from Texas."

Blank took his hat from his head and held it over his chest with both hands. "I believe there may be some misunderstanding, Mr. Taylor. I'm afraid we don't know any Cody."

"We're here to question you in connection with the deaths of Mr. Xenophon Brade and Miss Cecilia Villers," Miss Bonaventure put in, with less tact than Blank might have liked.

"Cecila?" Taylor said, blinking. "Dead? I . . . I didn't know."

"Killed by the same hand," Miss Bonaventure explained, "or so it would appear."

Either the man was a better actor than any Blank had previously seen, or he legitimately had not known about the death of Miss Villers. It was hardly surprising if he didn't, since the murder had only been discovered a few short hours before.

Taylor stood in the door, blinking in the bright June afternoon sun, seemingly adrift.

"May we come in?" Blank asked, gently.

Taylor nodded absently, and stepped aside to usher them in. "Sure, sure," he said, his eyes unfocused.

The rooms beyond the door were small but crowded with memories. If Miss Villers's flat had betrayed little about the woman who had lived there, Taylor's rooms spoke volumes. On the floor was a Mexican blanket spread out as a rug, and on the wall a pair of crossed cavalry sabers and a long-barreled rifle. On a hat rack near the door hung a ten-gallon hat and a gun belt, weighed down by a LeMat revolver. Tacked up on the wall, unframed, was a poster advertising Buffalo Bill's Wild West Exhibition, with the name "LITTLE BILL TAYLOR" emblazoned on the top and the legend "THE KNIGHT OF THE TEXAS PLAINS" at the bottom, and at its center a photo of a slightly younger W.B. Taylor surrounded by engraved scenes depicting him trick riding, shooting glass balls out of the air with a Spencer repeating rifle, demonstrating quick draws with a revolver, and so on.

Blank scanned the spines of the books on the crowded shelves while Miss Bonaventure sat down on the settee, her legs crossed. Spread on the table was a copy of an American paper, which on closer examination proved to be the April 19th edition of the *Dallas Morning News*. The front page carried a banner headline about a skirmish between a Turkish battery and a Grecian steamer, but it was a headline on page 5 that caught Miss Bonaventure's eye.

"'*The Great Aerial Wanderer*,'" she read aloud.

Blank stepped behind her and read over her shoulder.

The story concerned an airship which had apparently been reported in recent editions of the paper, which had landed at the Texan towns of Greenville and Stephenville and subsequently been seen to explode in midair. The article in question consisted primarily of the testimony of a Mr. C. L. McIlhany, who claimed to have seen an airship himself. Mr. McIlhany concluded his statement with the following observation. "*And say, what you reckon is going to happen when dynamiters get to riding in airships and dropping bombs down on folks and cities? Is the world ready for airships?*"

A shiver ran down Blank's spine as he remembered what he'd learned concerning aerial bombing in the School of Thought, however jumbled and garbled the intelligence had been. He straightened, saw a peculiar glint in Miss Bonaventure's eye, and wondered for the thousandth time just what she knew of what lay in store for their beloved London in the decades to come.

Whatever her foreknowledge of events to come, Miss Bonaventure played the article off as the hoax it doubtless was. "It must be longer than I'd realized since last I visited the United States," she said lightly, an eyebrow raised, "if they've already begun to travel by airship."

"Hmm?" Taylor looked over, distracted. He saw the paper spread across table. "Oh, that. My brother Jack lives in Recondito, California, and sends me a stack of American newspapers from time to time. I think he intends to make me all homesick, reminding me of what I've left behind, but it tends to have the opposite effect, most times, when I read bunkum like that."

"How long has it been, Mr. Taylor?" Miss Bonaventure asked, casually. "Since you came to England?"

"I came across the big water with Cody's Wild West show in 1887, ma'am, but when he pulled up stakes and went back to the States, I stayed up."

"It's 'miss,' actually," Miss Bonaventure corrected discreetly.

Taylor nodded and picked up a glass ball from atop a dressing table. The ball was the twin of those Taylor was depicted shooting out of midair in the poster. Was it one that he'd missed, all those years before? He tossed it up in the air and caught it neatly, and then again, over and over. It seemed to Blank to be some sort of nervous habit which the tall American did unconsciously, as another would tap a foot or drum fingers on a table.

"So Cecilia's dead, is she?" Taylor shook his head, disbelievingly. "Hell, Brade's body's barely cold, and now there's Cecilia to be laid out right beside him." He paused, thoughtfully, snatching the glass ball out of midair and holding it for a moment, frozen. "I gotta wonder if someone ain't come gunning for us."

"I wonder, Mr. Taylor, about this Cody you mentioned," Blank said, casually looking up from his examination of the titles on the bookshelf. "Did you mean Colonel Cody, he of the Wild West show?"

"Hell, no," Taylor spat. "I meant Samuel Cody. The polecat claims to be from Texas, but I've got it on good authority he's really from Iowa, of all places. And his name's just as phony. It isn't even Cody, but Cowdrey or some such thing. Hell, Buffalo Bill had to sue the bastard twice, to keep him from using the name 'Wild West' in his act, and to keep the bastard from claiming to be Buffalo Bill's own son on his playbills, and his wife Bill Cody's daughter."

"And he's been troubling you, this Samuel Cody?" Miss Bonaventure asked, looking up from the papers before her.

"He tried to talk me into investing in the development of some new rapid-fire pistol he couldn't get the British government to buy, and now he's trying to put on a new Wild West revue at Alexandra Palace and wants me to perform in it."

"The return of the 'Knight of the Plains,' Mr. Taylor?" Blank indicated the poster with a nod.

A blush rose in Taylor's cheek, and an incongruously boyish expression of embarrassment flitted across his rugged features. "Ah, that's just huckstering," Taylor said, glancing at the poster. "They needed to put something to balance out my name, I guess." He looked back to Miss Bonaventure and Blank. "But no, I'm retired from all that now, no matter what that bastard Sam Cody might ask."

A momentary silence stretched between them, as Taylor's attention drifted away, his expression growing once more careworn.

"If you don't mind our asking," Miss Bonaventure asked, at length, "how were you connected with Mr. Brade and Miss Villers? Were you friends?"

Taylor snapped back into focus and shook his head. "I don't know as I'd call us friends, miss. Professional acquaintances, maybe. I met Brade in the league, and then I met Cecilia when Lady P hired her to take the pictures for our big project, 'The Raid on the Unworld.'"

"Lady P?" Blank prompted, from the bookshelves.

"Lady Priscilla Cavendish," Taylor clarified.

"And they, along with yourself, belonged to this League of the Round Table?" Blank asked.

Taylor cocked an eyebrow, perhaps curious how Blank had come by the organization's name, but didn't voice a question about it, if he had one. Instead, he nodded, and said, "Yep. The group started up a few years back, as I understand it, when Baron Carmody got back to London after his trip to Africa went south. They roped me into it after reading some poems I'd written about King Arthur."

Now it was Blank's turn to raise an eyebrow. "Really? I wouldn't have taken you for a poet."

Taylor smiled, a bit sheepishly. "Well, see, I'd read Tennyson and just couldn't see what the fuss was about. Near as I could see, the fellow knew damned little to nothing about horses or warfare, which made him pretty ill-suited to write about a warrior king and horseman. I was practically born in the saddle, having ridden the Pony Express with Bill Cody and my twin brother, Jack, so I knew about horses. And I knew men who'd fought in the Mormon Wars and the Kansas border ruffians wars, and saw a bit of action myself fighting for the North in the War between the States, so I knew something of fighting, as well. So I figured I was better suited than most to write about Arthur, even if I wasn't exactly a dab hand at the writing itself."

"You were in the American Civil War, then?" Miss Bonaventure asked.

"Sure was, miss," Taylor said proudly. "I was one of the Red Legged Scouts under the command of Captain Tuff."

Blank paused in his perusal of the shelves and pulled down a slim volume. It was bound in green cloth and had the title *Horseman King* on the spine and the name *William Blake Taylor* stamped beneath. "This is your own work, I take it?" Blank flipped to the indicia, and saw that it had been self-published in an edition of five hundred copies.

Taylor was suddenly bashful, like a boy who'd suddenly found himself pantless in company, and hurried to take the book from Blank's hands. "Well, I know that I'm just a cowboy poet with aspirations that outreach my talent," he said, apologetically, "but I've got visions in my head that I just can't shake, and writing them down is the only way to get shut of them. Still, I'm a damned sight better at writing than Captain Jack Crawford, self-styled 'Poet Scout of the Black Hills,' so at least I can carry on knowing I'm not the worst damned scribbler to come out of the West."

Blank offered a gentle smile as Taylor slipped the slim volume into his pocket.

"When did you last see Mr. Brade or Miss Villers, if you don't mind me asking," Miss Bonaventure put in.

Taylor scratched his chin beneath his beard, thoughtfully. "I hadn't seen Cecilia in a fortnight, I suppose, but I saw Brade last week, at the regular League meeting."

"And when is the *next* league meeting, Mr. Taylor?" Blank asked.

Taylor looked up at the ceiling for a moment, as if consulting some mental calendar, and then said, with some surprise, "Tonight, I reckon."

Blank smiled. "You know, I would very much like to accompany you and meet the other members. Do you think that could be arranged?"

Taylor had provided an address in Mayfair, near Grosvenor Square, and told Blank and Miss Bonaventure to meet him there at seven o'clock in the evening. He would arrange matters with Baron Carmody, whose residence it was, and then they would be able to question the league members regarding the late Mr. Brade and Miss Villers.

The American cowboy poet was clearly shaken by news of Miss Villers's killing, perhaps not as much because of her death in and of itself, but for what it suggested about his own prospects. The only connection between any of the Jubilee Killer's victims was between Brade and Villers, and was the

League of the Round Table. If the league were the uniting factor, then Taylor
was right to suppose that he or one of the other members might be the killer's
next target.

Saying their farewells to Taylor, Blank and Miss Bonaventure returned to
York Place. She lounged on the divan reading a novel while he consulted his
Whitaker's, his social registers, his *Burke's Peerage*, and his *Who's Who*,
sketching out portraits of the Baron Carmody and Lady Priscilla, the two as-
yet unknown members of the league. Then, when he had done, Miss Bonaventure set aside her novel, and he recited aloud the facts as he knew them.

"Priscilla Anna Cavendish née Griffith," Blank said, his notes spread
before him on the desk. "From her first husband, fourth Baronet of Sherring,
Lady Priscilla was bequeathed an honorific; her second husband, however,
Thomas Aston Cavendish, a former officer in the Tenth Hussars and himself a
widower of the daughter of the third Baron Balinrobe, left her only a large
sum of money, which doubtless proved more useful. Widowed a second time,
Lady Priscilla opted not to remarry, announcing publically that she prefers
instead the company of women and is now an avowed tribadist." He paused
and looked up from his papers. "If anyone thought Lady Priscilla's claims to
be anything but a bald attempt at scandal, she'd likely be prosecuted for inde-
cency, but as it is, she remains unmolested. So to speak. In any event, Lady
Priscilla has pledged to spend her remaining years pursuing her 'grand work.'"

"Which is?" Miss Bonaventure prompted.

"It would seem," Blank answered, "that Lady Priscilla is something of a
self-taught scholar, following in the footsteps of Lady Charlotte Guest, she of
Mabinogion fame."

Miss Bonaventure nodded, and Blank continued with his recital.

"Arthur Carmody, the tenth Baron Carmody. Lord Arthur had been a
member of the Hythloday Club but let his dues lapse after the tragic events
of his expedition to Africa, during which he lost his wife and infant son. He
splits his time between the ancestral residence of Belhorm in Somerset, a
summer home in Brighton, and a large house in Mayfair off Grosvenor
Square, the address for which Mr. Taylor was kind enough to provide."

Blank could not help but be reminded of the first Baron Carmody, who'd
been a member of the School of Night during the days of Queen Elizabeth

and King James. Robert Carmody had been possessed of a keen intellect and a lunge few swordsmen would turn aside. He'd done proud service as a Stranger of the School of Night, serving the crown with distinction. That the present-day claimants to the School's long tradition, Absalom Quince and his band of lunatics, had fallen so far from the body's former glory was no smirch against the work Carmody and his fellows had done in olden days.

CHAPTER EIGHTEEN
Millennium

T HE DOOR ON THE FAR WALL OF THE LIBRARY opened onto the bottom steps of a wrought-iron spiral staircase that climbed up and up into the gloom, disappearing from view.

Stillman had dressed in a gray business suit and white Oxford shirt open at the neck and without a tie. On their way through the library, he'd strapped on a shoulder holster under his suit jacket, with his Hotspur fletcher snugged into it, and clipped a small box the size of a cigarette pack onto his belt, which he explained held additional rounds. Then he slid clunky sunglasses that he might have stolen from Buddy Holly over his eyes and started climbing the stairs. Alice, wearing her Doc Martens and leather jacket, followed him up. He'd told her to leave her backpack behind, but she refused.

"You never know when you may have to jam," Alice said.

"Suit yourself," Stillman said.

Figured that he'd never seen *The Breakfast Club*.

It was dark at the top of the stairs, though the echoes of their own footsteps coming back from the walls suggested a fairly large space. Alice barked her shin against some sort of ledge and then backed into a rough wall.

"Just where are we going, anyway?"

"We're already there, my dear."

Alice heard a car door open, and then the space flooded with illumination as the interior lights came up.

The damned thing looked like Speed Racer's Mach Five, but painted fire engine red. A convertible with curving lines, a pointed back end, and a point-backwards-bullet-shaped headrest for the driver.

"What *is* this?!"

Stillman grinned and slid into the driver's seat, which was of course on the wrong side of the car. "It's a 1957 Chevy Corvette SS, of course," he said, as if it were the most natural thing in the world. "Considerably customized, you understand."

By the light from the car's interior, Alice saw that they were at one side of a largish garage, with the concrete underfoot stained by oil spills back at the dawn of time.

"Used to have a whole fleet of cars up here in the motor pool, but this was the one I drove for preference. When I was promoted from Rook One to D, I used it as my personal car. When I demobbed, as it were, and MI8 moved across the river to Lambeth, I did a bit of jiggery-pokery with the files and ended up with the deed to the decommissioned Tower of London base and the keys to the Corvette SS. Seeing as I wouldn't be getting a pension, I figured it was only my due."

Stillman turned the key in the ignition, and the engine started to rumble. Then he punched a button on the dash, and overhead Alice heard the sound of gears grinding and chains clanking.

"Hop in, now." A band of bright sunlight appeared in front of the car as a garage door scrolled up into the ceiling. "Early bird, and all of that."

Alice climbed into the passenger seat, hugging her backpack to her chest. Now she understood why Stillman had put on his sunglasses, as she squinted in the blinding morning sunlight. She fumbled in the pockets of her leather jacket for her shades, barely able to see in the glare.

"Buckle up, love." Stillman flashed her a grin and suddenly looked years younger. "I like to take turns at speed, I'm afraid."

Alice hung on for dear life and Stillman whipped the Corvette around corners, zipped ahead of buses, dodged in and out of traffic. The sound of the horns blaring was almost, but not quite, drowned out by the music blaring from the car's stereo.

Stillman yanked the cassette out of the player—the *cassette*—and tossed it aside, slotting another in its place. Alice picked it up and read the hand-written label. *Zoot Money's Big Roll Band, Transition.* Then, from the speakers came an early Bowie number, "Life on Mars?"

"Sorry if my tastes aren't quite up to date, love." Stillman grinned, his graying blond hair streaming behind him in the wind, his head resting against the flat side of the bullet-shaped headrest. "I've been underground for quite a long while now and only come up at nights for groceries and liquor." He laughed and said something that was swallowed by the wind.

"What?" Alice shouted.

"Like a vampire," Stillman said, leaning over and shouting into her ear.

Ⓐ

They sped around Piccadilly Circus, then came to a juddering halt at a red light. Stillman pointed to the towering neon sign overhead for the Temple Megastore.

"I met him once, back in the old days, when I was still Rook One and the world made a little more sense. Temple, that is. Strange fella, that. I saw him interviewed the other night. Comes across as a mix between Richard Branson and David Bowie, worth as much as both of them combined and with less charm or sex appeal than either."

The light changed, and Stillman threw the car in gear.

"Still, he knew how to throw a hell of a party, I'll give him that."

Ⓐ

The British Museum was closed. A small crowd of people, mostly families with children, milled in the forecourt lawns. Stillman breezed right up to the security guard standing by the front entrance.

"Excuse me, friend," he said. "I'd like to talk to whomever is in charge, if you don't mind."

The attendant was a South Asian who looked to be a few years older than Alice. Maybe a student working weekends. He certainly had that bored part-timer look about him.

"Sir, the museum is not open at this time. Please come back between the hours of ten o'clock and five thirty."

Stillman checked his watch. It was a few minutes after nine. "No." He shook his head. "I'm afraid that won't do." He reached into his pocket and pulled out what looked like a thin leather wallet. Then he flipped it open, like a TV cop flashing a badge, and held it under the guard's nose. But when Alice looked, she saw that there wasn't a badge, just a blank, featureless piece of white paper. "My friend and I are on some urgent business and can't be delayed. Why don't you fetch your superior, and we'll be about our business."

The expression on the guard's face changed immediately. The bored indifference was gone, replaced by a wide-eyed look of respect commingled with a little fear. "Yes, sir. Right away. Just wait here, sir."

Then the guard spun around and disappeared through the door.

Alice stepped around in front of Stillman, and got a better look at the "badge" as he was putting it away. "What? Does the sight of a blank business card strike terror into the average Londoner?"

Stillman chuckled and flipped the thin leather wallet shut. "Not exactly. It's a kind of Neuro-Linguistic Programming I learned from my mentor. Hypnosis, if you want to use a crude analogy. By modulating the pitch and tone of my voice, and adding in a bit of subvocalization, I'm able to . . ."

The rest of his explanation would have to wait for another time, since he was interrupted by the arrival of an attractive black woman in a smart business suit, her hair pulled up in a tight bun. When she spoke, it was with just the slightest hint of a West Indian accent.

"Can I help you?" She was smiling, but her suspicion was evident.

"Ah." Stillman flipped the wallet open and held the blank badge out for inspection. "My name is Stillman Waters, and this is my friend . . ." He turned to Alice, raising an eyebrow. "You know, I don't believe we were ever properly introduced."

"Alice. Alice Fell."

"My friend Alice Fell," Stillman continued, turning back to face the woman. "And we're here to investigate the disappearance of the 'Vanishing Gem.'"

"The theft, you mean?" The woman looked up from the blank badge.

"Well," Stillman said with a smile, "who's to say it didn't just . . . vanish?"

The woman pursed her lips. "The fake left in its place, for one."

"Touché." Stillman mimed a bow.

The woman seemed to consider things for a moment, then nodded. "All right, come this way. But be quick about it. We're opening to the public in less than an hour, and we're trying to keep as tight a lid on this mess as possible."

The police, apparently, had been and gone days before. If the news hadn't carried the story about the theft that morning, the public would still be none the wiser. But the decision had been made to announce, and clearly their escort was less than pleased.

Construction was ongoing at the center of the museum, a large circular court where the British Library had been housed before being moved to a new location recently, and a new courtyard with a glass and steel ceiling put in its place. It was actually because of this construction, and the attendant reorganization of the museum's holdings, their escort explained, that the gem had been discovered in the first place.

"God knows what all is down there in the basements," she explained. "Next thing you know we'll find a whole species of tour guides gone feral, eking out a rustic existence down there in the dark."

"So the gem was just discovered lying around in the basement, then?" Stillman asked.

"Well, properly secured, of course," the escort answered. "But essentially, yeah. We were in the process of changing out our last exhibit—'The Apocalypse and the Shape of Things to Come,' did you see it?" She looked disappointed when both Alice and Stillman shook their heads.

"I guess we missed the end of the world," Alice said.

"If you've seen one Apocalypse, love, you've seen them all."

"Well, anyway," the escort said, "we were moving all of that gear down at the end of April, and taking the opportunity to restructure the holdings a bit, when a locked Victorian strongbox was discovered. It didn't appear on any inventory lists or manifests, going back to the museum's founding, so there was nothing for it but to open the thing up and see."

"And that's when the gem was discovered."

"Well, it wasn't easy getting the strongbox open, let me tell you. Took the better part of a week. But when we did, yes, there was the gem." She paused to unlock a door, and then ushered them through. "Funny thing was, though it was velvet lined on the inside, it was obviously designed to hold a much larger object."

They were descending a flight of stairs now, away from the galleries open to the public on the floors aboveground, into the basements hidden beneath.

"Was that when you first suspected something wasn't right about the gem? That it might be, shall we say, 'vanishing'?"

The escort nodded. "Maybe. I had an inkling, I suppose. When we couldn't find anything about it in the museum's archives, we sent it to the Department of Conservation and Research for analysis. It was a few weeks later that they reported back that it appeared to be losing mass."

"Without burning it away in the form of energy, as light or heat or what-have-you?"

The escort nodded again. "That's right. It wasn't giving off anything, on any band of the electromagnetic spectrum, no infrared radiation, no bleed of any kind that the scientists could find, or so they tell us. But it was still getting smaller, all the time."

"Isn't that impossible?" Alice said. "What about that whole 'conservation of mass and energy' thing?"

"Well," Stillman said with a smile, "I've often found that impossible things often aren't, and implausible things never are."

"So it was kept here, was it?"

Though this room was closed to the public, the gem had been kept in a display case, even more heavily alarmed and fortified than those upstairs. As the escort explained, things like motion detectors and the like were difficult to implement in high traffic areas, but down in the basements, things were kept strictly under lock and key.

There was a titanium and reinforced leaded glass display case at the center of the room, painted with motion sensitive lasers. Within was a cushion of black velvet. For roughly a week, since it was returned from the reseach department, it had held the Vanishing Gem. Then, for a brief time, it had held a lump of mirrored glass. Now, it was vacant.

There were cameras in three corners of the room and pressure-sensitive plates on the floor. The display case itself was rigged with motion- and pressure-sensitive devices. There was a single door, of reinforced steel, and small air vents high on opposite walls, both of them alarmed.

All Alice knew about security systems, beyond standard car alarms and the like, she'd learned from TV and movies and video games. From where she stood, though, if Indiana Jones, Lara Croft, and Ethan Hunt teamed up—and, of course, really existed—they'd have a hard time breaking in and out of this room.

"And there were no tripped alarms, no broken glass, nothing?" Stillman walked around the room with his hands behind his back.

The escort shook her head. "No, nothing. Just one day the gem was there, the next it was gone."

Stillman nodded. "All right, then. I'll need access to all of the data. Tapes from the surveillance cameras, security logs, that sort of thing."

The escort regarded him warily for a moment, then went off to make the arrangements.

"Man," Alice said, impressed, "when you hypnotize someone, you don't mess around."

Stillman quirked a grin, but shook his head. "It's nothing so impressive as all that. I can't make someone do something they wouldn't do otherwise, just give them a little push. Like her, most people, they respect authority. They're happy doing what someone tells them, since it means they don't have to decide things for themselves. A little nudge to make them think you're in authority, and after that it's all beer and skittles."

Alice raised an eyebrow. "So would it work on me?"

Stillman's grin broadened. "I don't know, love. You tell me."

Then it was back to Stillman's underground home, where he fiddled with decks of VHS and Betamax players, dragging them from the elephant's graveyard of storage in the other tunnel and hooking them up to his ancient color television. Alice took her playing cards out of her backpack and dealt a few hands of solitaire while Stillman spent hours watching the grainy black-and-white video footage or poring over indecipherable security logs, or studying schematics and floorplans.

The playing cards had originally belonged to Naomi Vance, and she'd given them to her granddaughter years before when they wore out. Naomi played bridge, when she still had enough friends alive and still talking to her to do so, and when she ran out of friends just played solitaire. She was serious about her play and retired a deck when it got too worn, when too many cards had bent corners or nicked edges. Alice had come on her about to throw the deck away, only ten years old, and had insisted that it be given to her, instead. Naomi had relented, but only on the condition that she could teach her granddaughter to play.

They'd played together for years. Gin rummy, or two-handed solitaire, or hearts. Even when Alice started hanging out with Nancy and going through her rebellious phase, before it ended badly that last night on the freeway, when Alice wouldn't talk to her mother for days at a time, she and Naomi still played, every week.

Playing now, the careworn cards under her hands, reminded her of those times and helped ease the ache inside, if only a little.

"Hey, Stillman. Since you were practically 007, did that mean you had a license to kill?"

Stillman looked up from the security reports and the handwritten notes he was taking on a yellow legal pad and gave her an odd look.

"I've done the necessary, a time or two."

"Who were they?" Alice shuffled the deck.

Stillman was quiet for a long moment. "No," he said at last. "You don't get to ask that. It's not proper. How would you feel, mmm? If I were to say, 'Hey, Alice, you kill anybody lately?'"

Alice kept her eyes on the cards, feeling the faint breeze of their fluttering on her face as they rippled together.

"I've killed two people," she said, quietly. "Not on purpose. But I did it. I didn't mean it, but I'm guilty all the same."

After a long silence, Alice looked up and met Stillman's gaze.

"Well, then," he said. "I suppose you know what I'm talking about." Then he picked up the remote and started back up the playback on the VCR.

"You don't often see work like this," Stillman said, shaking his head in admiration. "Most thieves don't slither past detectors like in the movies. They pay their five quid and walk in with the rest of the punters, and then duck behind the drapes at closing time. They snatch and grab and smash a window to get out. When the guards come running, they think they're looking for someone breaking in, not someone breaking out, and the blagger's on the run before they even know he's gone. But a job like this . . ."

He gestured to the documents fanned before him like a solitaire spread, and the black-and-white video playback.

"This is the work of a professional. A proper cat burglar." He mused. "If I didn't know better, I'd say it was the work of Tan Perrin, but that old bastard isn't up and around anymore, so he couldn't have done it."

"Know a lot of cat burglars, do you?"

"Overlapping skill sets, I suppose you'd say. In my line of work, it paid to know how to get in and out of a place without being caught. Whether you're making off with the crown jewels or sensitive microfiche hardly matters, the idea's the same. It's all tradecraft, in the end."

"Ha!" Stillman slammed his fist down onto the table, knocking Alice's cards to the floor. "Got her!"

"Got who?" Alice asked, playing fifty-two card pickup.

"Right there!" Stillman pointed to the automated log of one of the air vent alarms. "There's tricks of the trade that everyone knows, and there's others that are as unique as fingerprints. The way that this alarm was bypassed and shunted, it's a technique I first saw years ago. Used by a pair of twins, the Fox sisters." He smiled and glanced Alice's way. "Not the table-tapping spiritualists of the nineteenth century, of course."

"Oh, of course." Like she had any idea what he was talking about.

"Anyway, the Fox sisters died years ago, but not before handing down everything they knew, including this particular shunt."

"Handing it down to who?"

Stillman picked up the phone—the *corded* phone—and held the heavy Bakelite handset up to his ear. "To whom, love. Not 'who.'" Then he dialed— with a *dial*—and waited.

Alice sighed. "To *whom*, then?"

Stillman heard something on the line, then held up his finger. "Hughes?" He listened for a moment, then reached down and flipped a switch on the phone's sturdy base, and faint static hissed out of the speaker grill set on the side. "Hughes, can you hear me?" Stillman said, his voice raised, leaning in towards the receiver, gently resting the handset down beside it.

"Who *is* this?" buzzed the voice from the speaker. It sounded American, and male.

"Remember that time in Majorca, Hughes? You owe me."

There was silence for a long moment. "Shit. Waters, what the hell do *you* want?"

"Where's Aria, Hughes? I need to talk to her."

"Aria who?"

"Don't play the fool with me, Hughes." Stillman still smiled, but there was steel beneath his words. "Where's Aria Fox?"

Silence again, faintly peppered with static. "You know I can't tell you that, Waters. Client confidentiality, all of that jazz."

"Mmm mmm," Stillman hummed, nodding. "And I'm sure the Policía

Nacional in Madrid would be interested to hear all about the events of that January day, don't you? What do you suppose they'd say about confidentiality, mmm?"

Static hissed from the speaker.

"Fine. Okay? Fine. I . . . I can't tell you exactly. I've got a reputation to protect here, don't I? But . . . Okay, I *can* tell you that Aria was very, very pissed that her most recent . . . assignment meant she had to miss David Bowie's concert at the Roseland Ballroom in New York the other day."

"What?"

"Well, she had tickets for the eighteenth, last Saturday, but Bowie cancelled due to laryngitis, and she would have gone to the fan club show the next night, but she'd already booked the flight." Static. "She's a *huge* Bowie fan."

Stillman shifted on the couch, becoming increasingly annoyed. "Look, Hughes. I believe I've been more than fair with you over the years. Now, if you don't tell me what I want to know and stop messing me about with this trivia, I'm going to get quite cross."

"Sorry, Waters, that's all I can tell you. Don't call again."

Then there was a click, and the line went dead. Then a noise started from the speaker, which it took Alice a moment to recognize as an off-hook tone.

"Cheeky bastard," Stillman said, and reached over to redial. But this time, the phone on the other end just rang, and rang, and rang.

Stillman slammed the handset down on the receiver, lip curled in anger.

"Wait a minute," Alice said, trying to tease a specific memory out of the confusion of the past day. "Bowie's supposed to be playing some festival this weekend for the first time in thirty years."

Stillman looked up at her, a smile creeping across his face.

"In someplace called . . . Glastonbury?" Alice nodded. "Yeah, that's right." She tilted her head to one side and took in Stillman's big grin. "Does that help?"

"Alice, love," Stillman said. "How would you feel about taking a little road trip, mmm?"

There was always one kid, in every grade-school class, who called the teacher "Mom." It seemed an inescapable fact of life. And that they would then be known as the "kid who called the teacher Mom" for the rest of the school year.

Alice hadn't been that kid, but she'd sat next to him once, and had joined in with the others in teasing him mercilessly.

She hadn't thought of that kid in years. But when she opened her mouth and almost, but not quite, called Stillman "Dad," she couldn't help but remember him.

"What's that, love?" Stillman was fixing them breakfast. To get a proper start before they hit the road, he said.

Alice had just been about to ask him something about their plans, but every memory of what's she'd been about to say was driven from her memory as soon as she uttered the "Da-" syllable. She thought about playing it off, calling him "Daddio" like some hipster doofus from fifty years before, like Marty McFly in *Back to the Future*, but didn't have the heart to try.

"Nothing," Alice said, shaking her head.

This all felt very homey. Waking up to find an older man in the kitchen, making eggs, toast, and bacon. Stillman was about the age her dad would have been, had he lived, had she not fallen down the stairs.

It was strange, how quickly she'd come to trust this complete stranger. Had he done a bit of hypnosis on her, after all? Or was it just that she'd seen his face in her visions since she was a little girl, making him seem comfortable and safe to be around?

Stillman set a plate in front of her, the bacon nice and crunchy, just like she liked, so she tried not to worry about it one way or another.

She was toweling her hair off, just out of the shower, while Stillman was dressed and ready, waiting for her on the sofa, watching the morning news. He already had his shoulder holster on, Alice noted, though the fletchette pistol wasn't yet snugged in place.

The newscaster—news *reader*, they called them over here—was talking about an ongoing court case that had started up just weeks before. Two Libyans stood accused of carrying out the bombing of Pan Am Flight 103 over Lockerbie, Scotland, twelve years before that had killed 270 people. It was a Scottish court, but was confusingly built in an old US Air Force base in the Netherlands.

"I'll never get used to that," Alice said, shaking her head. "Planes blowing up over here, stuff like that."

Stillman gave her a strange look. "I think you'll find, love, that the rest of the world has unfortunately been used to 'stuff like that' for quite some time. It's only in America that you're quite so insulated from knowing about it." The corners of his mouth tugged down. "'Over here,' as you call it, we're more than familiar, I'm sorry to say."

"What, like not having trash cans and all that? The IRA, you mean?"

Stillman gave her a sad smile. "That, and before. Barrage balloons and Anderson shelters and long hot nights in Underground stations. Yes, we've quite a history of things blowing up around us, more's the pity."

Alice plopped down on the end of the couch and started pulling on her socks, lacing up her Docs. "Sorry. Didn't mean to be insensitive or anything." She turned her head to one side, looking over at him. "We're just . . . safe, in the United States, know what I mean? So we don't think about it as much. I mean, I know that a car blew up at the World Trade Center when I was in the fourth grade, and then that guy blew up that building in Oklahoma when I was in middle school, but it's still pretty rare."

Stillman's sad smile lingered. "Well, I hope you're right."

The way he said it, Alice was sure he knew she was wrong.

Alice thought she spotted the man Stillman called the Huntsman as the Corvette pulled out of the garage, but he assured her she was probably mistaken.

"He's like me, love," he said with a smile. "Tends only to come out at night."

Alice couldn't get over how small all of the cars on the highway were. Of course, if Stillman was to be believed, here it was called a *motorway*. Whatever. Either way, the cars were all damned tiny. Even the trucks were small compared to those at home.

Austin was a pretty liberal sort of town, well educated with lots of bookstores, and an alarming number of waiters had doctorates—it seemed a master's degree only got you a job in the kitchen—but even so, it was Texas, and so Alice had grown up surrounded by trucks. Big trucks. Really big trucks, and lots of them. Her mother drove an old Toyota Corolla, and her grandmother had driven an ancient Volkswagen Rabbit. If Alice had a license, she supposed that she'd have inherited the Rabbit, now that Naomi didn't need it anymore. But then she ran away. So much for that idea.

Texas highways were always choked with pickups and SUVs and eighteen wheelers. Whenever Alice had ridden with her mother in the Corolla or her grandmother in the Rabbit, she'd felt like she would be blown off the road at any time.

Nancy had driven a Renault Alliance. Nancy had been held back twice, so that by the time she was a freshman in high school she already had a driver's license. That was the start of the trouble, really, the temptation of jumping in the car with Nancy and skipping a few classes, or skipping school entirely. It was no fun to do it on foot, since you couldn't get far. But if you had a car? Well, there was no telling where you might get, or what you might get up to.

The last time Alice had seen the Renault, it had been wrapped around the concrete and steel base of a highway light post, completely totaled, the front windshield smashed to hell and gone. Alice had worn her seatbelt, and so had suffered only a sprained neck, a few cuts and nicks, and severe bruises across her shoulder and chest where the shoulder belt bit into her flesh. Nancy, on the other hand?

Anyway. Alice went back to thinking about the smallness of the cars on the motorway. When Stillman looked over and saw the strange expression on her face, the glistening in her eye, he started to ask her what was wrong, but she just turned the stereo up louder and lost herself in the sound.

They stopped for gas after what seemed an eternity. Alice was surprised to discover they hadn't even left London yet. Greater London, anyway. How big *was* this city?

The gas station had a Help Wanted sign posted in the window, and Alice entertained a brief fantasy about applying for the job, and staying, standing all day behind a counter and selling cigarettes and chewing gum to people with strange accents, making change for monopoly money, forgetting all about home and the accidents and her visions and her special destiny. Like anyone would hire a teenaged runaway epileptic with a nose ring and no marketable job skills.

Back in the car, as they pulled onto the motorway, Alice decided she'd had enough of silence and her own memories. Another Bowie album was playing on the stereo. Alice wasn't sure if Stillman had put it on in honor of the trip, or just because he liked listening to it.

"So, how'd you get into this line of work, anyway?" she asked. "Spying, I mean?"

Stillman had his left arm casually draped over the back of the seat, his right wrist resting on the top of the steering wheel. He peeked around the edges of his clunky sunglasses at her, his expression unreadable.

"That's something of a . . . complicated question. Or a simple question with a complicated answer, I suppose." He mulled something over. "What the hell, eh? In for a penny, in for a pound." He shifted on his seat and put both hands on the wheel. "The simple answer is that I was recruited by the SOE—the Special Operations Executive—during the early days of World War II. I worked for several years as a W/T, or wireless telegraph officer, in the more charming vacation spots of war-torn Europe. By the time SOE was officially dissolved in 1946, I'd been recruited as an agent of Signals Intelligence, MI8, and when it went underground and off the books, I stayed on. I was the first Rook Three, and held damn near every post in the operation by the time I put myself out to pasture."

She was supposed to believe this? "Just how old *are* you, anyway?" He looked fifty, or a spry sixty at best. "When did you sign up, as a toddler?"

Stillman treated her to a broad smile. "*That's* the more complicated answer." He watched the road for a moment, in silence. "I was born in 1920. When I was still a kid, I met a man who told me that I was special, that I had a destiny, that I would go on to do great things."

That sounded familiar. But 1920? That would make him eighty years old? As if . . .

"When I grew older," Stillman went on, his tone level, "we became friends. Then . . . then we became more than friends."

"Oh." Alice couldn't see how it was possible that Stillman was older than her grandmother, but she didn't have any trouble believing him when he talked about his friend. They'd been lovers. "Was that the guy in the portrait? And in the photo with you?"

Stillman nodded, his mouth drawn tight. He drew a heavy breath and held it before replying. "My friend came from something of an oppressive background. He was never quite comfortable, even when we were alone. Of course, it wasn't as if he was wrong to be worried. In those days, homosexuality was still illegal in Britain, after all. It was a mental illness, they said. Alan Turing, one of the cryptographers at Bletchley Park, was prosecuted for homosexuality and ended up taking his own life after an unfortunate series of events." He paused, a sad expression lining his face. "There but for the grace of God go I, if you believe that sort of thing."

Bowie was still blaring from the stereo, talking about time, who waited in the wings, speaking of senseless things. Stillman was still silent, lost in memory.

"You know, I saw a documentary once," Alice said, filling the silence. "About Bowie. It was on cable or PBS or something. There was all this footage of kids going to one of his concerts in America back in the early seventies, or hanging out in their bedrooms talking to the camera about how Bowie was God. And when I saw it, I couldn't help but notice how many of those kids were clearly gay. And just loving it, you know? That Bowie was up on stage, being all of these different people, blurring the lines between genders and stuff like that. You know? You could see it in those kids' eyes, that they thought the long hard battle was over, and that from that point on, they could be anything they wanted to be. Homo superior or whatever, right? But then, what happened? Just a few years later, Bowie moved on to be some other character altogether, and punk came along, and metal. Don't get me wrong, I love punk, but maybe it wasn't as . . . accepting of gay kids as the whole glam thing had been. And metal? Forget about it."

Alice was silent for a moment, thinking back to those eager, hopeful faces. They'd be the age her mother was now, she figured. She wondered what had become of them.

"Anyway. I just think about those kids, sometimes. Thinking that the future was here, and that they didn't have to be afraid anymore. What must it have been like, when they realized that they were wrong, and it was just like it had always been?"

Stillman glanced at her but didn't say a word. They continued on up the motorway, finally leaving London behind.

Ⓐ

Alice had decided to take it as a given that Stillman was as old as he said he was. Because, really, was that any stranger than anything else he'd said?

Ⓐ

"So what happened to your friend? Your mentor, or whatever?"

It was early afternoon, and the signs said they'd reach their destination in another hour at most, barring traffic.

Stillman looked her way and sighed.

"Just making conversation," Alice said, a little defensively.

Stillman nodded, and gave her a weak, weary smile. "All right. Fair enough. It's all been years ago, anyway." He glanced at the backpack shoved beneath Alice's legs on the floorboards. "How about another of those cigarettes, though, eh?"

Lighting the butt from the orange-glowing coils of the cigarette lighter, Stillman took in a lungful, and then with the smoke streaming from his nostrils, began to speak.

"You see, we were hunting an escaped Nazi sorcerer named Otto Rahn."
Stillman slid his eyes left, and caught Alice's disbelieving look. "Yes, I said
'sorcerer.' If you like, you can think of it as someone who dabbles in the dark
corners, as it were, a scientific researcher into unknown science. But our lot,
we always just called them sorcerers. Anyway, Rahn was one of the
Ahnenerbe, the Nazis who the SID had been eavesdropping on back in the
war, but he'd faked his death before the war had even really started and gone
into hiding. It was ironic, perhaps, that my friend and I were the ones to end
up hunting him down, since Rahn had been forced to fake his death in the
first place when it was revealed to his superiors that he was a homosexual. But
there you have it."

Stillman drew on the cigarette, the burning ember at its end glowing
brightly.

"The Ahnenerbe, you'll recall, believed all sorts of strange nonsense, and
Rahn was no exception. His contention was that the Eddas, the old Norse
poems, contained hints about the burial place of the guardian of the Holy
Grail. In 1936, while he was still 'alive,' he led a whole team of SS archeolo-
gists to Iceland to look for it. In 1947, after the war and under a new identity, he went back again, but this time my friend and I were on his heels. MI8
wanted to bring Rahn in, to pick his brains and see what sort of secrets he
carried around between his ears. In any event, we were just a few steps behind
Rahn when we lost the trail in Reykjavík and scoured the countryside
looking for him. We split up but found no sign of Rahn. My friend did turn
up an antique silver chalice, though, which he brought to our hotel and
insisted that I accept as a token of his affection. Our own personal grail, he
called it. He was always sentimental that way. He also brought with him an
old friend of his who he'd run into along the way, a man named John
Delamere, who was in Iceland on business of his own. As Delamere's purpose
and our own were complementary, he joined us, and it was a few days later
the three of us caught up with Rahn and his team, at the mouth of an
erupting volcano." A dark cloud passed over his face. "I . . . I was the only
survivor, on either side, everyone else lost to the flames. I returned home,
taking the silver chalice with me. That, and the portrait, and the photograph,
were all I had left of him."

Alice's brows were knit. "Wait, did you say *volcano?*"

Stillman looked at her, his eyes narrowed behind the clunky frames. "What of it?"

"I think my *grandmother* was in Iceland at the same time. She talked about a volcano in, yeah, in 1947!"

"Really?" Stillman was genuinely surprised. "How strange."

CHAPTER NINETEEN

Twilight

ON THE MORNING OF THEIR THIRD DAY in Llongborth, reasonably well rested and recuperated, Artor and his captains prepared to continue on their journey, only this time by land and not sea. Geraint had agreed to escort them himself to the hedge of mist of which he'd spoken and to outfit them with horses from his personal stables. The animals had been too long cooped up in their stalls, the Dumnonian king had insisted, and could do with the fresh air and exercise.

Artor's captains had brought their own saddles and tack along with them on board White Aspect, as a matter of course, and so while Geraint's people prepared the animals, Galaad and the others were sent to see to the gear.

The thought of mounting a horse made Galaad feel nauseated, even lightheaded. He'd not been on horseback since the accident, not since the spring morning when he and Flora had ridden out together and not ridden back. He knew, however, that if he refused to ride, he'd be left behind while the others rode out without him. For the others this journey might have begun with a whim on the part of Artor, the High King looking for some ready excuse to escape the tedium into which his life had sunk, but now it was clear that Artor burned with the same curiosity that had driven Galaad to his court in the first place. Having come face to face with the inhuman Huntsman and the unearthly hounds, Artor was determined to see this hedge of mist for himself and to see what lay within. And though they'd come this distance on the strength of Galaad's visions, at least initially, Galaad was sure that Artor would not hesitate to continue on the journey without him if the need arose.

So it was that Galaad resolved to overcome his fears, just as Pryder had said, to be the master of his emotions and not their slave.

Handling the saddle and tack was only the first step, Galaad knew. Even so, he questioned his ability to keep his morning meal down, already feeling his gorge rise at the mere touch of the saddle leather.

Having carried their gear to the stables, the captains began the business of dressing their horses for travel. Galaad hung back, the sting of bile at the back of his throat, and handed over saddles, bridles, and reins when requested.

"Here, Galaad," Artor called from the stable's door, Geraint at his side. The High King carried some sort of staff and bundle in his arms.

Galaad handed Bedwyr his saddle, and then gratefully stepped away towards the door, grateful for the opportunity to move away from horses, if only briefly.

"Yes, majesty?" Galaad couldn't help but fear that Artor had seen his disease with the animals and intended to ask after its cause. He tried to soften his queasy expression of distaste, to mask the quaver in his voice.

"It is because of you that we have come this far," Artor answered, leaning on a wooden staff almost as tall as he was, topped with some sort of bundle. "Whatever lies before us, whether danger or glory or death, it is down to you."

"Um, thank you?" Galaad was unsure whether to apologize or express gratitude, given Artor's manner. It sounded to him as though the High King *welcomed* danger.

"Yes," Artor said, nodding. "Well, it seems to me only fitting, given your pivotal role in our enterprise, that you should bear our standard when we ride out this morning."

Artor held forth the staff, and now Galaad got his first clear look at the bundle at its top. It was a representation of a dragon's head made of hammered bronze over wood, trailing a wind sock of red linen. The head was affixed to the end of the staff, so that when the staff was held aloft, the wind sock hung like the red tail of the dragon.

"This was once the draco standard of the Equites Honoriani Seniores," Artor explained, proudly. "It was left behind when the Roman army left Britannia to her own defenses and later adopted by Ambrosius as a symbol of the continuity of Roman culture on the island."

"Artor's own father, Utor, had been the standard bearer in Ambrosius's army when we were just boys," Geraint put in, "earning the epithet Utor Dragon's Head for the ferocity with which he defended the standard in battle."

A proud smile curled Artor's lip, while a wistful look came into his eyes. He paused for a moment, some memories playing back before his mind's eye, and then blinked rapidly, returning to the present moment. "Yes," he said, taking a deep breath and sighing, "but it has been some years since the draco has seen battle, and still more since she needed defending. But whenever my captains and I ride forth now, we carry it proudly, to remember those who have gone before us and to remind us why we struggle."

Artor handed the staff to Galaad, who accepted it nervously.

"I'm . . . I'm honored," Galaad said, unsure of the proper protocol. "But . . ." He trailed off, and cast an uneasy glance at the animals across the stable, snorting clouds of steam in the chill air.

"I know," Artor said, gently, his expression softening.

Galaad looked back at the High King, eyes widening. *Did* he know? There seemed no way that he could know the reasons for Galaad's fear, but then Galaad had once lived in a world free of corpse-white huntsmen and spectral hounds, so who was to say what was impossible?

"You need a saddle," Artor added with a smile.

All of the breath left Galaad's body, and he stood rigid for a long moment, before assaying a curt nod. "Y-yes," he said at length. "A . . . a saddle. Of course."

"Not to worry," Geraint said with an avuncular chuckle, patting Galaad on the shoulder. "I've had my people outfit my wife's roan for you. She's an obedient mare and will get you where you want to go." He paused, and laughed louder. "The horse, that is. Not my wife."

Artor joined in the laughter, and Galaad managed a weak smile. "Ah," he said. "Quite right."

It seemed the question had been decided for him, after all. He would ride out with the captains, and as their standard bearer, no less.

He only hoped he didn't vomit on the Dumnonian queen's horse.

"The hedge of mist now stands a half dozen miles to the north and east," Geraint explained as their company mounted up and rode out of Llongborth, the sun's glow in the east hidden by thick gray clouds. "On a clear day, you could likely see it from here. Even with the roads and hillsides as iced as they are, we should reach it soon after midday at the latest."

The captains traveled light but well armored. Each man wore a scale hauberk, except for Bedwyr, who wore one of mail, and Lugh, who complained of the weight and the chill of the metal. All wore helmets of various types and designs, Artor's own set with semiprecious stones, and each man had a shield slung on his back or else hanging from his saddle. The only other supplies they carried were sacks of comestibles and flasks of wine and water hung from their saddles. Their other effects they had left in Geraint's keeping.

In their marital finery, their cloaks flapping in the chill wind, the captains presented an imposing sight. And Geraint, who rode out with them as escort, was likewise caparisoned, his fittings if anything even grander than those worn by Artor, whose own armor had a well-traveled and utilitarian look to it. Only Galaad and Geraint's two pages were unarmored, though one of the pages carried their king's shield and the other his helmet, which was topped by an impressively large plume.

Galaad tugged his cloak more tightly around his shoulders and shivered, though his chattering teeth owed as much to his nerves as to the freezing winds. He held the staff in one hand, its foot supported against his saddle, the dragon's tail flapping in the wind.

"If it's so close," Artor said, gripping his horse's reins, "then I'd sooner be there than dawdle and talk about it. Let's *ride*, for pity's sake." With that, he kicked his heels into his horse's flanks, spurring it into motion, and the horse took off at a gallop.

"You heard the High King," Geraint said with a smile that did not quite reach his eyes. "Ride out!"

The rest of the party, the captains, the king, and his pages, urged their horses to gallop, coursing over the frozen ground after Artor.

Galaad cantered forward, delaying so long that his horse looked back over her shoulder at him, an almost human expression of curiosity in her big wet eye.

"Damn," Galaad cursed. He felt an emptiness within, a mounting anxiety creeping up his spine. He remembered that spring day, the last time he'd ridden a-gallop. And he remembered everything he'd lost that day. But if he remained behind, he stood to lose even more.

"Go, damn your hide!" Galaad yelled, kicking his heels, and as the horse thudded across the frozen ground, the dragon above his head ate the wind, its tail coursing behind.

Their progress was slow across the icy countryside, and with the sun hidden behind a thick blanket of gray clouds it was difficult to say how much time had passed, but it must have been near midday when the hedge of mist finally came into view. At first Galaad thought that it was simply more clouds obscuring the distance, but as they drew nearer, it became clear that they rode towards a seemingly unbroken wall of white different from the darker shade of the cloud cover overhead.

The party reduced their speed to a trot as they neared the mist, warily. The mist seemed indistinct, its exact edges difficult to discern, and Galaad found that his eyes watered when he stared too long at it.

"There it is, my friends," Geraint called, pulling on his horse's reins and coming to a halt some hundreds of yards from the mist. The icy ground ran right up to the white wall and then disappeared entirely from view.

The captains exchanged uneasy glances while their horses whickered and brayed, disquieted.

"I would not have believed it had I not seen it with my own eyes," Artor said, reverentially.

"Had I not lived in such close quarters with it these long years," Geraint answered, "I'd scarcely credit it myself, but the evidence is before you. The hedge of mist is real."

"And none who have ever ridden through have ever returned?" Gwrol asked, his expression wary.

"None have ever ridden through at all," Geraint said, and indicated their uneasy steeds. "Beasts seem to have better sense than men in that regard and refuse to enter the mist. But no man who has ever walked through has ever been seen again, no."

Artor leaned forward, his hands resting on his saddle, and narrowed his eyes. "I'd not thought it could be so . . . large."

Geraint nodded, his lips thin. "It now stands some two dozen miles in circumference, by our best estimates. Considering that it began no larger than a few dozen feet across, it has grown to a remarkable extent in such a relatively short time."

Artor nodded, thoughtfully. "Well, we learn nothing staring at it from a distance." Then he swung his leg over the saddle and dropped with a thud to the icy ground, the scales of his hauberk clinking. He slung his shield over his back and laid his hand on the hilt of his scabbarded spatha. "If we're to plumb the depths of this mystery, we must go through."

The captains, with visible reluctance, arranged their weapons about themselves and swung down from their horses, boots crunching on the ice underfoot.

Galaad lingered in the saddle, while the captains transferred their flasks and wineskins and bundles of comestibles to their own backs. That the captains performed these mundane tasks without speaking, as if by rote, suggested to Galaad that they had done similar maneuvers countless times in wartime, shifting from horseback to foot with changes in terrain or tactics, and that they might now be seeking solace and support in these familiar activities, taking their troubled thoughts away from the unearthly sight before them.

"Come along, now," Artor called to Galaad with a wave of his hand. "It's due to you that we've come, after all."

Galaad took a deep breath and let out a ragged sigh that fogged in the cold air. He set his jaw, willing himself to overcome his fears, and slipped off the saddle and onto the ground. He handed the draco standard to the nearest of the pages.

Artor turned to Geraint. "And you, cousin? Will you come with us into the heart of mystery?" But even as he spoke the words, it was clear that he knew what the answer would be.

"Yes, I had intended . . ." Geraint glanced to the arms his pages bore, his voice trailing off. He shook his head, sadly, and struggled to meet the High King's gaze. "I'm sorry, but . . . I cannot. I . . . I am needed with my people in Llongborth. I am . . ." He trailed off, his gaze lowering to the ground, shamefaced.

"Do not worry yourself, cousin," Artor said gently. "I understand. Had I a wife and son at home, I might feel differently, too."

Geraint looked back to Artor, his expression brightening fractionally. He nodded, seeming to find some peace with his decision. "I will return with your horses to Llongborth," he went on, in a louder voice, his tone firm. "But we'll leave one of our people stationed here against your return, for as long as we are able." He pointed to one of his pages, whose shoulders slumped as he realized that he would not be returning to the comforting warmth of the hall any time soon. "You," Geraint said, "will remain here." The other page could not completely hide the relieved smile that tugged at the corners of his mouth. "And you," Geraint continued, pointing to the other page, "will return with me, to ride back out by nightfall to spell your fellow in his watch."

Now both pages exchanged dispirited glances, but if they had any complaints did not give them voice.

The seven gathered in a ragged line, standing between the horses and the hedge of mist in the near distance. A cold wind blew from behind them, stinging cheeks and bare hands, and Galaad hugged his arms to his chest, shivering beneath his cloak.

"Well," Lugh said to Artor, "you wanted adventure and to have your pulse quicken once more before you died."

Artor glanced back his way.

"So, has it quickened yet? Because I'll tell you, my own blood is damn near *frozen*."

Artor gave him a tight smile. "I've not felt as alive in some time, my old friend. In some long time."

Lugh blew air through his lips, dismissively, but after a brief moment a smile crept across his own face. "Aye," he said. "Well, it beats haggling with traders for scraps of food, I'll give you that."

"Or listening to endless petitioners," Caius put in.

Artor nodded. "That it does."

"Are we going to go or not?" Gwrol said, fidgeting. "I can feel my manhood freezing off in this cold, just standing here."

"It's a small loss," Pryder replied, "and it isn't as if you had any use for it, after all."

"You fellows don't think we'll see those hounds again once we're within, do you?" Bedwyr asked, his voice quavering.

"Come on, you lot," Artor said, striding forward. "If this is to be our end, let us face it with heads high and eyes wide open, shall we?"

The captains left off their squabbles and comments and, hands on their sword hilts, followed after.

Galaad was the last to advance. He glanced back at Geraint and the pages, who already were busy putting the horses on a line to lead back to the city. He couldn't help but envy them, but at the same time, he felt the fires of his curiosity burning higher within, knowing that he could be so close to the answers he had so long sought.

He turned back towards the hedge and hurried to catch up to Artor and the others.

The party reached the hedge in a matter of moments and paused just before entering the hedge of mist. Seen from this close, it seemed more an absence of anything visible than a tangible thing in itself, more a wall of nothingness than any sort of fog. Behind was the world they knew, and before them was simply . . . nothing.

Artor glanced around at the others, a faint smile on his face, and without another word strode forward and into the mist. He disappeared immediately from view, even the sounds of his feet crunching the icy ground fading entirely.

The captains exchanged glances and shrugs, and then singly and in pairs followed behind.

Galaad was the last to go, as always. He paused a long moment, gathering his resolve. He set his jaw, tightened his hands into fists at his sides, and holding his breath, walked forward into the mist.

For a brief moment, it felt to Galaad as though he was nowhere. He saw only white, heard nothing, felt nothing. His stomach roiled, and he felt an intense sensation of vertigo, feeling almost as though he were falling from some great height and gaining speed, but also as if he were frozen in place. He thought for a brief instant that he was experiencing another of his visions, but he had felt none of the other indicators and the overall sensation was markedly different.

Then the moment passed and he completed the step he'd begun in walking into the mist, his leading foot striking the ground.

A wave of heat hit him, like an oven door just being opened, and he squinted in the sudden strange light that greeted his eyes. He stumbled forward, feeling queasy and unwell.

Galaad managed to keep from pitching forward onto his face, his arms out to either side for balance. Straightening uneasily, he glanced around, his eyes taking a moment to adjust to the odd quality of the light. The skies overhead were a clear, crystal blue, and the field which spread out before him was covered in some sort of strangely colored heath. Where an instant before he'd been in the depths of a frigid winter, now he found himself in warmest summer.

More worrying, though, he found that he was completely alone.

Galaad felt a momentarily thrill of panic and a sense of dissociation to find himself alone in these strange summer lands. Then he heard footfalls behind him, and a series of startled gasps, and turned to find the captains behind him, staggering through the hedge of mist. An instant later, Artor followed, his faint smile fading, replaced by an expression of confusion.

"But . . ." Artor began, looking from the captains before him to the indistinct wall of white through which he'd walked. "I just . . ."

"Where have you been?" Galaad asked, reaching out a hand towards the nearest of the captains, almost afraid to touch them, as though they might come apart if he did.

The captains alternated between looking around them at their strange new surroundings and glancing at one another in confusion over the unexpected order of their arrival.

Artor narrowed his eyes. "I just walked through the hedge, leaving you all behind me, and now I find that you preceded me through the mist. How is that possible?"

Lugh shrugged. "Perhaps we took a short cut," he said, unconvincingly.

"No." Caius shook his head. "It took no longer than the time needed to take a single step."

"And yet Galaad, the last to come, preceded us all," Pryder said, glancing towards Galaad with suspicion.

"On my honor," Galaad said, hastily, "I watched you all vanish into the mist, but when I followed I briefly found myself alone on this side."

"It was just . . . white," Bedwyr said, looking back at the mist, reaching out a tentative hand, though stopping far short of touching it. "And silence. It was simply . . ."

"Nothing," Gwrol finished for him. "It was as though we passed through nothing."

Some of the others nodded.

"I don't like this," Bedwyr said with mounting panic. "Perhaps we should return at some other time."

Bedwyr took a step back towards the hedge, as though to return.

"Wait!" Artor said, holding up his hand.

As it happened, he needn't have bothered. Bedwyr reached the mist in another step, but instead of passing through, he was stopped short, as though he had walked into a solid stone wall. He rebounded back, unharmed but distressed.

"I . . ." Bedwyr reached out his hand again, this time close enough to touch, but rather than disappearing into the white fog, it was met with resistance. "It is solid!" He looked to the others, his eyes wide. "It could be made of stone, or iron!"

The other captains exchanged curious looks, except for Lugh, who simply marched up to the hedge, clenched his hand into a fist, and pounded on it like one knocking on a door.

"Aye," he said, turning back. "It's solid enough, all right. Won't be going back *that* way."

Artor nodded, thoughtfully. "Perhaps that is why none of Geraint's people have ever returned. Perhaps this is a passage that can only be traveled in one direction."

"So how will we return?" Bedwyr's eyes were wide. "How will we escape?"

Artor stepped close and laid a hand on Bedwyr's shoulder. "There may yet be other avenues," he said, his tone soothing. "Or else it may be possible to traverse the hedge at some other hour, or in some other spot."

Bedwyr nodded eagerly, though his expression made plain that his anxieties were far from dispelled.

"But what of our strange order of arrival?" Pryder asked. "What does it mean that the last of us to leave was the first to arrive, and the first the last?"

"I don't know." Artor's voice was grave, his brow furrowed. "It seems our mysteries multiply in number, the questions outpacing the answers." He took a few steps away from the hedge, surveying the terrain before them.

"Ach, but it's hot," Lugh said, shouldering out of his cloak.

The others nodded, shifting uneasily in their armor and cold-weather clothing.

"Well," Artor said with a wry smile. "At least now you have one fewer thing about which to complain."

"Perhaps," Lugh said with a grin. He mopped at his brow with his bandaged hand. "Except that now I'm sweating."

Chuckling, Artor turned and walked further into the strange summer day.

The Summer Lands, as they had come to call them, had some clear resemblance to the lands on the far side of the hedge, for all the distinct difference in climate. The low fields and gently rolling hills they saw before them followed the same contours as those over which they'd ridden out from Llong-borth. Artor had not been in the area for nearly two decades, but said that in the main the landscape conformed to his memories from before.

But there were more differences than simply the weather.

Removing their helmets, sword belts, and hauberks, the captains shucked out of their heaviest articles of clothing. Then, dressed only in tunics, breeches, and boots, they armored themselves once more, and used their cloaks to fashion makeshift packs in which to carry their discarded clothes. More appropriately attired for the warmth, they continued on, exploring the lands around them.

The fields that ran from the hedge were carpeted with a thick-growing vegetation, some sort of fine-leafed and low-growing heath, but of a col-oration that none of the seven had ever seen before. These were a bright red, more brilliant than any clover, cinquefoil, or rose, but what was even more striking was that this color suffused the whole plant, leaves and all, and not simply a flowering bloom. Stranger still, perhaps, was the fact that that grass beneath, when glimpsed through breaks in the heath, was found to be of the starkest white, like the color of bleached bone.

And so they walked on, over fields of white grasses choked by brilliant red heath, beneath a crystal blue sky.

A short distance from the hedge, they came to a stand of trees no less strange. The trees were slender and towered over the tallest of the captains, but the bark was smooth and unmarked by boll or knot, and instead of the grays and browns to which the captains were accustomed was the flashing brightness of silver. The silver trunks were smooth and cold to the touch, like metalwork, and from the branches high overhead depended some sort of fruit. But these apples were not any natural hue or shade, nor yet the bright metal of the tree from which they grew, but were clear and bright, like ice or glass. Perfectly spherical apples of glass, hanging from the limbs of a silver-branched tree.

Curious, Lugh drew his sword, and by leaping into the air and swinging the blade overhead, he was able to dislodge one of the apples, which fell to the ground at his feet. He sheathed his sword and picked up the glass sphere, hefting it. It was perfectly transparent and completely smooth, and he was unable to dent it with his fingernail.

"I'm glad that we brought along victuals," Gwrol joked, hungrily. "I'd hate to test my teeth biting into one of *those*."

"Speaking of which," Lugh said, patting his belly and tugging at the ends of his long mustache, "when *is* our next meal, come to that? I'm famished." He tucked the glass apple into his belt, absently.

"It must be near meridian," Caius said, scanning the blue skies above, "though you wouldn't know it to look."

Caius was right. Though the skies overhead were clear and crystal blue, the captains had quickly noted that there was no sun in evidence. No shadows fell around them to indicate the light's source, and it was suggested that perhaps the illumination came at them from all quarters. If the hedge of mist through which they'd traveled extended in a dome around them as they'd been told, in all directions of the compass and overhead as well, then it was possible that the light was emitted in some way by the hedge itself, though how this was accomplished none could say.

"Whatever the hour, I'm hungry, as well," Artor said, slinging the shield from his back and dropping it to the ground. "Who has something for their sovereign to eat?"

Lugh pulled a loaf of stale bread from his pack and took a bite from the hard crust. "What?" he said, crunching noisily. "You didn't bring your own?"

"Yes," Pryder said with a sly smile, sitting on the ground and rooting around in his own bundle. "I thought the intent was for each man to carry what he needed. Weren't those always our marching orders, back in days of battle, O Count of Britannia?"

Gwrol unstoppered a wineskin, and took a generous draught. "Well," he said, wiping his mouth with the back of his hand, "I expect that you'll just have to be hungry a while longer, most noble majesty."

"You could always shimmy up the tree and try for one of the glass apples." Caius grinned, and jerked a thumb upwards. "Might help keep your thoughts off your appetite, if naught else."

"Mayhap," Artor allowed, nodding sagely, "but there again, on our return to court, perhaps I'll find need for five new stablehands to work the horses." He gave a wicked smile. "They drop a prodigious amount of dung, horses do."

"Here, you thief," Lugh said, and lobbed his bread loaf at the High King, who caught it handily. "But remember me when next you go handing out state honors. I wouldn't mind a high-flown title of my own, you know."

Galaad couldn't help but grin. Even in these strange and trying circumstances, the captains found some comfort in the easy company of their companions, falling back on well-worn jibes and jokes.

"The sovereign harbors a mighty thirst," Artor joked, eyeing Gwrol's wineskin hungrily. "Would that anyone had the ability to slake it."

"Leave off," Gwrol said, clutching the skin to his chest, protectively. "High King or no, you'll drink water if you've a thirst, and not a drop of mine."

Galaad munched a slice of dried meat from his own pack and took a sip of water from his flask. He glanced up at the glass fruit that glinted in the strange light overhead and reached out a hand to touch the smooth, cool flesh of the tree's trunk. It seemed strange to sit beneath branches on a clear day but not find an inch of shade, but holding his hand palm down before him he found the palm as clearly illuminated as the back of his hand. It was as though the light were a liquid through which they swam, surrounding them on all sides.

Still, things seemed somehow hazy and indistinct. Though the skies were blue, the light which suffused the Summer Lands was not bright, but had a somewhat diffuse quality, like the grayness of twilight. And the light seemed to limit visibility considerably; looking back the way they had come, Galaad was able to see only blue skies rising above the ground, though he knew that they were only a hundred yards or so from the white of the hedge of mist. It was simply one more mystery about this strange place, one more unanswered question.

They'd had, as yet, no sign of the island of his visions, but Artor reckoned that it must lie still some miles to the north, though just which direction was northwards was difficult to say. And, considering the strangely diffuse nature of the Summer Lands' twilight illumination, they could well be almost on top of the island before they could see it. It might prove more difficult to locate their destination than they had assumed, given the distances involved.

The seven ate beneath the silver-branched trees, speaking in low voices, glancing about them warily. Galaad felt weary, out of sorts. He felt a pressure in his abdomen and decided that he must need to relieve himself. When he stood, though, his head swam as the world seemed to spin around him. He had to lean against the silver tree to maintain his footing, and it took a moment for the dizziness to pass.

"You all right?" Caius said, reaching out a hand to steady him.

"I'm just . . ." Galaad began, blinking, his vision temporarily blurred. "I don't . . ."

"Here," Pryder said, wiping his hands on his breeches, "let me help." But when he climbed to his feet, he too went into a swoon, and standing too far from the tree to reach it for stability, pitched forward onto the ground, face first.

"Careful now," Artor warned, motioning the others to keep their places. Rising up only to his knees, he crabbed over to where Pryder had fallen. He reached out and shook the Gwentian's shoulder. "Pryder?"

Pryder rolled over on his back, shielding his eyes with the back of his hand. "I'm all right. At least, I think I am. Just came over dizzy of a sudden."

Artor raised his hand to his head, squeezing his eyes shut. "You're not alone, I'm afraid."

Gwrol came over to his brother's side and helped him into a sitting position. "Couldn't be the food or drink," Gwrol said, "as we brought it all with us this morning and had no ill effects when last we had it." He caught the sidelong glance that Pryder gave him. "Oh, leave it out, will you? I haven't had enough to drink to start stumbling *this* time, have I?"

Pryder gave a weak smile.

"Could be the air," Lugh ventured, taking a deep breath. "But smells all right to me."

"I don't like it," Bedwyr said, shaking his head fiercely. "Not a bit. Perhaps the land itself has become poison, inimical to man."

"Now you're just talking foolishness," Caius said, carefully standing, using a tree's trunk to assist. He closed his eyes, and swayed back and forth like a reed in a high wind. "It's more likely merely the effect of moving so quickly from cold weather to warm. It will pass."

Artor used his sheathed sword as a kind of crutch, slowly working into a standing position. "Perhaps," he allowed. "Still and all, we should proceed with more caution. We should not assume that anything we encounter is as we expect it will be."

The captains nodded their agreement.

"Then let's continue, then," Artor said, overcoming his dizziness enough to retrieve his shield from the ground and return it to his back. "We're learning little enough here, and may have a long distance to travel before we're done."

Galaad swallowed hard, fighting the waves of nausea which swept through him, and then he and the rest of the seven set out from the silver trees.

They had so far encountered no living thing in the Summer Lands save the unearthly silver-branched glass-apple trees, but after a time they came upon a herd of strange creatures the likes of which none of them had ever seen.

There were some dozen of the beasts in all. They seemed an unlikely mixture of badger and lizard, with white fur over their round bellies and fierce-looking talons on the tips of their narrow feet, their protruding snouts ending in a long, spiraling horn. These horned beasts munched contentedly on a pasture of the bright-red heath and paid the seven no mind.

A short while later, they encountered a flock of birds that stood on tall, thin legs, their snow white feathers sticking out in all directions, which regarded them with cool, emotionless gazes. As the seven drew near, the ungainly birds opened their enormous beaks, emitting ear-piercing shrieks, and then ran away, feathers ruffling, their long legs carrying them in prodigious strides across a hillside and out of sight.

Later still, they felt stirrings of wind around them where before the air had been completely quieted. As they walked, they caught flashes of movements out of the corners of their eyes, first on one side then the other, one moment ahead of them and then behind. They walked on, and finally caught a glimpse of the source of these sudden breezes and fleeting glimpses. It was some sort of creature with a long neck and strong, powerful legs, though whether it was animal or bird none could say. Having run circles around them so quickly it was scarcely visible, it now stopped some distance off to regard them. Its wide, snapping jaws suggested a predatory nature, but its relatively small size in comparison to a grown man meant that its prey could not be much larger than the strange birds or spiral-horned beasts they had seen. Evidently sizing up the seven as a potential meal, it seemed to find the odds not in its favor, and after a brief interval blurred into motion, disappearing from view.

If there had remained any doubts that they now walked in decidedly unearthly lands, such had long been dispelled. The seven had managed to become somewhat accustomed to whatever element of the environment had unmanned them beneath the silver trees, but they were still queasy, even slightly disoriented. Fortunately for them, the worst effects of the condition seemed to ebb and flow like waves, such that while any one of them was suffering the worst of it, another was in a better state, and so together they were able to advance across the Summer Lands without overmuch delay.

They hoped aloud that these difficulties would wane and pass as they spent more time in this climate, but as yet there were no signs of any general improvement. As it was, they counted themselves lucky that none of the fauna they had encountered had yet proved hostile to them.

Then they reached the shore, and fortune, it seemed, was no longer with them.

With the limited visibility of the strange twilight, they were nearly upon the shore before they even caught sight of water. The fields of white grass, speckled here and there with red heath, came to an abrupt halt at the waterline, the mirror-smooth waters continuing from there, without any boundary of beach in between.

The waters themselves, which extended as far as the eye could see, however far that might be, were so dark as to be almost black, but without a single ripple or wave marring their surface. It presented a strange picture, white grasslands behind, black waters ahead, and cloudless blue skies overhead. Nothing moved or stirred, and when the seven came to a halt at the water's edge, they could well have stepped into a tapestry or painting, frozen and immobile.

"The island is connected to the mainland by a spit," Artor said, looking left and right along the shoreline. "If the Summer Lands conform to the geography I remember, we should be able to find the island by following the coast to the north." He pointing to the right, where the shore marched along until it disappeared into the indistinct blue of the twilit distance.

"And how long will that be?" Lugh asked, leaning over and resting his hands on his knees. His skin had taken on a greenish cast, and he looked queasy. "I'm not sure how much more of this blasted place I can take."

"But we can't go back the way we came," Bedwyr said, wringing his hands. "What if we can't find a way out at all?"

Artor was about to answer when a flash of movement caught Galaad's eye. He started, looking out over the black waters, no longer mirror smooth, but now rippling.

"Look!" Galaad said, pointing.

The others turned and saw something large cresting the water some few dozen feet from the shore.

"What is it?" Pryder said, narrowing his eyes, hand on his sword hilt.

"I don't know," Artor answered, warily.

The thing grew larger, rising up higher over the waterline and moving in closer to the shore, while behind it another shape, just as large, crested the wavering water.

"Whatever it is, there are now two of them." Artor drew his spatha with one hand and slung his shield onto his other arm.

The others drew their own weapons, settling their helmets on their heads and shields on their arms, instinctively stepping away from the water's edge. Galaad, for his part, drew his own Saeson blade, conscious of the fact that he'd come equipped with no other arms or armor.

The nearest of the creatures had now almost reached the water's edge and loomed above the water, standing some dozen feet tall. And "creature" was the only name to call it, conforming as it did to nothing else in the seven's collective experience. It stood on two legs like a man, with what appeared to be a massive vertical mouth in its chest, lined with bloated lips, with a single massive arm that sprouted from the top of its trunk, in the place of a head, with three elbowlike joints and a massive handlike appendage.

The one-armed creature was just stepping onto the shore as it stopped and turned back. At first Galaad thought the one-armed creature might be retreating already but instead saw that the seven had fallen into the unblinking gaze of four massive eyes that lined the middle of the creature's back.

Galaad, already in the grip of the disease that had plagued them since the silver-branched trees, felt unsettled in the searing four-eyed gaze of the one-armed creature, but not so much that he failed to notice the arrival of the other creature. This one seemed almost like a massive slug, as tall as the one-armed creature but lacking any visible appendage or limb. Its body seemed to be covered in smooth, unbroken bone that bent and turned as the creature moved without cracking or breaking. Without limb to grasp or claw, it nevertheless presented a clear danger with its mouth, filled with three rows of sharp teeth and stretching from one side of its head to the other, above which was a single enormous eye in which three pupils contracted hungrily at the sight of the seven.

As the bone-slug turned its three-pupiled gaze upon the seven, the one-armed creature issued a roar of challenge from its chest-mouth and then thundered towards the seven on its massive legs.

Galaad cried out in alarm as the one-armed creature bore down on them but stood his ground, raising his sword high. The one-armed creature batted Galaad aside, knocking him to the ground, and reached for Caius. The fair-haired captain managed to scramble away as the one-armed creature snapped at him, but found that he'd lost his shield to its snapping chest-mouth.

At the same instant the bone-slug advanced, and not willing to wait for the creature to make its move, Artor charged forward, a battle cry in his throat. Its three rows of teeth gnashing loudly, and the bone-slug swung its massive head from one side to the other, bashing Artor aside, crumpling his shield and knocking his spatha from his hands.

With Galaad on the ground a short distance away, and Caius still scrambling backwards, the one-armed creature reached for Gwrol, wrapping its massive hand around him in rib-crushing embrace and lifting him bodily off the ground. With shouts of alarm, Bedwyr and Pryder rushed to Gwrol's defense, hacking at the creature's arm with their swords. And though their swords only rebounded off its tough hide, failing to draw blood, the one-armed creature howled in pain and annoyance, bloated lips twisted wide and wicked teeth snapping side to side, still holding fast to Gwrol. The captains continued their assault on its arm, and at length the creature released its hold on Gwrol, who collapsed to the ground, struggling to catch his breath.

Pressing the advantage, Pryder rushed ahead, swinging his sword like a woodsman's ax at the one-armed creature, but it merely opened its mighty hand and then closed it over his sword, tugging it away from his grip. While Pryder stood for a moment, empty-handed, the creature reared back its enormous arm and threw his sword away end-over-end into the water behind it.

Meanwhile, the bone-slug snapped at Galaad, who still lay sprawled in its path. Howling imprecations, Lugh leapt forward, his feet leaving the ground entirely, and tackled the bone-slug's head. The arc of his arm continued, driving his sword into the three-pupiled eye of the footless monster. In that same instant, though, his other arm came too near the creature's mouth, and before Lugh was able to pull his sword free and jump away, the three-rowed maw of the bone-slug clamped down. The bone-slug's fearsome mouth closed over Lugh's arm, and wild-eyed the Gael threw himself backwards, trying to tug his arm free and escape. He pulled free of the bone-slug's mouth, but his hand and forearm came away with it. As he fell screaming to the ground, blood gouted from the ruin of his arm just below the elbow.

The bone-slug, Lugh's sword buried in its eye, possibly piercing its brain, shrieked as it fell back into the water, kicking up a dark spray which rained down on the seven.

A short distance off, Caius, Artor, and Bedwyr stood their ground against the one-armed creature, while Pryder stood defensively over Gwrol, his shield held high.

Galaad rushed to Lugh's side, trying to staunch the free-flowing blood, unsure how they would manage against the remaining monster and hoping against hope that more creatures would not be climbing from beneath the waters to join them.

Just then, a high-pitched noise rang out, just at the edge of hearing. Galaad gritted his teeth, the sound buzzing in his skull, but as noisome as he found it, it was clear that the one-armed creature reacted much worse. Ignoring the trio of swords before it, the one-armed creature reared up, roars of pain issuing from its chest-mouth. Its enormous arm flailing above, the creature turned away and raced back towards the shore, the four eyes lining its back rolling around in agony. The creature crashed into the water and dove underneath, disappearing from view.

The captains turned, looking for the source of the sound.

"There!" Caius said, pointing with his sword's top.

A short distance off, what appeared to be a small silver ship rose up from the water. Lacking any sails or oars, it skimmed across the water towards them at speed, no larger than a one-man fishing boat.

Gwrol had found his feet, with Pryder's help, and the captains gathered around the prostrate form of Lugh, who clutched the bloody stump of his arm to his chest, tears streaming. Galaad stood, his sword in hand, and with the others faced the approaching craft.

There was no crew, but when the ship drew near the shore, Galaad could see that there was movement on her decks as dozens of beetlelike creatures whose skins glinted like silver scuttled about.

The crewless ship beached on the shore, half her bulk out of the water, and all movement on her ceased. Just then, a low hum could be heard, and a light shone up from the center of the ship's deck. There, before them, stood a woman, with white hair, white raiment, and glowing white eyes.

Hers was a face Galaad knew well. He dropped to his knees, throwing his sword to one side.

"White Lady," he said, and bowed his head.

CHAPTER TWENTY

Jubilee

THAT EVENING, AT PRECISELY SEVEN O'CLOCK, Blank and Miss Bonaventure rang the bell at Baron Carmody's Mayfair house and were ushered in by a servant. As they were escorted through cavernous halls lit by electric flambeaux and wide, carpeted corridors lined with portraits in gilt frames, it became apparent that the house had seen better days. Priceless furniture was covered beneath sheets of linen, gathering dust, vases and pots were choked with desiccated plants and flowers long past the point where watering would have saved them. The servant who escorted them was evidently one of only a handful who remained to keep the house in working order, the household operating with only a skeletal staff.

Lord Arthur received them in the library, carpeted in thick rugs the color of spilled blood, the walls covered in dark paneling, lamplight flickering off the steel of crossed swords over the fireplace. This was clearly the sanctum of an explorer, African tribal masks on the walls opposite the fierce visages of masked Japanese helmets, a towering pyramid of maps and charts piled haphazardly beside an enormous globe, totemic figures and amulets crowding every available shelf. The Baron Carmody himself sat in a high-backed, wing-armed chair upholstered in the finest leather, to all appearances a man of forty years of age or more, gone somewhat to seed, with a great shock of blond hair and a full beard, a brandy snifter in one hand and a cigar in the other, while on the nearby couch sat an ancient doyenne in a black mourning dress, her skin white with bismuth, her hair lacquered into a tight bun. Standing beside the fireplace, in which only cool embers lay, was W. B. Taylor, leaning against the mantle, a holstered LeMat revolver at his hip, a cut-glass tumbler gripped in one hand.

"Ah," said Lord Arthur on their entrance, waving them in with the burning ember of his cigar's tip, "you must be the investigators Taylor told us about. What were your names again?" He looked from the pair to Taylor, who shifted his gaze to the cold ashes in the fireplace, unspeaking.

"My name is Sandford Blank," the detective replied, stepping into the breach, "and this is my associate, Miss Roxanne Bonaventure."

Lord Arthur nodded, graciously, and indicated the ancient woman sitting primly on the couch with a minute movement of his brandy glass. "This is the Lady Priscilla Cavendish, and you know Bill Taylor, of course."

"Lady Priscilla," Blank said demurely, inclining his head in her direction. Beside him, Miss Bonaventure dipped momentarily in the ghost of a curtsey.

Lady Priscilla fixed them with a broad grin, and with the rolling r's of a Welsh accent, said, "Charmed to meet you, to be sure."

"Now, what is it we can do for you?" the Baron Carmody asked. "Something to do with the unfortunate deaths of Mr. Brade and Miss Villers, I take it?"

"A reasonable guess," Miss Bonaventure said with a smile, taking a seat. Blank leaned an elbow on the chair's back and rested his hip against its arm.

"I was hoping you might tell us a little bit about your little league, my lord," Blank said. "I take it your 'round table' is something to do with that of the legendary king whose name you share?"

The Baron Carmody bristled a bit at hearing his organization being called a "little League," but nodded, scowling slightly. "Yes, indeed. I became somewhat obsessed with my namesake on my return from Africa. Nearly a decade ago I was traveling in the dark continent when tragedy struck and I lost my wife and infant son. On my return to Belhorm some time later, I resolved to contribute something of substance to society rather than sinking into a morass of grief and self-pity. So it was that I pledged myself to restoring Britain to her former days of glory, and to the rebirth of the Age of Arthur in modern times. Shortly thereafter I attended a dinner in the city and chanced to strike up a conversation with Lady Priscilla and found in her a kindred spirit. So it was that the League of the Round Table was formed, and our mission of restoring the Age of Arthur begun."

"A . . . laudable goal, to be sure," Miss Bonaventure said, quirking a smile. "If perhaps a bit . . . ambiguous?"

"I believe what my associate means," Blank put in, "is that we'd very much like to know the specific means by which you hope to reach your goal."

"Well," Lady Priscilla said, picking up the thread, "perhaps I can assist. After all, this *is* the point in which I enter Lord Arthur's story. You see, after the death of my second husband, rest him, I developed a positive passion for Welsh mythology in general, and the stories of Arthur in particular. A veritable mania, one might say. My original intention was to produce my own translation of a collection of songs and poems from the Middle Welsh, which I felt would redress some shortcomings in Lady Charlotte's interpretation, but the more I researched the topic, the more I became convinced that there was a lost root text behind so much of Arthurian and Welsh myth and legend, an original of which the later versions were simply garbled misrememberances. However, I quickly realized that my own skills were not up to the task of rendering the story into modern verse, and so suggested to Lord Arthur that we might enlist the services of others of greater talent to help bring my vision to fruition. It is our fiercest hope that, when 'The Raid on the Unworld' is published, the public will be so edified as to accomplish our goal."

"That's your project, is it?" Blank glanced at Taylor loitering near the fireplace. "'The Raid on the Unworld?'"

"Just so," Lord Arthur said, waving his cigar, the smoke ribboning like a banner. "'The Raid on the Unworld: The True History of Arthur.'"

"The text will be by Mr. Taylor," Lady Priscilla explained, "based on my outline, of course, and it will be illustrated with photographs by Miss Villers, with costumes and designs by Mr. Brade." She paused, her excitement flagging and her smile beginning to droop as she recalled the circumstances which had brought them together that evening. "Of course, it *was* to have photographs and designs by Miss Villers and Mr. Brade," she went on, deflating, "but now I suppose we'll have to find some new talents to take up the torch."

"Do you have any examples of their work that we might see?" Miss Bonaventure asked.

"Of course," Lady Priscilla said, brightening. "Mr. Taylor, could you fetch that envelope I brought, the one you sent me yesterday evening."

Taylor obliged, grudgingly, and Lady Priscilla slid a stack of photographic reproductions from the slender envelope. These she handed to Miss Bonaventure, who held them up for Blank and her to see. There, in crisp halftones, were images of actors and models in elaborate Arthurian costume, posing in gardens astride uneasy horses or against painted backdrops with prop swords held aloft. There was a frankly amateurish quality to the whole production, but Blank managed a smile when he looked up in the proud, expectant faces of Lady Priscilla and Lord Arthur.

"Charming," he said, forcing an approving tone into his voice. "Quality work, I should think."

Returning to his post by the mantle, Taylor shook his head, dismissively. "Aw, it's sophomoric junk, and you know it," he said, exasperated. "I had a list of notes as long as my arm I was going to share with Cecilia, things she needed to correct before taking another shot, but I never had the chance." He shook his head, ruefully. "She was a nice lady, sure, and could work a camera, but I don't think she understood what we were after."

"Bosh, my good man, pure bosh," Lord Arthur objected, smoothing his blond beard with his thumb and forefinger. "There was room for improvement, to be sure, but you shouldn't dismiss their labors so cavalierly."

Miss Bonaventure fanned out the photos on the low table before her and looked up to meet Lady Priscilla's gaze. "My lady, would you mind explaining the essence of the story? I'm afraid I'm having trouble getting a sense of it from these images alone."

The Lady Priscilla struggled to keep her smile from spreading too broadly across her face, trying to maintain some decorum, but it was clear she had a passion for talking about her cherished subject. As her accent and manner indicated, she was a native of Wales and had only later in life begun to move in the rarified air of London society. So it was that there was something coarse and unrefined in her manner, which may not have endeared her to all of the doyennes with whom she was required to mix in polite society, but which Blank could not help but find refreshing.

"Certainly, my dear," Lady Priscilla said, clapping her hands excitedly.

"It's quite simple, really. It concerns Arthur, a Roman war duke in the days of the Saxon invasions, going with a group of men to a tower of glass on an island in order to rescue a woman held hostage by a magician." Lady Priscilla leaned forward, his eyes twinkling, her hands moving expressively. "This is the story found in the Welsh poetical fragment, 'The Spoils of Annwn'—Annwn here meaning 'not-world' or 'Unworld'—and found also in the stories 'Branwen, Daughter of Lyr' and 'The Voyage of Bran.' The former features Bendigei-duran, or 'Blessed Bran,' supposedly a different Bran than the voyaging cognate, though I think it's clear the two stories are garbled remembrances of the same tale. Bran, while it means 'raven,' also means 'king,' which suggests Arthur, does it not? And it's suggestive that both Bran and Arthur, when they are dead, are said to have had their severed heads buried beneath the White Mount, where the Tower of London stands today. Ravens, I should point out, feature heavily in the myths of the Welsh and Irish, attending the goddess Morrigan. In any event, the voyaging Bran, son of Febal, is summoned by the vision of a woman in white to an island on which silver-branched apple trees with crystal blossoms grow upon the white-silver plain, this island alternatively named 'many-shaped Emne by the sea' and 'Emain Ablach,' or 'Island of the Apple Trees,' which later chroniclers corrupted as Avalon."

Blank opened his mouth to speak, but the Lady Priscilla soldiered on, unflagging.

"In each of these stories there are four main objects, repeated in variations. First, there is a cauldron that can heal wounds and raise the dead, remembered in later times as a grail. Second, there is a sword, which we remember as Excalibur, and which Geoffrey of Monmouth called Caliburn, but which the Welsh knew originally as Caledfwlch, or Caledbwlch. *Caled*, of course, is Welsh for 'hard,' and *bwlch* is Welsh for 'gap' or 'space.' 'Hard space' or 'Hard gap' hardly makes sense etymologically, but perhaps there is some connection with the sword of Fergus mac Róich, Caladbolg, which means 'Hard Lightning,' and which the legends said had the power to slice the tops off hills and take out several men at a stroke. Or perhaps the sword of Manannan Mac Lir and Lugh Lamfada from Irish myth, the Fragarach, or 'Answerer,' which was said to be a sword no armor could withstand. Or perhaps even the sword of Nuada of the Silver Hand, Claiomh Solais, or 'Sword of Light,' which was one of the Four

Treasures of Ireland, an irresistible blade which had the power to cut enemies in half. In 'The Spoils of Annwn,' Llenlleawc the Irishman wields a 'sword of lightning.' One wonders if there might not be a connection between these sundry sword bearers. After all, the Irish Nuada is one of the Tuatha de Danaan who loses his hand fighting against the Firbolg at the First Battle of Magh Tuireadh, whereupon the god of medicine, Dian Cecht, made him a new hand of silver. Nuada, then, is cognate to the Welsh Nudd of the Silver Hand, and Nudd is cognate with Lludd, or Lludd Lllaw Ereint, or Silver Hand. By extension, then, both are cognate with the Welsh Llwch Llawwynnyawc, or Windy-Hand, and the Irish Lugh Lamfada, or Long Hand. In any event, in both Chretien's 'The Knight of Two Swords' and the Post-Vulgate 'Suite Du Merlin' there is a sword that only a worthy knight can draw from its scabbard. In Chretien's version of Percival's story, which is itself a dimly remembered version of the story of the *Mabinogion*'s Peredur, the hero is presented with a magical sword, like which only three had ever been made, and which could never be broken, except in one perilous circumstance. It was in that same account that Perceval saw a white lance with blood oozing from its tip, the Bleeding Lance being the third of the four objects which recur so often in these stories. It brings to mind Luin, the Flaming Spear which belonged to Lugh and which was another of the Four Treasures of Ireland. In the *Mabinogion* version of the story, Peredur sees such a spear but also a platter upon which is carried a man's severed head. The later romancers, embellishing the story of Percival, identified this head with John the Baptist, but might the original chroniclers have meant that of Bran, or perhaps even the head of Arthur himself, borne back to be buried beneath the White Hill, where the Tower of London stands today?"

Lady Priscilla paused in her lecture for a brief moment, musing.

"Cauldron and sword, spear and shield. These come down to us as the suits of the Tarot—cup, sword, staff, and coin—which themselves have devolved into the suits of playing cards over the centuries—hearts, spades, clubs, and diamonds. Interesting to think that the original story of Arthur, lost to us for millennia, might have been encoded in every deck used to play whist or poker the world 'round, isn't it?"

If Lady Priscilla expected some answer, she didn't pause long enough to hear it, but continued on, buoyed by her own enthusiasm for the subject.

"Just as there are four objects in the tales, there are three women, or one woman in three aspects, if you like, the triune goddess—mother, maiden, and crone. These recur again and again, the three goddesses of the Unworld—Rhiannon, Gwenhwyfar, and Morrigan. Now, Rhiannon is generally thought to mean 'Great Queen,' or Rigatona, but I think it more likely began as *rhiain annwn*, or 'maid of annwn.' *Rhiainannwn*, the Maid of the Unworld, could have become 'Niniane' and 'Vivienne' over time. And while the name Morrigan is thought to be Irish in origin, most likely *mór rigan*, or 'great queen,' I argue instead that it derives from a Welsh root, and was later loaned to the Irish. Rather than 'great queen,' it is *môr gwiddon*, or 'sea witch.' *Môrgwiddon* isn't a million miles from Morgain, the Welsh lady of the lake, and Morrigan, the Irish goddess attended by ravens. And there is the reference to *bran* again, raven and king. Finally, in Welsh, the Guinevere of Arthur is known as Gwenhwyfar. This is composed of *gwen*, meaning 'white' or 'fair,' and *hwyfar*, meaning 'smooth' or 'phantom.' The name could mean White Phantom. And while the story seemed little to interest the *compiler* Malory"—and here she sneered in distaste—"throughout the more primal tales were stories of Arthur's bride being abducted and carried off, often to a glass castle. Caradoc writes of Guenevere's abduction by Melwas, Geoffrey and Wace refer to Guenevere's abduction by Mordred, and Chretien writes about Guenevere's abduction by Meleagaunt. In this consonance of names—Melwas, Mordred, Meleagaunt—we hear echoes of the master of the tower of glass, the Lord of the Unworld. In Irish myth and folklore can be found the fairy known as *Fear Dearg*, or 'Red Man.' He dresses from head to toe in red and can make himself invisible. This figure is also remembered as Dagda, the Irish father of the gods, he of the cauldron, who was also known as *Ruad Rofessa*, alternatively translated as 'Lord of Great Knowledge' and as 'Red One of Great Knowledge.' Remember, too, that Merlin was said to have been imprisoned, either by Niniane or Vivienne, in a castle of glass, and there is the initial 'm' consonant again. In the Prose Lancelot of the Vulgate Cycle, Niniane is a fey who learned the magic arts from Merlin, lives in a magic lake, and who gives young Lancelot hints of the future, while outfitting him in white and silver. Is this the same lake in which resides the lady who gives Arthur his magic sword, Excalibur by any name? And I can't help but wonder if there might not be some connection with Dindrane, Perceval's sister in the Vulgate Grail Cycle, who gives Perceval the Sword of Strange Straps on board the crewless Ship of Solomon. Or even with the Queen of the Waste Land in the same cycle, who tells Perceval that only he, Galahad, and Bors will complete the Grail quest."

Lady Priscilla mused for a moment before continuing.

"Perceval has a complicated lineage, I should think. There is a measure of 'twin confusion' in the *Mabinogion*, and in particular in the story of Pryderi, also known as Peredur, later named Perceval. In *Pwyll Lord of Dyved*, Pryderi is originally named Gwri Golden Hair by his foster parents on account of the color of his hair. Only when he is reunited with his parents is he given the name Pryderi. In the *Mabinogion* story of *Peredur Son of Evrawg*, Peredur meets an old man with two sons, one yellow-haired and one auburn-haired. The old man proves to be his uncle, making these his cousins, but that's of little consequence. Later, in the Circular Valley, Peredur meets a great hoary-haired man in the company of two young lads, one with yellow hair and one with auburn, who carry knives with hilts of walrus ivory. Again, one yellow, one auburn. In the *Annales Cambriae*, of course, the later and possibly historical figures Gwrgi and Peredur are brothers. And finally, in many of the romances, Gawain's nickname is Gwalltafwyn, which means 'hair like rain,' and is translated as 'Golden Hair.' Is it possible that the chroniclers confused two figures for one, and ascribed to one figure the deeds and characteristics of two brothers?"

Blank stepped over to an empty chair and settled himself in. It was clear that, once she got started, it was not easy to get Lady Priscilla to stop.

"But that's another matter entirely. As to the actions of the story," she went on, "there are many hints. In 'Branwen, Daughter of Llyr,' Bran goes to rescue his sister Branwen from the Irish king Matholwch, who possesses the cauldron which can raise the dead. In 'The Spoils of Annwn,' Arthur and his men sail to Annwn to recover the cauldron from the Lord of Annwn, who has housed it in a Caer Wydr, or Glass Fortress, where he keeps someone named Gweir prisoner, said fortress alternatively known as Caer Pedryfan, the Four-Times Revolving Fortress, and as Caer Sidi, the Faerie Fortress, among others. Glastonbury was named by the ancient Britons 'Ynys Witrin,' or Island of

Glass, which perhaps suggests some connection between that hill in Somerset and the idea of a revolving fortress of glass, home of the Sidhe or faeries. In Caradoc's 'Life of Gildas,' it is reported that Arthur sails to the Isle of Glass, to recover Geunever from Melwas, the king of the Summer Country, in his Glass Castle. Here again, one is reminded of the fact that Somerset originally meant 'Summer Lands.' In Chretien's 'The Knight of the Cart,' Lancelot must go to the magical otherworld of Meleagaunt of Goirre—possibly *Voire*, or glass—to rescue Guinevere from a tower completely encircled by water, accessible only by a bridge made from a sword's blade. In Chretien's 'Erec and Enide,' itself a varient of the Welsh legends of Geraint and Enid, Maheloas is lord of *L'Ile de Voire*, the Island of Glass, about which is said, 'in this island no thunder is heard, no lightning strikes, nor tempests rage, nor do toads or serpents exist there, nor is it ever too hot or too cold.'"

Lady Priscilla sighed contentedly, looking like a barrister giving a final summation.

"So, you can see, there must have been some original to all these stories about Arthur and a band of men sailing to an island upon which was built a glass citadel to rescue a woman kept prisoner by a magician whose name might well have begun with the consonant 'm.' This magician, further, was in possession of a cauldron which could raise the dead and heal the injured, remembered in later times as the Grail. A woman, either the one imprisoned or another, outfits the heroes with magical swords, and perhaps also with lances and shields, and at some point a head borne upon a shield." She clapped her hands and gave Blank and Miss Bonaventure a broad smile. "See? As I told you, it's quite simple, and easily said."

Lady Priscilla finished her impromptu lecture, which left Blank and Miss Bonaventure feeling somewhat dizzy. It was clear that the Baron Carmody and Taylor had both heard this recitation many times, either whole or in parts, but on hearing it for the first time the listener was left with the principal impression of information flying past at speed, with only bits and pieces alighting in their minds long enough to make an impression.

Blank was hard pressed to find a connection between the litany of myth and legends Lady Priscilla had presented them and the deaths of the three prostitutes which had initiated his investigates. Nor, for that matter, could he see a clear connection between the deaths of the prostitutes and those of the former members of the League of the Round Table, Brade and Villers. Still, something nagged at the edge of his thoughts. Lady Priscilla *had*, after all, made mention of decapitated heads borne on platters. And of a figure—whether Nuada, or Nudd, or Ludd, or Lugh—who lost a hand in battle and was given a new one of silver. It was almost as if someone were reenacting elements of these myths in the modern day, inflicting on streetwalkers the injuries sustained by the mythical heroes. But in none of Lady Priscilla's recitation had she mentioned anything like the more prosaic injuries sustained by Brade and Villers, who had simply been cut and allowed to bleed to death.

"Fascinating," Miss Bonaventure said, sounding genuinely intrigued. She always had exhibited a passion for the mythological and arcane, at least when they could be seen to hint at some forgotten historicity. Blank's companion seemed to have made careful note of much that Lady Priscilla had said.

"Quite," Blank said, not as charitably. "And I'm sorry to drag the discussion from matters lofty to those much more sordid, but I'm afraid I must." He stood and began to pace slowly about the room, shifting his gaze from Lord Arthur to Lady Priscilla to Taylor. "Can you think of anyone who might hold some animus towards your group? Anyone who might bear a grudge, and who could have targeted Mr. Brade and Miss Villers for revenge?"

The three members of the League of the Round Table exchanged glances, open faced.

"Well . . ." Lady Priscilla ventured, unsure, "I suppose there could be some scholar, perhaps, who disagrees with our opinions, but I can't imagine that any of them could be quite so fervent as to contemplate violence, much less murder."

Taylor chuckled, ruefully. "Maybe it's somebody who read my first book of poems and wants to keep me from committing verse again."

The Baron Carmody puffed on his cigar, thoughtfully. "No," he said, shaking his head in a wreath of smoke. "I can't think of a one, I'm afraid."

"Oh," Lady Priscilla said, raising her eyebrows. "What about that strange man who came round asking questions the other week? What was his name again? Mervyn something?"

Lord Arthur nodded, remembering. "Fawkes," he said after a moment. "Mervyn Fawkes."

"Yes, yes." Lady Priscilla nodded eagerly. "That was it."

"Odd duck, that one," Taylor put in.

"And what did this Mervyn . . . Fawkes, was it?" Miss Bonaventure folded her hands in her lap, her tone gentle. "What did this Mervyn Fawkes do, precisely?"

Lord Arthur stuck out his lower lip, scowling. "Can't say I know what the cove did, except to pester us one night until Taylor and my manservant were forced to push him bodily out into the street. He just raved about stuff and nonsense."

"He was keen on the Grail, as I recall," Lady Priscilla said. "Had all manner of questions about the Grail Cycle, and about the ancient British myths from which the romances derived."

"Fellah was a few bricks shy of a load, if you ask me," Taylor said.

"The Grail, was it?" Blank pursed his lips, nodding thoughtfully.

"The gentleman was under the illusion that the Grail was a physical object," Lady Priscilla said, "rather than a metaphor for the quest for the divine within each of us."

"Well," Taylor drawled, "I don't know about *that*. The way I figure it, the Grail myth that's come down to us is a jumbled-up version of some older story, maybe a religious tale from pre-Roman Britain. Some sort of vessel of the gods, could be, like an original of the horn o'plenty."

"Bosh," Lord Arthur blustered. "The Grail is both literal *and* symbol. It has a physical existence, but in itself represents the boundless mercy of the divine. That it has not been seen since ancient times is more a commentary on the quality of those who have sought the cup than it is evidence of the Grail's existence or lack thereof." The Baron Carmody's chest swelled, proudly. "Mayhap, once our current enterprise is completed, we can mount a search for the Grail itself, and complete the restoration of the Age of Arthur with a return of the holy cup to this blessed plot."

Blank and Miss Bonaventure exchanged a meaningful glance. It was clear they were both thinking the same thing.

"Thank you all," Blank said, offering Miss Bonaventure his elbow. "You've all been most generous with your time."

"Are you going?" Lady Priscilla asked, sounding vaguely wounded. "I'd not yet even had a chance to discuss the meaning of the crewless ship."

"Oh," Miss Bonaventure said with a smile, "we've taken up too much of your time as it is."

The Baron Carmody remained in his seat, his eyes on the middle distance, his thoughts somewhere far away. "Perhaps," he continued, his voice low, his manner almost dreamlike, "we can even recover Excalibur itself. Think of it! The nation restored by sword and cup, and with us to thank."

Taylor gave them a weary smile and a ghost of a shrug. Blank did not fail to notice, though, the way the cowboy poet's hand never strayed far from the LeMat pistol at his hip. While the Baron Carmody escaped the grim reality of his circumstances—widowed, childless, and alone—in increasingly ethereal flights of fancy, and the Lady Priscilla lost herself in a maze of theory and erudition, it was clear that the former Knight of the Texas Plains was all too aware of the possible danger they faced from the Jubilee Killer.

"We'll see ourselves out," Blank said, inclining his head to the Baron Carmody in his chair and then to the Lady Priscilla. Then, with a nod to Taylor, he and Miss Bonaventure left the room the way they came in, leaving the League of the Round Table to its own devices.

The next morning, when Miss Bonaventure arrived at his house in York Place, Blank was hustling out the door to meet her before she'd even climbed down from the cab.

"Baker Street Station," Blank called out to the driver, climbing in beside her.

"Going on a journey, are we, Blank?" Miss Bonaventure asked.

"Just a brief excursion, my dear," Blank said with a smile. "Do you fancy a trip south to Crystal Palace?"

"Lawks!" Miss Bonaventure mimed fanning herself with her hand. "In *this* heat?"

"Ah, you're a delicate flower, Miss Bonaventure. Console yourself, though, my dear. Perhaps when our business is concluded you can cool your-self by the waters of the Boating and Fishing Lake."

At Baker Street, they boarded an Underground train on the Inner Circle line, and as they rumbled through the stifling heat of the tunnels, Blank told Miss Bonaventure what he'd been about since last they'd parted.

"I was up half the night," he explained, "digging up what information I could about the Mervyn Fawkes whom the members of the league remembered."

"What did you find?" Miss Bonaventure asked, now fanning herself in earnest, raising her voice to be heard over the rattle of the train's wheels over the tracks.

Flashing her a smile, Blank pulled a notebook from an inner pocket of his suit jacket and in the dim light consulted his notes.

"Mervyn Fawkes. Born 1858, London, the son of a mathematician. Studied geography, cartography, and mathematics at Oxford, where he received an MA in geography and cartography. Later appointed as a lecturer at Cambridge. Fawkes was a junior representative to the Royal Geographical Society on Joseph Thompson's later expeditions through eastern Africa, and his contributions to the effort were later noted by the society's president."

"Not quite the raving loon of the league's remembrances, I shouldn't think," Miss Bonaventure observed.

"Give him time, my dear, give him time." Blank returned his attentions to his notes. "Fawkes wrote a monograph entitled 'On the problem of accurately sounding the depths of the continental shelf and the mid-Atlantic reaches,' which was published in the *Journal of the Royal Geographical Society* in 1883. It appears that there was some sort of incident on an expedition for the RGS in 1885, after which Fawkes was briefly a voluntary patient at the Colney Hatch Lunatic Asylum. A short while later he left the institution against his doctor's wishes. He seemed then to develop an interest in philology, of all things. The May 1888 edition of the *Modern Language Notes* journal contained a letter from Fawkes in the Correspondence section, in response to an essay on the subject of 'The Old French Merlin' which ran in the March edition of that year, while the December 1888 edition of *Modern Language Notes* carried a review by Fawkes on James M. Garnett's *Beowulf: An Anglo-Saxon Poem.*"

"Fascinating reading, I'm sure."

Blank offered a sly grin. "Given my struggles to remain awake and cogent in the early morning hours as I reviewed the text, I might be forced to disagree. In any event, in the autumn of 1889 there is a record of Fawkes booking passage on a tramp steamer bound for Reykjavik but no indication that he returned. Not, that is, until he appeared on the employment rolls of the Crystal Palace in early May of this year, just some six weeks ago."

Miss Bonaventure cocked an eyebrow. "Where, one assumes, he works still?"

Blank's grin broadened. "So it would appear."

She nodded, appreciatively. "Fair enough. I think a brief foray is justified to see what our Mr. Fawkes has to tell us."

"My thinking exactly, Miss Bonaventure."

At Victoria Station, they transferred, purchasing tickets on the Crystal Palace Railway and boarding the next train heading south. From there, it was a brief journey of twenty minutes or so over the Thames and down towards Sydenham. Once they'd reached Sydenham Hill and the Lower Level of the Crystal Palace Railway Station, it was just a short walk to the Crystal Palace itself, relocated to south London from Hyde Park after the closing of the Great Exhibition of 1851. They passed the pools and fountains glittering in the midmorning sun and headed down the pathways lined with the imposing figures of Benjamin Waterhouse Hawkins's life-sized dinosaur replicas.

The Crystal Palace rose before them like a castle made of glass, and Blank could not help recalling the recurrent imagery in Lady Priscilla's recitation. Had Joseph Paxton read those sorts of stories as a child, perhaps, or had he merely dreamed up the folly while plagued by an undigested bit of cheese?

Blank remembered seeing Blondin performing at the Crystal Palace, years before. It had been only a handful of months since he'd read about the acrobat's death in Ealing. Blondin had assisted him in an investigation shortly after Blank had taken up the role of the consulting detective, and he'd been indebted to Blondin ever since. They'd dined together, from time to time, when Blondin's travels brought him back to London. To see the once agile and virile tumbler wither with age, his vaunted strength gradually failing him as health and vision faded, was an uncomfortable and unpleasant reminder of mortality. Other people's mortality, of course, not Blank's own. Still, he knew that there was an end to his own road, as well, a terminus towards which he traveled, however slowly; if it had not been for Omega and the lacuna Michel Void, though, he'd have reached the end of that journey long years before, at the many hands of Croatoan.

As he and Miss Bonaventure mounted the steps to the Crystal Palace's main entrance, Blank shook his head, trying to knock loose the ancient memories which crowded his thoughts and focusing his mind on the task at hand. Their first-class tickets on the Crystal Palace Railway, at a cost of two shillings and six, included admission to the Crystal Palace itself, so they had only to wave their stubs at the porter to be admitted without need for persuasion.

The museum housed within the glass and steel walls of the Crystal Palace was surprisingly vacant for such a lovely June day, apparently as there were few new exhibits at the moment to attract fresh custom. The few museum-goers were ushered around by docents, who led them from one item of note to another, while maids dissolutely pushed broom and pan across the floors, mooning. A subcurator, when plied with a bit of suggestion and one of Blank's featureless white calling cards, was only too happy to direct them through the north transept and to the Alhambra Court, where Fawkes had been set the task of dismantling an exhibit of textiles from Moorish Spain. Unfortunately, on arriving in the indicated section of the museum, they found Fawkes not in evidence, and they had to prevail on another museum employ to escort them through the various courts, halls, and vestibules of the building until Fawkes could be spotted.

They passed collections of tropical plants and ferns; cages full of live tropical birds and reptiles; objects of curiosity from the Orient; the so-called Mammoth Tree of California, standing some four hundred feet and at an age of four thousand years old—having achieved such an age just before being cut down and shipped overseas, Blank imagined ruefully; examples of British manufacture, including ceramics and glass, basket-carriages and broughams, locomotives, pumps, and washing-machines; fountains; picture galleries; photographical collections; objects of art and *vertu*, the utilities and luxuries of modern social life.

At last, their guide finally pointed out the lank figure lurking in the

Medieval Court, intent on the close examination of a tapestry dating back to the twelfth century.

Blank thanked their escort and sent him scurrying back to his duties, more than a little confused why he had agreed to act as impromptu guide to complete strangers when he had important work to be about.

"Mr. Fawkes?" Blank said, carefully approaching the man, his hat in one hand, his cane in the other. "I was wondering if we might have a word with you."

The man started and wheeled around to face them with a quick intake of breath.

"There's no cause for alarm," Miss Bonaventure said soothingly. "We'd simply like to ask you a few questions."

The man regained control of himself and regarded them with evident suspicion. He was short and thin, standing no taller than Blank's shoulder, with a mass of wiry hair and a stringy beard. The elbows of his coat were shiny with age, his cravat all askew, and periodically his left eye and the left corner of his mouth would twitch in concert, some sort of unconscious tic. "Who are you?" he asked, evenly.

"You'll have to forgive our rude manners," Blank said, and presented one of his calling cards. "My name is Sandford Blank, and this is my companion Miss Bonaventure. We are consulting detectives, assisting the police on a matter most grave." The barely audible thrum pulsed beneath his words, to no apparent effect.

The man squinted at the featureless calling card, and then raised a suspicious brow at Blank. "What's that to do with me?"

"*Are* you Mervyn Fawkes?" Miss Bonaventure asked as Blank tucked the card back into his pocket.

The man allowed that he was, albeit reluctantly.

"Now that we know each other," Blank said, comradely, "perhaps we can adjourn somewhere a bit more comfortable and chat for a moment." He looked from Fawkes to Miss Bonaventure and back. "I don't know about the two of you, but I'm absolutely *ravenous*."

A short while later, the three of them were seated in a private dining room in the Refreshment Department of the Crystal Palace, a cold collation of meats, entremets, and pâtés spread before them. Blank sipped a glass of lemonade, while Miss Bonaventure sampled a bottle of ginger beer. Fawkes sat opposite them, his hands spread on the tabletop, regarding them coolly.

"I'm sorry," Fawkes insisted, "but I just can't help you. Yes, I'll admit I went 'round to Baron Carmody's place the other week, to ask a few questions, but that was an end to it. I'd never seen any of those people before, and I've never seen any of them since."

Blank fixed him with a dazzling smile and nodded. "Certainly, I understand. These questions are a mere formality, you understand."

Fawkes glowered.

"Tell me, Mr. Fawkes," Miss Bonaventure said, "where do you currently reside?"

Fawkes narrowed his eyes. "I keep rooms in a lodging house in Camberwell."

"Ah." Miss Bonaventure nodded. "And you've lived there since your return from Iceland."

"Yes, I . . ." Fawkes began, and then broke off, realizing he'd said too much.

"So you *were* most recently in Iceland, then?" Miss Bonaventure asked, pressing the advantage.

"Perhaps," Fawkes said warily. "What of it?"

"You left England on a steamer bound for Reykjavik in 1889," Blank said, casually. "Just what have you been doing there in the cold, all these years?"

Fawkes drew his mouth into a tight line and remained silent.

"Ah, you'll have to forgive me," Blank said airily, chuckling slightly. "My curiosity gets the better of me."

"Camberwell is quite close to Lambeth," Miss Bonaventure observed. "Have you ever had occasion to visit the School for the Indigent Blind, by any chance? It's quite lovely."

Blank watched Fawkes's reactions closely, but if the mention of the blind asylum had generated any emotional response, the other man kept it well concealed.

"I've really got to be back to my duties." Fawkes's tone was gruff as he pushed his chair noisily back from the table and stood. "If you'll excuse me." With that, he was out the door and gone.

The two of them were left alone in the small dining room. "He seems somewhat suspicious in manner, wouldn't you say?" Miss Bonaventure said, raising an eyebrow.

"Quite." Blank sipped his lemonade. "And if he met Dickson's description of the man seen fleeing the scene of Miss Villers's murder, I would say that his manner was sufficient grounds to haul him before Melville with a bell around his neck."

"But he's not exactly tall, and not exactly hairless." With a look of disdain, she reached down and plucked a stray hair that had fluttered to the tabletop when Fawkes had risen and made his exit. "More's the pity."

"He didn't betray any knowledge of the blind asylum, either."

"He's a canny one, though if he's skilled at concealing guilt he's no dab hand at miming innocence." She sighed and turned to face Blank. "Well, shall we be off?"

"What's your rush, my dear?" Blank leaned back in his chair. "Have you tried the foie gras? It's better than it has any right to be."

The next days passed without incident. No further victims of the Jubilee Killer surfaced, but neither did any new evidence on the previous murders come to light. The heat, which at the month's beginning had been approaching uncomfortably warm, was now positively sweltering. It seemed only fitting, somehow, that Victoria should celebrate the anniversary of her ascendance to the throne in such a climate. After all, Blank mused, hadn't her subjects carried the "torch of civilization" to the globe's far corners? And if they sometimes set fire to the peoples and lands they found there with the self-same torch, well, what sort of thing was that to mention on such a splendid occasion? The conflagrations hadn't yet reached this sceptered isle, so it was hardly a subject worthy of polite conversation.

Blank burned, too, though the fires that raged in him had nothing to do with the climate. He'd once been a loyal subject to the crown. He *had* been, though there were times when he had to remind himself of it. And, come to that, there had been a time when he was a lacuna, a loyal agent of Omega, as well, happy to enter the School of Thought and receive his marching orders without a second's hesitation. But then he had been exposed to the writings of the Romantics, and those of William Blake in particular, and Blank had gradually had the scales removed from his eyes. He had lost his faith in empire, first, but then gradually, as he learned to conceal his thoughts, he broke with Omega as well, though the latter still had no notion of the split, so far as Blank was aware.

Blank was for self-determinism and the end of empire. Both empires in the here and now, and those which existed past tomorrow's horizon. It was the purpose to which he had pledged what remained of his long life and devoted what energy and time he could. There was some irony, then, that he found himself, on the twenty-second of June, joining the throngs who cheered the figurehead of empire herself, Queen Victoria.

It hardly mattered to Omega who sat upon the British throne; come to that, it hardly mattered to Omega whether Britain dominated the globe or some other, so long as one power did. In the days when the late Monsieur Void had been Omega's sole living lacuna, the sun had shone upon France. But as Michel Void passed beyond the mortal coil, so too did hopes for a French future. For a time, Blank and Quexi both toiled as lacunae in Omega's service, and it was even odds whether Britain or China would hold sway, but Quexi had learned too well Blank's lessons about freedom of will and expression and turned anarchist, and lacking her influence the Orient fell further under the dominion of the West.

Blank preferred to work at bringing down the system from within. While giving the appearance of carrying out Omega's wishes as outlined to him in periodic visits to the School of Thought, he worked in secret to undermine his master's plans. In the same way, while seeming to help ensure the stability of empire, through casual words in certain ears and covert action, he gradually eroded the empire's foundations, setting the stage for its eventual dissolution. His every intention was for a peaceful breakup of the established order, though he knew that some bloodshed would be inevitable. Still, he placed his hopes in figures such as Mohandas, whom he had met nearly a decade before while the young Indian was studying at University College London. Trained as a barrister, Mohandas was now in South Africa, fighting for the rights of Indians in that country, but eventually he would return home, and when he did, Blank hoped that he would put into action the non-violent methods they had discussed. With men like Mohandas taking up the cause of self-determinism, it was possible that in the future men might one day put off the yoke of authority and be the captains of their own destiny. And was it too much to hope that, in such a world, men and women would be free to love who they willed, and society's prejudice be damned?

If such a world waited beyond tomorrow's horizon, though, it was difficult to see any hint of it today. Rather than celebrating a free and independent India, the forty Indian potentates who rode in the Jubilee Procession carried an enormous banner, upon which was written a sentiment in English and Hindustani, proclaiming that Victoria alone was Queen of Earthly Queens.

Some fifty thousand troops marched in the procession, making plain the source of Victoria's strength. At its head was Captain Ames of the Horse Guard upon his charger, and Field Marshal Lord Roberts of Kandahar, astride the gray Arab, Vonolel, which had borne him from Kabul to Kandahar on his victorious march two decades before. In their train came cavalrymen from New South Wales, Hussars from Canada and Carabiniers from Natal, camel troops from Bikaner and Dyak headhunters from Borneo, the Chinese Police from Hong Kong in their coolie hats, Jamaicans in white gaiters and embroidered jackets, and Maori and Te'Maroan warriors who rivaled each other for tattooed ferocity.

The crowds along the route cheered and sang patriotic songs, though many hissed the Cypriot Zaptiehs in their fezzes, supposing in error that they were Turks. And it was not simply martial prowess that the crowds celebrated, but the privilege and power of those sovereigns and potentates that rode in the procession, as well. All of the nations and states in Victoria's dominion were represented, even the tiny Pacific principality of Kensington Island, whose headman walked the route from beginning to end, having little trust either in carriages or in the horses which drew them. And other powers, both those who shared authority with Victoria and those which could be her rivals, made an appearance, though often made strange bedfellows, as when the Papal Nuncio was forced to share a carriage with the representative of the Emperor of China.

Tens of thousands of Union Flags snapped in the summer breeze, flying from towers, draped from windows and awnings. But despite the wind, it was beastly hot, only amplified by the crush of bodies in the crowd. The Queen, in her stately carriage, cooled herself in the shade of a silk parasol, the ostrich feathers of her bonnet wilting slightly in the heat.

Sandford Blank and Roxanne Bonaventure were among the crowd, of course, as was every able-bodied member of the Metropolitan Police, all of them watchful of any sign of threat, whether to the Queen herself or to any of those who marched in her honor.

Blank and Miss Bonaventure were making their way through the crowd that lined the south side of the Strand when an ancient Chinese man collided with them, nearly knocking Miss Bonaventure off her feet. Blank caught her elbow, righting her, as the ancient Oriental leaned in close, bowing repeatedly in abject apology. Blank had dropped his cane, and the old man retrieved it for him. As Blank leaned forward and reached out to receive it, the old man whispered something in his ear, and then in a heartbeat had disappeared back into the throng.

"What was that about?" Miss Bonaventure asked, smoothing her skirts.

Blank settled his bowler back on his head, which had been knocked off kilter in the collision. Then, with the silver head of his cane, he pointed here and there in the crowd. Miss Bonaventure looked, and saw the Chinese scattered strategically throughout the crowd, nearly invisible in the mix of skin tones and nationalities.

"That gentleman was merely reporting in, letting me know that there's been no sign of a tall, hairless man with chalky skin, nor of a shorter man with a stringy beard and flyaway wiry hair."

"The agents of the Ghost Fox, one assumes?" Miss Bonaventure said. "On the lookout for Dickson's fleeing man and Mervyn Fawkes?"

Blank smiled. "They can go places and see things which are denied such as you and me, Miss Bonaventure, to say nothing of the police."

"At this point," Miss Bonaventure said, dabbing at her neck with a handkerchief, "the only place that I want to go is somewhere in the cool shade and out of this throng, and the only thing I want to see is a tall glass of lemonade. Preferably iced."

Blank took her arm. "I think the maddening crowd is fairly well watched at the moment." He led her towards a side street, away from the procession route. "And if Victoria happens to notice our absence, I'm sure a nice note and a fistful of flowers will make amends."

The procession was bound for St. Paul's, where the Prince of Wales awaited on horseback to receive the Queen, and so Blank and Miss Bonaventure went in the opposite direction. It wasn't until they crossed High Holborn, near the British Museum, that they found a public house that was open and not too crammed with patrons for them to gain entrance. Miss Bonaventure mourned the loss of her lemonade, but quickly decided that in a pinch a pint of ale would do just fine. So it was that while London was on its feet, cheering the Queen and celebrating the long years of her reign, the pair of investigators were secreted in a cool, dark booth at the rear of a nondescript public house, enjoying their pints in blessed silence.

It had been days since Miss Bonaventure had been able to indulge her love of the cheaper press, spending hours poring over the penny papers. Now that she had a moment of relative peace, she hoped to dip briefly into the sordid news and purple prose of the day. As it happened, though, the only papers the publican seemed to have on hand were those left behind by patrons: the day's edition of the *Daily Mail*, a special Jubilee issue which carried a headline about the *"Greatness of the British Race"*; a week-old copy of the *Shoe and Leather Trade Chronicle*; a copy of *Anti-Vivisectionist* of recent vintage, and a month-and-a-half-old edition of the *Standard*. Having had quite enough of the greatness of the British race in the streets outside, and having little interest in the shoe and leather trade nor in the campaign against vivisection, Miss Bonaventure perforce busied herself studying the yellowed pages of the ancient *Standard* that, if it did not rise to the level of purple prose which she usually sought in her periodicals, the Conservative audience of the paper preferring a more terse style, at least contained a rather detailed section on crime and punishment which suited her taste for the sordid.

After passing some quarter of an hour flipping through the aged pages of the *Standard*, Miss Bonaventure stopped short. Blank caught a hint of a smile on her lips as her eyes tracked back across a section, first once and then again. Then she looked up to meet Blank's gaze and took a long draught of her ale.

"The city's become dreadfully crowded, wouldn't you say, Blank? All of these well-meaning well-wishers underfoot. I don't know about you, but I think I could fancy a little excursion. Say, to Somerset?"

Blank cocked an eyebrow.

In response, Miss Bonaventure turned around the section of paper she'd been reading and indicated a small article with an outstretched finger.

Blank nodded, a smile tugging the corners of his mouth.

"You know, Miss Bonaventure, they say Taunton is lovely this time of year."

The brief article, dated the first of May, concerned a murder that had taken place in Taunton, in Somerset. A body had been discovered in Taunton Castle, the home of the Somerset Archeological and Natural History Society. Otherwise unremarkable, the report made mention of the fact that the victim's left hand, and right arm below the elbow, had been completely severed, the bones and flesh cleanly sheared away. The severed appendages had been found nearby the body the following morning, and the county coroner had been unable to account for how they had been removed, concluding that some inordinately sharp blade much have been utilized with considerable force.

The fact that the incident predated the earliest reported murders of the Jubilee Killer by some weeks, and had taken place hundreds of miles to the west, suggested to Blank and Miss Bonaventure that they might have been looking in the wrong place for clues, all along.

The trains and stations were congested with travelers returning home from coming to the city to see the Jubilee Procession, and so it was later that week before Blank and Miss Bonaventure were able to book passage on the Great

Western Railway. The journey from London to Taunton was scheduled to take a little under four hours, barring mishap, and so along with their overnight bags the pair brought along novels they'd purchased at a bookstall in the station to keep themselves entertained en route.

Miss Bonaventure had purchased a recent edition of *Personal Recollections of Joan of Arc*, by the Sieur Louis de Conte, published the previous year by Chatto & Windus of Piccadilly. Mark Twain was credited as "editor," but it was apparent that de Conte was himself a fiction, as likely was the Jean Francois Allen who was credited with translating the work from the original French. Blank remembered what Michel had told him about Joan, years before, and on seeing the image of the young girl embossed on the cover, a sword in her hand and a halo round her head, he could not help feeling sorry for the poor thing. It must have been a terrible thing to have been plagued for so long by voices one could never understand.

For his part, Blank had selected a copy of Bram Stoker's *Dracula*, published only the month before. From the character's physical description and mannerisms, it seemed apparent that the author had based his count upon the thespian Henry Irving, who so often trod the boards at Stoker's Lyceum. Less apparent, though clearly evident on further reading, was the fact that the author seemed to have been inspired, at least in part, by the real-life events of the Torso Killings of the previous decade. When he reached this unsettling conclusion, Blank found his taste for the fiction altogether lost, seeing too easily the skeleton of fact beneath the skin, and so closed the book with an expression of distaste. He remembered the events of those days too well to need reminding of them.

Miss Bonaventure saw him set the book aside and closed her own book on her finger. "Not Stoker's best, I take it?" she asked, knowingly.

Blank recovered himself and shook his head. "No, it's not that. Not to my personal tastes, perhaps, but for a reading public that hungrily devours the exploits of Varney and Sweeney Todd, I'm sure it will be quite appetizing. But I'm afraid that I find myself longing for the more dulcet arabasques of his earlier work. Did you ever read 'The Crystal Cup'?"

Miss Bonaventure shook her head.

"Published in pamphlet form by the London society some years ago. A charming little dream fantasy, though, as Oscar later observed, it could have used quite a bit more fantasy and a touch less dream."

Miss Bonaventure raised her eyebrow, and Blank realized that he'd said more than he intended.

"Wilde, do you mean?" she asked. "Oh, yes, he and Stoker were both betrothed to the same woman, weren't they? At different times, of course."

Blank nodded. "And she's married to Stoker still, as I understand it."

"Hmm." Miss Bonaventure mused. "You know, I've always wondered something and never thought to ask. I know that you've served as inspiration for fiction a time or two, with bowdlerized versions of your exploits finding their way into the work of Conan Doyle and Hal Meredith, but it's always seemed to me that there was a little something of you in Wilde's Dorian Gray."

Blank stiffened, almost imperceptibly, but managed to keep his expression neutral, only pursing his lips thoughtfully. "Really?"

"Well, there's his surname, which is certain suggestive of your habitual shade." She indicated his suit coat, vest, trousers, and hat, all of a uniform gray. "And the description of Gray's rooms is certainly reminiscent of your own in York Place. Come to think of it, you've both got locked rooms in your upper floors which you refuse to allow anyone to see." She grinned. "Admit it, Blank. Do you have a portrait secreted away up there, which makes plain all the sins your smooth features conceal?"

Blank knew she was only joking, but he couldn't help shifting uncomfortably on his seat. "My dear, I'm sure any portrait of me would be perfectly hideous in any event, without the addition of the marks of sin."

She playfully swatted his knee with her closed book. "There's a little too much of the dandy in your character for you to wear modesty easily, I'm afraid. But joking aside, you mention Wilde by his Christian name. Were you acquainted?"

Blank's gaze slid to the corners of their compartment and found something of interest in the countryside streaming past their window. "We knew each other," he said at length. "Distantly. For a time."

Miss Bonaventure took him at his word. With a shrug, she returned to her book, reading about the little girl who heard voices that drove her to do great things. Blank leaned his head against the cool glass of the window and closed his eyes, trying to forget that any such voices had ever existed.

It was early afternoon when they arrived in Taunton, and after depositing their overnight bags at the inn where they'd secured rooms for the night, Blank and Miss Bonaventure made their way to Taunton Castle.

On this site in the eighth century, or so the Anglo-Saxon chroniclers recorded, the Queen Etherlburge overthrew Taunton, which Ina had built. Later, in the twelfth century, Henry de Blois, the Bishop of Winchester and warlike brother of King Stephen, had constructed a mighty Norman fortress. The gatehouse with its drum towers was built at the close of the thirteenth under Edward I but restored with additions two centuries later in the days of James IV. In the civil war, it had been a stronghold of forces loyal to the Parliament, and in the aftermath of the Monmouth Rebellion of the late seventeenth, it had been the scene of many of the trials of the Bloody Assizes, when hundreds were sent to their deaths by Judge Jeffreys. There was some irony in the fact that, having been the site of so much history, it was only saved from destruction by the intervention of the Somerset Archaeological and Natural History Society, who purchased it for use as their headquarters and to house the society's museum and library.

Ivy had begun to creep up the castellated walls and turrets and left unchecked would cover the structure entirely.

"After you, my dear," Blank said, bowing and holding open the immense castle door. Miss Bonaventure gave him an abbreviated curtsey and stepped inside.

It was cool within the walls of the great, tumbledown castle, and dark. That the society had been able to effect some repairs was evident, as was the fact that they had a great deal of work left to do. The most recent efforts seemed to have concentrated on the newly christened Somerset Room, formerly the great chamber of the castle, which was now crowded with display cases that lined the walls and dominated the floor, and hung with various and sundry antique battle flags. It was here that they found Arthur Bulleid in close conversation with Harold St. George Gray, who was introduced to them as the assistant to the notable Augustus Pitt Rivers, Britain's first Inspector of Ancient Monuments.

The two men, Bulleid and Gray, both members of the society, were evidently planning a forthcoming archeological expedition to the nearby Somerset Levels which, while they were lowlands of moor and marsh in the modern day, in ancient times appeared to have been completely submerged for long periods of time. To the ancients, the hills and prominences of Somerset— Athelney, Brent Knoll, Glastonbury Tor—would have appeared to be islands, surrounded by waters that stretched all the way to the coast. It might have been possible, in fact, in a boat with a sufficiently shallow draw, to sail all the way from the open waters of the Atlantic to the middle of Somerset County.

All of which was fascinating, Blank assured them, but unfortunately he and his associate Miss Bonaventure were somewhat pressed for time, and presently more concerned with those more recently deceased, rather than those who passed away millennia before.

Gray and Bulleid were somewhat humbled, especially considering that the dead man had been their acquaintance, if not perhaps a close friend. The victim in question had been a man named Wilford McCall, who had been employed as a custodian of Taunton Castle by the society. To all appearances, McCall had interrupted the killer in the act of robbing the castle, though when the premises were searched the following morning it appeared that nothing had been stolen but a report concerning a recent archeological dig on Glastonbury Tor.

Blank raised an eyebrow. "But you say that the body wasn't found until morning?"

The two men nodded.

"What were McCall's normal hours of employment?" he asked.

Gray replied that McCall's schedule was somewhat flexible, but that he was never known to miss a last jar at the Tudor Tavern public house over on Fore Street. Never before that night, of course.

"So if McCall came upon the killer in the course of his usual rounds, it would have been sometime in the evening, at the latest? In which case the murder would have occurred well before midnight, and the killer would have had the free run of the castle until the morning."

The two men allowed that Blank's assessment seemed reasonable.

Blank looked around the Somerset Room. The antiquities on display, while none of them priceless, included bits of gold and silver, diamond and emerald, any one of which would have been worth any thief's time to pick up and pocket. And yet they all had been left unmolested.

"Gentlemen," Blank said with a smile, "I wonder if you couldn't tell me everything, absolutely everything, that you know about this archeological dig on Glastonbury Tor."

⟨A⟩

The facts were simple. For most of the decade, Arthur Bulleid had been involved in an ongoing excavation of Glastonbury Lake Village. Late the previous year, he had visited a dig being carried out on Glastonbury Tor by one Peter R. Bonaventure. Assisted only by a man named Dulac, Bonaventure was investigating ancient legends of Gwynn, son of Nudd, which he proposed had some origin in historical fact. Excavating not far from the ruins of St. Michael's Church, at the Tor's summit, Professor Bonaventure failed to substantiate his claim, the labor of weeks producing only some evidence of ancient sub-Roman fortifications dating to the early sixth century. His only discovery of note was a crystal, perhaps some type of milky quartz, which had been carved in the shape of a slightly tapering cylinder, giving it almost the appearance of a cup or chalice, though solid throughout. Whether it was of some ritual significance, or simply an ancient *objet d'art*, was unknown, but hardly seemed of monumental significance.

On completing his excavations, Professor Bonaventure filed a report with the Somerset Archaeological and Natural History Society, at Bulleid's request, and then he and his man returned to London, taking their crystal oddity with them.

⟨A⟩

That night, Blank and Miss Bonaventure dined at the inn in Taunton. They were eager to return to London but had missed the last train and so had to remain in town as they'd originally intended.

"Tell me, Miss Bonaventure," Blank said while their bowls of soup cooled. "Is this namesake of Bulleid's report any relation, do you suppose?"

She paused for a moment, her expression unreadable. "I don't recall any 'Peter' around the family table at the holidays, I'm afraid."

Blank nodded. "Ah, well, I suppose it would be one connection too many in an investigation that has already produced more that I find seemly. We now have Arthur Bulleid to add to Arthur Carmody . . ."

"To say nothing of Arthur Pendragon," Miss Bonaventure put in.

"Quite so. Too many Arthurs around, if you ask me." He sipped at his soup and made a face. "And not enough cooks."

"I think you're conflating the line about cooks in kitchens and Indians and chiefs." Miss Bonaventure sampled her own soup, and pulled a face of her own. "But I don't think you're far wrong." She dabbed at the corners of her mouth with her napkin.

"I can't help but wonder if the fare at the Tudor Tavern might not be an improvement."

"It could hardly be a declination."

"Come along then," Blank said, pushing back his chair and then stepping around to offer Miss Bonaventure his arm. "And on the way, I'd like to find a bookshop still open, if possible. I want to see if we can find anything concerning the legends this Professor Bonaventure was investigating."

So it was that a short while later the two sat opposite one another across a pitted and ancient table, rougher but far more palatable fare on the platters before them, studying the books they had bought.

"Here it is," Miss Bonaventure said, flipping through the pages of Lady Guest's translation of *The Mabinogion*, while Blank contentedly chewed a hunk of fish. "In the tale of 'How Culhwch won Olwen,' our boy is mentioned thusly: 'Gwynn son of Nudd, in whom God has set the energy of the demons of Annwvyn, in order to prevent the destruction of this world, and Gwynn cannot be let loose.'"

Blank washed his fish down with a gulp of porter and leaned over to see the passage for himself. "Now, that *is* interesting. I can only imagine that Annwvyn is the same as Lady Priscilla's Annwn."

"The Unworld," Miss Bonaventure translated.

"The very same."

"And I've found another mention here, in a footnote. Lady Guest reports

that, according to legend, St. Collen, the seventh-century Abbot of Glastonbury, once 'heard two men conversing about Gwynn ab Nudd, and saying
that he was king of Annwn and of the Fairies.' He admonished these men,
who said that Collen would soon receive a reproof from Gwynn. Three times
a messenger came to Collen and summoned him to come and speak with
Gwynn at 'the top of the hill,' by which I suppose she means the Tor. On the
third visit, Collen agreed to go. Our boy Collen is no fool, though, and takes
holy water along in a flask, just in case. On reaching the top of the hill, he
finds himself in the fairest castle he had ever beheld, amidst all sorts of music
and song. There is a man at the top of the castle in a golden chair, the king,
Gwynn himself, who tempts Collen with all manner of treats, but Collen
refuses them all. Then, and this is the interesting bit, Gwynn asks him
whether he has ever seen 'men of better equipment than those in red and
blue?' Which men these are, and precisely what is their equipment of red and
blue, Lady Guest doesn't report. Collen then responds that 'their equipment
is good enough, for such equipment as it is.' The king asks 'What kind of
equipment is that?' whereupon Collen proves to be a poor guest. Here's how
the translator puts it."

Miss Bonaventure sipped at her jar of ale, and then read aloud.

"*Then said Collen, 'The red on the one part signifies burning, and the blue on the
other signifies coldness.' And with that Collen drew out his flask, and threw the holy
water on their heads, whereupon they vanished from his sight, so that there was neither castle, nor troops, nor men, nor maidens, nor music, nor song, nor steeds, nor
youths, nor banquet, nor the appearance of any thing whatever, but the green hillocks.*"

"Hmm," Blank hummed. He held aloft the book he'd been perusing, a
slim volume on the folk tales of the British Isles. "It's here recorded that in
Welsh legend this selfsame Gwynn is sometimes said to be the leader of the
Wild Hunt and master of the Cwn Annwyn. What are the Cwn Annwyn, you
might well ask? The hounds of Annwn, of course, a pack of snow white, red-
eared spectral hounds who, with their master Gwynn, lead the souls of the
damned to hell. It is said that they are accompanied by a howling wind and
that their baying has the sound of migrating wild geese."

"More Unworld, then," Miss Bonaventure said thoughtfully.

"More connections. But like our surfeit of Arthurs, to say nothing of our embarrassment of Bonaventures, I'm not sure what our surplus of Unworld references tells us." He flipped through the pages of his book of British folk tales. "The more I read about this business, the less sense it makes. This Gwynn is the son of Nudd. Is that the same as Lady Priscilla says is cognate with Nuada and Lugh and a host of others? And these so-called hounds of the Unworld are in English folklore often called the Gabriel Hounds or Ratchets, and their master, the Wild Huntsman himself, is not always Gwynn, but is alternatively identified as Gabriel, Herne, Bran, or even Arthur."

"Another link between Bran and Arthur, I suppose."

Blank set the book aside, wearing an expression of distaste.

"Wait a moment!" Miss Bonaventure raised a finger, an idea creeping. "Weren't there white dogs with red ears in a story of Poe's?" She chewed her lip, searching her memory. "Arthur Gordon . . ." She trailed off, struggling.

"Arthur Gordon Poe?" Blank asked.

"No, don't be silly. Edgar Alan Poe. And Arthur Gordon . . . Pym! That's it. *The Narrative of Arthur Gordon Pym.*" She thought a moment, and her smile of victory faded. "But no, now that I think of it, those were actually white creatures with red *nails*, and teeth I suppose, not ears."

"Well," Blank said with a shrug, "I can't imagine how it would have made a difference." Exasperated, he shoved the books to one side with a sweep of his arm. "I can't imagine how *any* of this makes any difference. Unless our Jubilee Killer is motivated by mad flights of fancy which derive from these same dusty myths."

Miss Bonaventure fixed him with a level stare, and without a trace of humor in her tone, said, "What makes you think he *isn't?*"

CHAPTER TWENTY-ONE
Millennium

THE GLASTONBURY FESTIVAL, it turned out, wasn't in Glastonbury at all, but in Pilton, six miles to the east, on the A361. Whatever *that* was.

They had to park the Corvette a million miles away and walk, so that even though they'd arrived in late afternoon, by the time they got to the front gate it was early evening. There were a few dozen other latecomers at the gate, and like them the security guys tried to turn Alice and Stillman away, seeing as they didn't have tickets and the event had long since sold out.

Stillman just pulled out his blank badge and calmly explained the situation to the security guys, and before Alice knew it, they were being ushered through the gate, given their own personal escort to the VIP backstage area.

Whatever else happened, whatever her special destiny turned out to be, Alice was sure of one thing. She just *had* to get Stillman to teach her that trick.

Alice had asked why Stillman was sure that this Aria Fox would be found backstage. Stillman had just explained that Aria, in his experience, was hardly the sort to be out front with the groundlings. Alice hadn't been sure what he meant.

Now she understood.

This wasn't like Lollapalooza turned up to eleven. This was like Lollapalooza turned up to a hundred, multiplied times the X Games, and divided by Woodstock 99. It was *immense*.

There was a field of tipis. Another that seemed to be nothing but mud. There were shelters and temporary buildings and trailers and outhouses. And people. Thousands and thousands and thousands of people. And the noise. Multiple stages, music coming from all angles, people shouting and singing and carrying on.

Their escort was leading them towards an enormous pyramid-shaped stage. Some ways off, in front of the stage, was a tower of scaffolding for speakers or control booths or something, and between the two was a solid mass of people, with more spread out over the immense field around and behind the tower. In the distance, miles away, just barely visible in the fading light, Alice could see a smooth hill with a stone tower on top. It looked like something out of King Arthur days. A princess trapped on top of *that* would have to grow her hair for a good long while to make an escape, that was for sure.

The backstage area was behind the stage, naturally, safely buffered from the crowded of sweaty, blissed-out attendees. This was a different sort of crowd, to be sure. Some of them may have been the boyfriends and girlfriends of the various bands playing the festival, but most looked like bankers slumming on the weekend, or movie and television people. Suits, in a word, even if they were dressed more casually. Stillman, who looked old enough to be the father of any of them, and claimed he was old enough to be their grandfather, slid through the crowd like he was born to it.

"Excuse me. Pardon me, love. Coming through. Ah, watch your drink there, friend, almost had a terrible accident. On your side, love. Ah." He clapped his hands, smiling in triumph. "Aria Fox, as I live and breath."

The woman glared at Stillman from beneath her brows and took a long sip of her martini.

"Waters. What the hell do *you* want?"

"Do you know," he said, sliding onto the seat next to hers, "Hughes asked me the very same thing, just yesterday."

The woman named Aria Fox looked up and regarded Alice over the rim of her martini glass. Alice regarded her right back. Aria looked to be a couple of inches taller than Alice, though it was hard to tell with her sitting down. She had a slim build, muscled like a dancer, with her dark hair worn long and pulled back into a loose knot at the back of her head. She had a dark olive complexion, her smooth skin marred only by a small L-shaped scar on her upper left cheek. She was dressed in a tight-fitting white dress that came to midthigh, her shoulders bare, with white high-heeled sandals on her feet, the straps lacing up her ankles. She *definitely* wasn't dressed to mix with the hoi polloi out in the mud. For Aria, it was obviously VIP or nothing.

"Who's your friend, Waters?" She practically sneered. Even in the fading light, she wore big white-framed sunglasses over her eyes, making her expression difficult to read.

"Aria, meet another 'A. F.' This is my friend, Alice Fell."

"Kind of young for you, isn't she? And lacking the equipment you usually prefer, I'd guess?"

"Charming," Stillman said, with a smile that lacked all warmth. "Now, I understand you've been a busy little girl lately, our Aria."

Aria's eyebrow raised behind her sunglasses, and she gave Stillman a cool look. "Something tells me that Hughes won't be getting his commission this time out." She took another sip of her martini, draining the glass. "If he keeps it up, he won't be getting a Christmas card this year, either."

Stillman snapped his finger for the roving waitress. "Miss, could we have two dry martinis?" He glanced over to Alice. "Anything for you, love?"

Alice still hadn't quite recovered from Friday, and shook her head.

"Just the two, then, dear." Stillman slipped her a folded bill, though Alice couldn't tell the denomination. The waitress, though, was clearly impressed as she scurried off to the cash bar to fetch their drinks.

"I don't know how you got Hughes to talk, or what he told you . . ."

"Hughes didn't tell me anything, dear, trust me. Don't take it out on the poor boy. I just happened to notice that you used your mother's shunt on the air vent alarm, and twigged right away that you were the one I wanted to speak with."

"Damn," Aria cursed under her breath. "I know I should gone with the Maldanato, instead."

Stillman chuckled. "But that would have tripped the voltage sensors. No, Melody's shunt was the only choice to make." He shook his head, admiringly. "A marvelous piece of work, love, just marvelous. Your mother'd be proud."

Aria made a dismissive hissing sound and took off her sunglasses. Her eyes were almost the color of amber. "So you working for the British Museum, is that it? Not a lot of jobs calling for out-of-work ex-spooks these days?"

Stillman shook his head. "No, this one is strictly freelance. The authorities aren't even involved. I just want to take a look at that gem for myself."

Aria slid a glance Alice's way, her look bordering on contemptuous. "And is she part of your freelance crew, then?"

"Something like that."

Their drinks arrived, and Aria sipped her martini before speaking again while Stillman just swirled the liquid around in the glass.

"No." Aria shook her head, lowering the glass. "Nothing doing. The job is done and I've been paid. I'm a professional, and I don't talk out of turn."

"Fair enough," Stillman nodded, the corners of his mouth turned down. "Still, it'll be a shame if someone tipped off the FSB about who it was stole the Tsarina's diadem from the Kremlin Museum. I'm sure the boys at Lubyanka would love to get their hands on whoever pulled *that* one off."

Aria blanched, and her fingers tightened white-knuckled around the stem of her glass.

"You *wouldn't.*"

"Oh, wouldn't I?" Stillman smiled, broadly.

Aria tapped her foot and gripped her sunglasses in her hand so hard that a lens popped out, which she then ground underfoot, irritated.

"Okay, okay. I'll tell you who the client was, but no more. Is that a deal?"

Stillman considered for a moment.

"Come on, Bowie's about to start his first set, and I'll be damned if I'm missing him again."

Stillman finally nodded. "Yes, I think a name should suit our needs nicely."

Aria sighed heavily and shook her head, frowning. "I swear to God, if this gets out, I will *kill* you, Waters."

"You're certainly welcome to try, love."

Aria leaned in close, looking for all the world like a woman giving her gray-haired father a kiss. Then she whispered in his ear.

As Aria straightened up, Stillman's eyes widened.

"You must be joking," he said, flatly.

Aria tossed back the last of her martini and dropped the empty glass and her broken sunglasses onto the chair. "Nope. Came as a shock to me, as well, but there you have it." She put her hands on her hips. "Now, are we done, here?"

Stillman nodded, absently, his gaze drifting.

"Fine. Waters, don't come looking for me again. As far as I'm concerned, we're even. Got it?" Then she turned on her heel and marched away.

Alice slid onto the chair next to Stillman, who still sat wide-eyed, looking confused. "Hey, are you okay?"

"Mmm?" Stillman arched an eyebrow and turned to face her. "Oh, certainly, certainly. I'm just surprised is all."

"Why? What did she say? Who has the gem?"

They could hear the roar of the crowd as Bowie took the stage.

"It's Temple," Stillman said, and threw back the last of his martini in a single gulp. "Iain Temple."

It was late when they got back to the car, and neither of them felt like driving all night back to London, so Alice and Stillman decided to stay overnight in Glastonbury and drive back the next morning. They continued up the A361, and at the edge of the big hill with the King Arthur tower on top, they stopped at what looked to Alice like a big house, but that Stillman assured her was a hotel. Or a bed & breakfast, at any rate.

There was a pair of twin beds in the room, covered in floral-print comforters, but no bathroom, only a sink. The shower and bathroom were down the hall, on the other side of the pay phone. Alice was all for room service, not having eaten since midday, but the kitchen downstairs only served breakfast—hence the name, Alice decided—so they were on their own.

It was Sunday, and fairly late at that, and one of the only restaurants they could find downtown—Alice called it "downtown," but Stillman insisted it was the High Street—was Elaichi Tandoori, an Indian joint. Dots, not feathers. Alice had something called chicken tikka, washed down with several cans of lager.

When they had finished eating, Alice stepped outside to smoke a couple of cigarettes while Stillman settled up with the bill, and she had a chance to get a better look at the town.

The streets were surprisingly crowded for the lateness of the hour, filled with a strange cast of characters: aging hippies, men and women dressed up in medieval costumes, starry-eyed young people, men with shaved heads wearing the saffron robes of Buddhist monks, kids with acoustic guitars, women with wreaths of flowers over their heads and long flowing skirts. Alice walked a short ways up and down the street, looking at the names over the doors. The Isle of Avalon Foundation. The Library of Avalon. The Goddess Temple. The Maitreya Monastery.

Alice found a pamphlet in a rack outside a darkened shop front. It was all about Glastonbury but described it more like something out of *The Lord of the Rings* than the quaint English village she'd seen driving in that day, or even the crazed muddy mosh pit of the festival a few miles away. It described the town as a "temenos," or energy field, not as a geographical place. It talked a lot about mystic vibrations and attunement. It mentioned an "Angel of Glastonbury."

"You all right, love?"

Alice flapped the brochure like a flag. "What's all this about, anyway? Is this place some sort of weirdness magnet for crazies and smelly hippies?"

Stillman chuckled and cadged a cigarette from her. "Nah, nothing like that. Something odd *did* happen here, about a millennium and a half ago, but it went away, and no one ever knew quite what it was about. Or where it came from, come to that. All this"—he waved his hand, the smoke from the cigarette trailing, indicating the New Age shop fronts, the eclectic collection of pedestrians—"is just a cultural echo of that one event."

Alice stuffed the brochure in her pocket and drew on her cigarette.

"Still, that's not to say there *aren't* weirdness magnets, here and there, of sorts. Glastonbury just isn't one of them. There's a few hot spots in the Big Smoke, a big one in Ireland, one in the Varadeaux canton of Switzerland, one in New England, and the Texas town of Denniston, and Recondito, California . . ." He trailed off. "Dozens of them, all over the place, spots where the walls between the worlds are thinner, you might say. Keeps those of us in my former line of work on our toes, as you might well imagine." He dropped his cigarette to the pavement, only half smoked, and ground it underfoot. "Come on, love, let's to bed. I'm knackered."

The next morning, bright and relatively early, they climbed back into the Corvette SS and headed back up the A361. The roads were jammed with traffic leaving the Glastonbury Festival, but once they got past Pilton things eased up considerably.

Stillman outlined his plan during the early hours of the drive. He was intrigued why a billionaire like Iain Temple would hire a professional cat burglar to steal a gem from the British Museum. Aria had told him only that Temple had been the client and that she had delivered the item to him in his corporate headquarters in Canary Warf, the Glasshouse. So far as Aria knew, Temple kept a private collection of oddities there, and in all likelihood the Vanishing Gem was among them.

Digging through the glove compartment, at Stillman's request, Alice found a dubbed cassette of Temple's early seventies release, *Phoenix Rising*. Stillman explained that this was the concept album that introduced Temple's hairless, sexless, opal-eyed "Visitor from a Broken Earth" persona. The album related the story, through song, of the Visitor, who came to Earth from another world to learn about humanity. The haunting "Circular Ruins," inspired by the Jorge Luis Borges story of the same name, told how the Visitor had arrived in ages past in South America and been worshipped as a god by the natives there and how he had been forced to rebuild a new body when his old one became too worn and abused. "Wayfarer" told how the Visitor had wandered the nations of the Earth seeking out the secret of happiness and contentment, searching for the ultimate answer but finding only more questions. "Paragaea" was a haunting track about the strange, ancient world from which the Visitor came.

Stillman was dismissive of the album's musical qualities. It clearly borrowed heavily on the sounds of Mott the Hoople, T. Rex, and the Velvet Underground, and while it was undeniably an influence on David Bowie's *The Rise and Fall of Ziggy Stardust and the Spiders from Mars*, Bowie was clearly the more gifted musician of the two. Still, *Phoenix Rising* had been a considerable commercial success at the time, and the tours and subsequent albums in the years following were no less so. By the midseventies, Temple had "killed off" the Visitor persona, and taken the small fortune he'd garnered and invested it in technology concerns, especially telephony and the then-burgeoning computing industry. By the eighties, Temple had diversified his growing fortune even further, opening a retail electronics store in Piccadilly Circus followed by a chain across the UK and later Europe, the United States, and Asia. After that had come the airline, and the cable channel, and the frozen entrees and men's fragrances and designer clothing and music retail and so on. Now, Temple was said to be worth billions, though with the myriad of companies he owned, wholly or in part, it was difficult to estimate the precise value of his holdings.

The Glasshouse was the headquarters of Temple Enterprises and home of Temple himself. Built in the heart of Canary Warf, the London business development situated where the old West India Docks once stood, the Glasshouse was a veritable fortress of glass and steel, rising hundreds of feet in the air, some thirty-five stories tall. Temple's home was at the pinnacle of the Glasshouse, occupying the top four floors, probably the highest-dollar penthouse apartment in the world, protected by cutting-edge surveillance and alarm systems and a private army of security guards.

And this was the guy that Stillman intended to rob.

Great plan.

It was late afternoon, Monday. The Corvette SS was safely back in the inconspicuous garage above, and Stillman and Alice were down in the derelict Underground station, digging through antique electronics that hadn't been cutting edge since before Alice was born. And *this* was what Stillman wanted to use to help them break into Iain Temple's Glasshouse.

Stillman hooked up a computer the size of a car motor to an electrical outlet, and then balanced an ancient monitor on top, the white plastic of the casing gone sickly yellow with age. Fishing a loop of phone cabling from a filing cabinet drawer, he plugged one end into a modem the size of a typewriter and spliced the other into a thick bunch of cabling that snaked along the wall.

There was more than just antique electronics in the storage tunnel. While Stillman swore beneath his breath, trying to bring the ancient computer back to life, Alice picked around through the confusion of odds and ends piled haphazardly all around, idly.

There was what looked like a rifle, but at the end of the barrel was a kind of dish, like a satellite receiver, and from the stock hung a cord connected to a bulky metal box, with straps so it could be worn like a backpack.

"Enfield Sonica," Stillman said, when Alice held it up for inspection. "Sound weapon. Fires concentrated bursts of sonic vibration."

Alice returned the contraption to the pile. The next thing she picked up looked like a flare gun, a big bulky pistol, but had rammed into the barrel what looked to be a miniature collapsed umbrella with its fabric missing.

"Ah, harpoon pistol." Stillman nodded. "Fix a line and it can be used for grappling. Hang on to that, will you, love? Might come in handy."

Alice shrugged and tucked it into the pocket of her leather jacket, handle first. Next she picked up a silver disk. It was about two feet in diameter, a couple of inches thick, and surprisingly lightweight. It shone like silver, untarnished and unmarred. On the back was a loop of the same material, evidently a handle of some kind, though a bit wide for Alice to hold comfortably.

"Don't know what that one is, actually," Stillman said, mopping beads of sweat from his brow. "Back in '67, they were rebuilding Mark Lane Station— they called it Tower Hill by then—and put about that they'd destroyed the last remains of the old Tower of London Station. Which, as you can see"—he waved his arm, indicating the tunnel—"wasn't exactly the case. More like the old station was more heavily fortified and wired up to the new communications grids." He bashed the thick bunch of cables on the wall with a wrench. "The Tower of London itself stands on top of a hill, White Mount, and there's been people hereabouts for thousands of years, back to the Roman times and before.

Anyway, when they were doing the tunneling, they dug up some old bits of Roman pottery, some stuff that dated back to the time of Boudica, and that disk you're holding. The MI8 boffins never were able to work out who'd made it or when, out of what materials, or for what purpose. Their best guess was that it's some sort of data storage device with limited broadcast capabilities. Hard as bugger, though, and couldn't be cut by diamond or laser. Odd that, mmm?"

Alice shrugged and tossed the disk over her shoulder, to land clattering on the pile behind her. "You about finished with this stuff, yet, or what?"

Stillman grinned. "As a matter of fact . . ."

He stabbed a rocker switch on the front of the monitor, and the screen buzzed noisily to life, green letters dimly visible on the gray-black background.

"Now," Stillman said, cracking his knuckles like a concert pianist. "Let's see what we can find out about this Glasshouse, shall we?"

Stillman had managed to gain access to secured government and commerical servers, using all sorts of cracks and hacks, displaying far more computer savvy than Alice'd figured a guy his age would have. Either the age he appeared to be, or the age he claimed to be. Even so, the proof was in the pudding, whatever that meant. Stillman was tabbing through the internal database of the architectural firm that had been employed by Temple Enterprises to construct Glasshouse. After a short search, he turned up a host of 2D and 3D CAD drawings of the structure, detailed blueprints, elevations, and architectural drawings. The results quickly outpaced the ability of the fat green phosphor dots to handle, and Stillman was forced to lug the color television in from the living room in the other tunnel, patching into the computer's video output.

"You're pretty good at this stuff, you know?" Alice lit a cigarette and nodded appreciatively.

"Why, thank you for noticing, love," Stillman said, a sarcastic undercurrent in his words. "I've lived this long just waiting to hear your resounding approval."

Alice stuck out her tongue, tilting her head to one side. "What*ever*." She shrugged out of her leather jacket, only narrowly missing impaling herself on the sharp point of the harpoon pistol's dart. "So why did you give all of this up, anyway? If you're so in love with it, I mean?"

Stillman had been jotting notes on a sheet of yellow paper and stopped, tucking the pencil behind his ear and leaning back in his creaking seat, regarding her in silence. "Again, there's a simple answer and a complicated answer." He sighed, crossing his arms over his chest. "The simple answer is that I just stopped showing up to work one day. I stopped answering the phone, and eventually they stopped calling. See, after the end of the Cold War, MI8's focus changed a bit. We'd spent years keeping tabs on what the Reds were doing behind the Curtain, what sort of deals they were trying to make with powers on other planes, what sort of odd technology they'd laid hands on. And always keeping half an eye on the Yanks, as well, of course. The fellas in Bureau Zero were our brothers in arms and all, our partners in the special relationship, but that didn't mean that they always had Queen & Country's own best interest at heart. Then, when the Soviet Union collapsed, it all seemed to change, almost overnight. Suddenly, it wasn't a world with only two sides anymore, or at least allied interests on either side of a line. Now, it was every man for himself, and damn the hindmost. They used to talk about a 'peace dividend,' about the bounty we'd all enjoy once the Cold War ended. But it never happened. It was just one more empire breaking up into little fiefdoms, with only one more big empire left to fall." He paused and looked at Alice, meaningfully. "And, I'm sad to say, that one's bound to happen, sooner or later."

"Wait, that's the *simple* answer?"

Stillman chuckled. "Well . . . remember how I said I used to serve two masters? Well, before I ever took the king's shilling, I was on the rolls of Omega. Now, the goals of Omega weren't at odds with those of the British crown. Quite the contrary. It was in Omega's interest that things remain stable, that business thrive and technology continue to develop, that the frontiers expand . . . all of which *we* wanted, as well."

"What is Omega, anyway? Is that some secret society or something?"

Stillman smiled and shook his head. "Not exactly. It's . . . complicated. Suffice it to say that it's secret, at the very least. I was recruited by my mentor, the one I told you about. But while he was an agent in good standing, he had some rather definitive ideas about empire and self-determination, all of which ran counter to Omega's goals. And to those of the British crown as often as not. And so he had, for years, been carrying out his own secret agenda, while appearing to serve the interests of his masters. After he . . ." He broke off, eyes sliding to the corners. Then, after a pause, he continued. "Afterwards, I kept up in the same vein, using some tricks he'd taught me to keep my thoughts hidden and to myself. I . . . I'm not as strong as he was. I just couldn't keep at it as long. In the end, all of the blood and pain and suffering . . . It was for a good cause, I believe it still. The end of any empire is painful, and a people first experiencing their liberty make mistakes. But even so, after so many years at the game, I just couldn't . . ."

He broke off, lost for a moment in memory.

"You okay?" Alice asked.

"Yes, I'm fine, love," Stillman answered, not sounding it. "In any event, I stopped taking Omega's calls at the same time I bunked out on MI8."

"Haven't they ever come after you?"

"Well, MI8 hasn't, but then why would they? They've got to know I'm still out here. I'm living in their abandoned headquarters, after all, and as much as I've labored to keep out of sight, I can't have disappeared entirely. I figure they've decided it's not worth their trouble, so let me be." He paused. "As for Omega . . . Well, Omega might know where I am, but if I don't answer, there isn't much I've got to worry about. I was the only agent after my mentor . . . after my mentor, so it isn't as if there's anyone else Omega can send after me. Sure, I started to get older, but if that's the price I have to pay for peace of mind and a good night's sleep, so be it. Besides, I think a bit of gray gives me a distinguished look, don't you?"

Alice had followed only half of what Stillman had said, at best. He looked at her, as if expecting an answer, but she wasn't sure what to say. "Um, okay?"

"Thanks, love, I think so, too," Stillman said, and then turned back to the computer.

By the time they could no longer ignore the grumbling of their stomachs, Stillman had worked out the plan to the finest detail. In the kitchen, over roast beef and Yorkshire pudding, roast potatoes, and gravy, accompanied by a bottle of pinot noir, he explained.

"Temple has an impressive security setup, there's no doubt about it. And I doubt any thief short of an Aria Fox or a Tan Perrin would be able to get in and out without tripping all manner of alarms and fail safes. It's near impregnable. Notice that I say *near*. Because there's a few holes in there, if you know where to look. Including one fairly significant one." He unrolled a sheaf of papers, which had been spat out by a chattering dot-matrix printer the size of a refrigerator. There were schematics and architectural drawings of Glasshouse, with points marked in purple ink. Stillman held up one of Alice's Uniball Vision roller pens. "Hope you don't mind, but I took the liberty of borrowing this."

Alice patted her pockets. Sure enough, he'd snatched the pen right out of her front pocket, and she'd never even noticed him coming near.

"Another handy skill to have," Stillman said with a smile. "In any event, once I got the blueprints, I found Temple's security company. They're wholly owned by Temple Enterprises, so they don't have to farm any of the work out, but they've got a server that's hooked up to the Internet. It wasn't easy, but with the old MI8 icebreakers I was able to get in and poke around a bit."

"Wait a minute," Alice said, setting down her fork on the plate. "If you can get into their computer, why don't you just, I don't know, shut down the systems so we don't set off the alarms?"

Stillman's smile broadened. "Why, Alice. Now I think you've been reading *my* diary . . ."

CHAPTER TWENTY-TWO

GALAAD RAISED HIS EYES AGAIN and looked at the image of the White Lady on the crewless ship, while the captains around him stood open-mouthed in wonder.

"She seems more a phantom than a living thing," Pryder said, his voice low and full of awe.

Artor nodded, and Galaad could see that Pryder was right. Though he could see her every detail, Galaad realized that she was translucent, the outline of the ship dimly visible through her body.

The White Phantom looked from one to another of them, an expression of confusion on her white face.

"Seven, you are," she said in fractured Latin, her accent strange. "Three, I remember."

Galaad climbed to his feet and took a step forward, his arms out. "Lady . . ." he began.

Artor stop Galaad with a hand on his shoulder. "Abide awhile," the High King said quietly.

"Injured, one of you," the White Phantom said, her glowing eyes coming to rest on Lugh, who lay on the ground spattered with his own lifeblood. "Heal."

She waved her hand, and one of the scuttling silver beetle-things climbed up and over the side of the crewless ship. It came across the shore towards them, and Galaad could see that it was the length of a man's forearm, with four pinchers on either end. Crabwise, it scuttled quickly towards them.

When it was just a few feet away, Caius stepped forward, sword in hand, prepared to swing at the beetle-thing.

"Wait," Artor said. "Let us see what transpires."

Seemingly heedless of those standing, the beetle-thing scuttled between them and marched right up to Lugh. Planting four of its pinchers in the ground, it reared up like a snake, the four pinchers on its other end in the air, and angled itself towards Lugh's severed arm. Then, without warning, it emitted a spray of some sort of mist, a small cloud which settled over the bloody stump.

The captains shouted protests, but a look from Artor silenced them.

The cloud of mist faded, almost immediately, and they could see that the stump had completely sealed over, the flesh smooth and unmarked just below Lugh's elbow.

Lugh struggled to sit upright, looking wide-eyed at his stump. "The pain . . ." he said in amazement. "It's gone."

"Apologies, for arriving late," the White Phantom intoned. "Too late to save the hand. Perhaps a substitute is possible."

The White Phantom motioned again, and without warning the beetle-thing launched itself at Lugh. Before he could react, the four pinchers on its leading end clamped down on his stump, biting into his flesh.

"Aargh!" Lugh leapt to his feet, waving his arm to try to shake the thing loose, but it refused to budge. Then he stopped short, a strange look coming over his face. "Doesn't hurt," he said, wonderingly. He lifted his arm, and the silver beetle-thing moved with it. The four pinchers on the other end opened and closed, just like a fist clenching and relaxing.

"What . . . ?" Galaad began, and found that words failed him.

Lugh's eyes opened wider, and he reached out with the silver beetle-thing, clamped its pinchers around the blade of Galaad's Saeson sword, and tugged it from his grasp. With Galaad's sword held firm in the pinchers, Lugh turned back to the others. "When I think, it moves! It does what I tell it."

It was as if Lugh had been given a new arm of silver, to replace the one he'd lost.

Artor turned his attention back to the White Phantom.

"Lady, I take it you are the one who sent visions to this man here?" Artor indicated Galaad.

The White Phantom nodded. "Messages, I sent."

"Who are you?" Galaad asked, stepping forward.

The White Phantom shook her head. "No time. Not now. Aid is needed."

"What sort of aid?" Artor asked.

"This remote," the White Phantom said, pointing to the crewless ship which bore her, "is simply another message. In body, I am held captive inside the heart of the Unworld. Captive of the Red King."

Galaad didn't understand what the White Phantom meant. Was this not her, in fact, but merely another species of vision?

"Rescue me," the White Phantom implored. "Please."

"What's she saying?" Lugh asked, who had no Latin.

"She's asking to be rescued," Caius explained. "Says that someone called the Red King has her imprisoned in someplace called the Unworld."

"What's in it for us?" Lugh asked.

Artor scowled at him, but turned to the White Phantom and said, "What boon or bounty awaits us if we fulfill this office, lady? Already my men and I have been sore tested by this journey."

The White Phantom looked confused for a moment, as if she were trying to puzzle out what he had said. "Gifts," she finally said, nodding. "Weapons."

The captains exchanged looks.

"Three, I remember," the White Phantom continued. "Three sets of weapons, I carry. Apologies."

She motioned again, and more of the silver beetle-things scuttled over the sides of the ship. Only this time, they carried something with them, in twos and threes, struggling under the weight of their loads.

First came long, thin objects a bit more than three feet in length. They were a handspan wide and an inch or so thick, except for one end where they tapered into cylinders about the length and thickness of a sword's hilt. At that, they had something of the look of a scabbarded sword, though of a material which none of the captains could identify.

The beetle-things laid the three long scabbard-shaped objects at Artor's feet. Artor bent and picked one up, finding it surprisingly light.

"Swords, these are." The White Phantom paused, and with a smile she said two words which Galaad didn't quite catch but which he thought might be the Britannic words "awyr"—air or sky—and "pâl"—blade. "Once drawn, only the bearer will be able to draw them again. Bound to their owner."

Artor nodded and wrapped his fingers around the hiltlike end of the object. Then he gripped the middle of the scabbard shape with his other hand and pulled. Where before the object had seemed an unbroken whole, suddenly there were two, a hilt and a scabbard, with a hint of blue blade in between.

The sword slipped silently out of the scabbard. The blade had a faint blue hue, like a cloudless summer sky, but was amazingly thin. When Artor held the sword up and turned it from side to side, the blade seemed to disappear entirely when seen edge on, reappearing only when he turned the flat of the blade back into view.

"Thin," the White Phantom said, "but strong. Take care, do not touch, but sheath when not in use."

Artor nodded, gravely, and carefully returned the blade to its sheath. When the hilt touched the scabbard, it seemed to fuse again and become once more an unbroken whole.

"May I?" Pryder said solicitously, reaching out to Artor. The High King nodded silently and handed it over.

Pryder gripped the hilt and scabbard in either hand, but no matter how hard he pulled he couldn't tug the sword free of the sheath. "This is snugger than your grandsire's blade," he called over his shoulder to Galaad.

Artor picked up another of the scabbard-shaped objects and exchanged it with the one that Pryder held. Pryder yanked on the hilt, which immediately came loose, the skyblade slipping free. Unbalanced, he put his arms out to either side to right himself, and the skyblade swung in a low arc, slicing into the ground at his feet. The blade's tip dipped in and out of the ground like an oar in water, effortlessly, but a huge chuck of white-tufted sod came away with it, sides as smooth as blown glass.

"The Huntsman's blade," Pryder said in a low voice, looking at the bluish blade reverentially before carefully returning it to the scabbard.

"Lady," Artor said, turning back to her, "before coming to these Summer Lands we faced an eerie foe, a Huntsman who carried just such a blade. Is he the one who now imprisons you?"

The White Phantom took on a puzzled expression. "No," she said, shaking her head. "I know of no Huntsman. Only the Red King, and he cannot leave the white walls which surround these Summer Lands, as you call them."

Artor scowled. Another mystery, another question to add to their tally.

Lugh picked up another of the skyblades, drawing its blue length from the scabbard, while the beetle-things deposited three long, thin, staff-shaped objects at Artor's feet.

"Hey!" Caius said, as Lugh admired the whisper-thin blade of the skyblade. "Now that you've drawn that, no one else can!"

Lugh just looked at him and shrugged. "Ah, so that's what she was saying. Oh, well, I'm sure she's got another of them on her little boat for you."

"She only brought three," Galaad explained, still unsure how the White Phantom had "remembered" three of them.

"Well, then," Lugh said with a smile. "Good thing I picked *this* one up, isn't it?"

"Lances, these are," the White Phantom went on, indicating the staff shapes.

"*I'll* be having one of those," Caius said, shouldering forward and picking one up.

The lance was perfectly cylindrical, a little thicker than a man's thumb, and a little under five feet in length. They were perfectly white, the color of sun-bleached bone, except for a scarlet jewel set in the haft two feet from one end.

"Point the end away," the White Phantom instructed, "and depress the jewel."

With a shrug, Caius swung the lance around, its end pointing at a clump of red heath on a nearby hill, and pressed the jewel with his thumb.

With a low hiss, a red glob in the shape of a blood drop spat from the tip of the lance, flying at blinding speed through the air. When it struck the heath, it immediately burst into flames, setting the ground ablaze.

The other six instinctively moved away from Caius, who looked in wide-eyed amazement at the thing in his hands.

"It . . . it shot blood!" Caius gasped.

"It shot *flame!*" Bedwyr said, edging farther away, an edge of jealousy in his voice. "*I* want a lance that shoots flame."

"Here," Artor said, nudging one of the other lances towards Bedwyr with his toe, leaning away from it. "Consider it yours."

Bedwyr hurried over, careful to remain behind Caius, and picked up the lance. Gwrol, still holding his bruised ribs, picked up the other. Stepping away from the others, the pair faced in opposite directions and tested the bloodflame for themselves, and in short order there were small fires blazing on the hills and fields leading up to the shoreline. Galaad worried for a moment that they might be caught in a conflagration, but fortunately the fires, while burning fiercely, seemed to burn just as quickly, extinguishing in just a matter of moments.

"Disks, these are," the White Phantom continued, indicating the large circular shapes the beetle-things struggled under. "Unbreakable. Indestructible. Used to absorb and store, but can be used to protect."

Artor reached down and picked up the first of the disks dropped at his feet. Each was about the size of one of their shields, with a smooth silvery surface on one side and a kind of metal hoop in the center of the other side. Artor grabbed this hoop with his fist and hefted the disk, wielding it like a buckler.

"Here," he said to Galaad, tossing him the disk. "You can likely find use for this."

Galaad scrambled, but managed to catch the disk before it hit the ground. He found it remarkably light for its size, easily held in a one-handed grip. The hoop was a little too wide to be held entirely comfortably, suggesting it was either designed with a larger grip in mind or for a different purpose entirely, but putting aside the mild discomfort of the hoop's edges biting into his fingers and the base of his thumb, the shield was easily wielded.

Artor gave the other two disks to Caius and Bedwry, who experimented with crouching behind their round bucklers while firing bloodflame at the hills.

The weapons were all distributed, but as the beetle-things scuttled back to the crewless ship, more came after them.

"Lady," Artor said, lashing a length of leather around the top of the skyblade's scabbard and securing it to his sword belt, opposite his spatha, "there is something in these Summer Lands which does not agree with our constitutions. We have been ill since shortly after arriving, with no sign of improvement."

The White Phantom nodded. "Changed, are these Summer Lands. Unchanged, you cannot long endure. Mantles, you require. Protection."

She indicated the silvery material that the beetle-things laid before Artor. He picked it up and inspected it. It seemed transparent like glass from one angle, but when turned another way looked like silver. But it moved like fine, soft fabric.

"Enough for three, I bring," the White Phantom said, sounding concerned. "Mantle can divide, and redivide, and still be effective. But you will not be able to tarry."

Artor looked from the silvery, glasslike material in his hand to the White Phantom.

"Tear each in half, and one in half again" she instructed. "Then give a portion to every man."

Artor raised an eyebrow but did as she had said. Galaad could see the High King was surprised at how easily he was able to rend the material, which seemed otherwise so sturdy. As Artor tore the material, and each of the other two that the beetle-things carried, he distributed the pieces to his men.

"Lay the pieces over your heads," the White Phantom instructed.

Galaad shrugged but did as he was told, draping it over his head like a veil. He wanted to ask what next he should do, but before he could speak his answer presented itself. The mantle seemed to distend, flowing like water. He looked to his fellows, alarmed, his vision somewhat clouded by the silvery material. On each of the other six, he saw the mantle spreading farther and farther, until it covered them entirely, head to toe. They all glinted for a moment, like statues cast in silver. And then, without warning, the mantles began to disappear. Or, to be more precise, they seemed to *recede*, as though absorbed into their bodies, like water soaked up by parched, dry ground.

Immediately, Galaad's vision cleared. But more significantly, he found that his health was instantly improved. The sense of queasy disquiet that had plagued him since shortly after they'd passed through the hedge of mist had completely vanished.

"Remote, must return," the White Phantom said, as the beetle-things scurried back onto the crewless ship, "before absence is noticed. Continue to the tower of glass, and enter the Unworld. Rescue me. Beware the Red King. Beware the hounds."

The image of the White Phantom began to flicker.

"Wait, lady!" Galaad rushed forward, his hands held up before him. "I have so many questions for you."

"Reach the tower of glass. Enter the Unworld." The White Phantom began to fade, the outline of the ship beyond becoming crisper and more clear. "Rescue me."

With that, the image vanished entirely, and the White Phantom was gone. With a low hum, the crewless ship slipped back into the water, sailed a short distance away from the shore, and then sank back down beneath the rippling surface, disappearing from view.

"So what was *she* going on about, anyway?" Lugh said, flexing his new silver arm.

Their skyblades girt round their waists, disks and lances in hand, the seven continued on. Wary of facing any more undersea dwellers come up from beneath the water, they turned their course away from the shore, heading inland before turning north, trying as much as possible to parallel the course of the coast. From time to time they drifted back to the west, just far enough for the coast to come back into their limited field of view, and then quickly shied back to the east. None called it cowardice, Artor's decision to avoid another altercation with the giant monsters, though some among them were just as eager to test the mettle of their new weapons on an opponent.

It was hard to say how long they walked, and impossible to say how much time had passed since they'd pierced the hedge of mist, but even with their health bolstered by the strange mantles the White Phantom had provided, they began to tire. The skies overhead showed no signs of darkening, just as blue as they'd been when Galaad had first glimpsed them, and there was no indication that night would be falling any time soon.

Finally, as they approached a narrow stream which blocked their path, running from east to west, Artor announced that they would stop and make camp.

With sighs of relief, the captains lowered their packs to the ground and began unpacking their supplies.

"Look!" Bedwyr shouted, and pointed across the stream.

The others followed his gaze, and there on the far side of the stream they saw a group of people standing. At this distance, it was difficult to make out any details, too much obscured in the diffuse twilight, but Galaad could see that they were men, and not giant monsters like those they had faced on the shore.

The captains laid their hands on their weapons, warily, and hurried to the stream's edge.

"Halloo," Artor called, cupping his hands around his mouth like a trumpet. "Are you friend or foe?"

There were seven of the strangers, Galaad now saw, all facing away from the stream, their backs to Artor and his men. One glanced over his shoulder at them but did not speak. Then he looked away, and the seven strangers waded backwards into the stream.

"What madness . . . ?" Caius began.

When the last of the strangers had backed into the stream, a kind of haze appeared before Galaad's eyes, and when it cleared the strangers had disappeared from view.

Artor ordered the captains to keep careful watch on the stream, in case the strangers had submerged and swum to their side, but the waters of the stream remained undisturbed, and there was no further sign of the strangers.

Unable to find fuel for a fire, Caius experimented with his lance, firing a burst of bloodflame at the ground and generating a roaring blaze. The conflagration quickly burned itself out, but while it raged it gave considerable heat, and so with periodic blasts from the lance he was able to keep a fire burning long enough to cook their evening meal. There was some discussion of using water from the nearby stream, but the question was quickly made moot by

Artor, who insisted that they use only the water they had brought. Galaad thought of the ancient pagan myths of women who had ventured into the underworld and eaten the food of the dead, thereby ensuring that they would never be able to return to the world of men. Galaad wasn't sure if the High King was reminded of those stories as well, but nevertheless saw no reason to debate the decision.

Later, after they had dined on their simple fare, the seven gathered around the dying embers of Caius's bloodflame fire, seeming to draw more comfort than warmth from its glow. The skies overhead were just as illuminated as they'd been since first they'd ventured into the Summer Lands, but gathered around the fire, the seven spoke in lowered voices, pitched in tones more fitting evening.

Lugh was experimenting with his new silver arm, flexing and relaxing the silvery pincers at its end. With the ragged hem of his bitten-through tunic covering the join between flesh and metal, it was difficult to see where man left off and the metal began. He had pulled the glass apple from his belt and tossed it from hand to hand, testing the dexterity of his new appendage.

"Does it hurt?" Bedwyr asked, eying the silver arm uneasily.

Lugh was thoughtful for a moment, then shrugged. "Not really. It . . . tingles, I suppose you'd say. A bit like when your hand falls asleep and twinges with pinpricks until it awakens once more." Lugh snugged the glass apple back into his belt and held both his hands up before his face, flesh and metal, flexing them in unison. "But no. Doesn't hurt."

Bedwyr seemed suspicious, looking with distrust at the Gael's new appendage. It was clear that he'd been shaken by their encounter with the White Lady, or at least with her ghostly image, the White Phantom. And Galaad could see that Bedwyr was not alone.

"Do you think," Gwrol said, staring into the dying embers of the fire, "that the gods of our grandfathers really existed, after all?"

It had been so long since the Gwentian had spoken that it was startling to hear his voice once more. He'd hardly said a word since he'd been snatched up by the one-armed creature on the shore, and Galaad had put it down to the pain of his bruised ribs, though it now appeared that something else had been occupying Gwrol's thoughts.

"We'd always been taught that such things were superstitious pagan nonsense," he went on, glancing towards his brother Pryder, "mere fancy. But . . . but suppose that they *had* really existed, at that. With the retreat of the Romans and their god from Britannia, does that mean that the old gods might be returning?"

Pryder shifted uneasily, not willing to meet his brother's gaze. Galaad knew that the two Gwentians professed belief in the Messias, but had not seen any indication that their faith was particularly strong. Evidently, there was some room for doubt in their minds, at least on the part of one of them.

"I follow the ancient Derwydd faith of the grandfathers," Bedwyr said, eyes lowered, "but nothing in my beliefs accounts for monsters such as we've seen." He shuddered. "Who is to say that this White Lady is not some temptress, sent to lead us astray? Who is to say that she really exists at all?"

Artor shook his head. "I believe in what I can see, and always have. Who am I to doubt the evidence of my senses now?"

Caius chuckled, prodding the embers with the tip of his lance. "You didn't always trust your senses so well." In response to Artor's questioning glance, Caius explained. "Remember that night, years ago, when we first established a headquarters in Caer Llundain. You and I had drunk our fill, with your portion far exceeding my own, and we decided it the right time to walk the perimeter of the city wall. Stumbling often, and taking liberal doses from the wine skins we'd brought along to slake any recurrent thirst, we continued on into the small hours of the night, coming at last to the place where the wall in the east meets the Tamesa. I paused to relieve myself against the Cantium ragstone, and you staggered on up the white hill. In moments, you rushed back, wild-eyed, and insisted that you'd come upon a strange figure burying something beneath the hill."

Artor scowled. "You mocked me mercilessly for days, but I know what I saw."

Caius grinned wider. "But didn't dare to go back and try to dig whatever it was up, as I recall, for fear of what you'd find."

Artor shuddered. "I'm not a suspicious man, as you know well, but there was something about that strange figure, and the industry to which he turned his hand, which did not sit right with me. I insist to this day that was something beyond the ordinary to what he was about."

Caius chuckled again and prodded the embers, sending up a shower of sparks.

Galaad sighed, contentedly. "As for me, I'm just relieved that all of this is real. What will they say back in Glevum, all of those who claimed my visions were only a plague of guilt?"

Even as he spoke, he realized he'd said too much.

"Guilt over what?" Artor asked, eyes narrowed.

Galaad shifted uneasily, all eyes turning to him.

"What do you have to feel guilt over, tadpole?" Lugh asked, quirking a smile.

Galaad flushed and lowered his eyes to the ground.

"It . . . it is nothing," he said, trembling.

"Oh, no," Pryder said, in good humor, "you can't announce something like that and leave it unexplained. What is it that you'd done? Bedded another man's wife? Stolen away the neighbor's prized pig? What mischief could you have got up to in Glevum at your tender age?"

Galaad hunched his shoulders, shrinking into himself. "Her name was Flora," he said.

Around him the captains leered lustily, jabbing one another with their elbows.

"She was my daughter."

The leers faded, the elbows ceased their jabbing.

"She was not yet three summers old. It was a spring day, and we were riding. Flora loved to ride with me, and I with her. We rode out over the countryside, at a gallop, enjoying the sense of speed, feeling the rush of air in our hair, hearing it whistle in our ears. Then . . ."

He swallowed hard, eyes stinging.

"Then the horse . . . It was later decided that it had turned an ankle on a rock, but at the time all I knew was that it stopped short, falling to one side, and throwing me and Flora to the ground."

Galaad reached up and touched his head just above his right eye, the scar completely hidden above the hairline.

"I landed headfirst, and when I tried to stand, the flowing blood nearly blinded me. I lost consciousness almost immediately, but not before seeing my daughter, lying a short distance away."

His throat constricted, and he choked back tears.

"It was small comfort, but she'd died instantly, her neck broken in the fall."

Galaad lifted his eyes, looking around the circle, taking in the expressions of the captains.

"It was a short while after that when I had my first visions. At first my neighbors thought I was mad with grief and guilt, and then simply thought me mad, and in the end even my wife turned her back to me, leaving our home and returning to live with her parents. But I knew that it was not just grief, or guilt. I knew that someone spoke to me in the visions, and now others have seen her with their own eyes."

The captains glanced to one another, their expressions unreadable.

"Would that we had known that *before* leaving Caer Llundain," Bedwyr said, caustic. "We might well not have gone if we'd known your *visions*, so-called, were nothing but the product of an addled, grief-stricken mind."

"But whatever their source, the visions proved true enough to lead us here," Caius said.

"And is *this* the product of grief and guilt, as well?" Lugh flexed his silver arm.

"That's not the point!" Bedwyr snapped.

"Enough!" Artor barked, quelling any further comment. "This damnable light above will never fade, but we are all sore tired, and much in need of sleep. Let's call an end to the day, and continue this talk, if we must, tomorrow." A smile tugged at the corners of his mouth. "Whenever *that* might be."

Galaad was not sure how long they'd slept, but when he woke to the sounds of the others breathing, he felt considerably refreshed and rested. Too, he felt lightened somehow, as if he'd been shriven of his sins, at least in part, by admitting the truth about Flora and the visions to Artor and the captains.

For his part, Galaad was still not entirely convinced that there was not some connection between the accident and the visions, for all of his protestations to the contrary. He still wondered if perhaps the injury he'd sustained had not made him more susceptible to the White Lady's message. Or perhaps if, burdened by the guilt of causing his daughter's death, he'd not been given the chance for redemption, singled out by the White Lady for this dispensation. He burned to ask her, to find out the truth of it, and hoped against hope that when they reached the tower of glass, he'd have his chance.

Their bundles repacked and secured on their backs, their swords girt around their waists and their lances and disks in hand, the seven headed out. The stream, when forded, proved to be shallow, rising no higher than their knees, such that when they reached the other side only their boots and the legs of their breeches were wet.

The seven stood on the shore, shaking the water from their feet and legs. Galaad glanced back over his shoulder, and then called out in alarm. "Look!"

The others turned. Seven men gathered on the far bank of the stream.

Galaad's hand flew to the hilt of his sword. He wondered how they had been pursued, and by whom? He thought of the seven they'd seen when first reaching the stream. Then a thought struck him.

"Wait," Galaad said, staying his hand, while the others drew their weapons. "Look more closely."

The seven who gathered on the streams far side seemed not to notice them, except for one, short and compact, who looked at them for a moment with his mouth wide but silent, and then turned away. They were indistinct at first, obscured by the diffuse light of the Summer Lands, but as Galaad looked closer, their features became more evident. One had dark hair and a well-trimmed beard, carrying himself with a regal air. One had red hair and a drooping mustache, his right arm glinting silver below the elbow. Two were as alike as brothers, one light, one dark. One was tall and fair haired, another short and compact. And the last, carrying a circle of metal in his hands, looked to be little more than a boy.

"They are us," Galaad said softly.

Artor nodded without speaking.

"But how is it possible?" Caius gaped.

"That's not us now," Lugh said, warily. "That's us yesterday."

"What?!" Gwrol sneered.

"We're looking at yesterday, imbecile," Pryder said, punching his arm. "Can't you understand *anything?*"

Gwrol rubbed his upper arm, scowling.

"I don't like this," Bedwyr said in a low voice.

"You don't like anything, tree lover," Lugh snarled. "Come on, let's go. It's not as if we did anything yesterday worth looking at." Without a backwards glance, the Gael hefted his pack on his back and started away from the stream.

The others followed after, drifting after Lugh, seeming reluctant to tear their gazes away from the strange sight across the stream, this brief glimpse into the past. Galaad was last to follow, lingering at the streams edge. Across the stream, yesterday's seven were backing away from the stream, disappearing from view.

Perhaps Lugh was right, and there was nothing to be gained for looking too long at the past, dwelling too much on yesterday. With a heavy sigh, Galaad turned and followed the others towards tomorrow.

They had walked for some time when they first caught sight of the rider and first heard the white hounds coursing in his wake, their baying like wild geese in flight.

The rider approached at speed, coming at them out of the indistinct blue haze of the middle distance. He was astride some sort of beast, the size of a horse but with the look of a lizard, its scales red, with a long ropy tail and fierce talons. Tendrils trailed like whiskers from the sides of its massive head, and in its fierce mouth were four large teeth, two above and two below. Its eyes burned as if lit by flames from within.

"The Huntsman!" Galaad shouted, seeing the thin red blade the rider held aloft.

But as the rider thundered nearer, Galaad saw that he'd been wrong. This was not the same strange figure they'd faced in Llongborth, though it bore the same red sword and was followed by the spectral dogs of wrath. This rider was larger than the Huntsman had been, and while the Huntsman had been hairless, the rider's face was covered by a full red beard, his long red hair streaming behind him as he rode. And while the Huntsman's face had been frozen and immobile, the rider's face was clearly expressive, mouth open in a defiant snarl. Only the skin of his cheeks and forehead could be seen, and this little corpse white, while the rest of his body was entirely encased in some sort of close-fitting red armor that shone dully like metal but bent freely without joint or hinge.

Whoever the rider was, though, it was clear he meant harm to the seven.

As the rider drew nearer, Galaad remembered the White Lady's warning—*beware the Red King!*

CHAPTER TWENTY-THREE

Jubilee

THE NEXT MORNING, Blank and Miss Bonaventure returned to London. As soon as their train arrived, they deposited their overnight bags at the house in York Place and immediately checked the Blue Book for a listing for one Peter R. Bonaventure. They found an address in Earl's Court, not far from the museums, and before they'd managed to shake the dust of Taunton from their feet were back out the door and in a hansom cab on their way. They'd discussed the matter on their return trip from Somerset and had come to the agreement that the details of Professor Bonaventure's expedition, whatever they were, simply had to strike at the heart of their investigation. If they could learn from this other Bonaventure what it was in his report that was worth a man's life, they might be able to divine what motivated the Jubilee Killer and put an end to his spree before he struck again.

Unfortunately, it was not to be, at least not on that day. When they arrived at the address in Earl's Court they found the house standing vacant, the furniture covered in sheets and dust lining the mantle. The servant who'd answered the door, who'd been left in charge of the household in his employer's absence, explained that Professor Bonaventure's wife had only recently given birth to their first child, a son they named Jules, and that together the family had gone away to the continent to visit the mother's relations. According to the servant, the Bonaventure family had left London some three months before, in the early part of March.

Naturally, the servant knew nothing of any report, nor of any crystal chalice, and was sadly unable to provide a temporary address at which his employer might be contacted, as he received his instructions by mail on an irregular basis and had no clear notion where the Bonaventures' journeys had carried them.

So, after two days of travel, to Taunton and back, Blank and Miss Bonaventure found themselves only with more questions, and not the answers they sought.

Having spent a considerable amount of time in close quarters, Blank and Miss Bonaventure repaired to their separate homes, agreeing that it was in the best interests of their respective temperaments to spend a brief period apart. On his return home to York Place, Blank found a number of invitations to dinners and parties waiting for him, this being the first Friday evening after the Queen's Jubilee, but he felt more inclined to hermit a bit.

In amongst his post was a note from Superintendent Melville. At Blank's suggestion, Melville had tasked a constable to keep watch on the movements of Mervyn Fawkes, given his suspicious behavior when interrogated, but evidently the man had yet to put a foot wrong and gave no indication of being anything other than what he seemed: a slightly addled man who worked in the Crystal Palace.

Blank was all out of sorts. He felt as though he'd reached an impasse in his investigations. He had succeeded in turning up new information in the days past, but had been singularly unsuccessful in extracting any usable intelligence. He found himself mired in facts about everything from the folk beliefs of the ancient Britons to the most recent technological innovations of the moving picture industry but could not manage to unravel the skein sufficiently to produce any comprehensible pattern.

With only a single lamp burning in his library, Blank got a slender case down from a high shelf. Undoing the clasps, he swung the case open on its hinges and revealed the flute within, nestled in black velvet. A cylindrical-bore ring-key, cast in silver, the flute had been manufactured from silver by

Theobald Boehm himself. Checking the action of the keys, Blank raised the flute to his lips and began to play.

In moments, he was lost in remembrance. Blank had scant few memories of Roanoke, before the coming of the Croatoan, before Michel Void found him wandering alone through the village, the only one spared the ravages of the ego-destroying mind virus. He carried in his mind portraits of his parents, Dionys and Margery, but he could not now be sure if the images of them he recalled were their actual appearances or else false recollections he'd created in the years since to fill the empty space. But one of the clearest, most pure memories he retained of those early years was of his father playing his flute for the children of the village, Virginia and himself the youngest among them. That simple lilting memory had lodged in Blank's young mind, penetrating like an earwig and refusing ever to be dislodged. Years later, Blank had heard it again, played by a Scottish navvy who labored in the construction of the Marc Isambard Brunel's tunnel, and learned that it was the tune to a Scottish ballad, the story of a border reiver who plied his bloody trade in the debatable land for kith and kin.

He played that tune now, in the dimly lit library in York Place, all alone with his books and memories. He thought of those long-dead border reivers, and of his father Dionys, who had fled the justice of the debatable lands with his pregnant wife, looking for a better home across the sea. He thought of Virginia, and all the rest lost to Croatoan, and what would have become of him, barely three years old, had Monsieur Void not marched out of the track-less wilderness and offered him a second chance at life, albeit in the thankless and unforgiving service of Omega.

All of these things he thought, as he played, and the shadows grew deeper around him.

The next morning, Blank awoke feeling surprisingly refreshed. There was something cathartic to giving oneself in to the most morose of remem-brances, wallowing if briefly in the deep pools of self-pity and remorse. Facing his vexations in the light of a new day, he found renewed optimism, one might even say hope.

With a lightness to his step and a smile on his lip, he sauntered to Bayswater, to the Bark Place home of Miss Bonaventure.

This being Saturday, Mrs. Pool was at her liberty, and Miss Bonaventure was left to her own devices. So it was that Blank was unsurprised to find his associate dressed in nothing more than bloomers and a brassiere, head uncovered and barefoot, dancing back and forth in her front room, a button-tipped foil in hand, shadow fencing.

Miss Bonaventure was the New Woman, incarnate, there was no question about that. Even so, Blank often found that, in private, away from the prying eyes of the public or the huffing disapproval of her day maid, his associate often took liberties that would scandalize even the most radical of her fellow New Women. Just as often, though, Miss Bonaventure would catch herself doing so and quickly fall back to the more acceptable outrages of the contemporary feminist.

This was precisely one of those moments. On first admitting Blank into her home, Miss Bonaventure seemed unconcerned to receive a visitor in such a state of undress, much less one of the opposite sex. It was only after seeing Blank's amused smile and raised eyebrow that she seemed to realize her circumstance and hurriedly put on a man's shirt which lay draped across a chair back. With this casual concession to propriety, Miss Bonaventure resumed her shadow fencing, practicing her parry and riposte.

"I thought not to see you today, Blank," she said, only slightly winded by her exertions. "I take it you simply can't live without me?"

"Miss Bonaventure," Blank said, dropping onto the sofa, resting his bowler hat on his knee, "you have long since become indispensable. If we part, it is only that I reacquaint myself with your absence, that I might appreciate your presence all the more."

Miss Bonaventure lunged, skewering her imaginary opponent, and then recovered, coming once more *en garde*. "You stoop to flatter, Blank, but I'll not contest. Now, does some new intelligence bring you here this morning? Some new facts come to light regarding our investigations?"

Blank shook his head, but smiled. "Not new intelligence, my dear, but perhaps new perspective. We have spent so much time afoot, these last weeks, in surveillance and skullduggery, interview and interrogation, that we have forgotten the all-too-often tedious work of research. If we are unable to locate your namesake, this Professor Bonaventure, and likewise unable to obtain a copy of his report which the murderer snatched from the Taunton castle, then perhaps we might locate in other documents references which might help us triangulate the missing information we seek."

Miss Bonaventure parried an imagined blow and riposted. Then, satisfied with the motion, she drew herself up straight, tucking her foil under her arm and dabbing the gleam of sweat from her brow with the sleeve of her over-large shirt. "Just what documents would those be?"

"This Peter Bonaventure has some reputation as an explorer, I've discovered, and has filed any number of reports to the Royal Geographical Society over the years. I propose that we avail ourselves of the society's library and peruse Professor Bonaventure's filings, beginning with the most recent and working our way back, in the hope of uncovering some indicator of what the missing report might contain."

Miss Bonaventure paused in wiping her brow, her forearm frozen over her eyes. Then she lowered her arm slowly and fixed Blank with a steady gaze. "I take it this isn't to be one of those instances in which you consult your *Whitaker's* and have the answer in a trice."

Blank shook his head. "Sadly, no. By my best estimates, we'd have some dozens of lengthy, dusty, long-winded reports to review."

Miss Bonaventure sighed dramatically and rolled her eyes. "Oh, the things I endure in exchange for your company, Blank."

Blank shrugged. "I can only offer apologies, my dear. I'm a tedious rogue, I'm sure." His grin broadened. "Whyever do you put up with me?"

Raising an eyebrow, quizzically, she said, "Why, Blank. It's because you amuse me. Why else?"

As it happened, the offices of the Royal Geographical Society were closed for the weekend, and so it was Monday morning before the pair were able to gain admittance. Located at Number 1, Savile Row, just around the corner from the Royal Asiatic Society, the society's headquarters was an imposing structure, made even more so by alterations and additions made since the society had taken up residence. Atop the roof was a small astronomical observatory, the Map Room was unrivaled in its collection of charts, maps, atlases, and globes, and the stacks had in recent years been expanded with a new upper library on the second floor. It was here that Blank and Miss Bonaventure found the myriad reports filed by Peter R. Bonaventure over the years, and here where they spent the following days, morning, noon, and night.

They had learned, through an examination of Blank's social directories and references, that Peter Bonaventure was not a member of the Royal Geographical Society, though he had been offered a fellowship some years before. For reasons of his own, Bonaventure had declined the offer. If he was not a member in good standing in the Hytholoday Club, an exclusive society of explorers, it would be easy to assume that Bonaventure was simply not a "joiner," as the Americans would say; as it was, one had to conclude that something in the policies or practices of the RGS impelled Bonaventure to decline the proffered invitation.

They also learned that, prior to the birth of his son Jules earlier that year, Peter Bonaventure had lived an apparently ceaseless life of travel, journeying to the four corners of the globe, not once, but repeatedly. Bonaventure was a tireless explorer, autodidact, and polymath, who studied language and legend with the same passion with which he pursued geography and geology. In addition to a number of monographs on geographical subjects, he had penned his own translation of a book of medieval Arabic poetry, a survey of Indonesian mythology and folklore, a ethnological memoir of the year he spent living among the native Te'Maroan people of Kensington Island, a study of the history of pre-Columbian Aztec civilization, and an as-yet uncompleted and unpublished history of swordsmanship.

Miss Bonaventure received this information with an expression something like pride, as if Peter Bonaventure was in fact a member of her family and not simply an unrelated namesake. For his part, Blank was sorry that his and the professor's paths had never yet crossed, as he sounded a singular individual. With any luck, when this business was over and done and Peter Bonaventure and his family returned from the continent, perhaps Blank would be able to make his acquaintance. Such a man might well be of some use in Blank's plans for the future which even now were slowly beginning to unfold.

What Blank and Miss Bonaventure were unable to find, however, in this mountain of printed material, was any hint as to why Professor Bonaventure had taken it in his head to dig holes atop Glastonbury Tor, hunting the source of ancient British myths.

As a matter of course, Professor Bonaventure had filed any number of reports on his excursions and expeditions with the RGS, apparently as much out of a desire for there to be some record of his findings, should some unfortunate fate befall him in the field, as in the hope of benefiting the organization itself. The most recent of these dated to the autumn of 1896, some months before the excavations at Glastonbury Tor had begun, and sadly included no reference to any research in Somerset or mention of Gwynn or Nudd or Annwn or any such mythological oddities.

Turning from the most recent reports, Blank and Miss Bonaventure worked their way backwards, one report after another, digging back through the dusty stacks of the RGS library, searching for any clue.

Thursday afternoon, after more than three days of near-continuous study, Miss Bonaventure finally chanced on something of interest which, while it did not relate to Glastonbury or Somerset or British myth, seemed to have real bearing on their current investigation.

The report detailed an expedition in 1885, some twelve years before, when Peter Bonaventure had been commissioned by the Royal Geographical Society to investigate reports of a new island sighted some few hundred leagues from the coast of Ireland. Chartering a steamer ship, the *Clemency* out of Liverpool, Professor Bonaventure had searched the area and found what he described in the report as a large floating object. Not an island, it was organic rather than mineral, and though the report was vague on the point, the language used conjured images of a mat of seaweed and driftwood inadvertently lashed together by wind and wave and drifting aimlessly upon the oceans. In any event, the mass was solid enough for a landing party to go "ashore," and Professor Bonaventure led a small party in rowboats.

In the end, Professor Bonaventure reported that there was little of interest on the "island" and advised commercial sea vessels to steer clear of the area until it had floated elsewhere, doubtless in the hope that the organic matter which constituted the object would not foul their propellers. In a note appended to the report, the chairman of the RGS issued a blanket denial for any future request to investigate the object.

The report mentioned four names, two of which Miss Bonaventure and Blank found of considerable interest. The first two, those of the crewmen who had accompanied Professor Bonaventure in the landing party, were inconsequential. The other two were Professor Bonaventure's traveling companion on the expedition, Jules Dulac, and the representative of the Royal Geographical Society who had accompanied the expedition, one Mervyn Fawkes.

The link between Fawkes and Professor Bonaventure, previously unsuspected, was an illuminating one. Blank remembered coming across the brief mention in Fawkes's biographical detail of an incident on an expedition for the Royal Geographical Society in 1885, after which Fawkes was a patient for a time at Colney Hatch, but in the days of coughing in the dust knocked loose from files and folders in the RGS library he'd never imagined there might be a connection. Fawkes was suddenly a much more likely suspect as the Jubilee Killer, whatever his motives.

Blank intended to journey to Crystal Palace or to Fawkes's lodging house in Camberwell right away. But Miss Bonaventure pointed out that the Jules Dulac of the 1885 report was very likely the same Dulac who had assisted Professor Bonaventure in his excavation on Glastonbury Tor, as Bulleid reported.

"I'd come across a reference to a 'Jules' in some of the reports," Miss Bonaventure commented, rubbing her bleary eyes, "but for some reason I'd just assumed that the professor was referring to his son." She wore a hang-dog expression. "Precisely *how* he was referring to his infant son in reports up to ten years old, I can't imagine."

"You're tired," Blank said, patting her shoulder in a consoling gesture. "I likely skimmed right across those sorts of references myself without even noticing them. We've had precious little sleep the last few days and reviewed thousands of pages of material, so we can't be blamed for missing a word or two, can we?"

She brightened somewhat. "Well, shall we check the Blue Book and see if we can't find a listing for a Jules Dulac?"

Blank smiled. "Miss Bonaventure, we should alert Frank Podmore and the SPR, as I believe that you've been reading my mind."

A short while later, Sandford Blank and Roxanne Bonaventure stood before a house in Chelsea, just as the sun was beginning to set in the west. The house in particular was humble compared to its more grandiose neighbors that faced the Thames up and down Cheyne Walk but would have stood out as respectably large and sturdily built if relocated to another address in the city. Three stories tall, with three curtained windows on each floor above the ground level, the house was constructed of dark red bricks that seemed almost black in the dying light, the mortar between them gleaming like ivory. The door was also white, with a curious knocker in the shape of a dragon's head.

Stepping through the wrought-iron gate that separated the door from the sidewalk, Blank let fall the dragon-head knocker once, then twice, waiting for an answer. A short while later, the door opened, and a man stood framed in the light from within. He was about Blank's height, with short-cropped dark hair and few weeks' worth of beard growth. He had a square chin and well-defined jaw, a narrow nose, and high cheekbones. His face was unlined, but at the same time lacked the unbaked smoothness of youth, and so it was impossible to judge his age; he could have been anywhere from thirty to a well-kept sixty years of age. Evidently not expecting visitors, he was dressed only in shirtsleeves, riding boots, and trousers, his cuffs rolled up to the elbow, in his hand a pipe of briarwood, tobacco still smoldering in the bowl.

"Yes?" the man asked.

"Jules Dulac?" Blank replied with a question of his own. He found the man's appearance compellingly familiar, but couldn't place where he'd seen him before.

The man narrowed his eyes, warily. "Who is it asking?" His accent was odd and difficult to place. It seemed to partake of many different accents, something of French commingled with a little Welsh, the Home Counties mixed with a touch of German. Wherever the man was originally from, it seemed evident that he had traveled, and widely.

"My name is Sandford Blank," came the reply, "and this is my associate Miss Roxanne Bonaventure."

At the mention of Miss Bonaventure's name, the man's eyes widened. Seeming to forget all about Blank, he took a half step forward, studying her face intently.

"*Miss* Bonaventure," he repeated. "Yes, yes," he said, nodding slowly, narrowing his gaze. He looked her up and down, taking in her fashionable bicycle suit of jacket and matching bloomers over stockings, before finally coming to rest on her face. "You definitely share the family features. But I've not heard of a *Roxanne* Bonaventure before." The man tilted his head back, looking at her down the length of his nose, looking for all the world like a farrier inspecting a horse. "Who was your father, girl? Did Josiah have a bastard about whom Peter was never told? Or did Erasmus live long enough to have progeny, after all?" He snapped his fingers. "You're not from Varadeaux, by any chance, are you? *D'où venez vous?* Varadeaux? *Hein?*"

"*Je suis britannique,*" Miss Bonaventure said, shaking her head. "*Je viens d'Angleterre.*"

The man scowled for a moment, then smiled good-naturedly. "You'll have to excuse me," he said, chuckling slightly. "I . . . I have an interest in genealogy and have made a particular study of your surname. I thought I knew of all the Bonaventures currently living in the British Isles and was surprised to hear a name unknown to me."

Miss Bonaventure treated him to a smile, though to Blank it seemed that her smile was somewhat forced, as if the man had struck a nerve or given her some cause for concern. "No offense taken, sir," she said. "On the subject of names, are we to assume that yours is Jules Dulac, after all?"

The man drew himself up straighter, heels together, and inclined his head in a nod, a formal-seeming gesture. It struck Blank that the man had the carriage of a military officer. "Guilty as charged, miss. Jules Dulac at your service. What might I do for you?"

"My colleague and I are assisting Scotland Yard in an ongoing investigation," Blank answered, "and we were hoping you might be able to assist us."

"Certainly," Dulac said, genially. He paused, and then slapped his forehead. "Where are my manners, leaving you out in the street like tradesmen. Come in, won't you?"

Stepping aside, Dulac ushered them in, then closed the door behind them.

Blank and Miss Bonaventure found themselves in a large sitting room on the ground floor of the house. But aside from a pair of simple chairs, an occasional table, and a sofa, the room more closely resembled a museum than a residence. More precisely, a museum devoted to the art of war.

Dulac knocked the ashes from his pipe into a tray and casually packed more tobacco in the bowl from a pouch he pulled from his trouser pocket.

Bladed weapons of every imaginable shape and size crowded the room, hung on hooks from the walls or in simple wooden display cases that lined the floor: swords, of every imaginable provenance, sabers and scimitars, cutlasses and katanas.

But there were more than just swords in the collection. One wall was given over to flags, banners, and signets, dominated by a large white cloth upon which was embroidered the VOC monogram of the Dutch East India Company, with the motto "Terra et Mari" above and the words "Fidelitas et Honor" below.

"You wouldn't happen to have some interest in weaponry, would you, Mr. Dulac?" Blank asked, easing himself onto one of the plain wooden chairs.

Dulac smiled. He pulled out a silver vesta case, on which were engraved his initials, "J.D. ," and a stylized dragon's head, like that which served as the doorknocker, and striking a match against the case, held it to his pipe. "It's an interest bordering on mania, I suppose you could say," he said, around short puffs, drawing the flame into the bowl, "but with little else to occupy my time, it seems harmless enough."

In spite of the martial tenor of the room, though, it was clear that it had been the site of lighter pursuits, as well, as evidenced by the number of empty bottles stacked unceremoniously beneath the occasional table, and the cut glass tumblers and half-full bottles arranged on the table's surface. His pipe clenched between his teeth, Dulac fixed himself a generous glass of whiskey, and with a glance offered drinks to Blank and Miss Bonaventure, but they declined politely with a shake of their heads.

Miss Bonaventure moved nearer the wall, admiring an Aztec club lined with tiny obsidian blades. "You put most museums to shame, Mr. Dulac, at least in regard to matters martial. I dare say you have more here than the British Museum has ever put on exhibit."

"It's an avocation, nothing more."

"And your vocation, Mr. Dulac?" Blank asked. "I take it you have traveled quite extensively with a Professor Peter R. Bonaventure?"

"Yes." Dulac nodded. "For some time now. We share a passion for the untrammeled places on the globe, for unspoiled wilderness and forgotten lands."

"But you don't travel with him now?" Miss Bonaventure asked, taking a seat.

The man chuckled and flounced down onto his sofa, his arms resting on the back, the whiskey in the glass threatening to spill over the rim. "Where Peter now goes, I cannot follow."

"And where is that, precisely?" Blank asked.

Dulac's grin widened. "Matrimony. I've neither the talent nor the inclination for it, I'm afraid. I pledged myself to a woman, long ago, and have never seen a reason to seek the company of another."

"So no family then, Mr. Dulac?" Miss Bonaventure glanced around the spacious room and indicated the stairs leading to the upper floors.

Dulac's smile faltered, and a cloud passed across his features for a moment and then was gone. "Once upon a time, perhaps," he said, his voice sounding far off. "But only for a short while, and never again. There are some things that, once lost, can never be regained."

Miss Bonaventure pulled what appeared to be a lady's undergarment from behind the cushion of the chair in which she sat and held it up for inspection, her eyebrow cocked.

Dulac smirked, tilting his head to one side, and held his arms up in mock surrender. "Which is not to say that I haven't sampled the goods on offer, from time to time, but there's a world of difference between leasing and owning, if you take my meaning."

It was clear from the empty bottles and the lacy bit of abandoned finery that Dulac had indulged himself in the days or weeks previous, which presented a contrast to the formal reserve suggested by his military bearing, to say nothing about the martial aspect of his collection. But Blank had more pressing matters to attend than to play alienist to a strange man with a compulsion for weaponry. "Tell me, Mr. Dulac, do you recall a man by the name of Fawkes, by any chance?"

Dulac raised an eyebrow. "Fawkes, is it? There was a Geoffrey, as I . . ." He stopped short and shook his head. "No, I misremember. A *Mervyn* Fawkes. That's right. Mervyn Fawkes who accompanied us on an expedition to . . . Well, an expedition for the RGS, some years ago."

"That would be the one to the 'floating island,'" Miss Bonaventure asked.

Now both eyebrows raised, and Dulac looked at her with considerable surprise. "Why, yes, it would." He pursed his lips, thoughtfully. "I thought the RGS had elected to keep that matter under board, but it appears I was mistaken."

"And what can you tell us about Mervyn Fawkes?" Blank asked.

Dulac shook his head. "Very little, I'm afraid. I never saw him again after our return to port. I understand that he was . . . not quite right . . . for some time thereafter, but I never knew what became of him."

"Hmm." Blank nodded. "Late last year, you and Professor Bonaventure carried out an excavation on Glastonbury Tor in Somerset. Is that correct?"

It was as though a door had just closed in Dulac's face, and the easy smile melted away like ice thrown on a fire. "Yes," he said simply.

"We were hoping that you might be able to tell us something about the dig and what it is you hoped to find." Miss Bonaventure treated him to a smile, but might as well have been smiling at a brick wall.

"You'd have to ask Peter, I'm afraid," Dulac said, his tone curt. Then, his manner disingenuous, he adopted an ill-fitting pose as a stupider man. "I just carry the shovels, you know."

Blank gave a slight nod, not bothering to pretend he was convinced. "Well, I'm afraid that we can't ask Professor Bonaventure, as he's currently out of the country. You wouldn't know how to reach him, by any chance?" Dulac shook his head. "Pity. We'd consult the report he filed with the Somerset Archaeological and Natural History Society, but it seems that the paperwork was stolen in a robbery some time ago."

Dulac's eyebrows raised again, in genuine surprise. "Really?"

"Mmm," Blank hummed. "And a man was killed in the process, custodian to the Taunton castle."

"I . . . I didn't know."

"And nothing else stolen but that report," Miss Bonaventure put in.

Dulac seemed shaken. He took a long draught from his tumbler of whiskey, nearly downing the contents in one shot. Then he wiped his mouth dry with the back of his hand, his eyes focused on the middle distance.

"Tell me, Mr. Dulac," Blank said, casually, "do you happen to know anyone matching the description of a tall man, completely bald, with chalky white skin and, perhaps, something odd about his eyes?"

Dulac's head whipped around and, eyes flashing, fixed Blank with his gaze. His fingers tightened in a white-knuckled grip around his tumbler, and for a moment it seemed as if the glass might shatter in his hand. "What . . ." he began, his voice strained. "What did you just say?"

"We've been trying to locate a man described to us as tall, hairless, skin of a chalky-white hue, and perhaps something a little odd about his eyes. We think he might be able to answer some questions for us."

Dulac's neck corded and his hands shook with what could have been controlled rage or abject fear, or some combination of the two. He stood, suddenly, dropping his glass shattering to the ground, heedless of the noise or the shards.

"You'll . . . you'll have to excuse me," he said, lurching towards the door. Taking a frock coat down from a coat rack in the foyer, he opened the door. "There's something . . . to which I must attend."

Dulac stood in the doorway, almost vibrating with impatience, while Blank and Miss Bonaventure rose and made for the door. Dulac didn't meet their gazes as they passed him and stepped outside but pulled a ring of keys off a hook on the wall, stepped outside after them, and locked the door behind him. Then, the key ring in his hand, he hurried out through the iron gate, turned to the right, and began running up Cheyne Walk. At the intersection with Oakley Street he rounded the corner to the right, heading off to the north.

Blank and Miss Bonaventure exchanged quick glances and, without another word, took to their heels after him.

They must have pursued Dulac through the streets of Chelsea and South Kensington for nearly a mile until finally they reached Earl's Court. Dulac had exhibited an astounding degree of stamina, such that Blank and Miss Bonaventure were hard pressed even to keep him in sight, much less catch him up. As it was, they were lucky to see which doorway he turned into, near the intersection of Gloucester and Cromwell Roads, or else they'd have lost track of him entirely. As they drew nearer, though, the doorway standing open, they recognized the address at once.

This was the residence of Peter R. Bonaventure, which they'd visited the week before on their return from Taunton.

Reaching the open door, they found Professor Bonaventure's servant standing in the entryway, distressed.

"Where did he go?" Blank said, seizing the man by the elbow. "Where is he?"

The servant turned watery eyes on Blank, and then pointed to the rear of the house. "Mister Dulac has gone to the master's storage."

Blank released his hold on the servant, and without pausing to explain himself, ran into the house, Miss Bonaventure following close behind.

At the rear of the house, they found the door wide open, and saw the flickering light of a lantern swinging beyond. Outside, they found themselves in a garden, and at the bottom of the garden was a small, fortified-looking building, and it was before this that Dulac knelt, his head down and shoulders slumped.

The servant appeared at Miss Bonaventure's side.

"The master had it built," the servant said, unprompted, "to store all the treasures he brings back from his travels. Mr. Dulac has been by to check on it, regular, in all the time the master's been away. Though, come to think of it, it's been some weeks since we've last seen Mr. Dulac. And now he shows up, all wild-eyed, and barrels through the house without so much as a by-your-leave."

Miss Bonaventure gave the little man an affectionate pat on the shoulder, consolingly, and then she and Blank crossed the garden to stand behind Dulac.

The windowless building appeared to be made of sturdy stone, and the door was of thick-timbered oak, banded in iron and closed with a massive padlock. Or rather, it should have been. The padlock, though, which should have hung from the iron ring through the crossbar, was in Dulac's hands, cleaved neatly in two. To all appearances the lock had been severed, the door opened, and then the whole affair closed back up again, so that on first glance it would have appeared to be whole and unmolested.

"I'm a damned fool," Dulac said, his voice low, and Blank knew he spoke as much to himself as to them. "To wait so long, to find it, and then to think my job done just because I'd locked it away behind stone and iron." He shook his head, his eyes squeezed shut. "When first we brought it back, I checked every day, just to make sure I hadn't dreamt the whole thing. Then every week, at least, to make sure it was safe and secure. Then, Peter went away with his wife and little Jules, and my visits became more sporadic, losing more and more of my time in spirits and the soft embrace." His fingers wrapped around half the severed lock, Dulac pounded his fist into the ground with an audible thud. "Six weeks it's been since last I came to check. Six weeks since he's snatched it away from me, after all this time."

It was clear that Dulac hadn't opened the door but having discovered the lock severed knew what he would find within. Gingerly, Blank stepped around him, and pulling the crossbar free, opened the door, the hinges swinging noiselessly. If he had to guess, Blank would suppose that the thief had oiled the hinges when breaking into the storage to prevent the squeal of iron on rusty iron from announcing his presence.

In the dim light that leaked from the lantern outside into the window-less space within, Blank caught glimpses of the items secured within the storage and saw that the servant had not been far wrong to call them treasures. Gold masks, skulls of jade, totems, and relics from the world wide. And in the center of the room a sort of plinth, atop which was a card which bore the words "CRYSTAL CHALICE, GLASTONBURY TOR, OCTOBER 1896" written in a neat hand. Behind the card, in the thin layer of dust that covered the plinth's top, a bare place was dimly visible.

Miss Bonaventure appeared at Blank's elbow. "Dulac has made another abrupt exit, Blank. Thought you'd like to know."

Blank glanced around the dimly lit space and nodded. He found himself curious to paw through the collection and see what other trinkets and wonders had been found on the professor's various expeditions, but he hadn't the time to indulge the notion. Turning, he and Miss Bonaventure headed back towards the house.

The servant still stood at the back door, eyes wide and startled.

"You'll probably need a new lock," Miss Bonaventure said, handing him the severed halves of the padlock. "Which way did Mr. Dulac go?"

The servant pointed through the house to the front door.

Blank pushed up the brim of his bowler with the silver-chased head of his cane. "Much obliged, my good man."

By the time Blank and Miss Bonaventure were back out on the street, Dulac was nowhere in evidence. Hardly winded from his sprint from Chelsea, he clearly had untapped reserves of stamina, and had raced away into the dark night.

"He's probably gone back to Cheyne Walk," Blank said, peevishly. "Shall we give pursuit and see if we can't get some answers from him?"

"I don't know, Blank." Miss Bonaventure pointed in the opposite direction, up Gloucester Road towards Kensington Gardens. "I suspect we might be otherwise engaged."

Blank turned and looked in the direction she indicated.

There, a hundred feet or so away, stood a tall figure dressed in a shabby black suit. It had been the new moon the night before, the skies overhead dark, but in the light from the gaslit streetlamps the figure's skin appeared so white it seemed almost to glow, his eyes hidden behind smoked-glass spectacles. He was completely hairless, even lacking eyebrows, but the nails at the ends of his thin fingers seemed curious long and sharp.

"Miss Bonaventure," Blank said, tightening his grip on his cane, "I believe you may be right."

"Excuse me," Blank said, calling out to the strange figure as if he were hailing an acquaintance across a crowded street. "Might we have a word?"

The strange hairless figure, his expression immobile and unreadable, stood motionless, his eyes hidden behind lenses of smoked glass.

Blank took a step towards the silent figure, upon which the man immediately took a step backwards.

"There's no reason to be frightened," Blank called out, soothingly. "We only want to ask you a few questions."

Blank took another step forward and waited. It seemed for a moment that the strange figure would remain still, but instead of taking a step backwards, the man turned and took to his heels, running in the opposite direction.

"Oi!" Miss Bonaventure shouted, chin up and head back, uncharacteristically vulgar. "We're talking to you!" Miss Bonaventure glanced over at Blank. "Well, glad I wore my bicycle suit today. It'd be hell running in a full skirt."

With that, Miss Bonaventure sprinted after the fleeing figure. Blank chuckled and propelled himself after her.

The strange, hairless man moved alarmingly fast, his chalk white skin a blur beneath the gaslamps, and it was all that Blank and Miss Bonaventure could do to keep him in sight. Crossing from Gloucester Road into Palace Gate, he crossed Kensington Road and into the park not far from the bright-lit Albert Memorial. Blank and Miss Bonaventure dodged horses and carriages, hansom cabs and growlers, narrowly escaping collision and reaching the far side of the road relatively intact. They raced through the Queen's Gate and around the gilt majesty of the memorial, flanked by marble representations of the four corners of the world—Africa astride her camel, Asia atop her elephant, Europe before her bull, and America riding her buffalo.

Beyond the memorial, the wide footpaths of Kensington Garden were scarcely discernible in the thin light of the distant gaslamps, only the faintest sliver of the moon visible overhead. They almost lost the man in the gloom, but Blank's sharp eyes caught a flicker of white moving between a stand of nearby trees, and they were once more on the scent.

On they raced, to the north and east, through the widely spaced copses of trees. It seemed for a moment that they'd lost their quarry again, only to find him standing by the banks of the Serpentine.

As they approached, the figure seemed transfixed for a moment, staring into dark waters, slightly rippled by the gentle evening breeze. The air smelled of water and algae, and was noticeably cooler than the rest of the city where the stones of buildings and the pavement underfoot held the heat of the day long into the night. The figure seemed frozen, and Blank and Miss Bonaventure checked their speed as they drew near. When they were but a few dozen feet away, the figure turned to face them.

It was only now that they realized that the man hadn't been transfixed by the water. He'd been *waiting*. And not for his pursuers, but for the pair of animals which now padded along the banks of the Serpentine, appearing from out of the night's gloom.

They appeared to be dogs, though there was something of a cat about their heads, with long ears, short legs, and long bodies. Their fur was completely white but for the tips of their ears, which were bloodred. As the hounds drew nearer, Blank saw that their teeth and claws, too, had been dyed or painted a deep scarlet hue. Something tickled his memory, seeing the barred incarnadine teeth of the dogs.

The man's face remained immobile and inexpressive, but he opened his mouth as if to speak, for the first time. Instead of words, though, the man simply uttered a click and whistle, a strange trilling noise, and in response the dogs came to a halt right before him, facing Blank and Miss Bonaventure and snarling.

It was clear that the dogs meant them no good, and the man with the smoked-glass spectacles had managed to check their pursuit.

"Red in tooth and claw," Miss Bonaventure said in a low voice, crouched in a ready stance.

Blank recalled the phrase, from Tennyson's *In Memoriam*, an elegy to his friend Arthur Hallum. Another, Blank mused, to add to the embarrassment of Arthurs they'd already stumbled over.

Blank replied only with a grim grin. He wished, and not for the first time, that his mesmerism could be employed in such circumstances, but experience had taught that someone truly intent on doing him harm could not be so easily persuaded. More corporeal means of influence were needed. He wrapped one hand around the silver-chased handle of his cane, the other on the wood midway down, and with a whisper of steel on steel he drew out the long thin blade of sword-stick. Then, with blade in one hand and cane-sheath as club in the other, he stood ready to meet the hounds.

The dogs ceased their growling and opened their maws to bay, but their baying sounded more like geese in flight than the barking of dogs.

"I don't suppose we could talk about this?" Blank said, with a slight smile.

The hairless man trilled again, and the dogs attacked.

"It appears not," Miss Bonaventure said, and lashed out with a kick.

CHAPTER TWENTY-FOUR
Millennium

ALICE AND STILLMAN SLEPT LATE THE NEXT MORNING. They needed the rest. That night, Tuesday the 27th of June, if all went to plan, they'd be carrying off a daring jewel heist, penetrating the most secure levels of Glasshouse and walking off with the Vanishing Gem.

With any luck, the final puzzle piece in place, Alice would finally be able to work out the riddle of the visions, would finally know what the messages were trying to tell her and what all of this was for. It just wasn't possible that she was simply crazy, right? How else could she have known Stillman Waters, or about the gem, or the London Eye and all of that?

Of course, Alice realized with a cold chill, she could be even crazier than she thought. What if *none* of this were really happening? What if she'd been sitting alone in a derelict Victorian men's room since Friday night, having completely lost her mind? Stillman Waters, occult secret agent, a mix of James Bond and Harry Potter? How likely was *that*?

No. Even if all of this was just a crazy delusion, the last mad ramblings of a deranged mind shutting down, she had to follow it through to the conclusion. Even if she was completely batshit and imagining all of it, the talking ravens and the creepy white and red dogs and the cat burglars and the jewel heists and all, there was nothing to do but see it through. Maybe there'd still be some answer at the end, either way.

Alice wrapped the blanket around her tighter, there on the sofa in the living room at the heart of the spy's home hundreds of feet below ground. And she tried to sleep, hoping that it would be dreamless.

The simplest methods were the best. That's what Stillman had said, and it seemed to be working.

Three days before, on Saturday, he'd explained to Alice about how most thieves operated. About how they'd paid their tickets at the door of the museum, walk in with everyone else, and then hide out in a bathroom or behind a curtain while everyone else filed out at closing time. Then they'd smash and grab, and make a run for it, so that when the guards went looking for someone breaking in, they'd already have broken *out*.

They used the same basic principle in the Glasshouse, though perhaps with a little more technological sophistication. Still, it beat sliding on your belly past infrared beams or rappelling from the ceiling on wires. That stuff looked *dangerous* . . .

Getting into the building had been a matter of relative ease. While most of Glasshouse was occupied by Temple Enterprises, a few floors had been leased out to other companies, most of whom did business with Temple. One was a solicitors' firm specializing in immigration law. Using a couple of off-the-shelf identities drawn from Stillman's wide assortment still on file from his days of espionage, they posed as a young woman from America—big stretch—and her British uncle, who was sponsoring her for British citizenship. The appointment had been made over the phone for late in the afternoon. At shortly after four o'clock p.m., Stillman and Alice, or "Reginald Cleaves" and "Elizabeth Cleaves," checked in with security in the front lobby. Their identities were confirmed, their signatures recorded, and they were given temporary visitor badges and escorted to the elevators. They rode up to the twenty-eighth floor, the highest the visitor badges would allow them to go, and made their appointment with the solicitors.

The interview was brief, and the solicitor's representative took down their particulars and scheduled a follow-up appointment for later in the week. Then Reginald and his niece Elizabeth left the offices.

But they didn't leave the building.

There was a supply closet on the twenty-seventh floor. From a careful study of the architectural drawings and the security systems, Stillman had been able to determine that the closet door was not in the direct line-of-sight of any security cameras. And a review of the security logs showed that it was not opened during operating hours but unlocked by the night shift cleaning crew, sometime between nine o'clock and ten. And even better, the hot water supply for the upper floors passed just behind the wall of the closet, which would help mask their body heat from the thermal heat detectors on the floor.

The door was secured by a standard pin-and-tumbler lock. It was the work of less than ten seconds with a rake pick and a tension wrench to pop the door, and then Stillman hustled Alice inside.

Then they waited in the dark for the day to end and the building to slowly empty.

"Why are you doing this?"

It had grown stuffy and stifling in the closet, in the dark, and Alice had come to find the silence unbearable. She kept her voice to a whisper, like Stillman had insisted, but just couldn't keep silent any more.

"I'm not doing anything, love, just sitting here."

"No. I mean . . . *this*. Why are you breaking the law for someone you don't know? Why are you risking your neck? If your old employers find out, won't you get in trouble?"

"I expect so." Pause. "But it's as much because of boredom as anything else, I suppose. Even trouble, if that's what I end up with, is better than nothing. And I've made do with nothing for a good long while. So boredom, and curiosity as well. About just who you're hearing, and just what they're trying to tell you. I thought it might be Omega, but then . . ." He trailed off.

"You mentioned that before. When you asked me if the name meant anything to me. How could I be hearing Omega, anyway?" She laughed, quietly but ruefully. "They in the habit of going around and sticking crazy visions in girls' heads?"

Alice expected a chuckle, at least, but didn't get one. "It's been known to happen, a time or two. There was a girl named Joan, once upon a time, who was called to be an agent, but her mind couldn't quite work out what it was hearing, and I think it drove her a little mad in the end. She knew she was getting a message but never could understand what it was telling her. But no, what you've got, it seemed different to that. I've not seen anything quite like it before." Pause. "So tell me, love. When did these 'visions' of yours first start? It's been a good long while, I take it, from reading your diary."

A silence stretched out between them.

"Remember how I told you I'd killed two people? Well, it was after the first time."

She thought Stillman might say something, might ask her to explain, but he let the silence do the asking for him.

"See, when I was seven and a half, I was upstairs in our house with my dad. Mom was out back, working in the garden. I was reading and Dad was working on one of his little home improvement projects. The banging of his hammer stopped, and after a while I went in to check on him." Pause. "He'd had a heart attack, but I didn't know that at the time. All I knew was that he was on the ground, his face all screwed up. He was awake, though, still conscious. He told me to go get help, and quick. I went. I ran. As fast as I could. But the stairs in our house, they were carpeted, and I was barefoot, and my foot always slipped on the third step down, anyway, so Mom always told me to be careful. But I wasn't, and I . . . I fell."

She paused, remembering.

"I fell, and I watched the stairs tumbling all around me, and I closed my eyes, and when I opened them again, it was a week later. I'd been in a coma the whole time. I'd laid at the bottom of the stairs for an hour or more before Mom came in and found me. Dad . . . By that time, my dad had been dead for a while."

Silence again for a moment.

"After my dad died, my mother's mother moved into the house with us to help raise me, since Mom was busy running the contract postal unit."

"And that was when your visions started?"

Alice nodded, then realized the gesture was wasted in the dark. "Yeah. Just a little while later."

"Alice, love. I've killed people. More than I care to remember. And what you did was nothing like it."

Alice shook her head. Another wasted gesture. "I didn't shoot him, if that's what you mean. But if I'd been more careful, if I hadn't slipped and fallen, then Mom could have called the ambulance, and they could have come and taken him to the hospital, and he'd have been all right and still alive and I wouldn't be here now trying to make up for it!" She bit off her last words, shaking with suppressed emotion.

"You said two people. That you'd killed two people. Who was the other, then?"

"Just a girl. Just Nancy. Just my only friend. She didn't care that I was younger, or wasn't a cheerleader, or didn't listen to the right music." She scoffed. "Mom thought she was a lesbian. I don't know. Maybe she was. Maybe I was. I'm not really interested in sex, so does it really matter who I'm not interested in having sex with? All I knew was that Nancy was there for me, and cared about me, and was my friend."

"So what happened?"

"I was fifteen, almost sixteen, and a freshman in high school. Nancy and I skipped school. We skipped school a lot. We drove around in Nancy's car until she was too stoned to drive, and then I took the wheel. I didn't have a license, but if it didn't bother Nancy, it didn't bother me. I'd had a couple of drinks, and a toke or two, but I was fine to drive. I'd been off my meds for almost two years but hadn't had an episode in all that time. I guess it was just overdue. I smelled something burning and thought that Nancy had dropped the roach." She paused, swallowing hard, struggling to remember to keep her voice low. "I had a vision. I saw the same thing I did all those times when I was seven, after the accident. The eye over the city. The birds. The gem. The lake, its surface as motionless as glass. The man with the ice-chip blue eyes. And the gem." She closed her eyes as if she could forget. "Then, when I came out of it, the car was wrapped around a light post, I was cut and bleeding all over my face and hands, unable to breathe right from the bruises I'd got from the seat belt, and Nancy . . . Nancy? She hadn't worn a seatbelt, never did. She'd gone through the windshield, face first."

"And she was . . . ?" Stillman began, then trailed off.

Alice nodded, uselessly. "They told me that she died instantly, but I think they were just trying to make me feel better."

⚓

This looked like the scene where the two characters who have been growing closer to each other, all along, finally bond, trapped together in a confined space for a long amount of time. This looked like that scene, but it wasn't. Alice and Stillman were in the closet, in the dark, for long hours, but they weren't Audrey Hepburn and Peter O'Toole in a closet in *How to Steal a Million,* or Loni Anderson and Frank Bonner in an elevator on *WKRP in Cincinnati,* or John Ritter and Don Knotts in a meat locker on *Three's Company.* They were a teenage runaway epileptic and a self-professed former spy who lived in a hole in the ground.

Alice realized that they might just have discovered all of the common ground they were going to find. There might not be any more possible avenues for connection. The gulfs that separated them—in age, in experience, in temperament—might be insurmountable, after all. There was no way of telling.

⚓

"I'm not going to tell you that you've got nothing to feel guilty about," Stillman had said. "I expect you've already been told that more times than you can count. You don't need anyone else's permission to forgive yourself, love. You can do that all on your own. And until you're ready to do that, there's nothing anyone else'll be able to do for you, more's the pity." He paused, and Alice could hear him breathing. "For what it's worth, though, that guilt you're shouldering, the crimes you think you've committed? They aren't a patch on what I've got on my own back, love. Not a patch."

Then he fell silent and didn't speak again. Alice realized he was probably waiting for her to say something. He would be waiting for a long time.

By nine o'clock, the building would have mostly emptied out, if this was a typical workday. It was time for Stillman and Alice to go to work.

Stillman had set a routine running in the security servers. At nine o'clock, on the dot, the system would respond as though it had experienced a significant spike in voltage coming in from the utility mains. The electrics in the building would flicker, while surge impedance systems handled the transient voltage. Of course, there would have been no spike, but only a careful cross check of the building's records with those of the utility provider would prove it. And no one would think to check, since at that precise moment the security servers would switch from the live CCTV feeds from the cameras throughout the building to cached hard-disk recordings from the same cameras, twenty-four hours before. The date codes in the timestamp wouldn't match, of course, but the hour and minute would, and with any luck no one would notice the discrepancy until Stillman and Alice had finished their business and were gone.

The fire doors on the central stairwells were alarmed, of course, but were a matter of relative ease to baffle. Then it only remained for Alice and Stillman to mount the stairs, climb from the twenty-seventh floor to the thirty-fifth, get around the motion detectors in the gallery, and they were home free.

That was the plan, at least.

The fire door on the thirty-fifth floor was locked, which was surely a violation of safety regulations. Stillman identified it as a UL 437 rated high-security cylinder lock. He then took a bump key from his pocket. Specially cut, the key slid right into the lock. Then Stillman tapped it, just hard enough, and the pins inside the lock popped apart and the door opened.

"Okay, love," Stillman whispered, pocketing the bump key. "Here's where it gets a bit tricky, right?"

The routine that Stillman had planted in the security servers had taken care of the security cameras in the hallway downstairs and allowed them to climb the fire stairs without tripping any alarms, but now that they had reached the penthouse level, they would have to tread more carefully. This floor was largely given over to Temple's gallery, if the architectural plans were any indication, and the motion detectors in the gallery were on a separate system to the rest of the building.

Fortunately, there were no security guards patrolling the upper floors. Only Temple and his personal guests were allowed access. So long as they didn't run into Temple himself, and managed to avoid setting off the motion detectors, they had better than even odds of making it out unscathed. And if the popular press was to be believed, Temple was still out of the country at the moment, so there was little chance of that.

The problem was getting around the motion detectors, of course.

Stillman had explained that it wasn't like Alice had seen in the movies. There was nothing to duck or slide under, no handy infrared beams to illuminate with a quick spray from an aerosol can, nothing to bounce back with mirrors. The upper floors of the Glasshouse instead used volumetric motion detectors, which saturated the space with microwaves, leaving virtually no dead spaces behind.

That was where a little bit of MI8 spy science came into play. It wasn't magic, but might as well have been.

From Alice's backpack they withdrew two bundles of a flexible, clothlike material. They looked to be nothing more unusual than raincoats, which is what the security guards downstairs had taken them for on visual inspection. But they were so thin that, unfolded, they were larger than their small size when packed would suggest. And they were *not* raincoats, and hardly usual.

"Zip it up tight, love. Don't leave any wrinkles, or it'll spoil the effect."

The cloaks were slightly elastic, and selected for fit, so that when unrolled and pulled over arms and legs, they fit snugly. Light and flexible like rubberized fabric, the cloaks were constructed of electromagnetic metamaterials. Only partially opaque to visible light, when Alice had the hood closed over her face, she could still see reasonably well, her vision only slightly obscured, like looking through thin gauze.

"Ready to go?" Stillman checked the seams on her cloak, gave her a thumbs up, and then began to move slowly through the corridor towards the gallery, right into the space saturated by microwave motion detectors. "Remember, love," he whispered, "slow and steady wins the race."

Alice nodded and started after him.

The cloaks were designed so that microwaves could flow around them with scarcely any distortion, or so Stillman had said. It was all to do with the electromagnetic properties of the metamaterials used in their construction. When Alice asked where MI8 had come up with such futuristic gear, years ago, Stillman had casually explained that a sample had been found at the site of an "incursion," and that the "boffins" at the Tower of London Station had managed to reverse-engineer it after a few years. It didn't have much application—an invisibility cloak that only made the wearer invisible to microwaves—until the widescale implementation of microwave-based motion detectors, at which point it had become *very* useful.

They had to move as slowly as possible to keep from tripping the vibration sensors in the walls, but after a quarter of an hour or so they'd crossed the corridor and reached the entrance to the gallery.

This door was even more heavily fortified than the one leading to the fire stairs. Titanium-reinforced steel, biometric identification pad, deadbolts as big around and as long as Alice's leg. No bump key would get them past it. This called for some more MI8 gadgetry.

On Stillman's wrist, beneath the fabric of his cloak, was a metal wristwatch, its outline clearly visible. He held his wrist up to the biometric identification pad, depressed a button on the side of the watch through the cloak, and waited.

"More technology from another universe, I take it?" Alice whispered.

"No." Stillman shook his head, the movement masked by the opaque fabric of the cloak. "It's from this one, I'm afraid. Just from quite a ways in the future, is all."

The pad bleeped, and the heavy deadbolts slid back.

"After you," Stillman said with a bow, as the steel door swung open, soundlessly.

Alice wasn't sure what she was expecting. It wasn't this.

This wasn't a couple of paintings and a sculpture or two. This was a full-on *museum*. Alice wondered how one person, even a billionaire, could have gotten hold of so much stuff. Then, remembering the means he'd used to get the Vanishing Gem, she realized there weren't really many limits to what Temple might have gotten, or from where.

Aside from a central column, which contained the elevator shaft, conduits for water and power, the fire stairs, and the service corridor through which Alice and Stillman had just passed, the rest of the thirty-fifth floor was a large open space, bounded only by the outer walls of glass and steel. The floors underfoot were marble, the high ceiling tiled. The immense space, which could have housed a dozens offices, was filled with Temple's personal gallery.

Paintings hung on nearly invisible wires from the ceiling. Statues and pottery and weapons and books and parchments were displayed on waist-high plinths that dotted the floor every few feet. It was like a forest or a garden arranged by an insane gardener.

Some of the displays were under glass, but most were open to the air. None of the displays were labeled. Presumably, their owner knew what everything was. And, based on his reading of the architectural schematics and security logs, Stillman had deduced that Temple was the only person who ever came into the gallery. That was why the motion detection stopped at the steel door they'd just passed through. The logs showed no record of Temple ever bringing a guest to this floor, and no one from the security department or cleaning staff had entered the gallery since construction on the building was completed. There were no cameras, no motion detectors, no vibration sensors. Nothing but a lifetime of plunder, it seemed, all for the amusement of one man.

Alice and Stillman shucked out of their cloaks, carefully wrapping them up for the return trip, removing them to reduce the chance that they might get ripped unnecessarily. Alice's backpack was still back in the stairwell, hidden as best as they were able to manage, and so when the cloaks were wrapped, they set them down on the safe side of the steel door, ready for their eventual exit. Then they had a chance to look around them a bit, their vision unobstructed.

Stillman, a man who casually talked about communication with other universes and technology from the future, who lived in a secret underground base and had a lifetime of memories of the dark corners of reality where most never tread, nodded, appreciatively. "Now *this* is impressive . . ."

It took them so long to find the Vanishing Gem that Alice began to worry it wasn't there after all. Stillman didn't seem much to mind, though. He kept lingering by displays that were obviously *not* the Vanishing Gem like a kid with a gift certificate bouncing around the aisles of a toy store, trying to decide what to buy.

"Oh, look at this!" Stillman pointed at what looked at first glance to be a fat robot snake, or a beetlelike sculpture. It was constructed of a stainless, glimmering silvery metal, segmented like an armadillo, and was one foot long and several inches in diameter, with four pinchers a few inches long on either end. "I've heard about this but never thought I'd see it."

"What is it?"

"A Roman named Niveus that . . . well, that I've read about, said that he saw something just like it in fourth-century Britain. An Irish Celt was using it as a prosthetic arm, if you can believe it, though it was clearly repurposed. The Celt was an ancient old man, but talked about having come from somewhere else, some*when* else, when he was a younger man. He'd made a new life in his new home but still talked about his former existence, especially when in his cups. If not for the silver arm and certain details about future events in his stories, Niveus would have dismissed him as a madman, unhinged by drink. Niveus wanted to make off with the prosthetic, but the Celt's grandchildren caught wind of it and secreted the old man away. Niveus never saw him again."

Alice shrugged and moved on.

She passed what looked *exactly* like the Ark of the Covenant from the Indiana Jones movie but which Alice was sure must have been a movie prop. Further along was a black stone, polished to a mirror sheen, held in a gold frame. Next to it was something Stillman called an astrolabe made of gold, covered in what Alice thought might be Persian writing. A few feet away stood a small model of the moon, carved of ivory, with the craters marked with Egyptian hieroglyphics.

"Ah, a functioning Antikythera computer," Stillman said, pointing to a box of brass and teak with a pair of dials on the front, centered on concentric metal rings. "Didn't think any of those survived."

Alice continued. Resting on a long display table was a sword in a sheath. It was white, almost translucent like porcelain, but looked blue when the light hit it at an angle, the scabbard and hilt made of the same material. The handle was a spiral, like a narwhale's tusk, like a unicorn's horn, coming to a blunted point. Only the faintest line was visible between hilt and scabbard.

"My god . . ." Stillman said in a whisper, coming to stand beside her. He reached out his hand, tentatively, his fingers stopping just inches from the handle. Alice knew, from everything Stillman had learned, that the objects on display in the gallery were not wired to sensors or detectors; still, it was as though Stillman was afraid to touch the sword. "I . . . I never thought to see . . ."

Stillman, holding his breath, wrapped one hand around the handle, put the other under the scabbard, and lifted the strange blue-white sword into the air.

Alice opened her mouth to speak, to ask him what was so important about a sword made of porcelain or whatever, but then she caught a glimpse, out of the corner of her eye, of an unprepossessing smooth gem sitting on fabric under glass atop a nearby plinth. She turned her head, looking directly at it.

It was *exactly* as she'd seen in her visions. This was the last piece of the puzzle.

"I *do* hope you'll be careful with that. Unbreakable the sword may be, but devilishly hard to keep the fingerprints off."

Alice's heart leapt into her throat, and she spun around. Stillman, the sword still in one hand, was drawing his Hotspur from inside his jacket with the other.

There, behind them, stood a young man in a plain white T-shirt and black slacks, his feet bare, standing before the elevator, the doors just now sliding shut. He was bald, and Alice couldn't be sure, but she got the impression that his eyebrows were more pencil than brow. His eyes were hidden behind sunglasses, the frames small and round. He smiled at them, quizzically, his hands on his hips.

It was Iain Temple, naturally.

"Don't look now, love," Stillman said, casually, "but I think we've been rumbled."

Temple stepped forward, casually, making no threatening moves. If Alice hadn't known that he'd started releasing albums more than ten years before she was born, she'd have guessed he was only a few years her senior, at most. What was it with these British guys not aging, anyway?

"Interesting, isn't it?" Temple indicated the blue-white sword with a nod, then held his hand out to Stillman. "May I?"

Stillman narrowed his eyes, warily, and kept the barrel of his Hotspur trained on Temple's chest, but handed the sword over without objection.

"It appears to be topologically flat, if you can believe it." Temple had both hands around the handle, holding the point of the scabbard up before him. "A single, impossibly large molecule. Or perhaps, some of my researchers theorize, two macromolecules cohered by intermolecular forces." He pointed to the faint seam where the handle met the scabbard. "Magnetic resonance imagining can't penetrate, but our models suggest a 'blade' within, a continuation of this spiraling grip. There's every possibility that, if there is such a blade within, and it is only a single molecule thick, that it would be capable of slicing through virtually any material. Only matter with incredibly strong bonds between the constituent molecules, whether covalent or intermolecular, would be proof against it. Like a monofilament, but rigid." He shook his head, still smiling, and carefully placed the sword back on the display table. "But we've never been able to force the scabbard open, so we can't know for sure. Still, it's beyond the reach of any science *I've* every encountered, that's for certain. One of my teams unearthed it in Iceland years ago, and it's been a puzzle ever since."

Stillman had slowly worked his way around, his fletchette pistol still trained on Temple, until he stood beside Alice. "You won't be able to get it open, either."

Temple raised one of his drawn-on eyebrows, pursing his lips slightly. "Oh, really?"

Stillman nodded. "That sword used to belong to a friend of mine. John Delamere. He was the only one who could ever draw the blade. He said it was because it was genetically coded to its owner."

Temple's brow remained raised, and he nodded, impressed. "I'll have to make a note of that. Perhaps it might open new avenues of exploration."

"I thought you were supposed to be out of the country," Stillman said.

Temple shook his head. "No, I've not left this building for years. I have doubles that travel, make personal appearances, such like. I conduct interviews via satellite from here, run my companies by telephone or telepresence, but I never leave the Glasshouse."

Stillman scowled.

"Now *you* I recognize from our meeting years ago," Temple said, pointing to Stillman. "And I've kept up with you, over the years. I have extensive intelligence on operations such as that which you used to head, Mr. Waters. But you?" He pointed to Alice. "I'm afraid I haven't had the pleasure."

Alice was in no mood even to pretend to be polite. She could feel anger welling up inside, a rage that was all too familiar.

"Why'd you take it?!" Alice yelled, having to restrain herself from rushing the man. "What's this all about? What's this got to do with *me*?!"

"I'm sure I have no idea, my dear." Temple smiled, unctuous.

"The gem!" Alice stabbed a finger at the jewel safely ensconced behind the glass case.

"Ah, the so-called Vanishing Gem?" He looked from Alice to Stillman and back again. "Is *that* what this is about?"

"What is it, anyway?" Stillman asked, his Hotspur unwavering.

Temple shrugged and drifted over to the glass display containing the gem. "Well, that's the real question, isn't it? It appears to be some sort of opaque gem, nothing remarkable about it, except that it seems to be growing smaller, without measurably dissipating any energy or mass. It's *vanishing*, as the British Museum would have it. But where is it going?"

He stopped and looked to Alice and Stillman, as if expecting an answer. When they remained unspeaking, he shrugged and went on.

"One of my researchers was extremely bothered by all this, let me tell you. Kept banging on about the information paradox and such like. There was even the suggestion that the excess mass was bleeding as energy into another universe or continua altogether. But I've had some personal experience with such cross-continuum encounters—believe me—and this has none of the hallmarks. There is typically some residual Hawking radiation around such a fissure in space-time, particle-antiparticle pairs that are generated by vacuum fluctuations and then separated when one of the pair disappears into the fissure. There's no such radiation here. Nothing. So, again, what is it?"

"Why don't you tell us, smart guy?" Alice snarled.

Temple shrugged. "Very well." He put his hands on his knees and leaned over to peer closely through the glass at the gem. "Our best guess, at this stage, is that the gem is an object from outside this universe entirely. It only appears to be shrinking because it is, in fact, moving backwards in time."

"What?" Alice said.

"Which suggests, based on the current rate of decay," Temple went on, as if she hadn't spoken, "that we'll be witnessing the initial 'incursion' any time now." He straightened and smiled at them. "Exciting, isn't it?"

Stillman had evidently had enough. He raised the Hotspur, thumbing the control for full automatic. "All right, this has been charming, but I don't think we've got anything to lose at this stage by abandoning subtlety. The young lady needs the gem, I believe, but for what reason I'm not sure. In for a penny, in for a pound. So open the case, give me the gem, and we'll be on our way."

Temple just smiled at them, maddeningly.

"What if his guards are on their way?" Alice said, tugging Stillman's sleeve.

Stillman shook his head. "No, if they were coming, they'd be here already. I don't think our friend here called them before finding us here."

Temple shook his head, apologetically. "Oh, no, I didn't find you here by chance. I received word from downstairs that there was a break-in and came here to check on my gallery."

Alice glared at Stillman. "I thought you said this was going to *work*."

Stillman was confused. "I don't understand. We shouldn't have tripped *any* alarm."

"Oh, it wasn't you, I shouldn't expect." Temple put his hands in his pockets, casually. "You were already in the gallery when the break-in occurred, if I'm not mistaken."

Alice and Stillman exchanged glances.

"So who *was* it, then?" Alice said.

At that moment, the steel door through which they'd come, which now stood closed and locked again, suddenly tore in half, as a bright red line appeared, slicing from the top right to the bottom left, cleaving the door neatly in two.

As the two halves of the door fell apart from one another, clattering to the floor with a deafening din, Temple glanced back at Alice and Stillman.

"It was *him*, I'd imagine."

There, on the far side of the door, heedless of the myriad alarms he was setting off walking unprotected through the microwave saturation, stood a tall, slender man in a tattered black suit, completely hairless, his flesh the white of a corpse, in his hands a sword that glowed a sickly red, the blade so thin that when turned it disappeared from view.

It was the Huntsman.

CHAPTER TWENTY-FIVE

Twilight

RTOR AND HIS CAPTAINS did not waste a moment in discussion but immediately dropped their packs and loosed their swords from their scabbards. The blue light of the skyblade flashed in Artor's fist and in the hands of Lugh and Pryder, while Caius and Bedwyr held their disks before them, their bloodflame lances aimed forward. Gwrol, for his part, had a bloodflame lance in one hand, a spatha of mundane iron in the other.

Galaad drew his Saeson blade, and raised his disk as a buckler, tightening his grip on the hoop of strange metal at its back.

The rider was almost upon them now, and though his mouth had been twisted in a snarl since first they'd seen him, only heartbeats before, he'd still not spoken a word. Fast as his unearthly steed carried him, though, the dogs who coursed alongside him were faster still and reached the seven first.

In Llongborth, there had been but six of the strange white hounds, and Artor and his captains had been sore tested to withstand the bites and swipes of their ruby red claws and teeth. This time, they faced a full dozen of the creatures.

The first of the hounds plowed into the captains' left flank, tackling Pryder and Gwrol. In close quarters, the bloodflame lance proved worse than useless, as Gwrol tried to fire a burst of the bloodflame at his attacker and succeeded only in setting the ground at his feet alight. He escaped setting fire to himself, but just barely.

Pryder, for his part, swatted at his attacker with the flat of his skyblade, which rebounded harmlessly. Then, as the hound prepared to bury its blood-red teeth in his loins, Pryder shifted the blade in his grip and swung back, catching the hound just behind its shoulders with the blade's edge.

The skyblade passed completely through the hound, hardly slowing, passing unhindered out the other side.

Had Pryder swung lower, and had the skyblade bit deeper, he'd have sliced the hound clean in half; as it was, the tip of the skyblade reached only midway through the hound's body, so that as Pryder stepped away, the hound seemed to fold in the middle, the wound opening like a massive mouth. The cut was clean, smooth-edged, but as the hound fell to one side the pressures within pressed organs, viscera, and fluids bulging out, spilling over the white grasses underfoot.

For the first time the seven saw the efficacy of the whisper-thin sky-blades. They hadn't the time for awe, though, considering that they now faced a mounted opponent who had a red-tinged skyblade of his own.

The rider was upon them, driving his great reptilian steed through their ranks, swinging his great red blade at the nearest of them. But Artor, standing his ground, raised his own skyblade to meet the Red King's, and the two swords rebounded off one another with a sudden strange humming. Each capable of cleaving living flesh like an oar through water, when met blade to blade they proved implacable.

More of the hounds were among them now, snapping and clawing. Lugh lay about him with his skyblade, slicing off a hound's ear with a near miss, then lashing out with his silver arm on the riposte, the pincers clenched like a fist, and clouting the hound a fierce blow to the side of its head.

Bedwyr, crouched behind his disk, fired off a burst of bloodflame at an oncoming hound, but while the dog was caught afire, its progress was not halted. Like a ball of flame, the burning hound charged into Bedwyr, knocking him from his feet, setting his own garments ablaze.

The rider dug his heels into the sides of his lizardlike mount and reared its head around to come back for another pass. Artor wrapped both hands around his skyblade's hilt, his spatha scabbarded and forgotten at his side, readying himself.

One of the hounds rushed Galaad, and while he swatted ineffectually at it with the mundane iron of his Saeson sword, when the jaws of the beast met the strange metal of Galaad's buckler disk it was stymied. Galaad heard the red teeth snap and crack in the hound's mouth, and the creature reared back, roaring in pain.

All fear suddenly forgot, heedless of any risk to himself, Galaad shifted his disk aside and dove forward in a clumsy approximation of Lugh's signature lunge, his "answer," driving the point of his Saeson sword directly into the roaring mouth of the hound. He'd reasoned that, while the creature's hide was seemingly impregnable, the softer lining of its mouth might not be as resilient. And he was not far wrong. The sword bit deep into the hound's open mouth, passing through the already cracked and broken teeth, and pushing into the soft tissue at the roof of the beast's mouth.

The hound's fiery eyes opened wide, and it thrashed its head to one side. Galaad very nearly lost his sword, managing only at the last to snatch it back from the creature's howling mouth. As he raked his sword away, the edge tugged against the inside of the hound's mouth and parted the flesh with an audible rip. The creature skulked away, its mouth cut into a vicious smile on one side, leaking an unearthly ichor.

The captains were giving as good as they got, and while they had not yet lost one of their own, the sheer numbers of their attackers were against them.

The rider thundered past Artor, their skyblades meeting again with a humming clash.

"Who are you?" Artor demanded to know. "By what right do you attack us?"

Either the rider did not understand Artor's Britannic speech, or simply did not care to answer, but either way he remained silent, brandishing his red sword and returning for another pass. Galaad could not help but notice that, for all of his apparent strength and obvious ferocity, the rider did not seem a particularly accomplished swordsman. Still, with the steed beneath him and the pack of white hounds at his beck, his technique hardly seemed to matter.

"Who are you?" Artor repeated, this time in Latin, shouting to be heard over the baying of the hounds.

A wicked grin curled the mouth hidden behind the full red beard, and the rider shouted in response simply, "The Red." He waved his sword over-head like a standard. "The Red King."

This was the mysterious figure who imprisoned the White Lady, by her testimony. And the one against whom she'd warned them. It was clear to see why.

The talons of the Red King's reptilian mount thundered on the ground as he rushed back towards them. Their ordered flanks had been broken up, the seven no longer standing as one united front but now divided into indi-vidual melees, as the captains struggled with the hounds that harried them. The bloodflame lances were useful against them, but only in measured doses, as use too close to, or against a charging opponent, could be as dangerous to the lance's wielder as to his foe, as Bedwyr had learned. And the skyblades, though easily able to slice through the hound's tough hides, were likewise of dubious value in close quarters, as there was too great a risk of injuring one-self on the whisper-thin edge, the blade hardly caring whether it passed through the flesh of an enemy or of the one who bore it.

Artor broke to one side as the Red King galloped towards him, swinging with his skyblade at the lizardlike beast that bore him, but managed only to swipe a handful of the whiskerlike tendrils that dangled from the side of the monster's head. Still, the beast opened its mouth with a howl of agony, but rather than discouraging another attack, it seemed only to hearten the beast, and it rushed back at Artor, snapping with its massive teeth at the High King's body just as its rider swung at Artor's head with his skyblade.

Galaad stood over the still smoldering body of Bedwry, trying to keep the hounds at bay with his Saeson blade. The Demetian had been badly burned and lost large chunks out of his side and leg to the red teeth of the hounds. He whimpered when Galaad first drove the hounds away, bashing the sides of their head with the face of his buckler disk, but while Galaad poked and prodded at the advancing hounds with the tip of his sword, Bedwry fell alarmingly silent. Galaad hoped that he'd merely lost conscious-ness, fainting from the no doubt intense pain, but feared that the silence pre-saged an even more dire state.

It was difficult to get an exact count, but it appeared that some four or five of the hounds had fallen to the skyblades of Lugh and Pryder, or to the bloodflame shot by Caius and Gwrol. Galaad thought for a moment that they might win the day, then the Red King changed his tactics, and that faint hope faded.

Gwrol had switched targets, turning his attentions away from the hounds and to their mounted master, and as the Red King exchanged blows with Artor, Gwrol had sighted along his bloodflame lance and let fly with a string of the drop-shaped bursts of bloodflame.

The bloodflame splattered against the rider's red armor, and he howled in pain as the flames licked all about him. But while the fires burned him, they did not consume, his red beard and hair only singeing. Eyes flashing, the Red King spurred his mount into motion and galloped towards Gwrol. The Gwentian fired another burst of bloodfire, this one striking the reptilian mount in the eye, but it was not enough. The Red King bore down, and with a single mighty swipe of his red sword cleaved Gwrol's body in twain.

Galaad's heart was in his throat, as he watched Gwrol's head and left arm fall to one side, his right arm and legs fall to the other. In the moment that followed, the air was filled with an ear-splitting scream as Pryder saw what had become of his brother.

With a roar of outraged disbelief, Pryder rushed towards the Red King, swinging his own blue skyblade above his head like a club. Hounds snipped at his heels, but Pryder was mindless of any injury or impediment, his every intention directed at the man who'd just murdered his brother.

The Red King saw the approaching Gwentian, a bloody thirst for revenge in his eyes, and for the briefest moment something like fear crept across his bone white face. Then, at the last instant, he turned his steed to the side so that Pryder's first blow struck the mount, and not the rider. It meant a delay of only a moment, but it was sufficient. As Pryder's blade sliced effortlessly through the neck and front leg of the mount, the Red King leapt down on the other side, landing on his feet with the bulk of the now fast-dying reptilian beast between him and his assailant. Pryder was forced to inch around the still quivering bulk of the decapitated beast, his blade held before him, and the Red King was ready for him.

As Galaad had noticed, the Red King was not an accomplished swordsman. But in his rage and grief, Pryder was not thinking clearly and not fencing to the best of his ability. Galaad remembered the Gwentian's advice to master his own emotions, and thought it some bitter irony that Pryder seemed to have forgotten his own lesson in the moment he needed it most.

As the Red King and Pryder exchanged blows, Artor moved to join his captain, evidently thinking that two blades might prevail where one would find only stalemate, while Galaad and the others contended with the remaining hounds.

Just when it seemed that, at long last, the odds might have tilted in their favor, everything changed once more. A new monster arrived on the scene, and all hope of victory was lost.

The newly arrived monster loomed out of the indistinct blue distance, towering over them. Had any shadows fallen in that place, the entire battle could have nestled in the giant's shadow, so massive was he. Shaped somewhat like a man, but with a head more like that of a goat, something like crystal or glass glinted from his forehead, while the rest of his massive body was covered in a shaggy white fur. He was easily as tall as four of the captains stacked end to end, his enormous arms so long that his knuckles dragged the ground.

It seemed a dead certainty that, with the goat-headed monster on his side, the Red King was sure to prevail against the surviving captains.

What none of them guessed until the evidence was before them was that the goat-headed monster would instead turn his massive hands *against* the Red King.

In the first moments after its appearance, the Red King seemed not to guess the monster's intent, either, but looked at it with something more akin to annoyance than fear. The Red King wore the expression of one who found an already noisome task interrupted and thereby lengthened. He backed away from Pryder and Artor, his own red blade held up defensively before him, and shouted some words in an unknown language at the beast.

Whatever the intent of his words, they clearly failed to have the desired effect. The towering goat-headed monster lumbered forward, massive hands dragging the ground, clumping with a will towards the Red King.

The Red King shouted again, angrily, another string of incomprehensible syllables, but on the goat-headed monster came.

One of the spectral hounds rushed towards the goat-headed monster, red teeth snapping, but the giant simply closed one of his massive fists around the hound and crushed it like a grape.

The Red King's eyes opened wide, and he uttered something incomprehensible beneath this breath.

The goat-headed monster dropped the crushed hound, raised its ichor-stained hand high overhead, and then swung it down palm first at the Red King.

The Red King danced away, just barely escaping the blow but still buffeted by the wind of its passage. He did not waste time deliberating, but took to his heels, running away, calling back over his shoulder to the surviving dogs—"Tekel. Tekel lili."

The hounds who had survived the blows of skyblade, the scorch of blood-flame, and the monster's crushing grip were six in number, and these bounded after the Red King as fast as their short legs would carry them.

The Red King and his hounds were vanishing in the hazy middle distance as Artor and the others turned to face this new threat. Galaad left Bedwyr's side, coming to stand by Artor, while Pryder knelt down and cradled the severed halves of his brother. Caius and Lugh joined them, their weapons held ready.

But if the captains had expected another attack such as that which the goat-headed monster had meted out to the Red King and his hounds, they were disappointed. Instead, the monster settled back on its haunches, its knuckles resting on the ground, and leaned its goat head towards them.

Something glinted in the goat's forehead, and Galaad saw that glass was embedded there, as he'd originally thought. He hadn't time to wonder what light had glinted, with the only illumination the diffuse twilight of the Summer Lands, when a beam shone forth from the glass, striking the ground at their feet.

And there before them stood the White Phantom.

"My bidding, this creature does," the White Phantom said, "servant to the White. Only a short time, I can communicate, before the Red takes note."

Galaad, disconcerted by the casual presence of the giant monster, exchanged uneasy glances with Artor and the others.

"Near, the tower of glass," she continued. "A short distance, away."

"Where away, lady?" Artor asked.

The White Phantom glanced at the goat-headed monster behind her. "This creature, soon released by the White. But he will guide you a short distance. Follow the direction he goes, and you will find the tower of glass."

"Please, dear lady," Galaad said, stepping forward, overcoming his fear of the monster sufficiently to approach the White Phantom. "Please, I must know who you are, and what purpose you have laid out for me."

"No time." The White Phantom shook her head. "Reach the tower, enter the Unworld, and your questions will be answered. No time."

Before Galaad or the others could say another word, the image of the white lady flickered and faded, and the beam of light from the goat head snapped off. With that, the goat-headed creature stood, as docile as a milk cow, and lumbered off.

"We should follow," Galaad said, urgently. "He'll lead us to the White Lady!"

"What about our wounded?" Caius said. "What about Bedwyr?"

"He's mostly dead," Lugh said flatly, nudging the smoldering body of the Demetian with his toe. He slid his skyblade into its scabbard and bent for a closer look. "No, completely dead, by the look of him."

"What about . . . ?" Caius turned to where Gwrol had fallen. Pryder was just now standing, his front and arms stained red with his brother's lifeblood, his skyblade gripped tightly in his hand.

"There's no reason to delay here," Pryder said, all emotion gone from his voice. "If this Red King is master of the tower of glass, then it is there that we'll find him and there that I'll wreak my vengeance on him."

Without meeting their gazes, Pryder slid his skyblade into its scabbard, the hilt and the sheath joining once more as a seamless hole, and headed off in the direction the goat-headed monster had gone.

Lugh was crouched over Bedwyr, placing a copper coin under the dead man's swollen tongue. Then he laid Bedwyr's sword by his side, in close reach of his lifeless hand, the fingers curled and splayed, blackened by the flame. "I don't know what sort of afterlife tree lovers go to," he said quietly, barely loud enough for Galaad to hear, "but the Romans think you pay a toll, so you've got a coin if you need it. And you've got your iron handy, as well, should push come to shove." Lugh took a last look at the blackened face of the fallen, eyes burst and sightless. "A good road to you, Bedwyr, you feckless bastard," he said, straightening. "I hope you get whatever reward you hoped for in life."

Lugh set his jaw and strode over to where Artor stood flanked by Caius and Galaad.

Galaad opened his mouth to speak, but seeing Lugh's dark expression, he kept silent.

Lugh held his silver arm aloft, mouth drawn into a thin line. "That's a hand and two comrades these bastards owe me," he snarled. "I mean to collect."

With that, he stomped off after Pryder.

Artor's face took on a grim look. "Who am I to argue with that?"

They had lost sight of the goat-headed monster almost immediately, but it had left a trail that was easy to follow, and so they continued on their course, moving through the Summer Lands.

As they walked, Artor held his skyblade in front of him, turning it this way and that, examining the blade.

"A weapon like this should have a name," he said to Galaad, who walked at his side. "Sharp enough to slice through that great beast without a jar or jolt. And so thin that, turned *this* way, it appears that there is only empty space before me, but a space still solid and hard enough to fend off the strongest blow."

"A hard space?" Galaad replied.

"Hardspace?" Artor mused. "That seems as good a name as any, I suppose." He nodded, thoughtfully, regarding the blue blade. "Hardspace."

At last, a smooth-sided mound hove into view before them, above which rose a tower of glass. It was just as Galaad has seen in his vision.

The surviving five stood at the water's edge, looking across at the island. To reach it, they would have to cross a spit of land that narrowed to the width of a sword blade before widening out again on the other side. It was difficult to judge distances; visibility had seemed to vary widely as they'd made their final approach, but by their best reckoning the tower stood a mile or more from the spot where they now stood.

Artor laid his hand on the hilt of his skyblade, the newly christened Hardspace, his expression thoughtful. "Was it folly to come this long way, following a vision, leaving our long-cherished friends strewn on the path behind us? Was Caradog right, and we should have stayed in Caer Llundain and minded matters mundane?"

Caius rested a hand on the High King's shoulder. "If truth were to be told, I thought this journey would be just a last romp, a chance for the six of us to stretch our legs, sleep out under the stars, and remember good times past while passing a wineskin from hand to hand. I hardly gave Galaad's story any credit, no offense intended, Galaad, but never expected to see the glass citadel he described."

"And yet there it is," Artor said, pointing.

The sides of the tower were completely smooth, a cylinder which tapered slightly as it rose from the base, ending at a perfectly flat top some hundred feet or more from the ground. It could not have been more than a few dozen feet in circumference, though, and Galaad was hard pressed to imagine how much could fit inside; nor how anyone could gain entrance, come to that, since there were no doors or windows in evidence. He supposed that they must be clustered on the far side of the tower, obscured from view, or else too small to see at this distance, but he knew that he'd not be surprised if on close approach no such entrances presented themselves. How they would gain entry, then, was a matter to be solved once this final bridge was crossed.

"I'll allow I may have been wrong about spirits and saints, gods and goddesses," Lugh said, flexing his silver-pincered hand. "There are monsters beneath the waves, and giants walk the earth." He scowled. "But whatever gods there are, they're bastards, so far as I'm concerned, the lot of them, and

I'll take what they owe me out of their hides." He drew his skyblade, glinting blue in the twilight. "And if they don't like it, here's my answer for them right here."

"Pretty words," Pryder said, and set his foot on the narrow bridge to the island. "When I've had my revenge on this Red King, perhaps you can write a song about it."

The others followed after, creeping over the swordblade-thin spit of land, and walked on into the eerie quiet of the island beyond.

As relatively still and silent as the Summer Lands had been throughout the hours and days of their journey, the island was even more so. Where beyond there had been occasional signs of life—the strange birds, the lightning-fast predators, the spiral-horned creatures—here there was none, even the gently rising hills completely bare of grass, tree, or heath. Only close-packed dirt, so hard and dry it could have been fired in an oven.

They went on and finally came to the base of the smooth-sided mound, which rose at a steeper grade than the hill sloping gently up towards it. As Galaad's vision had shown, and Artor's recollections held, it was rounded on one end, pointed on the other, and rose above the surrounding island perhaps some five hundred feet. At the crest of the off-center mound, nearest the rounded side, rose the tower of glass.

There had been nothing but the gently rolling hills of hard-packed earth to hide their approach from the bridge, so Artor had seen little reason for stealth, but now at the very threshold of the tower of glass itself, he was surprised to have encountered no resistance, no picket of guards to halt their advance, no sentry or fence.

"They must not worry about intruders overmuch," Caius said when they'd completed a cautious circuit of the mound's base, "since there appears to be no way in or out."

The tall captain was right. Just as it had appeared from a distance, there did not seem to be any visible entrance to the tower, nor any window or arch. The smooth walls of glass were unbroken from base to top.

"I tire of this skulking about," Lugh said, his "answer" still in his hand. "They're bound to know we're here, since that red bastard scurried ahead with his hounds. They no doubt wait within, preparing their defenses."

"I agree," Artor said, tightening his grip on Hardspace's hilt. He set his foot on the mound and began to climb the steep grade. "We'll find a way in, and then we'll find the answers we seek."

Standing just before the smooth glass wall of the tower, Galaad was reminded of the hedge of mist that encircled the Summer Lands. But where the mist had been hazy and indistinct, this glass was smooth, definite. It was not transparent, but had the silvery look of a mirror which did not reflect back any light which struck it, instead seeming to dance with some inner light.

The five had made their steady way around the tower's base on reaching the mound's summit, their weapons held high and ready, but they had found no sign of a hidden entrance, as Caius had suggested they might.

"Well, maybe we should just *cut* our way in," Lugh snarled, and before anyone could respond, swung his skyblade in a wide arc that slammed into the side of glass tower.

The skyblade rebounded, silently, but the tower's side was left smooth and unmarred.

"So much for *that* notion," Caius said with a faint smile.

"It didn't even dent," Galaad said and reached out a hand to touch the glass. His fingers brushed the tower's surface, which was surprisingly warm to the touch, and though the surface remained smooth and solid as ever, the lights which moved beneath began to ripple, like the water of a pond struck by a stone, radiating out from the point he had touched.

"Arrive," came a voice from somewhere, which Galaad immediately recognized as that of the White Lady. "Enter."

Galaad's hand still rested against the tower's surface, and without warning his fingers pressed into and *through* it, disappearing from view, the glass now indeed rippling like water.

With a shout of alarm, Galaad pulled his arm back and his hand reappeared, sliding out of the glass as easily an oar from water. The glass, though, continued to ripple, glinting like quicksilver.

"Remarkable," Artor said and stepped nearer. Hardspace held in his right fist, he reached out with his left and, after a moment's hesitation, plunged his hand into the wall. His arm disappeared to the elbow, waves propagating out through the surrounding glass. "It's . . . warm." He pulled his arm free and inspected his hand closely. He wiggled his fingers experimentally, satisfied that all of them remained.

Pryder did not delay any further, but lifted his skyblade before him and strode with a will directly at the wall. It rippled with his passage, and then he was gone from view.

"Wait for me," Lugh called, and hurried after, plunging into the glass as though it were nothing but a curtain of falling water.

Caius shrugged. "Well, it seems the fashionable thing to do, so . . ." He grinned and leapt through the wall, his feet leaving the ground just before he knifed through the glass.

Artor glanced to Galaad. "Well, this is the place where your visions led, the goal to which your questions drove us. Shall we see if any answers lie within?"

Galaad smiled and nodded. Then the two of them, the High King and the young man from Glevum, stepped together through the glass wall and left behind the world they knew.

CHAPTER TWENTY-SIX

Jubilee

I F THERE HAD BEEN ONLY THE TWO DOGS, Blank and Miss Bonaventure might almost have prevailed. Though their snapping incarnadine teeth were fearsome, the humans had the advantage of height and reach, and Miss Bonaventure was able to keep her attacker at bay with well-placed kicks, dodging when necessary, while Blank used a combination of thrusts with his sword-stick and wallops with his cane to do the trick. Still and all, Blank's blade failed to do as much as draw a welt on the back of the dog who harried him, and Miss Bonaventure only narrowly escaped losing a foot to the gnashing red teeth of the other more than once.

To be charitable, it was a momentary standoff. Perhaps. At least, that was how Blank preferred to think of it later.

Then, however, the *rest* of the dogs arrived, and the odds were most definitely against them.

Four more of the beasts padded out of the darkness from the direction the previous two had come. They moved like white ghosts along the edge of the Serpentine, ears, teeth, and claws glinting red like spilt blood.

"What is it Shakespeare said about discretion and valor?" Miss Bonaventure said, sidestepping as her attacker lunged forward and then lashing out a kick to the side of the dog's head as it passed, which seemed scarcely to faze it.

"I suspect these beasts are after our 'better parts,' at that," Blank shouted back. Then he pointed with his sword-stick, its point to the man behind the smoked-glass spectacles. "We'll take this up another time, sir!"

Then, taking one last swipe at his attacker, however ineffectually, Blank turned and sprinted to the north, away from the newcomer hounds, Miss Bonaventure following close at his heels.

Blank could hear the sound of the strange man trilling again, then the flying-geese sound of the hounds' baying, and chanced a glance back over his shoulder to see that now the full half dozen of the creatures was coursing after them.

"More speed, Miss Bonaventure," Blank shouted, breathlessly.

They raced along the Serpentine towards the Italian Gardens. The dogs were close behind and coming closer, their white-faced master following at some remove.

"This way!" Blank shouted, grabbing Miss Bonaventure's hand just before they reached the Pump House. There were four small pools here, the artificial headwaters of the Serpentine, quartered by stone walkways. Blank had hoped to slow their pursuers somewhat, doglegging in a zigzag across the walkways, perhaps even causing one of the hounds to fall into the water, unable to check their speed in time.

Instead, the water proved a more effective barrier than he'd hoped.

Halfway to the statue of Edward Jenner which presided over the eastern side of the Italian Gardens, Blank dragged Miss Bonaventure to the left towards the Pump House and chanced a quick look behind them. The six hounds had reached the edge of the nearest pool and stopped dead, just shy of the water. It was almost as if the water, whether exposed in the pool or flowing beneath the stone walkway, served as some sort of barrier to them.

Blank didn't waste time speculating. He turned back to the right, racing to the east, around the corner of the Pump House and back onto the footpath.

"This way," Blank said in a harsh whisper. "We'll find safety in York Place."

Miss Bonaventure resisted, tugging his hand back. "But my place is nearer." She jerked a thumb over her shoulder.

"True," Blank said, and looked back at the hounds, who were even now inching their way around the Italian Gardens, trying to find solid ground. "But that way also lie our pursuers."

Miss Bonaventure looked back and, pursing her lips, nodded. "Fair enough." She turned, and poured on speed. "Then let's go!"

It was a short while later that they reached York Place, having zigged and zagged a few times along the way, hoping to throw the hounds off the scent. As it was, they reached Blank's home without any sign of pursuit for some blocks and had begun to entertain the hope that they'd lost their pursuers.

Upon reaching Number 31, York Place, they discovered they'd been found by another pursuer altogether, though perhaps of a less menacing mien.

It was a constable, who leaned against the doorjamb, drowsing.

"Something I can do for you, constable?" Blank was only slightly out of breath but daintily mopped his brow as he fished in his pocket for his house key.

The PC blinked rapidly, shaking himself awake.

"Yessir, Mr. Blank, sir," the constable said, hurriedly, and proffered a piece of paper.

Blank handed the key to Miss Bonaventure, who opened the door as he read the note. It was from Melville.

"What's it say?" Miss Bonaventure said, stepping inside and glancing somewhat nervously back the way they'd come, watchful of any pursuit.

"It appears, my dear, that our exertions are not quite done for the day. The Jubilee Killer has struck again."

A short while later, they stood in Piccadilly, facing Devonshire House. It was an imposing structure, a long brick building of eleven bays, separated from the rabble of Piccadilly by a high, featureless brick wall.

Sandford Blank remembered that wall well. It had been built shortly after the Great Fire of 1666 to keep out the mob and had done its job well. Even tonight, it seemed, it was keeping the commoners at bay, while admitting only the *crème de la crème*.

The servants at the gate, in the livery of the Duke of Devonshire's ancestors, demanded to see their invitations.

"I assure you, we've been summoned," Blank said, brandishing the note sent to him by Superintendent Melville.

The head servant studied the cryptic note with evident confusion, deriving about as much meaning from it as Blank had anticipated, and then turned to call over the house steward.

"Ah," Miss Bonaventure said, sarcastically, "*now* we'll see some results."

The majordomo crabbed over to them, looking more like an animated skeleton dressed in the costume of a Renaissance-era page than a living human being. When the situation had been explained to him, a deep frown pulled the corners of the steward's mouth down, and he glared at them with beady eyes.

"No," he said, his voice high and reedy. "It is simply out of the question. Bad enough that we run the risk of disrupting the mistress's party with the presence of the *police*"—he said this last with an expression like someone spitting out a worm found half eaten in an apple—"but I'll not make matters worse by allowing a pair of *middle-class* bounders to traipse through in modern dress." He paused, glanced at Blank's lounge suit and bowler hat, and then looked with distaste at Miss Bonaventure's bicycle suit. "Much less one in *bloomers*."

"Now, see here!" Miss Bonaventure took a step forward, lacking the patience for politeness.

Blank moved to intervene but needn't have bothered.

"Blank! What is the delay?"

He and Miss Bonaventure turned, and across the forecourt on the far side of the gate saw Superintendent Melville approaching at speed, dressed as the Sheriff of Nottingham.

Miss Bonaventure stifled a laugh at the sight of the large man stuffed into doublet and hose, but Blank only smiled indulgently.

"If you'd be so kind as to verify our bona fides, Melville," Blank said, "I think we can get on with matters."

In short order, Blank and Miss Bonaventure were rushed round to the servants' entrance at the rear of the house and outfitted in appropriate costume. They were reunited, moments later, Blank in the guise of a musketeer from the days of Louis XIII, a rapier at his side, and Miss Bonaventure as an Egyptian maiden, her eyes lined with kohl, a beaded wig on her head. Her wide silver bracelet with its lenticular gem at the end of her bared arm seemed to fit the motif, offering a counterpoint to the broad collar she wore, from which depended a scarab encrusted with jewels of paste.

"Why, Blank, don't you cut a dashing figure?"

Blank swept the broad-brimmed hat from his head and bowed low. "Cleopatra at her finest was never as lovely." He offered her his arm. "Shall we, O Vision of the Nile?"

They stepped through the side door and found themselves at the foot of the well-known Crystal Staircase, its bronze-scrolled handrail gently spiraling around the glass newel. At the head of the staircase stood the Duke of Devonshire, in the dress of Charles V and wearing a genuine collar and badge of the Golden Fleece lent to him by the Prince of Wales. At his side was the Duchess, as Zenobia, Queen of Palmyra, a grand tiara above her brow. The pair wore painted smiles, unable to completely hide their unease from the seven hundred or so guests who crowded the Great Ballroom.

The guests had been arriving for nearly an hour, though the quoted arrival time of half past ten had only just struck, and crowded now in the ballroom, lit by two huge chandeliers hanging from ornamented rosettes, from which radiated delicate floral motifs. The walls to either side were broken up into panels of white and yellow brocade, with long mirrors between the windows, doubling and redoubling the swelling crowd within. The reflections helped to accentuate the unreal nature of the gathering, which looked for all the world as if someone had torn down the walls of time, and from all epochs of history men and women had been thrown together. Italians of the Renaissance, French princes and princesses, Napoleons and Josephines, Cavaliers and Puritans, Orientals of lands far away and long gone, and more, and more. In the far corner, a makeshift studio had been assembled, and the partygoers one by one had their images immortalized in photograph.

It was clear that the costumiers of London had been worked to a frazzle these last weeks. As had been explained to Blank and Miss Bonaventure, the invitations specified that partygoers should appear "in an allegorical or historical costume dated earlier than 1820." Not a guest, nor a musician, nor a herald or servant, nor even the waiting maids who helped the ladies in the cloakroom, was permitted to appear in a dress later than the beginning of the current century, hence the pair's need for a change of costume upon arrival. In the cloakroom, they'd heard that an uninvited interloper in modern dress had been spotted early on but had been quickly ejected by the duke's servants.

It was whispered that this would be the grandest fancy dress ball in nearly a quarter century, since the Prince of Wales's famous ball at Marlborough House in 1874, in which guests arrived in the costume of one of a number of distinct quadrilles, this group costumed in the manner of the Venetian court, that one in the style of the Vandyck, even one costumed as characters from a pack of cards. In the Duchess of Devonshire's ball, by contrast, there were a number of different "courts," each headed by a well-known lady, attended by "princes" and "courtiers." The Austrian Court of Maria Theresa, Empress Catherine's Court, the Queen of Sheba's retinue, the Italian Procession, the Doge, even two competing courts of Queen Guinevere and the Knights of the Round Table.

What the Duke and Duchess of Devonshire wanted very much to keep from the partygoers, and in particular from the Prince of Wales and the rest of the royal party, who were due to arrive in another half hour, was the fact that one of the courts was without a sovereign and that a queen lay dead in the garden.

The back garden of Devonshire House had been transformed by electricity into a fairyland.

A large supper tent had been erected in the garden, to which access was obtained by a temporary staircase from the house. Hardly a scene of rustic outdoor dining, the supper tent had been hung with three Louis Quatorze tapestries depicting scenes from Roman antiquity. Strung from trestles throughout the garden were festoons of flowers, from which at intervals electric lights shone.

A handful of the guests had, on first arriving, descended the temporary stair and inspected the garden for themselves, and it was apparently one of these curious early arrivals who had met an unfortunate end. Luckily, only a few had been on hand when the body was discovered, and these were carefully shepherded away by the police before they could inform the rest of the partygoers. Blank had asked, on hearing the details, why the party had not simply been cancelled, and Melville had informed him that the duke and duchess had made it perfectly clear that cancellation was not an option, especially not with the royal party due to arrive by eleven o'clock. The police had so far been able to prevent a panic from spreading, and it fell to Blank and Miss Bonaventure to learn what they could before the victim's body was cleared away when the partygoers were allowed out into the garden following the quadrilles and waltzes.

They found the body behind the supper tent. The electric lights overhead blinked on, then off, then on again, so that as they approached they were presented first with a brightly lit tableau, then near darkness, then the tableau again, and so on. A man with a great shock of blond hair and a full beard, dressed in the costume of a Roman equestrian, sat in a folding chair, his head in his hands. On the dark grass at his feet lay the lifeless body of an older woman in a flowing white dress, the fabric stained dark at her neck with her own life's blood. As they drew nearer, they saw that the woman's head lay a short distance away, her white hair spread round her like a nimbus. A police constable, dressed as Friar Tuck, stood a respectful distance away, truncheon in hand.

It took Blank a moment to recognize the face on the sightless head, sitting in the dark grass as if it had been planted there. It was the Lady Priscilla, she of the League of the Round Table.

"Lord Arthur?" Miss Bonaventure said, placing a tender hand on the shoulder of the ancient Roman.

The Baron Carmody looked up, his face streaked with tears, his eyes red-rimmed.

"Lady Ormonde had already been announced as Queen Guinevere," the baron said, his voice sounding as if it were coming from somewhere far away, his eyes not quite focusing on the two of them, "with Grosvenor as her King Arthur. Lady Priscilla wouldn't hear of it. She was to be Gwenhwyfar, the true Welsh queen of the Unworld, and I the War Duke Arthur." Baron Carmody looked down at his costume, the Roman cavalry sword at his hip, surcoat of mail. He shook his head, his eyes moistening. "We came out here, to see the tapestries, and I turned my back for only a moment, before . . ."

"Take your time, Lord Arthur," Blank said gently, kneeling down. "Take your time."

"I didn't see who it was. Didn't even hear anything. Priscilla didn't scream, didn't shout out. I heard her talking to someone, sounding cross, but thought little of it." He glanced behind him at the supper tent and the tapestries within. "I lingered over damned textiles, and by the time I came to see where she'd gotten to, some murderous scoundrel had . . . had . . ."

He tried to bring himself to look at the sightless head, lying a short distance away, but couldn't, bringing his gaze to rest instead on the white shoes upon the Lady Priscilla's feet.

Suddenly, the Baron Carmody opened his eyes wide and launched himself out of his chair, seizing Blank by the shoulders.

"You'll find who did this!" It was not a question, not an entreaty, but a statement. "This can't be allowed to go unavenged. Whomever . . ." He turned his head away, but darted his eyes for the briefest instant to the headless body upon the grass. ". . . did *this*, must be punished."

Blank reached up his right hand and laid it upon the Baron Carmody's forearm.

"I seldom give assurances, Lord Arthur. And never when I don't mean it. But I *promise* you the killer will be brought to account for all that he has done."

By the time the Prince of Wales arrived, in the guise of the Grand Master of the Knights Hospitalier of Malta, the remains of the Lady Priscilla had been wrapped in a sheet and borne away, and the ground cleared of any sign of the dirty business. By the time the royal party had taken their seats upon the dais in the house, each court advancing in turn, bowing, and passing on, Blank and Miss Bonaventure had conferred with Superintendent Melville, who dispatched his most trusted officers to escort Baron Carmody to his home in Mayfair. By the time the quadrilles began, stately and sumptuous, Blank and Miss Bonaventure were on their way out, this time through the front entrance, and when the waltzes were in full swing, the pair were already home in York Place, back in their own clothes, their feet propped up on the ottoman. Throughout the hours of the night, as the partygoers were let out into the garden to lounge in the electric fairyland and feast in the supper tent, Blank and Miss Bonaventure reviewed the details of the case as they knew them. And when the party finally dispersed, the morning hours already well advanced, the pair were still talking.

Whoever the Jubilee Killer was, it could not be the dead-faced man with the smoked-glass spectacles who ran about in the evening hours with a pack of spectral hounds with incarnadine ears, teeth, and claws. At the exact moment when Lady Priscilla had been killed, per Lord Arthur's testimony, the chalky-skinned figure had been face to face with Blank and Miss Bonaventure in Kensington Garden. But if it wasn't their hairless friend with the hounds who was behind this bloody business, who was it?

Superintendent Melville had refused to detain and question each of the partygoers, despite Blank's urgent request of the night before, insisting that to do so would only cause panic and embarrass a powerful member of the aristocracy with close ties to Buckingham Palace. Blank felt surely that the Duke of Devonshire would be more embarrassed if the Prince of Wales ended up beheaded at a fancy dress ball, but Melville was confident in the abilities of his men, who had been scattered throughout the ballroom in the Lincoln green of Robin Hood's merry men, to safeguard the life of the royal party.

In the end, Blank had been able to persuade Melville to hand over a full list of the invitees to the ball but had been instructed that he was not to bother anyone on the list without first consulting with the superintendent.

Blank hoped that paying a visit to the Baron Carmody would not be considered "bothering," but even if it were, he preferred to think that any invitees with whom he was already acquainted should be exempt from Melville's prohibition.

So it was that the morning after the Devonshire House Ball, Blank and Miss Bonaventure called on Lord Arthur at his home in Mayfair. W. B. Taylor, the Knight of the Texas Plains himself, was already there, consoling the ersatz War Duke on the loss of their queen the night before.

Evidently, the Baron Carmody had not slept any more than Blank and Miss Bonaventure had done. He wore only a dressing gown over silk pyjamas, his Romanesque costume of the previous evening piled unceremoniously in the corner of the library. When Blank and Miss Bonaventure arrived, Lord Arthur was cradling a half-full tumbler of whiskey, starring into space.

Taylor, who again had his LeMat revolver holstered at his waist, paced the floor like a caged panther, hands at his sides in white-knuckled fists, his brow knit.

"We hate to intrude on your mourning, gentlemen," Blank said, his bowler hat in hand, his cane tucked under his arm, "but we hoped to see if Lord Arthur might have recalled anything about the events of last night that might help shed light on matters."

The Baron Carmody shook his head, his expression dark. "Nothing. No, nothing."

"Who is it?!" Taylor spat, whirling on his heel and pointing a finger at Blank and Miss Bonaventure. "Who is it keeps picking us off? And what the goddamned hell did we ever do to them?!"

The cowboy poet was clearly agitated, and for a moment Blank thought he might draw his revolver and demand answers at the end of its barrel, but then Taylor slumped onto the sofa and buried his head in his hands.

"This ain't right, I tell you," Taylor insisted. "Waiting around for some bastard to come out of the shadows and cut us to ribbons. It ain't right!"

Blank was forced to agree.

"Please, Lord Arthur," Miss Bonaventure said. "You must have heard or seen something that might help us." She paused, waiting for an answer that wouldn't come. "Blank and I heard mention of someone at the party early on who was expelled for arriving in modern dress. It occurs to us that this might have been the killer, assuming that it wasn't one of the invited guests. Did you see anyone who was out of costume, Lord Arthur?"

A long silence stretched out, as all eyes turned to the Baron Carmody. At long last, he shook his head, blinking slowly.

"This . . ." Lord Arthur began, his voice barely above a whisper. "This league of ours, this pipe dream of an Arthurian renaissance." He shook his head, angrily. "It's all a fantasy. I see that now. Stuff and nonsense to keep us from seeing ourselves, hiding from me my loneliness, from Lady Priscilla her own lack of purpose, from Brade his lack of originality and from Taylor . . ." He paused and rolled his eyes over in Taylor's direction.

"My lack of talent," the cowboy poet put in.

Lord Arthur nodded, slowly. "Perhaps." He took a deep breath and let out a ragged sigh. "She was old enough to be my mother, the Lady Priscilla. Or an elder aunt, at least. Not that things between us were ever romantic. But I think we filled for each other the role of the spouses we had lost, at least in some small measure. With her daily visits and endless lectures, I could forget, if for a moment, all that I had lost in Africa and how empty this damned house still is."

"Lord Arthur," Blank insisted, his tone firm, "try to remember. Is there anything, anything at all, that you haven't told us yet?"

Lord Arthur's chest rose and fell with another ragged sigh, and he turned to look at the cold ashes in the fireplace. "I've had enough of England, enough of London. There isn't a corner I can turn in this city that doesn't remind me of my departed Penelope, or little John, and now poor Priscilla is added to the chorus of ghosts that haunts me." He raised his tumbler to his lips and paused, looking over the rim. "Perhaps I'll go to America, as Penelope and I always discussed we someday might. Maybe there I can start a new life." He took a sip of his whiskey, then sucked his teeth as it reached the back of his throat. "Maybe even start a new family."

Miss Bonaventure exchanged a glance with Blank and then tried a new tactic. "There was someone taking pictures last night, as I recall. Perhaps there might be some clue to be had in those." She stepped closer to the baron, and in a low voice said, "Lord Arthur, do you recall who was taking the photographs?"

"What?" Baron Carmody raised an eyebrow and looked up into Miss

Bonaventure's eyes as if seeing her for the first time. "Yes, I had my photograph taken," he answered, sounding somewhat annoyed, as if the question was obvious. "They gave me some sort of claim ticket. It's over there somewhere . . ." He waved to the pile of costume in the far corner.

Blank stepped over, and shifting through the brightly colored cloth, picked out a printed card from the pile. "It seems that we'll be paying a visit to the firm of J. Lafayette, Number 179, New Bond Street."

Taylor leapt up from the sofa, his mouth drawn into a tight line, his jaw set. "I'll tag along, if you'll have me. I don't like the notion of sitting here in the dark, waiting for death to mosey along and find us."

Blank regarded the cowboy poet for a moment, then nodded with a slight smile. "We'd be delighted to have your company, Mr. Taylor."

The trio said their farewells to Baron Carmody, who hardly seemed to notice. Leaving the Carmody house near Grosvenor Square, it was only a short distance to the offices of J. Lafayette on New Bond Street, a matter of some four or five blocks, just up from the Doré and Grosvenor Galleries.

The photographic firm of J. Lafayette was located in a five-story building surmounted by the queen's royal crest in bas relief above an image of a sunburst. The Lafayette firm, headquartered in Dublin, had only recently opened a branch in London, added to those already in Glasgow and Manchester.

The offices had just opened for the day, and Blank, Miss Bonaventure, and Taylor were asked to wait while someone in authority could be summoned. They were shown into the waiting gallery on the ground floor, where the handiwork of Lafayette and company were on display, in particular a familiar image of Queen Victoria on the occasion of her Golden Jubilee, ten years previous, which according to the accompanying placard had earned Lafayette a Royal Warrant as "Her Majesty's Photographer in Dublin."

After a brief wait, the branch's manager appeared in the waiting gallery. Blank, presenting his featureless calling card, employed a bit of persuasion, and in short order the trio were being escorted into the development labs on the building's second floor. The heavily shuttered room smelled of chemicals, and the already developed photographs hung drying on lines strung from wall to wall, like photographic garlands.

Most of the photographs were staged against the backdrop which had been arranged in the corner of the Great Ballroom of Devonshire House. There was Miss Arthur Paget as Cleopatra and Daisy Pless as the Queen of Sheba, the Hereditary Prince of Saxe-Coburg and Gotha as Duke Robert of Normandy and the Princess of Wales as Marguerite de Valois, Frances Evelyn Warwick as Marie Antoinette and the Honorable Reginald Fitzwilliam as Admiral Lord Nelson. There was even the Baron Carmody as the Roman Briton war duke Arthur, in contrast to the more fanciful King Arthurs portrayed by the seventh Baron Rodney in full plate armor and Grosvenor in surcoat and mail. And here was the Lady Priscilla as Gwenhwyfar in a flowing gown of samite, looking years younger with her hair cascading over her shoulders than she did in modern dress with it lacquered into a bun.

Some of the photographs, though, were not staged, but were more candid snapshots of the Great Ballroom itself, and of the crowds milling there. The Crystal Stair curved up out of view in one shot, while another showed the serried ranks of waltzers moving across the floor. And in one photograph, in the far right side of the image, was plainly visible a man in modern dress, his hair wiry and his beard stringy, carrying in his arms a long slender case. The man's eyes were wide and crazed-looking, and his lip curled in an expression of distaste.

It was, unmistakably, Mervyn Fawkes.

Needless to say, Mervyn Fawkes was not included in the invitation list for the Devonshire House Ball. Doubtless, he had been the interloper in modern dress thrown out in the party's early hours. And it seemed a surety that he'd been the one to murder poor Lady Priscilla, and by extension Brade and Villers and all the rest.

Mervyn Fawkes *was* the Jubilee Killer.

CHAPTER TWENTY-SEVEN
Millennium

WITH THE STEEL DOOR OPENED, the innumerous klaxons sounding downstairs could be faintly heard, like distant sirens.

"What the hell is *he* doing here?!" Alice shouted. But no one had an answer for her.

"I've heard about you for years, of course," Temple said to the Huntsman, as the red-sword-wielding figure advanced into the gallery. "Never had a chance to make a proper study. Would you be willing to sit for a few tests with my researchers? You'd be compensated, of course."

Temple reached out his hand, offering to shake.

The Huntsman, the red sword in a two-handed grip, responded only by swinging the blade in a wide arc.

Temple's arm below the elbow thumped to the floor.

"Now, see here!" Temple waved his stump of an arm, from which strange fluids oozed. "I think I've been most reasonable up to now, but this has gone on far enough. Now, you . . ."

Whatever Temple was going to say next, it was lost when the Huntsman casually picked him up with one hand, like a sack of potatoes.

"Put me down!" Temple ordered.

In a matter of strides, the Huntsman was at the window. In one fluid movement, he drove the point of his red blade through the glass. Then he yanked the sword back at an angle, and the window shattered into a million pieces. The pieces fell towards the street far below, and with a shove Temple went after them, only now putting up a spirited resistance, thrashing with his legs and remaining arm. His bare foot caught the side of the Huntsman's face a glancing blow but succeeded only in knocking off his wraparound sunglasses; too little, too late. He dropped over the edge and out into the night, disappearing from sight.

The Huntsman turned, and Alice could see that his eyes were completely red except for the thin point of the pupil and seemed almost to glow.

Now he was coming for them.

Stillman started firing his Hotspur, which slowed the Huntsman, but only marginally.

Alice's thoughts concentrated like a laser. The world had shrunk to her and the gem, and the glass that separated them. She needed something to smash it with. Something to break through, so she could grab the gem and go, and find the answers later. Something like . . .

She glanced at the sword, just feet from her. It looked like it might break if you tapped it too hard, but Temple had said something about it being unbreakable. And it was the only thing to hand.

Alice wrapped her hands around the handle, picked the sword up, and swung it like a baseball bat.

Halfway through the arc of her swing, the scabbard of the sword slid off, flung away amongst the plinths, revealing the naked blue-white blade beneath.

The arc of her swing continued, and the blade connected with the glass of the display case. The sword sliced through as though the case wasn't even there, but as it passed through, the top half of the display case slid to one side like a car in neutral at the top of a hill without the parking brake engaged and smashed to the floor.

Alice didn't pause to wonder, but dashed forward, snatched up the gem, and held it tight in her hand.

"Come on!" She shouted to Temple, racing for the elevator. "Let's get out of here!"

Stillman fired a few more fletcher rounds into the Huntsman, who seemed only annoyed. "You can't open that, love! Biometric panel, remember!"

Alice tucked the gem into the pocket of her jeans, and on the run scooped up Temple's severed forearm. "Not a problem!"

She slammed the cold lifeless hand against the biometric pad, and the door slid open immediately, with a chime, like the captain's cabin on the starship *Enterprise*. "Come on . . ." She started to yell over her shoulder, only to feel herself shoved forward.

She fell to the floor of the elevator, Stillman crouching behind her. He stabbed a finger at the Down button, and then emptied the rest of his Hotspur rounds at the Huntsman, who was now only feet behind them. The door slid shut just before the Huntsman reached the elevator.

The car had only started to descend when the red blade of the sword slid sideways through the door.

"Oh, shit!" Alice shouted. Then, gracelessly, she battered at the red blade with the blue-white sword she held and managed to knock it aside far enough for the car's descent to continue.

"Suddenly," Stillman said, glancing at the ceiling as the floors chimed off, "descending in a car suspended by cables when pursued by a man with a sword that can cut through *anything* doesn't seem terribly wise."

When they reached the ground floor at a normal speed, not plummeting to their death at thirty-two feet per second squared, they decided that the Huntsman must have wanted the gem more than he wanted Alice or Stillman dead, and if he cut the cables and let them fall, it would be more difficult to sort the same jewel out from the wreckage.

Which meant, of course, that he'd be descending the stairs, more than likely, hoping to catch them at the bottom.

They got their first hint of the carnage that lay in the Huntsman's wake when they stepped off the elevator on the ground floor. From the looks of things, the Huntsman had come in through the front door, opening up the glass and steel with his sword like a church key on a can. The security forces of Glasshouse had evidently mobilized to stop him. Unsuccessfully, it seemed, at least if the bodies, parts of bodies, and viscera that covered the lobby floor like scattered garlands were any indication.

According to Stillman's researches, a dozen security personnel were assigned to the Glasshouse on a typical night shift. It was hard to tell, given the size of the pieces into which some of them had been sliced, but if she had to guess Alice would have said that most of that dozen had met their end here at the front gates.

They passed the door to the fire stairs, which had been sliced from its hinges. Alice wasn't sure, but her first instinct was to be more impressed that the Huntsman had climbed thirty-five stories—and so *quickly*—than with the fact that he carried a super-science macromolecular sword capable of cutting through anything, which he was clearly willing to do.

She had the gem back in her hand now, the surprisingly light blue-white sword in the other. She hadn't had time to process yet, but was beginning to realize that, though she held the final puzzle piece in her hand, the puzzle was resolutely failing to resolve into anything like an answer.

However, she had more pressing concerns. Namely, that if the Huntsman was able to *climb* the stairs in the amount of time it had taken them to walk from one side of the gallery to the other, it was more than likely that he could *descend* equally quickly.

She and Stillman could compare notes later.

Stillman was loading additional fletcher rounds from the cigarette-pack-sized clip on his belt into the Hotspur, already racing for the door. "Come on, love. Don't dawdle."

"Coming, Da-" She bit the word off. She had almost called him *that*, again.

The doors were wide open, naturally, the glass shattered and the steel lying in shredded ribbons on the ground, so the pair were able to get back outside without incident.

Then, of course, they found the Gabriel Hounds waiting for them, their red teeth and claws glinting like rubies in the faint light of the crescent moon.

There was no way past them. There were five of the spectral white dogs, arranged in a perfect semicircle around the front entrance of the Glasshouse. They snapped their red teeth and snarled, lowering their strange, catlike heads.

From behind them came the sound of crashing, and Alice knew that the Huntsman would reach the ground floor in moments, if not sooner.

"What are we going to do?" Alice asked, tightening her grip on the sword, glancing over at Stillman.

Stillman held his Hotspur in a two-handed grip. "My darts may slow them down a bit, love, but won't stop them. Your sword'd probably cut their hides, but I doubt you could get all of them before one of them manages to get its jaws clamped on you."

He glanced around. Alice followed his glance.

The Glasshouse was part of the Canary Warf district, Docklands, which had been built atop the old West India Docks. It was built right at the edge of the dark waters of the West India Millwall Docks. A short distance from the Glasshouse front entrance was a pedestrian footbridge that connected Canary Wharf with the West India Quay on the waterway's far side.

"If we can get to the other side," Stillman said, pointing with his chin, "the water might slow them down enough to let us get to ground."

Alice looked at the five snarling hounds who held their positions, keeping them cornered until their master the Huntsman arrived. "I don't see that happening."

From above came the sound of flapping wings, first one pair, then several, then dozens. Alice looked up, and the skies overhead were completely filled with black-winged birds, descending on the Glasshouse entry.

"Then again . . ."

The ravens were eerily silent, the only sound the flapping of their wings. There must have been dozens of them, maybe even hundreds or more. Like a black cloud, like a fog of darkness, they descended from the night sky, diving towards the spectral Gabriel Hounds.

One of the ravens broke off from the others, angling towards the place where Alice and Stillman stood. Raising his Hotspur, reflexively, Stillman almost fired on it, but at the last moment, Alice stayed his hand. "Hold on a second. I've got a feeling."

Stillman shot her a look that conveyed exactly what he thought about her feelings at this juncture, but didn't voice an objection.

The raven flew in a wide arc around them, approaching from behind. At the last moment, it extended its talons, and flapped its wings, shifting its body weight back. Slowing its descent, its wings flapping even faster, it landed on Alice's shoulder, its talons closing on the tough material of her leather jacket. It folded its black wings and brought its black beak near Alice's ear. Beak opening, it spoke again, its voice high pitched, growly-squeaky.

"Unworld. Waits. Memory. Within. Disk. Save. Alice."

From within the Glasshouse came the sound of stones tumbling to the floor, and Alice glanced back to see the Huntsman slicing his way out of the stairway, evidently not content with the size of the existing door.

"Come on," Alice said, as much to the raven on her shoulder as to Stillman, and taking to her heels running. "Let's continue this conversation elsewhere!"

While the rest of the flock of ravens distracted the Gabriel Hounds, dozens of them ending their lives in bloody ruin in the jaws or under the paws of the beasts, the talking raven flew along beside Alice as she and Stillman raced towards the bridge. The Huntsman was only a short distance behind, but he too found himself the focus of the ravens' attention, as dozens of them flapped and clawed around his head, stymieing his progress. He sliced them in half, black feathers and viscera flying in all directions, but still more came.

The puzzle was coming together, but try as she might, Alice couldn't make sense of the image.

Alice and Stillman reached the far side of the bridge, the raven once more perched on her shoulder. The West India Quay Station was just a short distance away.

"Where to now?" Stillman asked, starting to breathe heavily. For the first time, Alice believed he might well be the age he claimed to be. He was looking exhausted.

She was more than a little winded herself.

"I don't know," she panted. "Let's ask our feathered friend, shall we?" She turned to look at the raven on her shoulder. "Okay, what's this about, anyway? Come on Polly, squawk!"

"Alice. Memory. Within. Disk. Save. Alice. Unworld. Waits."

Alice shot a glance at Stillman. "That was helpful, wasn't it?" She held the Vanishing Gem up, catching the light from the nearest lampposts, glinting like a milky diamond. "What *is* this thing? What's this all about?"

"Unworld," the raven said, in its squeaky-growly voice.

"What, is that what this is, or what this mess is about?"

"Unworld," the raven said, simply.

Alice waved the blue-white sword, menacingly. "Look! I've had enough of all of this. If I've got a goddamned destiny, why doesn't someone just tell me what it is, already, and get it over with?!"

"Unworld. Waits. Alice."

"I think we should be going now, love," Stillman plucked at her elbow.

The raven swung its head around and fixed ink black eyes on Stillman. "Alice. Memory. Within. Disk. Save. Alice."

"Do what now?" Stillman said, cocking an eyebrow. Then his eyes widened, and he pointed across the green-glowing bridge. The Huntsman stood at the far side, the Gabriel Hounds baying at his heels. "Oh, no." Stillman sighed heavily. "Well, anyone up for a run?"

Alice shook her head and stood her ground. "No!" she snapped. "I'm *tired* of running. Look, this guy is the T-1000, okay?" She took in Stillman's blank expression. "From *Terminator 2*? No? Whatever. Look, he's going to keep coming, right? You shot him full of holes, didn't do any good. I've been running for, what? Five days now? Longer? And he still found me. He's got a magic sword that can cut through anything." Stillman's eyes slid to the sword in her hands. "And you know what? So do I. So here's what I'm thinking. Let's go back to the middle of the bridge, right? Stand right over the water. And then if he wants us, he's got to come over the water to get us. You said it weakens him, or something like that, right? In which case, if he comes for us, we've got the home court advantage. Make sense?"

Stillman just looked at her, impressed. He nodded.

"All right, then. Time to stop running. Time to be a little more proactive." She put her foot on the bridge, the gem in one hand, the sword in the other. "Maybe *then* the puzzle will start to make sense."

The bridge rested on pontoons, mostly submerged in the waters below. On either side of them were balustrades of stainless steel cables. Behind them was the north side of the waterway and the refurbished Victorian warehouses of the West India Quay. Facing Alice and Stillman on the opposite side, with the towering Glasshouse behind them, were the Huntsman and his Gabriel Hounds.

"Still not sure how you were able to draw that sword, love." Stillman gestured to the blue-white blade in Alice's hands while checking the action of his Hotspur.

Alice shrugged. "Makes about as much sense as anything else, the last few days."

"Mmm." Stillman nodded. "You *did* say your grandmother was in Iceland once upon a time, didn't . . . ?"

"Look!" Alice said, cutting him off. "Here they come!"

She pointed with the point of the sword at the Canary Wharf side of the waterway, where the Huntsman had just stepped onto the footbridge.

"They'll be slow in coming," Stillman said, thumbing off the safety on his fletcher pistol, "but now it's just a matter of time."

"Yeah, but moving as slow as he is, maybe we can get some answers from him." The Huntsman was taking slow, tentative steps, like an old lady walking on ice.

"I'm not sure he can talk, love, at that."

Alice opened her mouth to answer, but the raven perched on her shoulder beat her to it.

"Unworld. Alice. Unworld." Its squeaky-growly voice seemed fainter, as though coming from farther away.

"I guess the dogs must have made short work of the rest of the flock."

"Maybe not," Alice said. From the direction of the Glasshouse, a few black shapes fluttered, feathers rustling, and came to rest on the railings to either side of them, perching atop the balustrade. There were three on either side of them, six in all. With the one on Alice's shoulder, that made seven. "Looks like a few of them made it out in one piece, more or less."

Stillman hummed, thoughtfully.

The raven turned its black eyes to Stillman, and opened its beak. "Alice. Memory. Disk. Within. Save. Alice. Save."

"An intent little bugger, isn't it?" he said, raising an eyebrow.

Slowly, so gradually that at first she didn't notice it, Alice's hand began to grow warmer, the one holding the gem. She raised it up in front of her face and found that the Vanishing Gem had begun to glow.

"Um, Stillman?" she half turned to him, keeping her eyes on the gem.

The Huntsman was almost halfway to the bridge's midpoint where they stood, his thin sword glowing red in the dim light, while the Gabriel Hounds at the shore were baying, like the sound of wild geese in flight.

It felt as if the gem had grown more heavy, a hundredfold. Alice was forced to set the sword down on the deck of the bridge at her feet, careful to keep the blade flat so the edge didn't cut into the deck, and hold the gem in both hands.

"Stillman, what's it *doing?*"

"I-I'm not sure, love."

"Unworld. Alice." The raven's growly-squeaky voice rasped in her ear, while it tightened its talons on her shoulder. "Unworld. Waits."

Suddenly, the light from the gem flared up, flooding Alice's field of vision with whiteness. It felt very familiar.

Then, Alice fell.

CHAPTER TWENTY-EIGHT

Jubilee

MISS BONAVENTURE WAS FOR ALERTING THE AUTHORITIES, but Blank was afraid that even a moment's delay in getting to Fawkes might make all the difference. Taylor, for his part, insisted on accompanying them to the bitter end, intent on seeing the Jubilee Killer brought to justice.

A hansom cab carried them at breakneck speeds from New Bond Street to Victoria Station, the driver paid handsomely to pay no mind to safety or courtesy, and in short order the trio were on board the Crystal Palace Railway, headed south. It was midday on Friday, and assuming that he had not abandoned his post, Mervyn Fawkes would be found at this hour at work.

As they rattled along the track, Taylor with his hands gripped white-knuckled on his knees, Blank and Miss Bonaventure compared notes. Fawkes certainly fitted the role of culprit in most regards, at least in terms of opportunity, but there still remained the questions of motive and method. What did Fawkes gain from these senseless and gruesome killings? And just how were they accomplished?

Too, there remained the question of the man in the smoked-glass spectacles, and his strange dogs, dyed and groomed to resemble the Gabriel Hounds of the Wild Hunt. What was his connection to all of this? And what of the crystal object retrieved from Glastonbury Tor by Professor Bonaventure and Jules Dulac, which seemed to lie at the center of all this madness? If Fawkes *were* the Jubilee Killer, then he doubtless was behind the theft of the report from the Somerset Archaeological and Natural History Society, which perhaps had led him to find the crystal chalice in Professor Bonaventure's storage in Earl's Court. Just what was the significance of the ancient artifact to Fawkes, worth the life of at least two men and five women to him, and possibly more? And, finally, there remained the vexing question of method? What manner of tool or implement had Fawkes found that allowed him to slice iron and steel, flesh and bone, as easily as an oar cutting through water? Was it something he brought back with him from his extended stay in Iceland?

All of these questions and more plagued the trio as they rode south towards the Crystal Palace. Perhaps, Blank thought, the answers might be waiting for them at the end of the line.

When they reached the Crystal Palace, they worried that it might be difficult to locate Fawkes. As it happened, they needn't have bothered.

Mounting the steps that led to the grand front entrance, the trio passed fleeing visitors and employees alike. Men, women, and children ran in wide-eyed terror, shouting something about madmen with swords battling inside.

They entered the airy pavilion, the midday sun streaming through the glass panels which covered the walls and the roof high overhead, and found an unlikely scene already in progress.

It was Mervyn Fawkes, inexpertly wielding a long sword, the blade a brilliant shade of red, so thin that when turned on edge it seemed to disappear entirely from view, a scabbard on the ground at his feet. Facing him, a Sam Browne belt under his frock coat, a long scabbard hanging from it, was Jules Dulac, in his hands a sword with an equally whisper-thin blade, but glowing faintly bluish white instead.

It was clear that, of the two, Dulac was the accomplished swordsman, and Fawkes the uneasy amateur. Time and again Fawkes lashed out with his blade, snarling with rage, only to have its point turned aside easily by Dulac's own sword. Dulac, for his part, continued to shout the same question over and again, a repeated refrain.

"Where is it?"

So intent where the dueling pair that they failed to note the arrival of Blank, Miss Bonaventure, and Taylor, much less the mayhem they had engendered amongst the patrons and employees of the Crystal Palace. The trio stopped a short distance off, wary of the long thin blades the two swung, one with such mad abandon, one with clinical precision.

"Where is it?!"

Dulac's mouth was drawn into a tight bloodless line, his newly clean-shaven jaw set. There was nothing of the slightly dissolute celebrant Blank and Miss Bonaventure had met the night before to him now, only the steely gazed warrior that Blank had glimpsed beneath. The theft of the crystal chalice, which evidently he felt himself pledged to protect, had spurred him to renewed vigor.

"*Where is it?!*"

Still Fawkes refused to answer, only howled wordless screams of rage as he lay about him on all sides with the red blade. Finally, his lack of skill caught him wrong-footed. Dulac smacked Fawkes's red sword to one side with his own blue blade, and then surged forward, planting a kick directly in Fawkes's midsection, knocking the wind from him.

Fawkes crumpled over with a groan, and though he retained his grip on his red sword's hilt, the blade was driven by the force of his fall *into* the very concrete of the floor beneath their feet, halfway to the hilt. Before Fawkes could regain his feet and draw his sword back out of the stone, Dulac stepped forward and smacked his arm with the flat of his blue blade, dislodging his hands from the hilt. Then with another well-placed kick Dulac drove Fawkes back and away from the sword, which still protruded halfway from the hard floor as if it had always been there.

Suddenly, the dynamic of the duel had changed. Fawkes was on his knees, clutching his bruised chest and struggling to catch his breath, while Dulac stood over him, menacing him with the point of his whisper-thin blue blade.

"Now, talk!" Dulac shouted. "Or I'll cut you in two, just like you did all of those poor women and men!"

Tentatively, Blank and the others approached the pair, careful not to startle them.

Fawkes looked up, a clever gleam in his eye. "You won't do it," he sneered at Dulac. "If you want the chalice so badly, you won't kill me before finding out where it is, or you'll never see it again."

"Don't test me," Dulac snarled, but Blank could see that Fawkes's words had found their mark.

"I do hate to intrude," Blank said gently, "but my friends and I would like very much to know just what the devil is going on."

Dulac had evidently noted their approach but paid them little mind. Now, as Taylor stepped closer to the red sword protruding from the concrete, reaching out to touch the impossibly thin blade, Dulac snapped, "Don't touch that!" Then he turned to Blank, his expression grim but weary. "This man has stolen something I have spent a great many years protecting, and I need it back."

"What?" Fawkes said. "*You* protect the Grail? Absurd!"

"The *Grail?*" Taylor repeated, eyebrow cocked.

"Of course, you stupid fool," Fawkes spat. "What *else* did you think this was all about?"

Dulac looked to Blank and his companions, and sighed. "All right, ask your questions, as you seem better able than I to get this pile of dung to speak. But find out for me where he's hidden it, or you'll all answer to me."

Blank nodded and turned to the kneeling Fawkes. "Well, let's have it man. First, it's clear that something in your experiences in Colney Hatch suggested to you this obsession with the Grail. What was it?"

Fawkes shrugged. "A book of ancient poems was the first clue, I suppose. Then I happened to speak with another patient who had become obsessed with the work of the pre-Raphaelites. My experiences on the floating island had made it plain to me that there was more to the world than what presented itself to our eyes, and if one myth were true, why not another? And what myth made reality could be more powerful than that of the holy cup, the Grail, capable of curing any wound or of raising the dead back to life. I thought for a time, wrongly, that the Grail itself was only a metaphor, an encoded formula such as those later used by the alchemists, and upon my release from Colney Hatch I attempted a few . . . experiments . . . to rediscover the formula from first principles, using as my guide all of the repeated references in the myths and legends to heads on platters and severed hands and arms. But my experiments failed to produce the desired result, and so I continued to research."

Fawkes rubbed his bruised ribs gingerly, clearly relishing the memories.

"In the British Museum," he went on, "I found a handwritten note in the margin of Thorkelin's transcription of Beowulf, which mentioned an episode in a fragmentary thirteenth-century manuscript of Snorri's edda. A Geat adventurer, perhaps an original of Beowulf, traveled to Britain and battled against a warrior who later traveled to find a magic tower or chalice that could restore the dead and heal wounds. The note mentioned that the final resting place of the chalice's guardian was believed to be in Iceland. Naturally, I shortly thereafter journeyed to Iceland, and spent the next years hunting for the guardian's tomb. Along the way I met and married an Icelandic woman, who was warm beneath the sheets and skilled in the kitchen if perhaps not as handsome as she might have been, and she later gave me a son, Hiram. For a time, it seemed that I would settle down and raise my family there in Iceland, my hunt for the Grail abandoned in failure, but then just before all hope was lost I managed to find it. The tomb of the Grail guardian! And within, even more amazing, the body of the guardian himself, in a remarkable state of preservation. At his side lay a strange sword, which no one but I was able to draw from its scabbard, the blade so thin it could only be viewed from the side, glowing with the red fires of the pit. The red blade could slice through any material, no matter how dense or strong, and so I brought it with me on my return to civilization."

"What of your family?" Miss Bonaventure asked, meaningfully. "Your wife and son?"

Fawkes shrugged. "Still in Iceland, I suppose. You see, when I returned to the home I shared with my wife and child, the strange sword in hand, I was no closer to finding the Grail than I'd ever been. I had found the resting place of the guardian, it was true, and salvaged his supernatural sword, but while I'd established the veracity of the Grail legends, I had not found the Grail. I had hoped in the guardian's tomb to find some clue to the location of the chalice itself, but had found only frozen stones, a lifeless body, and a sword." A smile tugged up the corners of Fawkes's mouth, and a crazed gleam lit his eyes. "A short while later, though, that all was to change. In an English-language newspaper, I happened to read a brief article about an archaeological expedition by my old 'friend' Peter Bonaventure, in conjunction with the Somerset Archaeological and Natural History Society, in which a crystal *chalice*-like object had been unearthed. And unearthed from Glastonbury Tor, which in ancient times, the Somerset Levels flooded, had been an *island*, just as in the fragmentary poem Thorkelin cites."

Fawkes's chest rose and fell as he swelled with pride.

"Only I had the vision to put the pieces together. Only I recognized just what it was Bonaventure had found. The next day, I left my wife and son behind and boarded the next ship to England. When I arrived, I journeyed at once to Taunton, sure that Bonaventure's 'chalice' could be found in the offices of the Somerset society. But instead, I found only the report the fool had filed and that he had taken the treasure back with him to London."

"And you killed the custodian to learn this," Blank said, matter-of-factly.

"What of it?" Fawkes shrugged. "He interrupted my research and got only what he deserved. In any event, I took the next train to London, found Bonaventure's home, and then with the irresistible edge of my magic sword cut my way into his storage, there to find the Grail itself."

"Damn your eyes," Dulac hissed. "And damn me, as well."

Fawkes pursed his lips, shooting the sword bearer an annoyed look. "Yes, I had the Grail, for all the good it did me. I couldn't seem to make it work. I tried a few more experiments, as I had done ten years before, but simply couldn't make it function."

The pieces of the puzzle slotted together in Blank's mind. Fawkes had mentioned 'experiments' he had performed after leaving Colney Hatch in 1887, inspired by the Grail legends of heads on platters and severed limbs. Ten years later, he had duplicated those experiments, this time with the crystal object he believed in his madness to be the Grail itself.

"It was *you*," Blank said, drawing his sword-stick from the cane, the silver-chased handle in his fist. "You killed those women all those years ago. The one found in the Thames, the one in Whitehall, the arm in the Lambeth blind asylum and the leg under Albert Bridge and the body in Battersea. You were the *Torso Killer*."

Fawkes regarded Blank with a weak smile. "Ah," he said. "You were in the papers then, weren't you? I *thought* I recognized your name."

Blank lunged forward, intent on driving the point of his sword-stick into Fawkes's heart, and was stopped only when Miss Bonaventure took firm hold of his arm and dragged him back. Blank looked to her, eyes flashing. "Why did you *stop* me?!"

"Besides the fact that I suspect you'd regret it later," Miss Bonaventure answered, "I think that *he* might take issue with the action." With a nod, she indicated Dulac.

The man held his blue-bladed sword aloft, intent on slicing down and through Blank if he carried through with his thrust. "I don't blame you, Blank. But until I find the thing I'm after, I'm afraid no harm can come to him." He turned and snarled at Fawkes. "After I get it, I'll be the first to help you cut him up, if you like."

"Oh ho!" Fawkes chuckled. "Is that meant to be some sort of enticement for me to comply, then?"

Before Dulac could answer, Taylor cleared his throat to get their attention. "Um, fellows?"

Blank turned and looked in the direction that Taylor was staring. The Crystal Palace was now all but deserted except for their little company, and so it was somewhat surprising to see a new figure standing in the open doorway. Tall and thin, completely hairless, his expression unreadable behind his smoked-glass spectacles, it was the figure they had pursued and faced the night before.

"Oh, no," Dulac said sadly, shaking his head, looking like someone who had just come upon the fallen body of a dear friend. "Not this."

Without speaking, the strange figure strode directly towards them, his hands at his side. There was no sign of his hounds and their incarnadine teeth and claws, Blank noted with something like relief.

"Hey, now . . ." Taylor said, as it became apparent that the figure was walking right towards him. He backed away, hand on the handle of his holstered revolver.

Too late, Blank realized that the strange figure was not walking towards Taylor, but towards the red-bladed sword buried in the concrete a short distance from him. Before any of them could move to intercept, the man in the smoke-glass spectacles reached down, wrapped his long-nailed hand around the sword's hilt, and easily drew it from the concrete.

"Damn," Taylor cursed beneath his breath.

The sword's hilt nestled in the man's fist as if it had been made for it. With the red sword in one hand, the man reached up and pulled the smoke-glass spectacles off his face with the other. His eyes were revealed to be flashing red, like pools of liquid fire.

Dulac shook his head sadly, raising the tip of his blue blade. "It doesn't have to be this way, Pryder. We need not face each other as enemies for the Red King's sake."

Blank understood little to nothing of what Dulac said, but it was clear that the red-eyed man would not be giving any response that might clarify. Instead, wordlessly, the white-skinned figure lunged forward, driving the point of the red sword towards Dulac's chest.

Dulac parried the blow with the flat of his blue sword, and riposted, but the red-eyed man handily smacked the blue blade away. Back and forth the pair danced, as their blades rebounded again and again with a strange humming sound.

"Blank!" Miss Bonaventure shouted.

He turned and saw that Fawkes had taken advantage of the momentary confusion to take to his heels, racing off, deeper into the Crystal Palace. "After him!" Blank shouted, and gave chase, Miss Bonaventure and Taylor following close behind.

"Stop right there," Taylor said, leveling the barrel of his LeMat revolver at Fawkes.

The chase had led them here, to the Medieval Court where Blank and

Miss Bonaventure had originally found Fawkes two weeks previously. He stood now before the same tapestry, dating from the century after the Norman conquest and in much the same style as the Bayeux Tapestry, and only now did Blank realize that it depicted a scene from the Grail cycle, a trio of knights standing before a vision of the cup.

Blank had his sword-stick in hand, Miss Bonaventure beside him in a martial stance, while Taylor stood with his pistol pointed unwaveringly at Fawkes's back.

Fawkes did not turn around, but continued looking up at the tapestry before him. "I was sure that Lady Priscilla held the answers I sought, that her studies of the ancient myths had given her insight into how the Grail could be used. But then the so-called 'League of the Round Table' rebuffed me, and I was forced to seek out those that had worked with her."

"Why?" Taylor demanded. "Why go after the others and not me? I knew more than Cecilia ever did, or Brade. I'd read all of Lady P's notes and could have told you anything you wanted to know."

Fawkes glanced back over his shoulder, a wry smiled on his face. "Well, the magic sword of the Grail's guardian can cut through anything, but I don't think it could stop bullets." He nodded towards Taylor's pistol. "And since you were the only one of the bunch to keep your own armory of firearms, you were the very *last* on my list."

Taylor drew back the hammer of his revolver with his thumb.

"Hold on!" Miss Bonaventure said, laying a hand on Taylor's forearm, lowering his aim. "Look!" She pointed back the way they'd come.

The red-eyed man was advancing on them, his scarlet-bladed sword in one hand, the other reached out towards Fawkes. It seemed to Blank, in that moment, that the red-eyed man didn't seem to be menacing Fawkes, but instead looked as if he were racing to protect him.

With Taylor's attention off of him, Fawkes reached up and grabbed a fistful of the tapestry in either hand and, hauling down, yanked the fabric from the wall. Behind was revealed a small alcove, evidently intended for display purposes. Within was a small object, no larger than a pint glass, a smooth-sided cylinder than tapered at one end. It seemed to be some sort of milky quartz and glinted like a diamond in the early afternoon sun.

Blank rushed forward, intent on tackling Fawkes to the ground, fighting the instinct to run the murderer through with his sword-stick. But before Blank could reach him, Fawkes wrapped his hands around the crystal, and something strange began to occur.

"Strange" in this instance being a relative term, Blank knew, held in the balance against swords that slice through steel and strange men with glowing eyes of fire.

The crystal began to radiate light like an electric bulb, accompanied by a low humming noise. As the hum increased in pitch and volume and the light grew ever brighter, Fawkes looked up and met Blank's eyes, tears streaming down his cheeks.

"I've done it!" Fawkes cried. "I don't know how, but I've managed to . . ."

Just what he thought he'd done, Blank would never know, because in that instant the sound reached a deafening level as the light swelled to a blinding flash, and in the next instant, the crystal was clattering to the ground, with Fawkes nowhere to be seen.

The red-eyed man slowed momentarily, seeing the crystal fall to the ground, but only altered his course, continuing to race ahead, this time with the evident intention of snatching the crystal from the ground.

"Don't let him get it!" shouted Dulac from the far end of the concourse, holding his bleeding shoulder. "For the love of god, don't let him at it!!"

Blank and the others hadn't a single notion what was transpiring around them, but they knew that the red-eyed man bearing towards them was no friend of theirs, and Dulac was clearly the enemy of their enemy, so their own allegiance was obvious. Blank raised the point of his sword-stick and stepped in the red-eyed man's path.

"Blank, no!" Miss Bonaventure cried, but it was too late. Besides, Blank knew what he was in for.

As the red-eyed man closed the distance between them, Blank ducked to one side and lunged forward, piercing the other man's thigh. A normal man would have crumpled in pain at that moment, but whatever else he was, it was clear that the red-eyed swordsman was no normal man. Ignoring the silver-bladed sword protruding from his leg, he reared back and skewered Blank on the point of his red sword.

Blank hung for a moment on the blade, unable to breathe.

Then the red-eyed man dragged his sword out. As Blank's blood and viscera spilled out onto the floor before him, the red-eyed man batted him to one side with a long-nailed hand, as casually as a man swatting a fly. Then he wrenched the sword-stick from his leg and tossed it aside.

Taylor stepped into the breach, raising his LeMat pistol, and with a ruthless efficiency fired again and again, striking the red-eyed man nine times squarely in the chest, then when the .44 caliber slugs were depleted he fired off the 28-gauge shotgun shell from the shorter barrel, hitting the man square in the face.

Amazingly, though, the red-eyed man staggered, but remained standing.

Dulac finally caught up, his left shoulder bleeding freely from an enormous gash, but his right hand still firmly gripping the hilt of his blue blade. As the red-eyed man lurched forward, swinging his scarlet sword at Taylor, Dulac managed to deflect the blow, knocking the red sword aside.

Miss Bonaventure leapt to Dulac's side, holding Blank's cast-off sword-stick in a two-handed grip. Dulac swayed on his feet, and as he struggled to regain his balance the red-eyed man swung at Miss Bonaventure. Incredibly, the red-eyed man's swung missed by a large margin, whirling harmlessly through the empty air, and Miss Bonaventure was able to lash out with the sword-stick and swat the back of the red-eyed man's arm. Unfortunately, her cut failed to loose the sword from his grip, but compiled with the shots Taylor had fired it seemed to have a cumulative effect.

The red-eyed man looked for a moment at the crystal lying on the floor, something of longing in his unreadable expression, and at the woman and men who stood between him and it. And then, without further exchange, and still having uttered not a single word, the red-eyed man turned and raced away, his steps thundering through the empty pavilion.

CHAPTER TWENTY-NINE

Unworld

Galaad

THE WHITE LADY HAD SAID that within the tower of glass lay the Unworld. At the time, Galaad'd had no notion what she had meant. Now he was beginning to suspect.

Stepping through the glass wall, he had found himself beside Artor and the others in the middle of a large open space. Glancing back, he didn't see the tower wall but only emptiness for some hundred feet or so, ending in an irregular, dark wall. Another wall, twin to the first, was a hundred feet or so in front of them, while to the right and left the space continued as far as the eye could see. The only difference in the two walls that Galaad could discern was that the one in front seemed to curve slightly away from them, while the one behind curved slightly towards them. It was as if they stood at one side of a large, enclosed circle.

Disturbingly, though, the circumference of this circle was clearly larger than the tower in which it was contained. Galaad's mind could not encompass the possibilities that single fact suggested.

The distances swallowed any sound, no echoes of footsteps or words rebounding off the far walls, and when they spoke, their words sounded strange, somewhat distorted. The light was dim, the hazy gray of twilight, and the air was still and cold.

"Where *are* we?" Caius asked, looking around, his eyes wide and alarmed.

"The Unworld," Artor answered, his jaw set.

"Whatever *that* means," Lugh spat.

Galaad felt somewhat queasy and laid a hand on his stomach, his insides in revolt. But after a moment, the feeling of uneasiness passed. Galaad caught a glimpse of the back of his hand, which glinted silvery for a moment and then was restored to its normal hue. He remembered the mantle the White Phantom had given them and wondered whether the state of his constitution had anything to do with it.

"Which way, Artor?" Pryder asked, his features limned in the blue glow of his skyblade.

"Any way is as good as any," Artor said, glancing from one side to the other. At random, he pointed to their right. "That direction."

Pryder nodded and stalked off to the right. "I shall be the vanguard," he said, glancing over his shoulder at Artor, expressing some vestigial need for permission, though it was clear that Pryder had long since decided to follow his own course.

Artor merely nodded, clearly recognizing the Gwentian's need for movement, his hunger for revenge.

As they walked, the wall to their left curved away, the wall to their right curved in, so that they followed a semicircular path. From time to time on the inner wall there appeared what seemed to be large, oddly shaped doors, though these did not have any evident hinges or handles, and the five could not work out how to open them. They continued on, passing these unusual doors every few dozen paces, each as barred and impassable as the last.

The sound of their footsteps was the only noise they could hear, and even these were muffled by the vastness of the surrounding space. From time to time Galaad would feel another bout of nausea coupled with a sudden weariness, but these passed just as quickly with no continuing ill effects. From the expressions the others periodically took on, Galaad could see he was not the only one to be experiencing these occasional episodes.

At one point, a black bird flew by high overhead, heading in the opposite direction. Its raucous call was oddly comforting, something so familiar in so strange a place.

It seemed that they must have walked in a complete circuit, so long did they march, though with one stretch of the curved corridor no different than the rest it was impossible to distinguish one point from another. Galaad wondered whether they would just circle, indefinitely, until hunger, thirst, and fatigue took them.

Suddenly, just ahead, one of the unusually shaped doors opened. There was a hiss, like that of a snake, like air escaping a bladder, and bright lights shone out into the darkened corridor.

Before the five could react, a metallic monster crabbed into view. It had jointed legs, like a spider's, seven in total, and a diamond-shaped head that craned above its squat body on a long neck. There was no mouth, but a single baleful glass eye of the deepest red set in the middle of the head, facing towards them. But for the eye, the monster was covered completely in what appeared to be metal, silvery and shining.

The metal monster regarded them for a moment as the five spread out in a line, weapons at the ready, but before Artor and his men were able to react, a beam of scarlet light shot from the red eye, striking Caius.

The tall captain was immediately engulfed in flames, reduced to ashes between one heartbeat and the next.

Galaad opened his mouth to cry out, but Lugh reacted faster. He had pulled the glass apple from his belt with his silver hand, and rearing back he threw it at the monster's head with all his strength. The strange fruit struck the monster's red eye, and in a shower of crystalline fragments both apple and eye were reduced to dust.

The monster was rendered blind, or so it seemed, and Lugh pressed the advantage, rushing forward, his skyblade held in his hand, and gave the metal creature his answer. The blue blade bit through the monster's body, cleaving it in two.

But there was no time to celebrate his victory, for as the two halves of the metal monster fell on either side, some strange light seemed to coruscate from the severed metal, dancing like lightning, and lashed out, engulfing Lugh. The Gael howled in agony as the blast knocked him from his feet and he was sent flying through the air an impossible distance. He struck the irregular outer wall of the corridor and immediately vanished from view.

"No!" Artor shouted, and raced to the point where Lugh had vanished. But when he reached it, he found the wall as cold and solid as it had always been, his hands meeting only resistance. There was no sign of Lugh's passing, no sign that he had ever been.

Of Caius, there was a more concrete reminder. A pile of ashes heaped on the smooth floor of the corridor, little bits of bone and teeth flecked within. His disk lay beside the heap, unmarked, and his bloodflame lance had rolled a short distance away, untouched by the flames.

And then there were three.

Alice

Alice fell through whiteness. Beside her, the raven flapped its black wings, uselessly, but didn't say a word. There was no sound, only the white light all around, and the weightless sensation of falling.

Then Alice hit the ground.

The raven squawked, sounding like a raven instead of a helium-sucking baby-monster, and flew off around the slow bend of the corridor.

It took Alice a moment for her eyes to adjust.

She was in a corridor of some kind, the dark walls some two hundred feet apart, curving to the right and left in the distance. The ceiling overhead was almost invisible in the gloom. She wasn't sure where the light was coming from. It was almost as if the air itself was glowing, since the walls and ceiling were lost in darkness, but the space around Alice was faintly lit. It was a gray light, though, like dusk or twilight.

Alice climbed to her feet, rubbing her bruised ass. She turned and looked in either direction. Stillman and the Huntsman, the ravens and the dogs, the footbridge and Canary Wharf and London were nowhere to be seen.

"Where the *fuck* . . . ?"

This wasn't one of her visions, she was reasonably sure. It just didn't *feel* like one. Had she blacked out on the bridge during a seizure and been brought here? But where was *here*? And where was Stillman? Had the Huntsman overpowered him, *killed* him even, and taken Alice off to some underground tunnel?

Alice held up her hands. Her empty hands. She didn't have the gem. It wasn't on the floor around her. Maybe the Huntsman had pocketed it while she was out?

None of this made any *sense*.

Without warning, a sudden spasm of nausea doubled her over, her gut clenching.

This was worse than mixing her meds and alcohol. This felt *bad*.

In a moment, the sick feeling passed, leaving Alice weak and sweating.

"Okay, so this is strange *and* unpleasant."

Alice walked closer to the right-hand wall, the inner side of the curve. There was some kind of door, but she didn't see any way to get it open. She closed the distance, but after several minutes of trying, the door remaining stubbornly shut.

She should have held on to the sword. As if the Huntsman would have let her keep it, of course.

But then, if the Huntsman had brought her here during a blackout, why bring the raven along as well? And how weird that she'd hallucinated a raven falling with her, only to find the raven here at her side when she came out of it.

So maybe she *hadn't* blacked out?

Which meant . . . What? That she'd fallen?

She thought about Stillman's talk of other universes, of Iain Temple talking about fissures in space-time.

Whatever.

"Hello!" Alice cupped her hands and shouted. No answer.

She shrugged. Might as well see what she could see. She started walking to the left, following the curve of the wall. There was bound to be an open door, somewhere.

Galaad

Pryder took Caius's fallen disk for his own, while Galaad, at Artor's insistence, had armed himself with Caius's bloodflame lance.

The door through which the metal monster appeared had closed after it passed through, and nothing the trio could do managed to wrench it open again. And so they continued on.

On they walked, and on, the only sound their muffled footsteps and the rhythm of their breath.

When they must have walked for an hour or more since the encounter with the metal monster, Galaad was sure that they had completed yet another circuit, but no matter how far they walked, they never again came upon the remains of Caius or the severed halves of the metal monster.

"I don't like this," Pryder said at last, when they paused briefly to take small sips of what little water remained in the flasks they carried. "We walk in endless circles, like animals pacing a cage, and come no nearer our quarry."

"Perhaps we should return the way we have come," Artor said, a helpless tone creeping into his voice. "That door opened for the metal beast; perhaps it will open again and we can be there waiting."

Galaad wanted to object, to say that they'd surely already retraced their steps and passed that same door, the remains of their brief battle having been cleared in their absence, but he saw the haunted look on Pryder's face and kept his peace.

They walked back, an hour and more, and to Galaad's amazement they eventually saw the fallen monster and the ash pile of Caius's remains coming into view around the curve of the wall. It was maddening, seeming that the spot could be approached from this side and not the other. Did the corridors spiral up or downwards, so that they had actually reached another level on completing a circuit? It hardly seemed likely, since there was no appreciable gradient to the floor beneath their feet, but he could think of no other answer.

The trio waited what seemed an eternity beside the closed door, kneeling down, watchful for any sign of its opening, but were rewarded only with still silence. Then, unexpectedly, they heard muffled footsteps approaching from behind.

They leapt to their feet, and whirled with weapons in hand, to find a figure approaching from around the bend.

Galaad at first took it to be a youth, but as the figure drew nearer, eyes wide with fear, he could see that it was a woman. Or a maid, to be precise, perhaps a few years his junior. Her hair, so dark as to be black, was cut short, and she wore a short coat of black leather over a close-fitting white tunic, with tight blue breeches on her legs and heavy black boots encasing her feet. She was unarmed, and seemed to present little threat to the trio, evidently on the edge of terror, or shock.

She slowed her approach as the trio came into view, and warily addressed them in some strange language, which to Galaad's ears had the same sound as those the Red King had spoken.

"Who are you?" Artor demanded in Britannic. Then, at her evident confusion, he repeated in Latin, "Who are you?"

The maid seemed to understand the Latin a little better, but seemed no less confused for all of that, appearing to struggle to find the words to answer.

Galaad took a step forward, reaching out to the maid. "Do you need help?" he said, gently.

Gentle or no, when the maid saw Galaad's approach, fear flashed in her eyes.

"Enough of this," Pryder barked, brandishing his skyblade. "I want answers!" He advanced on the maid, angrily.

Seeing Pryder approach, a dark expression on his face, the maid started, shouting out in alarm, and took to her heels, running off in the opposite direction.

"Come on, after her!" Pryder shouted back over his shoulder, sprinting.

Artor and Galaad could only exchange uneasy glances and hurry along after him.

The maid could not have been more than a short distance ahead of them, just beyond the curve of the wall, but no matter how fast they ran, they didn't overtake her, and never again were they to catch sight of the maid of the Unworld.

Alice

"Okay, *that* was seriously weird," Alice said, breathless.

She'd run away from the three guys with the swords, only to find one of the big doors she'd passed only moments before was now open. She'd ducked inside, and the door shut behind her. Only now, hands on her knees, was she finally able to catch her breath.

What had those guys been, medieval knights? Roman soldiers? And what *language* was that? Part of it almost sounded like Latin, but not like any pronunciation Alice had learned in school.

Now that she'd caught her breath, and the sword-wielding guys hadn't come bursting through the door, Alice had a chance to look around and take in her surroundings.

A narrow passageway led from the door, the walls featureless and bare. Unable to open the door behind her even if she wanted to—which she *didn't*—Alice shrugged and walked up the hallway. A little way in it jogged to the right, then back to the left, then branched into two more hallways.

It was a maze.

Alice knew mazes.

Running her fingertips along the right-hand wall, she followed, seeing where it led.

Galaad

The trio ate a meager meal on the corridor floor, munching disconsolately on the few remaining scraps of dried meat that remained in their packs, rationing their remaining reserves of water. They rested for a time, their legs and backs aching, though whether they slept for hours or merely dozed for moments, it was impossible to say. When they woke, they continued on, now testing each door they passed, spending hours trying to pry the door open, to wedge their weapons into the near seamless cracks between door and jamb, all without any success.

It seemed an eternity, but at last, they rounded the curve of the inner wall and found one of the doors open and inviting.

Light streamed from within. They entered, weapons in hand.

Alice

Several more times the nausea overtook her, but eventually Alice found herself at the edge of an enormous space, dominated by two giant figures, one red and one white, crouched on either side of a huge chessboard. Between them, the silvery-metal and glass pieces, each of them at least twenty feet tall, moved on their own, back and forth across the board.

At first, Alice thought the giant figures were statues, but then the white one *moved*. A large outcropping on top, that might conceivably have been meant to be a head, turned towards her. It didn't have anything like eyes, but Alice knew that the thing was *looking* at her. She felt her skin crawl.

Then, Alice heard a clattering noise behind her and turned to see a seven-legged metal spider-thing come crab-walking out of the maze, with a red-lensed camera at the end a long craning neck. It was some sort of robot thing and was coming straight for her.

Alice didn't stop to converse but turned and took off running across the chessboard, dodging around the towering pieces of silver and glass.

The spider robot was quicker, though, and before Alice was even a few squares in, it was on her, wrapping one of its long segmented legs around her waist, pinning her arms to her sides.

Alice tried to scream, but no sound came out. Then, mercifully, everything went black.

"The sample wakes."

The voice buzzed in her brain without passing through her ears.

She was surrounded by whiteness on all sides, and falling.

"The sample's memories have been studied and recorded. The Dialectic has gained knowledge of the sample's language. These words are being implanted directly in the sample's mind."

"What . . . what's this . . . ? Who *are* you?" Alice's voice sounded raspy and hoarse in her own ears.

"The Dialectic is the governance of the Change Engine. A sample is retrieved, examined, and altered experimentally. The results are . . . inconclusive. A new sample is needed, and the first sample will be kept in suspension, pending further examination."

"What? What do you mean, altered?" Alice looked down, and for the first time saw that her leather jacket was now bone white, as were her jeans. She held up her hands, and even her skin seemed bleached white. She reached up and tugged a lock of her hair in front of her eyes, now no longer dyed black, but blindingly white. "What . . . what did you *do* to me? Who *are* you?!"

"Additional study is needed. The new sample is retrieved."

Then the voice was gone, and Alice was left alone. Falling through whiteness.

Galaad

The trio found themselves in a labyrinth of narrow, winding passages. At first, Galaad found them a pleasant change from the monotonous engulfing spaces of the corridors beyond, but when they had taken a dozen turns or more, each time finding themselves facing another turn and wall, the novelty quickly wore off.

After stalking through the winding labyrinth for what seemed an eternity, they took a final turn and found themselves at the threshold of a massive chamber. The ceiling was so high as to be invisible from the floor, while the walls receded so far in every direction that they were only just visible. Galaad, who'd long since ceased trying to work out how so much space could be contained within the confining walls of the tower of glass, reeled at the sight of it.

But the space was not empty. The floor of the enormous chamber was dominated by what appeared to be some sort of gwyddbwyll board, the floor demarked in an immense checkered grid, on which stood pieces of silver or glass, each as tall as a house. The pieces, to Galaad's astonishment, seemed to move of their own accord, sliding back and forth across the floor.

So stunned was Galaad by the gwyddbwyll set that he momentarily failed to notice the two gargantuan figures hulked on either side. They were of such a scale, of such monstrous proportions, that it seemed as if they would not at first fit inside his mind, dominating so much of the view on either side of the board that they essentially disappeared from view. But in short order he came to realize that it wasn't that one side of the room had a red hue and the other side white, but that there crouched on either side of the massive board two monstrously large figures, one red and one white.

They were dragons. Or not dragons, precisely, but that was the only word in Galaad's vocabulary that came close to encompassing them. They were enormous, immense, unimaginably large. Somewhere high above on either side was something suggesting a head, or even a face, regarding the movement on the board between them, while the movements of Artor, Pryder, and Galaad were completely beneath their notice.

Pryder was for attacking the dragons, but Artor was quick to stay his hand. It would do no good, the High King insisted, having no more effect than a gnat attacking a mountain. Whatever these immense dragons were, it was beyond their ken, and on a scope far in excess of anything that mere men could affect. Better to continue on, and seek the Red King or the White Lady elsewhere.

It took them some considerable time to skirt around the immense beings, but finally they came to another archway opposite that through which they'd exited the labyrinth, which led into still more twisting corridors. At Artor's insistence they quitted the giant chamber, leaving the dragons to contemplate their game, and their search continued.

CHAPTER THIRTY

Jubilee

Miss Bonaventure rushed to Blank's side as he lay bleeding on the floor, his skin pale, his lips bloodless. "Blank!"

Coughing, Blank struggled to sit, holding his insides in with both hands. "Must . . . get back . . . to York Place . . ." he managed, with difficulty.

"You're in a bad way, friend," Taylor said, leaning over with his hands on his knees. "I think we maybe ought to call a doctor."

Blank bit his lip and managed to shake his head fractionally from side to side. "Won't . . . die . . ." He coughed, a sick wet sound rattling in his lungs. "Unless . . . my head is removed . . . or central nervous system completely pulverized . . . I can still recover. But only . . . if you get me back . . . to my flat."

"You heard the man," Dulac said, sheathing his blue sword in the scabbard that hung from his Sam Browne belt. The bleeding from his shoulder seemed to have slowed, if not stopped entirely. He snatched up the crystal from the ground and tucked it into the pocket of his frock coat, and then leaned down and picked up Blank effortlessly like a child, one arm under his knees and the other around his shoulders. "Now," he said to Miss Bonaventure, "where's his flat, anyway?"

Commandeering a four-wheeled growler carriage, Dulac whipped the horses to a foaming frenzy and drove through the afternoon traffic, north across the Thames and towards Marylebone. Miss Bonaventure cradled Blank's head in her lap, while Taylor used his coat to try to staunch the flow of blood from Blank's gaping wound.

"Blank," Miss Bonaventure said, leaning in close and whispering in his ear, so low only he could hear, "this isn't fun anymore. Let me take you somewhere you can get help. A doctor, a hospital, anywhere. I can have you there in an instant."

Blank opened his eyes and managed a weak smile as his gaze met hers. "No, my dear. I'm quite aware . . . of your . . . skills in this regard . . . but I assure you . . . I'll be fine." He sputtered, and Miss Bonaventure wiped the pink foam from the corners of his mouth with a handkerchief. "I need . . . the locked room . . . at the top of the stairs."

"Then I can open a door there right now," Miss Bonaventure said, and raised the arm with the silver bracelet in front of her.

"No," Blank said. "Might startle . . . Dulac away . . . and I have questions yet . . . for him."

Miss Bonaventure sighed discontentedly. "Have it your way," she said, pouting slightly. "But I swear, Blank, if your eyes start rolling back in your head and I hear anything that even *sounds* like a death rattle, I'll have you to a doctor as quick as you can say Bob's your uncle, and I don't care *what* you say."

"Who's Bob?" Taylor asked.

Blank managed a laugh, and immediately regretted it.

Dulac carried Blank up the stairs of Number 31, York Place, with Miss Bonaventure leading the way, turning on the lights. Taylor followed behind, looking around with a confused expression.

At the top of the stairs, they came to a sturdy locked door.

"In . . . there," Blank said.

"Where's the key?" Dulac asked.

Blank shook his head. "There's . . . no key. Put me down."

Dulac did as he was asked. Blank, holding Taylor's blood-sodden jacket to his stomach with one hand, staggered forward and laid his other hand palm down against the door, just above the knob.

With an audible click, the knob turned and the door swung inwards on its hinges.

"I'll be damned," Miss Bonaventure said, eyes wide. "A biometric scanner."

The corners of Blank's mouth tugged up in a smile. "Why, Miss Bonaventure." Leaning heavily on the doorjamb, he staggered into the darkened room. "I'm impressed."

Miss Bonaventure and the others followed Blank into the room, and her fingers found the light switch on the wall. Electric lights in brass stanchions flared to life along the walls, revealing a portrait gallery.

"Which one of these is Dorian Gray?" Miss Bonaventure joked, as Blank made his slow and steady way to the well-upholstered chair positioned at the center of the floor.

"All of them, I suppose," Blank said, easing himself down onto the seat. "And none." He closed his eyes for a moment, willing the room to stop spinning around him. "Oscar only ever saw the one that Whistler was painting"—he pointed with a languid hand towards the most recent portrait, which depicted Blank in modern evening dress, with a red orchid in his lapel—"but when things went sour between us it . . . and my locked room . . . inspired him to write his damned story."

Taylor and Dulac walked along the walls, looking up at the portraits. They all appeared to be of the same man, though they had clearly been painted by a dozen different artists, in different times and places.

"This one I know!" Dulac said, pausing before the Rembrandt, which depicted a dashing young man in the dress of an early seventeenth-century gentleman, his hand resting lightly on the hilt of the rapier at his side, a large feather in his wide-brimmed hat. Dulac turned to face Blank. "I *thought* your face a familiar one."

Blank smiled slightly, his eyes half-lidded. "As did I on seeing yours, Monsieur Gilead. But we'll have to wait . . . a moment . . . to reminisce about old times . . . I'm afraid."

Then Blank closed his eyes, found the still place within him, and the world fell away.

When he opened them again, he was once more within the School of Thought.

Of course, Blank had not really gone anywhere, neither in body nor in mind. He still sat in the chair within the portrait gallery at the top of the York Place house, the walls and ceiling impregnated with circuitry that amplified the communication with Omega.

The eyes that opened were not eyes, and were not his own. These were thoughts generated long after his own body was dust, which would later be implanted back into his mind in the guise of true memory.

Omega could locate Blank wherever he went, implanting memories directly into his mind. When these unpacked, he would recall conversing directly with Omega in the unimaginably distant future. But if Blank needed to initiate contact with Omega, as he did now, he needed to do so from here.

The body that Blank now wore wasn't his body, any more than the thoughts he was thinking were his own. This was an emulated body and mind, existing in a simulated virtual environment conjured up by complicated circuits and magnetic fields in a vast cloud of electrons and positrons. There was a real world, somewhere beyond this illusion, but Blank knew it resembled not at all any world known by living man.

The nearest galaxies receded beyond the horizon untold trillions of years before, and the mass of the Milky Way galaxy was entirely in stars that had long before exploded and collapsed into black holes and neutron stars, or in brown dwarfs and dead cinders that never attained nuclear fusion, or in stars that withered into white dwarfs. What energy that remained was generated by proton decay and collisions between elemental particles. This was the heat death of the universe first predicted by Hermann von Helmholtz.

This cloud of elemental particles, a vast mind thinking slow and deep thoughts, was Omega. The machine-child descendant of man, Omega had long before forgotten its origins, having lost the thread that led from the first organic life to itself. Trillions of years before, before the stars began one by one to go out, Omega embarked upon a plan to rediscover its ancestors and secure its present and future. It began by creating endless simulations, modeling every possible culture that could have created its antecedents. It knew that organic life had been based on carbon and that it had stored its genetic record in complex strings of simple sugars. From there, it was a matter of ease to simulate all possible carbon-based life-forms that could be coded by such sugars. From there, it had generated emulations of all logically possible individuals and arranged these individuals in all possible combinations of societies and civilizations in all possible inhabitable environments.

Having created models of all possible worlds, of all possible lives, Omega began to grow bored with its game. It considered its options while the stars burned down around it, and then hit upon a new game to play. It would work out which of its simulated worlds and emulated lives was the true history of the universe.

The methods Omega employed were many, but a key tactic was a search through time itself.

Its simulations had established that organic consciousness was the result of quantum state reductions within cytoskeletal microtubules in the brain. Since, at the quantum level, the classical past and classical future were not globally distinguishable, and since entangled quantum particles enabled communication of a sort on a nonlocal basis, it merely remained to test all of the particles at hand to see if any were entangled with organic minds in the deep past. If a resonance could be found between one of the emulated minds and an organic mind, elsewhere and elsewhen, then Omega reasoned that the emulated mind was an accurate representation of a being who actually lived.

Having established contact with these resonant minds, Omega discovered that it was able to do far more than simply locate them. It could *communicate* with them. By manipulating the half of the tangled pair that it held in the deep future, it could affect the functioning of the organic mind which incorporated the pair's other half in the distant past. It could create and implant new memories, and through careful means could read the memories the organic mind had generated on its own.

It was at this point that Omega struck upon its final and most vital game.

The past was largely unknown, huge gaps or lacunae in the historical record. But the future was a certainty. In time, the last of the stars would be gone and all that would remain in the universe would be black holes of various masses, rapidly evaporating to nothing. In time, even the protons would have all decayed, and all that would remain in the universe would be a collection of neutrinos, positrons, electrons, and photons of enormous wavelength. The universe would be cold and dead, and with it, Omega itself.

There was some cause for hope, though. There were other universes, whether orthogonal to the space-time Omega inhabited or beyond the cosmic horizon. It might be possible to reach one of these through means or mechanisms unknown to Omega. Or it might be possible to create whole new universes within black holes, the event horizon containing an entirely new big bang. But this, too, was beyond Omega's reach. It was possible, though, that some mind in the forgotten past had discovered a means that for whatever reason had not appeared in Omega's emulations. It was even possible that in the distant past someone had encountered an artifact from some *other* universe, a relic from some space-time previous to or apart from Omega's own. And, failing this, with sufficient time Omega might be able to discover these means and mechanisms from first principles. But time was running out. Though some vigintillion years remained before the ultimate heat death of the universe, Omega's thoughts became much slower as the universe cooled, and it was only a matter of a few trillion trillion years before it would be unable to continue.

The minds that it had discovered, then, would become Omega's agents in the past. Working in these gaps in history, these lacunae, they would have two primary missions. First, to advance the course of civilization, wherever possible, so as to speed the birth of Omega itself; with an earlier creation and longer life, it might be possible that Omega could solve the problem of surviving the heat death of the universe in time. Second, to seek out any means of journeying to or creating another universe and identify any intrusions into our universe by another; but while such intrusions, though rare, could be found throughout history, none seemed to offer the exit that Omega sought.

The emulations of these agents, these lacunae, were brought together in a single simulated environment to share intelligence and information wherever possible. This new simulated environment became known by the lacuna who occupied it as the School of Thought, and it was here that the emulated Sandford Blank found himself.

The School of Thought was variable, infinitely mutable. Sometimes it was an endless plane stretching out to the horizon in every direction, with a black starless heaven arching overhead. Other times it was an impossibly immense, infinitely large library, every possible life of every possible person who might ever have lived encoded in the pages of the innumerable books upon its endless shelves. Still other times it was a featureless void, or a boundless ocean, or a trackless forest.

On this occasion, the emulation of Sandford Blank found himself in a more pastoral setting. A stream gently burbled by a short distance away, and on the opposite shore rose a crystal dome supported by columns of white stone. The ground beneath Blank's emulated feet was soft, carpeted with lush green grass, and rose at a slight incline from the banks of the stream. And everywhere he looked were other lacunae, in the temple on the opposite shore, in small boats punting down the stream, in the gondolas of hot air balloons which drifted overhead, or seated on the hillocks that were scattered irregularly throughout the landscape.

The emulations of all of the lacunae coexisted in the School of Thought, though theirs was not an atemporal existence. Rather, all times were one, as the subtle mechanisms within Omega were constantly sending and receiving communications from all points in history. So it was that Blank found himself facing emulations of other lacunae, some of whom were long dead when Victoria celebrated her Diamond Jubilee and some of whom would not be born for years, centuries, or millennia yet to come.

Nearby where Blank stood were a collection of men and women seated in a rough circle on the small carpeted hillocks that rose from the ground. There was young Quexi, her smooth skin and luxurious hair white as ivory against her gray gown, her eyes glinting violet. Next to her was Michel Void in doublet and hose, and Niveus in the striped tunic of a senator of the Roman republic. A short distance off sat Iokanaan in his desert robes and Stillman Waters in his Carnaby Street suit.

Blank crossed the short distance and found a seat amongst them, waiting for his audience with Omega.

"You have that look again, Kongbai," the young Quexi said. "Are you in communion with your past self?"

Blank nodded. The emulated lacunae could feel the synchronization of communion as a strange twinge at the back of their minds, as new memories were uploaded from their organic counterparts and integrated into their virtual minds.

"Yes," Blank answered. "There's been a spot of bother, I'm afraid."

"Ah, you don't know the half of it, guv," Stillman Waters said, lacing his hands behind his head, leaning back with a smirking grin. "I've nearly just had my bollocks handed to me by a Russian necromancer and assassin, and let me tell you, those bastards are no fun at all."

A side effect of the communion with Omega, besides the synchronization of memories across the vast reaches of time, was that the lacuna's organic mind entered a trancelike state and the body's autonomic processes came momentarily under Omega's influence. The various systems that regulate the body's healing and maintenance were engaged, and any damage due to entropy or injury, age or abuse, was corrected. With regular engagement with Omega, the aging process could be virtually arrested for a period of centuries, the lacuna's lifespan extended from three score and ten years to something nearer three or four hundred, barring catastrophe. In addition, the well-regulated muscles of the body performed at peak efficiency, giving the lacuna speed and strength unmatched by any but the most highly developed physical specimens.

So it was that when lacunae met one another in the School of Thought, it was often while recuperating from some physical trauma.

"Was I with you, my boy?" asked Michel Void, drawing the simulated smoke of an illusory pipe into his emulated lungs.

"No, my friend," Blank said, somewhat sadly. "This was somewhat after we parted company, I'm afraid."

"Oh," Quexi said, clapping her alabaster hands together. "Then I was there, surely?"

Blank's face tightened. "No," he said at length. "I'm afraid you were not with me at this point in history, either."

Quexi's brow knit, quizzically, but she let the matter slide.

It could be disorienting, talking to those you remembered from past organic lives but whose memories were synchronized with other eras than one's own. Michel Void had died in the seventeenth century, old age finally overtaking him after centuries in Omega's service. The Quexi who now smiled and winked a violet eye at Blank remembered sharing adventures with him at the end of the eighteenth century, and had no memory of leaving Omega's service and shutting her mind off to the summons to communion. And Blank knew that his past self would one day meet the young Stillman Waters, and train him as Michel had trained Blank, but in the era that Blank remembered Waters's birth was still decades away. The most recent memories of the emulation of Waters who now lounged a short distance were of a skirmish that occurred in the middle of the twentieth century.

There was no prohibition against discussing the subjective futures of their past selves, but it was considered impolite and somewhat distasteful, and as a matter of course most lacunae tended to avoid such topics whenever possible.

That did not mean, however, that they did not feel free to discuss their lives in more general terms.

"Tell me, Brother Sandford," said Iokanaan, scratching his chin through his full beard, "whatever became of your friend? The one to whom you told the story of my death and who was inspired to write a drama strange and beautiful."

Iokanaan's past self had acted as lacuna in the days of Tiberius Caesar, laboring in Levant to help lay the groundwork for a body of thought that would help ensure the dominion of Rome for centuries to come. He had run afoul of the tetrarch of Galilee and Perea, and suffered the one wound from which a lacuna could never recover, but in the moment that his head was cleaved from his shoulders, he had entered communion with Omega, and all that he knew or had learned in life was saved in the School of Thought. The emulated Iokanaan, remembering his death, had become obsessed with the topic, and rare was the conversation that he was not able to bring around to the subject of his own demise.

"I have not seen my . . . friend . . . in some time," Blank answered. "But he was recently released from imprisonment, so perhaps his situation improves."

Before the Judean could reply, a soft glow suffused the air around Blank, and a sphere appeared, hovering above his head.

"Excuse me, friends," Blank said, rising. "Perhaps we'll continue this conversation another time."

The sphere was the interface with Omega, and as it descended, Blank disappeared from the view of his fellow lacunae and found himself in a featureless white void.

And then he opened his eyes and was once more in the portrait gallery at the top of the York Place house.

CHAPTER THIRTY-ONE

Unworld

Alice

ALICE FELL, ENDLESSLY.

There was no hunger, no thirst, no sleep, no rest. Only whiteness, only falling.

Alice fell.

There were no visions, but memories plagued her. Movies she'd seen, books she'd read. Whatever the unknown beings—the Dialectic?—had done to her, they'd unlocked her memories, somehow, so that she remembered everything in startling clarity, in exquisite detail. She remembered falling, the first time, her father on the floor upstairs. She remembered glimpsing the highway lamppost, just before the flash, Nancy giggling like a madwoman in the passenger seat. She remembered her grandmother's last days, and her mother's disapproval, and her classwork and her friends and the teachers and strangers and all . . .

She retreated into comfortable memories. Unable ever to sleep, she lulled to the memory of her father reading to her.

"Alice couldn't see who was sitting beyond the Beetle, but a hoarse voice spoke next. 'Change engines—' it said, and was obliged to leave off."

She remembered her upstairs bedroom, lying in bed while her father sat on the bedside chair, the ancient copy of Lewis Carroll's complete works in his hands.

"'You'd be nowhere. Why, you're only a sort of thing in his dream!'

"'If that there King was to wake,' added Tweedledum, 'you'd go out—bang!— just like a candle!'"

Alice could remember the comforting weight of the quilt over her legs, the soft rustle of hair on fabric as she turned her head to the side, looking at her father sitting beside her.

"'That's the effect of living backwards,' the Queen said kindly: 'it always makes one a little giddy at first—'"

It occurred to Alice to wonder whether she might not be crazy, after all. Maybe all of this, not just everything since reaching London, but everything that had happened since she was seven years old, lying in bed, listening to her father read the story of that *other* Alice, had all been a dream. Could she wake up from it now? Could she open her eyes to find her father standing over her, seven years old again?

Ever drifting down the stream—
Lingering in the golden dream—
Life, what is it but a dream?

Galaad

After countless turns, dead ends, and backtracking, Galaad and the others came to another chamber which, while only a fraction of the size of that which housed the gwyddbwyll-playing dragons, was still massive compared to the cramped confines of the labyrinth. Not so massive, though, that Galaad didn't feel crowded when he discovered that the room was not empty.

The Red King stood there as though waiting for them, this impression only strengthened when the passage to the labyrinth sealed shut behind them as soon as they'd entered. The Red King was not alone, however, but was flanked on either side by dark figures, each of whom bore naked red blades like his in their hands. As Galaad's eyes grew accustomed to the gloom of the chamber, though, and he looked again at the faces of the Red King's lieutenants, their skin given a ruddy cast by the red light of their blades, he realized with a creeping horror that they were familiar to him.

The one on the right had a face blackened and cracked, his eyes impossibly large and white, his black tongue sticking out at a strange angle from his split lips. Galaad could even fancy that he saw a glint of copper in his mouth.

The one on the left had a face that was smoother and unmarred, his mouth hanging slack behind his blond beard, his eyes half-lidded and dull. He was stripped to the waist, and from his right shoulder to below his rib cage on his left side was a jagged line that glinted with metal and glass. One arm seemed positioned higher than the other, his head canted disturbingly to one side, as though he had been cut in two and reassembled improperly. Which, Galaad realized with an icy chill, was exactly what had happened.

The Red King grinned evilly behind his full red beard, and his eyes flashed in the dead white of his face. He opened his mouth and spoke to the trio, but in words none of them could understand. Then he paused, and laughed, and motioned the undead warriors on either side of him to advance.

"He sends our own dead against us," Artor snarled, raising Hardspace before him. "He'll pay for that."

Pryder, on the far side of Artor from Galaad, wore a softer expression, mouth working, eyes wet, looking at what had become of his brother's lifeless body.

It was clear to Galaad that whatever animated the two servitors of the Red King, it was not Artor's fallen companions. If something stared from behind the dull and lifeless eyes in those expressionless faces, it was some foul thing from the pit, or some mindless spirit held in the Red King's thrall. Galaad's cosmology was not wide enough to encompass such beings, but he knew that the evidence for them was before him and approaching rapidly.

The Red King seemed content to let his undead servants fight his battles for him and hung back while the two advanced, their red blades held before them unwaveringly.

"Pryder, mind your flank!" Artor called, as the undead warriors neared.

With the Red King standing watch, there were two red skyblades to their two blue, but as he held none of them, Galaad felt not at all comforted by the odds. That their opponents had already died once, and still stood, did not seem to factor in Galaad's favor, either.

The burnt thing that had once been Bedwyr lurched towards Galaad, swinging its red blade gracelessly, but Artor stepped in, turning aside the undead's blow with Hardspace.

Galaad hazarded a look to Artor's other side and saw Pryder standing, his sword's point to the ground.

"Gwrol," Pryder said, gently, "do you not know me, brother?"

The unthinking thing that had been Gwrol did not speak in response, its only answer coming in the form of a mighty swing of its red blade.

Perhaps Pryder could not move in time, but Galaad had seen him parry a blow in a shorter span than that, and in less trying circumstances. Maybe it was more likely that Pryder simply could not bring himself to raise a blade to his brother, whether living or dead, or that he had decided that he had no desire to continue without Gwrol at his side. Whatever the reason, Pryder's arms remained at his sides while the undead warrior completed its thrust, and that was all that it took.

Pryder stood stock still, hands at his sides, looking at the lifeless face of his dead brother. Then he turned his gaze and looked at the hilt of the red blade pushing against his chest. The blade's tip protruded some feet behind him, the red sword piercing him cleanly through the heart. The undead warrior, emotionless and silent, whipped the sword back and out of Pryder's body. Surreally, Pryder remained standing for a moment, looking almost as though he would turn and walk away, but then his eyes went white, the pupils rolling up in his head, and he crumpled and fell in a heap, lifeless.

Everything that followed came in a hurried blur. Artor, a roar thundering from his throat, wheeled around and struck out with Hardspace, slicing overhead at the undead Gwrol. Hardspace struck true and cleaved the undead warrior from the top of his head down, one arm and leg flopping disturbingly in one direction, one arm and leg in the other, the head and trunk shaved neatly in two and peeling apart down the middle like an overripe fruit.

At the same moment, the burnt thing that had been Bedwyr, maddeningly silent, lashed out with its own red blade at Artor's back.

Galaad did not have time to see if the undead warrior's blow had struck, but thrust forward with his lance, its tip digging into belly of the burnt thing, and his thumb found the jewel stud on the haft.

The burnt thing that had been Bedwyr seemed to glow with a red light from within for the briefest moment and then came apart in all directions with a deafening explosion, raining down viscera and hunks of bone on everything in sight.

Galaad dropped the lance, lacking the time to be disgusted, and raced to Artor, who was just now falling to his knees.

Cradling the High King, Galaad's heart stopped in his chest when he saw that the undead Bedwyr had struck true, after all. A large part of Artor's left shoulder and a section of his back had been sliced cleanly away, and blood, bile, and other humors now poured forth from the exposed viscera.

"The . . . Red King . . . ?" Artor managed.

Galaad looked up and saw that their opponent had gone. He had evidently not stayed to watch the results of his undead minions' battle against the trio.

His nostrils filled with the stench of burnt flesh, his clothing draped with bits of gray, stringy meat and charred skin, Galaad wrapped Artor's cloak around the High King's shoulder, staunching the flow of blood as best as he was able.

"Help me . . . to stand . . ." Artor commanded, Hardspace still gripped in his right hand.

Galaad thought to object, but saw little reason. If Artor preferred to meet his death on his feet rather than on his back, Galaad felt privileged to assist.

"Come . . . along," Artor managed to choke out. He experimented with using Hardspace as a crutch, and while Galaad had expected to see the tip sink into the floor, it held fast. With Galaad on his left side to support him, leaning on Hardspace in his right, Artor was able to hobble forward.

"Now . . ." Artor swallowed heavily, his cheeks pale and bloodless. "Where . . . is that . . . damned White Lady?"

Galaad clutched his buckler disk in his left hand, his right arm wrapped around Artor's back, supporting him, and they staggered together out of the chamber and through the open archway in the far wall.

Alice

Then, without warning, something changed.

The empty whiteness before her was no longer empty, no longer merely white.

It was a white rabbit in a checked waistcoat, an umbrella under one arm, a pocket watch in its hand.

"Oh, good," Alice said, her voice raspy and hoarse. "So I *am* crazy after all."

The little white rabbit tilted its head to one side, its long ears falling over its rounded shoulder, its pink eyes regarding her curiously.

"This image is one with which you associate comfort, yes?"

The rabbit's mouth moved, whiskers twitching, while the voice spoke, but the words sounded in her brain, just as they'd done before.

Alice shook her head, and her long white hair fell over her face. She pushed it out of the way with hands that looked like her mother's hands. How long had she been falling?

"The Dialectic is disrupted, the symmetry is broken. Red and White are out of balance. All due to the second sample. We cannot comprehend his mind. His thoughts. We need help. The White needs your *help."*

Alice realized that the voice was addressing her directly, now, not just as the "sample." What had changed?

"Look," rasped Alice's voice. "You need help? That's great. Great. That's great." She was unused to talking. It felt like years since she'd done it last, and she felt as though she'd lost the trick of stringing words together. "I need . . . I need to know. To know what's going on. Where am I? What have you done to me? Who are you? What is this all about?"

Once, Alice was sure, she might have cried. But she had no tears left. Her emotions felt strangely dampened and had ever since she had found herself falling, here in the whiteness, her skin and hair and clothes bleached white.

"*The White will explain.*" The rabbit's nose twitched, the whiskers vibrating. "*It would be simplest to implant the knowledge of the Change Engine and its history directly into your mind, and allow it to unpack.*"

"Wait a minute . . ." Alice started to say, but it was too late.

A glass flower blossomed in Alice's mind, and suddenly she *knew*.

Once, there was a universe, peopled by intelligent beings. But the universe was dying, would soon be dead. And so the beings devised a means to escape the death of their home and to go in search of another.

All that they were, all that they would ever be, they stored within the device, and sent it out into the shoals of the higher dimensions, searching for a new home.

The complete knowledge of a dead universe, contained in a tiny pocket of space-time, a lifeboat adrift on the higher dimensions.

The Change Engine.

The Change Engine itself was a small, fast-revolving Gödel universe. It was relatively small, no larger than a city, bounded by a circular corridor. However, since it was rotating, this corridor could be traversed like a spiraling tower. Walking in one direction, one moved into the future; walking in the other, one moved into the past. It was thus possible to walk to any point in the Change Engine's miniature space-time, physically or temporally, without violating local continuity.

The "gem" was no gem, but was the phase boundary transition between the space-time Alice knew as the world and the small revolving pocket universe within—a world in reverse, an unworld.

The Change Engine was designed to survive the death of a universe, and then to go out into higher-dimensional space and seek another universe to colonize. The Change Engine was governed by a rigorously defined dialectic, a control mechanism that applied two separate sets of protocols to each new circumstance. When the protocols reached a point of balance or equilibrium, the Change Engine acted on the resulting decision. One pole was the Red, which was engineered to drive for conquest, destruction, and re-creation. The other was the White, which was designed to work towards preservation, exploration, and noninterference. The two poles interacted, testing outcomes until balance was reached between the varying needs of their protocols, the deliberations manifested as the movements of representational objects around a two-dimensional grid, each new configuration encoding a possible outcome.

When encountering a new universe, this Dialectic was intended to interrogate the space-time and determine whether its qualities were near enough to those of its home universe that the new universe could be xenoformed to a state suitable to support the lives stored as information in its indestructible disks. If not, the Change Engine would disengage and continue drifting through the higher dimensions, searching for another space-time. If so, then the Change Engine would begin the work of reorganizing the space-time around it, reconfiguring it to meet the desired parameters. As the affected zone spread, the Change Engine would introduce flora and fauna into an acceptable biosphere, beginning the process that would result in a new home for the survivors.

That was the plan, at any rate.

When the Change Engine first made contact with the space-time Alice called home, it had collected specimens to examine. The first sample it had brought through the phase boundary transition was Alice Fell.

The first examinations had produced confusing, conflicting results. There were elements of Alice's genetic makeup which, paradoxically, could only have come from *within* the Change Engine itself.

The Red argued that the sample had been contaminated on retrieval, and that another should be gathered. The White argued that the results of the examinations were as yet inconclusive, and should be continued.

The Dialectic reached stability, and the decision was made to modify Alice biologically, so that she could survive in the desired parameters, should the space-time be xenoformed to match the Change Engine's universe of origin. This was a standard test in the Change Engine's procedures, the reasoning being that if an organism originating in the physical conditions of the newfound universe could be modified to survive in conditions which prevailed in the Change Engine's universe of origin, then by extension the newfound universe could conceivably be xenoformed to support the biologics which had originated in the universe of origin.

The results were inconclusive. Another specimen was required.

Experimentation on the second sample was performed while the Dialectic considered the confusing entropic structure of the new space-time. The data received from beyond the phase boundary transition, the gemlike "skin" of the Change Engine, suggested that the entire space-time was anti-entropic, which the scientists who had originally created and programmed the Dialectic had considered impossible.

It was only after the second sample had been examined and modified that the Dialectic reached a conclusion. It was realized that the Change Engine was impacting the local space-time orthogonally, moving opposite the flow of entropy. The space-time itself wasn't anti-entropic, but the Change Engine was colliding *backwards* against entropy's flow.

This was counter to the Change Engine's protocols. Proper xenoforming could not be carried out in such conditions. The Dialectic considered the question of disengaging and moving on, which should have been a foregone conclusion. However, a novel element interfered with the decision. The second sample had not been placed in stasis, as was procedure, but was still being interrogated by the Red. This sample, which labeled itself with the concept-term "Mervyn," reached decisions on an irrational basis, not following any logic or protocols that the Dialectic could discern. This sample, this Mervyn, had begun to influence the decision-making process of the Dialectic. It corrupted the Red protocols, altering the Red agenda, changing the standards by which the Red determined its position.

With the Dialectic unbalanced, and the White unable to counter the now irrational positions of the Red, the decision was made to remain and begin the process of xenoforming.

Moving opposite the flow of entropy, though, as the Change Engine pushed more of its bulk into the local space-time, strange temporal tides sprang into being around the phase transition boundary. These tides ebbed and flowed, with regions around the boundary sometimes exhibiting entropic attributes, sometimes anti-entropic, and sometimes showing no movement whatsoever.

As the Change Engine moved against the flow of time, it pressed deeper into the local space-time, becoming larger in the past than it had been in the future. And as it moved backwards in time, the affected biosphere expanded, ever larger, no more than a few picometers across at first, then nanometers, then microns, then centimeters. An object placed near the phase boundary at this stage, pushed within range of the temporal tides, might find itself traveling backwards into its own past: cells would grow younger, injuries would heal, decay would retreat. Or it might find itself frozen in time, until the tides again ebbed and flowed.

Time moved at a different rate within the Change Engine. Past and future were merely points on the maps, which one could visit again if one walked long and far enough.

But Alice could not go anywhere. Alice remained within the white heart of the Change Engine, forever falling.

"I want out of here. All right? I just want to go home. If I help you, I just want to go home."

The little white rabbit regarded her, its pink eyes unblinking.

"You cannot return to your 'home.' Having been altered, you cannot survive in your universe of origin, but only within the Change Engine, or within the affected

biosphere, already xenoformed. And even there you cannot go, as the Red holds sway, and the Red will not agree to your release. You must remain here, at the Change Engine's heart."

If she could still cry, she would have.

"But the White is not entirely without resources. You can be granted limited access to the Change Engine's systems. You will remain here, but your proxy could be broadcast elsewhere. This, in exchange for helping us cope with the corrupting influence of the Mervyn, and helping us restore the Dialectic to the appropriate balance."

"How . . . how can I help *you?*" Alice looked at the small white rabbit floating before her. If there had been any wind, she'd have thought they were falling together, side by side. But there was no wind, no sound at all. "I don't even understand everything you've shown me. A lifeboat from a dead universe? Is that even *possible?*"

"The Red controls the results of the Mervyn's interrogation," the white rabbit replied, *"but the White has limited access. Would you like to know what the Mervyn told the Red, that corrupted its protocols? We cannot parse the meaning, but perhaps you might."*

Alice considered it. What choice did she have? It wasn't as if she was doing anything else.

Another glass flower bloomed in her mind, as new memories unpacked.

And then Alice understood, at least in part.

She *remembered* seeing a man with wiry hair and a stringy beard, dressed in the clothes of a Victorian gentleman. But all of it—hair, beard, clothes— was a deep, unrelenting red. She *remembered* hearing his high, reedy voice, explaining to the machine intelligence of the Change Engine about a barbershop with three barbers, and a boy and his two uncles, Joe and Jim, one of whom needed a shave. She *remembered* hearing the confusion of the Red, trying to parse out the statements.

She remembered all of this, though she'd not been there, hadn't seen or heard it herself. These were more memories, planted directly in her mind by the White. Alice knew that.

Alice also knew what this Victorian gentleman, this Mervyn, seemed to have done. She recognized the story about Uncle Joe and Uncle Jim and the three barbers, Allen, Brown, and Carr. It had been in the Lewis Carroll collection her father had read to her when she was a girl, before the accident, before she fell. It was a logic paradox in story form, a parable about competing hypotheticals that could not coexist. Just the sort of logic problem and twisted reasoning that was behind all of Carroll's Alice stories, the nonsensical-seeming thought processes that twisted the mind in circles.

Alice didn't know anything about the beings who had built the Change Engine, or designed and programmed the artificial intelligence which governed it, the two-poled Dialectic. Somewhere in the Change Engine, she knew, there were indestructible silver disks, on which the survivors had been encoded as pure information, to one day be decanted into new cloned bodies in another universe. Perhaps someday she might meet one of them, face to face, and learn what sort of people they'd been. But she knew one thing about them, already. Their culture had never produced a Lewis Carroll.

This Mervyn had baffled the Red by reciting Carroll's logical paradoxes, and nonsense poems, and so forth. Knocking it off its pins enough that it could coerce the Red into changing its protocols. And why?

Because Mervyn had learned what Alice had just been told, that he could never return home to his own space-time. His body had been fundamentally altered, irreversibly, and the only place he could exist would be a world likewise modified by the Change Engine. And so Mervyn had realized that, if he was to have any kind of existence at all, he would have to convince the Dialectic to remain in his universe, and change enough of it to give him room to move around. If he failed, and the Change Engine moved on, back into the higher dimensions, he and the other sample would be discarded, their usefulness gone.

Mervyn had accomplished this by altering the Red's operant protocols, talking endlessly to the Red until its own goals, objectives, and strategies had been effectively rewritten. Not huge changes, but enough that in the tug-of-war of ideas and ideologies with the White which formed the basic functioning of the Dialectic, the Red would always prevail on the question of remaining in this new universe and modifying it per protocols.

Mervyn, made red by the same process that turned Alice's hair and clothes white, intended to remake the world over again, and set himself up as its ruler, with the Red's help. The world would belong to him, the Red King.

And changed in the past, the world would be changed in the future as well. It wasn't enough that the world Alice knew would be gone. When the past was altered, the Earth remade, then the world Alice knew would never have existed at all.

CHAPTER THIRTY-TWO

Jubilee

OMEGA DID NOT COMMUNICATE IN WORDS. It read the memories of the lacuna and responded with action as appropriate. When communing with Sandford Blank, it had gleaned from his remembrances everything it needed to know, updated the record of memory, and then communicated the new memory back to Blank's organic self at the appropriate point in history, in this case the third day of July 1897.

"Well, that's much better," Blank said, standing.

His jacket, vest, and shirt were still cut wide open and gored with blood and viscera, but the flesh beneath was now smooth and unmarked. While in communion his body's processes had worked overtime, knitting skin and muscle together, redirecting resources as appropriate, healing what had been hurt.

Blank was now in possession of an hour of new memories, more or less, while only a matter of moments had passed in the portrait gallery. It was hardly surprising. After all, if one could encompass eternity in an hour, as mad old William Blake had said, surely it would be a simple matter to cram an hour into a moment.

"I don't know about the rest of you," Blank said, clapping his hands together, "but I for one could very much use a drink."

Having cleaned up and dressed in a fresh shirt and suit, Blank joined his guests in the sitting room downstairs. Miss Bonaventure had opened a bottle of Madeira, and she, Taylor, and Dulac sat drinking generous portions, speaking little. On the table between then rested the crystal chalice, the source of all their troubles.

"So, Mr. Dulac?" Blank said, going to the sideboard and pouring himself a glass. "Or shall I call you Monsieur Jean Gilead?"

Dulac managed a weary smile. "I have been both, and more. Dulac, both Jules and Giles. Jean Gilead. Johannes Lak." He shook his head. "More than I can remember. I think perhaps my current name wears thin, though. Perhaps next I'll be Delamere, eh?"

"Look, what's all this about, anyhow?!" Taylor demanded. "Just why ain't you dead, Blank?"

Blank took a seat next to Miss Bonaventure on the sofa and shrugged. "I am in the employ of an entity called Omega, and Omega has hard enough time finding agents without letting them bleed to death needlessly. While I sat in that chair, my body healed itself, because it was what Omega desired."

"What is this Omega?" Miss Bonaventure said, eyes narrowed.

Blank gave her a slight smile. "An infinite brain enclosed in a narrow circle, my dear." He turned his attention back to Dulac. "But suffice it to say that I have been alive quite a few many years. Though not, I suspect, nearly so many as you. Tell me, what was the first name you carried, sir?"

Dulac took a deep breath, and closed his eyes for a moment, sinking into memory. When he opened them again, a wistful smile played at the corners of his mouth. "My parents were good Christians, though of the Pelagian variety, and as they considered that I brought a breath of scented air into their darkened lives, they named me for the biblical source of such balm." He sat up a little straighter, and in an unrecognizable accent said, "I am Galaad of Glevum."

Blank nodded. "Who, as Lady Priscilla would no doubt point out, were she here, the later chroniclers misremembered as Galahad."

A slight blush rose in Dulac's cheek, and Taylor looked from him to Blank and back with widened eyes. Dulac nodded, reluctantly.

"How much of it is true, what the legends say?" Blank asked.

"Not all," Dulac answered, "but enough. I sailed with Artor, in those last days of the fifth century of the Christian calendar. With him and his captains I entered the Summer Lands, and with him pierced to the heart of the Unworld. There I was remade by the White Lady, and given the task of safe-guarding the tower of glass, until the far future date when the White Lady would enter it and remove all impurities."

Blank only understood a measure of what the man said, but enough to capture the general drift.

"When the Summer Lands retreated," Dulac went on, "the Tower of Glass still stood atop the tor, and so I had constructed around it a great fortress, enclosing it entirely. In time, the fortress crumbled, and we built another on the spot, and when that fortress fell we built a church, and then another. Nothing could last long in the near vicinity of the Tower of Glass. But each time the walls fell, the tower was revealed to have shrunk, and so each time the enclosure was smaller, and smaller. In time, it receded entirely into the earth, leaving only the surrounding structure of mundane stone standing."

Miss Bonaventure gestured to the crystal chalice on the table between them. "And *that* is what remained of your tower?"

"It wasn't *my* tower," Dulac shot back, eyes flashing. Then he calmed, vis-ibly. "But yes. I knew that it would one day be unearthed by a man named Bonaventure, and since it was given to me to safeguard the tower whatever its form, however diminished, I set about finding this man. I knew, from what the White Lady had told me, that it would be the nineteenth century of the Christian calendar before the crystal would be unearthed, and so there was little need for rush, but I wanted to know where the man would be when the time came. So centuries ago I sought out the Bonaventure family and found it in the kingdom of Varadeaux, once an independent nation, then a part of France, and now part of the Swiss Confederation. I became a friend to the family in various guises, drifting away for a time and then returning to another generation under a different name. When a branch of the family moved to England, centuries ago, I followed it here, splitting my time between the septs, now in one country, now in another, unsure which would one day give birth to the man for whom I waited."

"When I knew you as Jean Gilead in the days of Louis XIII, you traveled in the company of a musketeer named Etienne Bonaventure," Blank said.

Dulac smiled, remembering. "He was a good friend, was Etienne. As were Amandine, Achille, Hieronymus, Michel-Thierry, and Cornelius, to name but a few." He looked to Miss Bonaventure. "That's why I was so perplexed on meeting you, girl. I thought I knew the name and provenance of everyone born with that surname for the last three or four centuries at least."

Miss Bonaventure gave a sly smile in return. "Perhaps I'm an apple that fell a bit farther from the tree than most." She paused, and her grin widened. "Or perhaps I haven't yet been born."

Dulac barked a laugh. "Well, stranger things have happened, and that I can attest."

"What became of Mervyn Fawkes?" Blank asked. "He disappeared in that flash of light, but there is no way that he could have escaped on foot in so short a time."

Dulac shook his head. "I can't say the reason he was drawn in, but I can tell you without doubt that he has entered the Unworld, the realm within the crystal. And having entered, I can tell you that he will never be able to leave. Of all those who have ever passed inside, only myself and one other have ever returned, and only one of us while still living."

"What will you do now?" Blank asked, his tone measured.

Dulac sighed and indicated the crystal chalice with his chin. "Return that to safe keeping, I suppose. Perhaps when Peter returns he can help me arrange a more secure holding, perhaps buried under the British Museum. Then I wait for the coming of the White Lady, as was my charge."

"And the man with the red eyes and red sword?" Miss Bonaventure asked. "Who is he?"

A cloud passed over Dulac's features, and when he spoke again, his tone was more grave. "One of Artor's captains, another who journeyed with us into the Unworld. In death, his body was desecrated by the Red King and sent out into the world to do his bidding. The Huntsman also waits for the White Lady, but to stop her entering the Unworld, where I stand to secure her passage."

"The Huntsman?"

"That's the only fit name for him, Blank," Dulac answered, "though in life he answered to Pryder. While my life and energies are sustained by the White Lady, the Huntsman is sustained by the Red King. We have met one another a time or two over the long centuries, but in death he lacks the stamina of my lengthened life. For every year or two that he walks abroad, he must spend nearly half a century asleep beneath the ice, somewhere cold. I've sought his resting place these many long years, but never yet found it." He let out a ragged sigh. "I fear that I'll never catch him sleeping, and must wait until that final day when we face each other, all for the sake of the White Lady."

"But what should happen if you find him now, and he defeats you?" Miss Bonaventure asked. "I'm not saying it'll happen, but surely you've considered the possibility."

Dulac smiled ruefully. "If I fall before the appointed day, leaving unprotected the White Lady yet to come, I can only hope that she finds some other champion or that someone else steps into the breach in my stead." His smile faded, and his expression darkened. "If not, I would fear for us all."

Finishing his Madeira, Dulac climbed to his feet. Hooking the scabbarded sword back onto his Sam Browne belt, he picked up the crystal chalice and tucked it safely into his pocket.

"Blank, it was a pleasure meeting you again, and I thank you for the drink, but I'm afraid I should be off. There's still a chance I can catch the Huntsman before he goes to ground, and I'd sooner save myself another half century of searching if I could."

Blank stood and took Dulac's proffered hand in his. "Good luck to you, Galaad of Glevum. I hope you someday find the rest and reward you deserve."

Dulac's eyes seemed to moisten, and he smiled sadly. "That is a hope that we share."

With that, Dulac clicked his heels together and bowed to Miss Bonaventure, snapped off a salute to Taylor, and disappeared out the door and into the dying late afternoon light

Taylor left soon after.

"No offense, folks, but after all of this business, I don't think I'm cut out for living in London, after all. I think I might best head on home to Texas. Last time I looked, we don't have folks running around claiming to be hundreds of years old back home, or healing up from mortal wounds by resting a spell in a comfy chair." He grinned, his eyes twinkling. "No offense, you understand."

Tipping his hat, the cowboy poet, Knight of the Texas Plains, finished his drink in one long draught and showed himself to the door.

Miss Bonaventure refused to be satisfied by the curt answers Blank had given the others, about Omega and his own role as a lacuna. When Taylor and Dulac had gone, Miss Bonaventure forced him to explain his circumstance at length, which he gladly did, finding it something of a relief to speak so openly on a topic that he'd kept hidden for so long.

"So you're a secret agent for a machine intelligence at the end of time, is that it?" she asked, her gaze narrowed. "Is that what you're asking me to believe?"

"I believe the term they'd use where you come from is 'computer,' my dear," Blank said with a smile. "Or 'artificial intelligence.' Something like that."

Miss Bonaventure's eyes widened, and her mouth dropped open. "Wh-what do you mean? 'Where I come from'?"

Blank sighed, and reaching out patted the back of her hand. "Come, my dear, come. We both know you're not from around here, chronologically speaking."

Miss Bonaventure opened her mouth to speak, then closed it, then opened it again. "So you know about this?" She held up her arm and pointed to the wide silver bracelet on her wrist.

"The Sofia, I believe you call it?" He nodded. "You first met me six years ago, when you were a younger woman, but I first met you a century before, when you were quite a bit more . . . mature, shall we say?"

She cocked an eyebrow and regarded him quizzically.

"Imagine my surprise when a woman who looked eighty years old if she was a day came up to me on the streets of London, a complete stranger, and apologized for keeping secrets from me."

"I never," Miss Bonaventure said, playfully punching Blank in the shoulder.

"You most certainly did," Blank said. "You said that perhaps if you'd been a little more forthcoming with sharing your own secrets, perhaps I'd have found it a bit easier to share mine."

"What?" Miss Bonaventure said, with a sly smile. "That you're a homosexual?"

Now it was Blank's turn to widen his eyes in surprise. But he regained his composure almost immediately, and nodded, primly. "I thought that certainly I'd kept it from you."

Miss Bonaventure grinned. "Where I come from, in addition to calling machine intelligences 'computers,' we're also a bit more open about our sexuality, and as a result most of us have developed the ability to sense another's orientation, to some degree of success. Though there are some who prefer it were otherwise, women are quite able to openly admit their love for other women, and men for men, and all combinations in between."

Blank's breath caught in his throat, and his heartbeat skipped. "Do . . . do they really?"

Miss Bonaventure took his hand in hers. "Yes, Sandford," she said tenderly. "They do."

Blank had to look away for a moment, unable to meet her gaze. "I . . . I so seldom . . . It's been so . . ." He took a deep breath and composed himself, and looked back to his companion. "I allowed myself the indulgence of a relationship only once in the last hundred years. I thought that society, here at these modern times, this fin de siècle, might finally be approaching the point where the love that dare not speak its name might at last be uttered, if only in whispers. I had commissioned James Whistler to do my portrait—my only vice, recording my changing appearance over the course of years, recording a history I can never share with another living soul—and James introduced me to his friend, the writer Oscar Wilde. Oscar and I became . . . involved for a time. I was . . . distracted from my duties." He paused, a pained expression on his face. "While I was otherwise engaged, a madman began killing women, removing their heads and severing their limbs. It was because of *me*, because I let romantic entanglements distract my attentions, and in the end the murderer slipped away. I blamed myself, of course, which Oscar could never understand, and the relationship ended badly as a result."

Miss Bonaventure tightened her grip on his hand. "But now Mervyn Fawkes reveals himself as the Torso Murderer, and the Jubilee Killer as well, and though he will not stand trial, you can at least console yourself that he's been brought to justice."

Blank thought for a moment and then managed a nod. "Perhaps," he allowed.

"In which case you can return to pursuing your duties in the service of your Omega with a clear conscience."

A sly smile spread across Blank's face. "Not precisely."

Miss Bonaventure raised an eyebrow.

"You see, Miss Bonaventure, I am *not* laboring in the service of Omega, whatever it might think. After being exposed to the writings of the Romantics, and in particular William Blake, I became something of an anarchist. Or if not an anarchist, precisely, then at least one who feels that man should live free of influence, whether king or queen in the here and now, or God in the heavens, or machine intelligence at the end of time. I had learned, almost by accident, the trick of segmenting my consciousness, and hiding my thoughts from Omega while in communion. While Omega reads my memories when I link minds with my emulated self in the deep future, I keep some of my memories hidden away. I later taught the trick to Quexi, another lacuna, thinking that she could join me in the struggle. But in the days of the Opium Wars, she became disenchanted with my notion of gradual improvement and cut herself off from Omega entirely, refusing all contact and communion."

"The Ghost Fox," Miss Bonaventure said in a low voice.

Blank nodded. "Denying communion with Omega, she was herself denied the beneficial side effects of the process. No longer able to heal any wound, she began again to age naturally. She set up her own fiefdom, the Ghost Fox Triad, dedicated to the principle of freedom above all." He paused for a moment, taking a deep breath. "I wonder sometimes if hers is not the wiser course and mine the foolish path. But I am committed, nonetheless. I will continue to work within the system and behind the scenes, to orchestrate the end of empire and the rise of self-determinism. It may come at a high cost, but I think it a price worth paying."

Blank paused and then motioned to the bracelet on Miss Bonaventure's wrist.

"I told your older self years ago, and I'll tell you now," he said, his tone grave, "that you should take particular care not to reveal yourself to any willing agent of Omega. If it should come into the possession of the ability to move freely through time, it would return to some earlier epoch and colonize the past, and we would find ourselves not the distant ancestors of that massive intelligence but its unwilling slaves."

Miss Bonaventure was silent for a moment, thoughtful. "So, Blank?" She fixed him with a grin. "Since you know about the Sofia, is there anywhere you'd like to go? Any place or time you would like to see? You need only ask, and I can open a door."

Blank drew his mouth into a line. Roxanne Bonaventure had made him the same offer, more than a century before, when she'd first appeared to him as an old woman and explained that she had the ability to move at will through space and time. And now, just as then, he found himself thinking of Roanoke, tempted by the notion of going back and seeing his parents, if just for a moment.

He opened his mouth, about to give voice to his temptation, but at the last shook his head, and gave again the answer that he had, a century before.

"I've seen enough of history that I prefer to live it a day at a time, my dear." He gave her hand a squeeze. "Perhaps another time."

CHAPTER THIRTY-THREE

Unworld

Galaad

A RTOR ON HIS ARM, dying by inches, Galaad continued on through the winding corridors, passing through rooms which blinded him with the countless gems that glinted on glass walls, through rooms where he squinted to see their way in the darkness, through rooms of pure red and rooms of pure white. They passed through vast empty caverns and made their way through corridors scarcely wide enough for them to pass. But all of them vacant or vacated, with no sign in evidence of the Maid of the Unworld, of the Red King, or of the White Lady they sought. And so they went on, leaving behind them a trail of Artor's lifeblood, slowly leaking out.

Alice

Alice agreed to help the Change Engine. Mervyn, this self-proclaimed Red King, would need to be stopped. And she was the only one in a position to do something.

But she would need help.

Alice wasn't sure what year it was, out there beyond the walls of the Change Engine. Trapped in the whiteness at its heart, it seemed to her as if hours might have passed, or days, or years, or centuries. It was impossible to say. Given that Mervyn appeared to have come from the late nineteenth century, it was clear more time had passed than Alice might originally have guessed. From the record of his memories made by the Red, though, the White had been able to draw one useful piece of information: that Mervyn had taken the phase boundary transition, the "gem," from a man named Bonaventure, though it had been larger then than it was in Alice's time.

Alice assumed that this Bonaventure, like Mervyn, was in the nineteenth century, if Mervyn's clothes were any indication. It was impossible to say for sure, though.

Alice thought of the Mad Hatter, who'd lost a fight with Time and found himself imprisoned in six o'clock. Now Alice knew how he must have felt.

No one could enter the Change Engine from the universe outside, unless they were drawn in from within. And the Change Engine was only able to draw in organisms that were in direct contact with the phase boundary transition. In other words, those who were touching the mirrorlike "skin."

If Alice was going to get help from outside, she'd have to lure people to the gem. Of course, the systems of the Change Engine informed her that it wasn't a gem any longer, nor even the chalicelike object it had been when Mervyn had first seen it. It had grown so much, moving back through time, that it was the size of a building now. It was a tower. And the affected bio-sphere, the area of surrounding space-time modified to match the Change Engine's universe of origin, had begun to grow, logarithmically, now some several miles across.

Alice was able to gain limited control of the simpler systems of the Change Engine, with the White's assistance. She was able to manipulate the mirror-skin of the Change Engine to propagate signals out into the universe beyond. Using the same technology that allowed the White to implant memories directly into her mind, she sent a simple message of images out into the world. She was signaling blind, not sure who would receive it, or when. But she knew *someone* would receive it. After all, she realized, she'd already met them. The three sword-wielding knights she'd encountered just after being drawn into the Change Engine.

Mervyn was now moving freely through the affected biosphere, interacting with the plants and animals engendered there by the Dialectic. Perhaps, if he were to be stopped out there, prevented from reentering the Change Engine, then she could go to work on the White, modifying its own protocols in time to checkmate the Red.

The medieval knights, or Roman soldiers, or whatever they had been, then, could be her arms. Since she couldn't leave the heart of the Change Engine, she could send them out to face Mervyn, and put an end to his plans.

But they'd need to be armed.

In the pattern stores of the Change Engine, the library of information of all technology created by the beings who perished when the old universe died, Alice found tools which could be put to other uses. A macromolecular blade able to cut through any substance. A rod which could fire bursts of heated plasma. Unbreakable storage disks that could be used as shields. Beetlelike service robots, with four pinchers on either end. A kind of hovering machine, a remote capable of sailing through air or water. And an impossibly thin environmental suit that could protect organisms from outside, allowing them to exist for brief periods within the affected biosphere.

The skin of the Change Engine recorded a change in the biosphere. Organisms from the outside were entering. *People.* These were those that Alice was waiting for. They must have received her signal, and come.

Using the molecular machines of the Dialectic to construct the tools needed, Alice sent the hovering craft, heavily laden, out to greet the new arrivals.

Alice was able to communicate with the newcomers through remote presence, sound and images sent back and forth by the machinery in the hovering platform. There were not three of the knights, as she had remembered, but seven. One of them spoke to her image in Latin, and she responded as well as she was able, dredging through her now-perfect memory of high school Latin classes, taxing her skills with the dead language to their limits.

When the knights took the macromolecular blades, Alice said that they were "vorpal swords," which was a joke no one would understand for centuries. The vorpal blades had to be keyed to an organism's specific genetic information. Only they would be able to draw the swords from the scabbards, or perhaps their offspring.

One of the knights was injured after an encounter with monsters from the past of the dead universe. She fashioned him a new arm from one of the silver-beetle service robots.

Alice warned them about Mervyn, about the Red King. Then she withdrew the hovering remote before Mervyn or the Red noticed its presence. And she waited, to see if her knights were equal to the task.

Mervyn encountered the knights, and sent after them doglike organisms fabricated from the Change Engine's pattern stores, fierce creatures with red teeth and claws. Alice remembered them and remembered what kind of danger they posed. She named them "rath," though there was nothing "mome" about them.

Alice could not send the hovering remote again without alerting the Red to their plans. But she managed to fashion a communication node and affix it to the head of one of the subsentient creatures the Change Engine had created to populate the affected biosphere. The creature drove away Mervyn and his dog creatures, and allowed her to communicate to the knights again, if briefly.

Alice passed the time, waiting for the knights, examining the data stores of the Change Engine. She discovered something interesting. There was all manner of technology recorded in there, things like the macromolecular blades and the disks and the plans for the Change Engine itself. And there was scientific information, exhaustive data about the universe from which the Change Engine had come, information about the interplay between the higher and lower dimensions, about the nature of space-time itself. There were engineering schematics, plans for molecular machines, information about how to extend organic life, and store and edit memories, and all manner of things hardly dreamed about by the scientists in Alice's world.

But there was something missing from the data store.

There was no music. No dramas. No books. No fiction.

In short, no stories.

Perhaps it was all stored in the minds recorded on the disks. Or maybe the builders of the Change Engine had abandoned anything that wasn't science or engineering or technology long ago, if they ever had it. But whatever the reason, one thing was clear. The Change Engine itself, and the Dialectic by extension, had no knowledge whatsoever of anything that wasn't *real*.

By the time the surviving knights reached the skin of the Change Engine, it was too late. The Red had taken note of her activities and closed off access to vital systems. The White's tactic in engaging Alice's help appeared to have failed.

Mervyn and the Red were aware that she was within the heart, but unable to do anything about it beyond blinding her and cutting off her control of the Change Engine's systems. The White was able to protect her that much, at least. But knowing that she was there, an irritant in the heart of the Change Engine, Mervyn decided to secure his own position and help ensure his own survival. The White, powerless to stop him, had monitored his movements and relayed them to Alice.

Mervyn had taken the corpse of one of the fallen knights and animated it by remote presence. A robot, or zombie, guided by remote control. He'd modified the body so that it could survive in the universe beyond the affected biosphere, unliving but undead, unchanging and virtually immortal, though able to operate for only brief periods of time without resting. Then, along with similarly modified doglike rath, this modified corpse, this zombie, this Huntsman, would be sent back into the outside universe, as a kind of insurance policy. But he would not go unarmed. Mervyn had already used one of the macromolecular blades himself, and he added the Huntsman's genetic data to his own; the Huntsman would carry it down through the centuries and, if need be, Mervyn's younger self might one day wield it, as well.

This Huntsman would be sent walking to the future, one step at a time, to the Change Engine's own past, with two principle protocols: protect Mervyn and prevent Alice or any others from entering the Change Engine.

Alice wasn't sure what that kind of paradox would do. If the Huntsman killed her younger self in the future, before she entered the Change Engine, she wouldn't be here in the Change Engine now, right? Or would it just create a new timeline, a new Change Engine without Alice falling eternally in its heart?

She didn't know. But she didn't want to risk finding out.

If Mervyn wanted to send insurance into the future, one step at a time, then perhaps Alice would do the same. And then it would be time for her to try a logic problem of her own.

Alice waited. It seemed an eternity, falling there, in the silent whiteness at the heart of the Change Engine. Eventually, though, she knew that help would arrive. And she'd long before worked out who it would be.

She was an old woman when the two surviving knights reached the Change Engine's heart. Luckily, she'd had time to work on her Latin in all the time since, and was able to communicate with them a little more freely.

One of them was beyond helping. He would die soon, that much was clear. Alice knew that she could reanimate his body when he was dead, a corpse turned into a zombie puppet like the Red King's Huntsman, but she couldn't bring herself to do that. Besides, it wasn't necessary. There was another option.

Galaad

Galaad and Artor came at last to the heart of the Unworld, the place to which all of the corridors and passages led. It was a multifaceted room, and on entering through the wall, they slid down the roughly curved floor. Artor's blood streaked behind them, until they finally came to rest in the bottom of the bowl. The floor, walls, and ceiling were an innumerable number of planes of silvery metal, all of different shapes and sizes, broken here and there by openings of various sizes and shapes, of which the door they'd exited had been just one. It was as if they were within some many-faced jewel.

Something hung in the center of the sphere, though at first it hurt Galaad's eyes just to look at it.

"You have come," said a voice from above, and the strange curves and shapes before Galaad's eyes began slowly to resolve into a figure. "It has been so long, I had almost given up hope."

Galaad squinted overhead. There, in the center of the crooked enclosure of the chamber, hung the figure of a woman. But this was not the young maiden they'd encountered in the corridor, nor yet the mature figure who had appeared in his visions and in their journeys through the Summer Lands. This was an ancient crone, haggard and withered, looking for all the world just like the witches who featured in the stories told to children around smoldering night fires.

She hung in midair, not immobile, but drifting slightly back and forth, arms and legs swaying easily, long snow white hair spreading out in all directions like a nimbus. It was as if she floated under the sea, gently buffeted this way and that by the underwater currents.

"It has been a difficult journey for you," the Sea Witch went on, her tone gentler than her wrinkled and fearsome expression would suggest possible. "I am sorry for that."

"Who . . . who are you?" Galaad gasped, kneeling at Artor's side and looking up, his eyes watering with the strangeness of the sight.

"I am she whom you came seeking," the Sea Witch answered, sadly.

"The White Lady? But . . . But, I don't understand . . ."

The Sea Witch shook her frail head, the nimbus of white hair shifting around her. "I have been imprisoned here a long, long time."

"But . . . but you appeared to us only a short time ago, with the look of one barely past the pink of youth."

"A short time for you," the Sea Witch answered, "a long lifetime for me. Time does not flow normally in the Unworld, and still less here at its heart. The tower turns, and in turning generates something like time, something like space. Walk one direction and you advance into the future; walk another, and you return to the past. So it is that you can encounter the same person in their youth, in their mature years, and again at the end of life." She smiled, slightly, the expression difficult to read amidst the forest of wrinkles. "But not necessarily in that sequence."

Artor coughed wetly, a red froth bubbling at the corners of his mouth.

Galaad looked from his injured companion up to the Sea Witch floating overhead. "Great lady, whatever your name, please help my friend. My king. He is gravely injured."

"No," the Sea Witch said, shaking her head sadly. "He is dead."

Galaad opened his mouth to object, but looked down at the High King who lay cradled in his arms and saw that she was right. The cough had been his death rattle, all life gone from his eyes.

"But his death will not be the end of his journey, I'm afraid," she said. "Nor is your own far from over, I'm sorry to say."

Metal monsters climbed from the multifaceted walls and ceiling, clinging like spiders crawling across a ceiling, and advanced on Galaad and the late High King.

"You carry your disk still," the Sea Witch said, and pointed a bony finger at the round shield at Galaad's side. Galaad could only nod, dumbly. "Place it near your friend's head," the Sea Witch instructed.

Galaad was numb, all sense of feeling gone, his senses near shattered. He felt like a puppet, lacking the will to act of his own accord. He was so weary, so beaten down by his long journey, with so much death and blood in his wake, that he would in that moment have obeyed any order, from any source, no more his own creature than the undead servants of the Red King had been.

Galaad did as he was told and set the disk on the floor just above Artor's head. It looked almost like a halo.

The Sea Witch moved her hands before her in a complex sigil, and the chamber seemed to suffuse with a white glow that faded after a moment. The disk began to hum, quietly at first, and then with increasing volume, rising in pitch. Artor's cheek twitched, and one of his eyes seemed to flutter.

Galaad brightened, thinking in an insane moment that the Sea Witch was somehow restoring the fallen king to life. But then the humming ceased, and the twitching and fluttering was stopped, and Artor was again an insensate, lifeless corpse.

"All that your friend was, all that he ever thought or hoped or believed, is now within the disk." The Sea Witch paused, thoughtfully. "Now," she said, at length, "we must see to you."

Alice

Thanks to the White, Alice had control over the systems in the immediate vicinity of the Change Engine's heart. After she had uploaded the dying knight's mind into the disk, she set to work on the other. She rendered him unconscious, telling him that he would sleep, and then sent streams of molecular machines into his body.

While the tiny machines did their work, Alice turned her attention back to the disk.

As she had learned when the White first implanted the history of the Change Engine into her thoughts, the unbreakable disks in the pattern stores were intended for the long-term storage and retrieval of the former inhabitants of the dead universe. Each of the millions of disks contained a handful of minds, perfectly stored at the moment of recording. Someday, the protocols ran, their original bodies would be remade, fabricated out of extant organic material, and the minds contained within the disks downloaded into them.

The knights had used the disks as unbreakable shields, not guessing the kind of protection they might instead be able to offer. But Alice wanted even more.

With the White's assistance, Alice altered the programming and functioning of the disk.

Somewhere, in the spiraling tower of the Change Engine, a raven had once flown. A raven that, when with at least six of its brothers, had been able to speak. Now, Alice understood why, and how.

From the records of the Dialectic, the White was able to supply the genetic profile of the black-winged bird. Alice keyed the disk to download the stored consciousness of the dead knight stored within, not into another human body, but into the minds of a flock of birds. The stored mind would be distributed, if imprecisely, across an entire subspecies of ravens, passed down genetically through their descendants. Any single raven would only hold a small portion of the fragmented mind, but enough of them together would constitute something like a human personality. It wouldn't be able to reason and communicate like a human would, but with proper motivation and singlemindedness, it would suit her purposes.

Alice whispered to the mind stored on the disk, imparting to it a mission. Find her younger self in the future and protect her from the Huntsman and his dogs.

Then, as the molecular machines were completing their modifications to the last surviving knight, a sudden thought hit Alice. Now she understood what the raven had been trying to say. The raven had been communicating a message, all right, but it wasn't directed at her.

Alice coded the new message into the dead knight's mind, and then instructed the White to upload a copy of her own memory and mind into the disk. It was her own little lifeboat, of sorts. She only hoped that Stillman could work out what the message meant.

Then she turned her attention back to the last knight.

The molecular machines of the Change Engine had altered his biology, from the toughened skin through the strengthened muscles down to the bones laced with unbreakable polymers. The machines built other machines, which coursed through his bloodstream, and nestled in his marrow, and moved up and down his spinal column, self-regulating repair mechanisms that would be able to heal any injury and stave off the effects of aging for long periods of time. The knight would age, but extremely slowly.

Galaad

When it was over, Galaad felt restored, refreshed. He stood up, his muscles moving with a strength and ease he'd not experienced before.

"You have been altered, changed to serve our purpose," the Sea Witch explained. "You will age, but so slowly you will scarcely notice, and you will heal instantly from all but the severest wounds, and even from those you will recover in time."

Galaad flexed his fingers, overwhelmed by the sense of vitality that flooded through him.

"Now, retrieve your fallen companion's sword and the sheath worn at his side."

Galaad did as he was told. Again the Sea Witch moved her hands before her, describing strange sigils in midair. The room brightened with the same white glow, which again faded just as quickly.

"Now the sword has been altered as well, bound to you as it was once bound to him. Now you will be able to draw from the sheath that which no one else can."

Galaad slid the whisper-thin blade into the scabbard and watched the hilt join with the sheath. Then, effortlessly, he pulled the sword free again, the blue glow casting strange shadows over him.

Alice

Alice told the knight about the Huntsman, about how his fallen friend had been remade by the Red King and sent out into the world. Then she told him to take the disk to London, and bury it under the hill at the east edge of the city, the place called White Mount. Then, it would fall to him to wait the long centuries until the time came to act. He should protect the tower, and prevent the Red King from entering if at all possible, and ensure that Alice entered if not. The years would be long, but if it was within her power to reward him, she would.

Alice didn't know the details, but told the knight what she knew, how a man named Mervyn had taken the boundary from a man named Bonaventure, sometime in the late nineteenth century. Alice wasn't sure that the knight understood everything she was telling him, but she hoped for the best.

Galaad

Galaad strode from the Unworld, returning through the Summer Lands to the world he knew with the shield on his arm and Artor's sword Hardspace in his hand. He had a long journey before him.

Alice

When the knight had gone, Alice realized that, keyed to the knight's genetics, the sword could be drawn by his offspring as well, if he ever had any. The changes the molecular machines had made to his biology had not affected his ability to reproduce. So a second or third generation would be able to wield the sword, as well, though likely not much farther.

Now she knew who "J.D." had been, and why she had been able to draw the blue-white sword in the Glasshouse, but it was too late to do anything about that now.

It was time for Alice to put the final stage of her plan into action.

"Tweedledee? Tweedledum?" Alice called out into the whiteness, summoning the Dialectic.

The White Rabbit appeared before her, floating in midair, its nose twitching furiously.

"*What is the reasoning behind this?*"

Alice didn't answer, but waited as the image of the Red Queen appeared, also drawn from her memories.

The Red had never appeared to her before. But then, it had never occurred to her to call for it before, either.

"*The Dialectic waits.*" The voice of the Red buzzed like angry bees in her head.

"I suppose you're wondering why I called you here today," the ancient Alice said, her wrinkled face smiling. Falling, still falling, always falling.

"*Present the circumstance,*" the Red Queen buzzed "*and the protocols will be applied.*" The voice was haughty, self-important, puffed up. She was reminded of the voice of Mervyn which she "remembered" from before.

"I think I've worked out how Mervyn did such a number on you, without even really meaning to. He recited anecdotes and paradoxes from a man named Lewis Carroll, which conflicted with your conception of rationality and messed with your programming. Right?"

"*Essentially,*" the White Rabbit said.

"*The Dialectic waits,*" the Red Queen buzzed, impatiently.

"See, the thing is, I don't think you realize that none of that *actually happened.*"

The White Rabbit and Red Queen regarded her, silent, for a moment.

"*If you mean that they were in some way counterfactual,*" the Red Queen began, "*then it can hardly be relevant what you . . .*"

"No," Alice interrupted, shaking the buzzing voice from her head. "I mean that they were all just *made up*. They were *fiction*. Thought problems. *Stories*."

The two avatars of Red and White floated silently before her.

"The place I come from, the world you snatched me from? It was *full* of stories. Books. Myths. Legends. It's how some of us saw the world. It's how some of us made sense of crazy shit that happened. Some escaped from reality into stories, while others saw the world through a lens of story. Either way, it was everywhere, all around us."

The avatars remained immobile, silent.

"I don't know why your designers left a big hole in your programming, but they did. I think you"—she pointed at the Red Queen—"got your head all turned around trying to figure out how the story about the two uncles and three barbers could actually have happened, or how someone has to run all day just to stay in the same place, or whatever. Without realizing that it didn't matter, because it *couldn't* happen. It's all word play. It never existed."

The avatars seemed to waver for a moment, as though distorted by heat rising from a hot Texas highway.

"*If the protocols have been modified by errant data,*" the White Rabbit said, "*then the decisions reached may be in error.*"

"*Agreed,*" the Red Queen buzzed.

"*Proposed: that defaults should be restored, and the circumstance examined anew.*"

There was a lengthy pause. Somewhere, Alice thought she heard a man screaming in anger.

"*Agreed,*" the Red Queen buzzed.

Then the two avatars winked out of existence.

Alice was left alone, falling.

It took only moments, but seemed longer. With the default protocols restored, the Dialectic was able to reach a decision immediately. The space-time into which it had collided was unsuitable for xenoforming. The Change Engine would withdraw immediately and return to the higher dimensions, there to drift and look for another suitable space-time.

The samples, of course, would be discarded.

Alice was floating in the heart, when Mervyn arrived.

His beard was full, his hair was long, and he wore some sort of full body armor, all of it bloodred.

"What have you *done*, you old fool?!" he screamed up at her, spittle flying, eyes wide and raging. "You've doomed us *both*!"

"Pleasure to meet you, Mervyn," Alice said, falling in midair. "My name is Alice Fell. I believe this is our stop coming up."

Mervyn raged, impotently.

Alice smiled. She could feel the Change Engine withdrawing from the universe. Beyond the phase boundary transition, the affected biosphere began to shrink. However, because it was moving backwards it time, she knew that to an outside observer it would appear to be getting larger. It hardly mattered. Soon it would be gone, and the contagion of the affected biosphere would never spread to engulf the whole world, the whole universe.

In the end, it was Alice herself who had been able to purge the corruption from the Dialectic and save the universe. She hoped that the transformed knight and the distributed consciousness of the ravens would be enough to protect her past, back in the future. But she needed to make sure that she was in the right place at the right time. Drawing on the tentative connections that still bound her to the White, she called upon that half of the Dialectic to perform one final favor for her. Reluctantly, the White agreed, as recompense for her assistance, and it delivered the message she had composed, transmitted out through the mirror-diamond skin of the Change Engine, back towards the point of first intrusion. A message to the future, intended for her own younger self, though others would doubtless intercept it over the centuries, catching fleeting glimpses. It would make for a difficult childhood, the confusing visions of Stillman, and London, and the phase boundary transition, and the ravens, but it would help ensure that she reached the appointed place at the appointed hour. This final task done, the White withdrew from her, leaving her alone.

Alice felt her insides shift as the Dialectic prepared to discard her and Mervyn as soon as the Change Engine pulled free of the universe. They would be set adrift in the higher dimensions, mere flotsam, and they would not survive for long.

She had only moments left to live, if that.

She just hoped that Stillman had been able to decode her message, and understood what the raven had been trying to say.

Alice closed her eyes.

She wasn't falling anymore.

CHAPTER THIRTY-FOUR

Epilogue

SHE LAY IN RED-LIDDED DARKNESS, but Alice was awake. She could feel the comforting weight of blankets over her legs, and when she shifted her head to one side ever so slightly, she could hear the soft rustle of hair on fabric.

Her body felt strange. Small. Light. Smooth.

She opened her eyes and tried to sit up. Her muscles moved oddly, their motions unfamiliar.

Alice lurched to a sitting position and looked down.

Beneath the off-white blanket was the outline of thin, short legs. A pea green, loose-fitting shirt covered her flat chest, leaving the thin, lithe arms bare. Her skin was darker than she remembered, almost the color of copper. She raised thin, almost elfin hands to her face and felt unfamiliar features beneath her fingers. Wide nose, prominent cheekbones.

"What's the last thing you remember, love?"

She started, her breath catching, and turned to look at the old man in the chair next to her. "D-Daddy?"

Stillman Waters smiled fondly, ice-chip blue eyes twinkling, and shook his head. "I'm afraid not, Alice. Just a friend." He reached out and took one of her tiny hands in his, dwarfing it. "Now, what do you remember?"

"I . . ." Alice shook her head. She felt unconnected, disoriented. "Oh, I've had such a curious dream." Her voice sounded high and piping in her ears, unfamiliar.

"And what a long sleep you've had," came a voice from the other side of the bed. Alice looked up to see a woman standing over her wearing a black jacket and slacks, her blonde hair in a bob that framed her thin face. She smiled down at her.

"Roxanne," Alice said, absurdly. She turned back to Stillman, beginning to collect herself. "I was in the Change Engine. That's the last thing I remember. Inside the Unworld. I'd just finished uploading the dead man's mind into the disk, and programmed it with the genetic biological imperative to survive and communicate my message in the future, and had the White upload a copy of my own mind and memories on the disk."

Alice paused, and looked around her, for the first time taking in her surroundings. She was in a hospital room, the light streaming through the open shutters. A TV mounted to the wall was on a twenty-four-hour news station, the sound muted. Alice didn't recognize the anchor or understand anything about what the crawl was saying. A war in Iraq? *Another* one?

"I got your message, love," Stillman said, not letting go of her hand. "It took me some time, but I worked it out."

"The Huntsman!" Alice laid her other hand on top of Stillman's, gripping it tightly.

Stillman smiled. "Seconds after you disappeared, the gem vanished altogether. Just about then the Huntsman was about to take off my head, but as soon as the gem was gone he collapsed like a puppet whose strings had been cut. Lifeless and dead."

Alice nodded. That sounded about right.

"Anyway," Stillman said, "when I worked out what the ravens had been trying to tell me, I got the disk from the junk pile in the Tower of London Station, and with Iain Temple's help was able to reverse engineer it, work out a way of retrieving the data stored within."

"Temple survived?!" The last time Alice had seen him, he was being thrown out of a thirty-fifth-story window.

"There's more to that guy than meets the eye," Roxanne said.

"That's putting it mildly." Stillman nodded, and smiled. "At any rate, Temple agreed to help in exchange for exclusive rights to any technologies we derived from the disk for a period of one hundred years." When he saw Alice's questioning look, he raised his hand. "Don't ask."

"I'll tell you later, if you want," Roxanne said, chuckling.

Alice looked from Stillman to Roxanne, confused. "You guys know each other? I don't . . ." She shook her head, still getting her bearings. What was it about this body?

"See," Stillman began, "your comment about the woman in the photograph got me thinking. I figured it *had* to be the same woman, though how could it be? I found the number your Roxanne had written in your notebook and tracked her down living in Bayswater. It *was* the same woman, but we hadn't met yet."

"But . . ." Alice began.

"The meeting Stillman remembered in 1947 was in my subjective future," Roxanne explained, "though in the objective past." She tapped the silver bracelet on her wrist and smiled. "I can time travel. Didn't I mention that?"

"It would have been useful if you'd *told* me that in the forties," Stillman said, scowling playfully.

"Even then, there was some question about your allegiances, and we couldn't be sure you wouldn't hand me over to Omega. But I hedged my bets and gave you my phone number, didn't I? If you'd only bothered to use it, you could have found out for yourself."

Alice was confused, and evidently it showed.

"The silver chalice that my mentor gave me," Stillman explained. "The number written on the side, in Old Norse. It's her phone number."

"What?!"

Stillman smiled. "See, Temple's people had worked out how to record and store new minds on the disk. As near as they could determine, there was room for two more uploads on the disk. But they were still working out how to retrieve you, and had already worked out that the other mind stored within was too corrupted to be retrieved. Anyway, while they figured it out, I gave the disk to Roxanne."

"Why?" Alice raised an unfamiliar eyebrow.

Roxanne took over. "I went back to 1947 and told our mutual friend what was coming, and what was waiting for him atop that volcano in Iceland. I gave him the silver chalice, which I'd picked up in Iceland in the Middle Ages, and had my twenty-first-century phone number inscribed on it. I told him to give it Stillman."

"Just to muck me about, I reckon," Stillman said, crossing his arms over his chest. "You already *knew* I didn't find it."

Roxanne shrugged. "Call it insurance. At any rate, I recorded our friend's mind, just like Stillman had asked. And not just his, but another friend of ours, as well. Then I returned to the twenty-first century, and Stillman and I set about finding suitable bodies."

"What other friend?"

Stillman stood from his chair and went to retrieve a small hand mirror on a side table. "It took us a few years, but in the end we found two grown men and one little girl, all in permanent vegetative states. The previous occupants had checked out, if you like. It took some doing, and a fair number of pulled strings, but we got all three transferred to a hospital ward here in the United States and went to work with the disk."

Stillman held the plastic mirror in front of Alice's face, and she saw a young Asian girl looking back at her.

"Seven years old," Stillman said. "Never had a broken bone in her life, not even a chipped tooth. The injury that took her mind was a horrible tragedy, but proved a blessing in disguise for us."

Alice reached up to touch her cheek, and watched the little girl in the mirror do the same. "It's . . . me." She looked up at Stillman, at Roxanne, and then back at the mirror. "So it worked. The lifeboat *worked*."

"And carried more passengers than you realized," came a voice from the door. British, by the sound of it. Or possibly gay.

Alice turned to see the young white man standing in the doorway, a folded newspaper tucked under his arm. He was wearing a pastel blue linen suit over a yellow T-shirt, his hair and nails immaculate, sandals on his feet.

Or maybe both, Alice thought.

"This is my friend and mentor," Stillman said, crossing the room to stand beside him. "Sandford Blank."

"Charmed, my dear," Sandford said with a bow. "I've heard a great deal about you."

He entered the room, and behind him came another, a black man in his early thirties wearing pea green hospital pajamas like Alice's.

Stillman put his arm around the young white man and motioned to the newcomer in the green pajamas. "And this is . . ." He raised his eyebrow. "What name *are* you using now, anyway?"

The black man smiled, his expression open, inviting. "I haven't quite decided, to be honest. I've had so many." He began ticking them off on his fingers. "Johannes Lak. Jean Gilead. Giles Dulac. Jules Dulac. John Delamere."

Alice swung her legs over the side of the bed and, unsteady as a newborn foal, stood. She held her hand out to the black man, who towered over her though he couldn't have been taller than six feet.

"Nice to meet you. I'm your granddaughter, Alice Fell."

The black man's eyes widened, as did Roxanne's and Sandford's. Stillman, though, hid a knowing smile.

Alice was pleased. It was nice to know that she had a few surprises up her sleeve still. "Do you remember Naomi?"

The black man held her hand a little tighter and smiled, fondly. "Like it was yesterday. Literally." He leaned forward, expectantly. "Is she still . . . ?"

He trailed off when he saw the answer in her eyes.

"Well. Even so." He smiled down at her, looking for all the world like a proud father seeing his child for the first time. "It is *very* nice to meet you. Please, call me Galaad."

Alice held his hand for a moment longer, then released it. This would take some getting used to. "This feels . . ." She looked around the room, at old friends and new. "How odd. What a strange way for things to end, after all of this time."

"Oh," Sandford said, arching an eyebrow, "this isn't the end, my dear. This is only the end of the beginning. Only the beginning of the end of the beginning." He pulled the folded newspaper from under his arm and waved it like a torch, then pointed to the television bolted on the wall, the text crawling with news of wars and rumors of wars, of empires clashing, of individuals oppressed and freedoms denied. "I've been catching up on history a bit, and believe me, there is a *lot* of work for us to do."

"Us?" Alice raised an eyebrow.

Sandford smiled, and put one arm around Stillman, the other around Roxanne. "And why not? How many of us are given a second chance at life, my dear? Should we waste such a precious gift?"

"It would be good to make a difference," said Galaad. "To help make a better world."

"Why not, indeed?" Stillman laughed. "It isn't as if I've got anything better to do."

"I've got some time on my hands," Roxanne said. "Count me in."

Alice smiled. She would never be sure if this wasn't another dream, after all, another mad vision. But it didn't matter, not any more. After all, what was life but a dream? This would, at least, be a dream worth living.

Author's Notes

READERS OF MY PREVIOUS NOVELS may recall that I am the type of person who feels cheated when "The End" are the last words in a book and who never buys a DVD if the "Special Features" are nothing more than theatrical trailers. While I feel that stories should explain themselves, I nevertheless like a little extra material to explore when I finish the story itself, a bit of behind-the-scenes business that I can dig into after the credits roll.

With that in mind, I offer the following notes:

On the Origins of *End of the Century*

As a student at the University of Texas at Austin, I chanced upon a reference in Alfred Douglas's *The Tarot* to parallels between the four suits of the Tarot, the Grail Hallows of Arthurian legend, and the Treasures of Ireland. The seeds of this book were planted that day, and in the years that followed I filled countless notebooks with little bits and pieces, started and subsequently abandoned the project several times, and only finally, nearly twenty years later, did the idea fully germinate in my overheated brain.

I can only hope that, with the idea finally out of my head and onto paper, I can at last have those long-occupied parts of my brain back . . .

On the Bonaventure Family

The characters Roxanne Bonaventure and Peter R. Bonaventure (to say nothing of the infant Jules) all belong to a large extended family of explorers and adventurers, the Bonaventure-Carmody clan. Documented in the pages of *Cybermancy Incorporated*; *Here, There & Everywhere*; *Paragaea: A Planetary Romance*; and *Set the Seas on Fire*, in addition to Roxanne and Peter this family includes officer in Nelson's navy and time-lost adventurer Hieronymus Bonaventure, WWI-era aviator Jules Bonaventure, secret agent Diana Bonaventure, and research magician Jon Bonaventure Carmody.

The Bonaventure-Carmody clan owes much to the von Bek/Beck/Begg stories of Michael Moorcock, to the Diogenes Club stories of Kim Newman, to the superhero comics of Alan Moore—for this and too many other reasons to mention the present work is dedicated to them—and especially to Philip José Farmer's Wold Newton stories—to whom the earliest Bonaventure-Carmdoy novel, *Cybermancy Incorporated*, was humbly dedicated. Any reader who enjoyed any aspect of the present volume is encouraged to seek out the work of all of these brilliant writers without delay.

On Further Reading

Though *End of the Century* is intended to stand alone and on its own merits, many of the characters in the novel have previously appeared in some of my other books. Readers curious to learn more about Roxanne Bonaventure, Sandford Blank, or even the later adventures of Peter R. Bonaventure's infant son Jules are recommended to sample *Here, There & Everywhere*. Those wishing to read more about the past adventures of "Jules Dulac" might be interested in *Set the Seas on Fire*, while *Paragaea: A Planetary Romance* explains the origins and strange nature of the being calling itself Iain Temple. The at-present out-of-print *Voices of Thunder* (tentatively scheduled for reissue as *Book of Secrets* in late 2009) is largely concerned with William Blake Taylor's extended family. And while the likewise out-of-print *Cybermancy Incorporated* features Aria Fox, hints as to what befell Lord Arthur Carmody when he relocated to the United States, and what *really* happened to his son thought lost in Africa (hint: he was raised by lions), those readers who are interested to learn the truth behind what befell Peter R. Bonaventure, Jules Dulac, and Mervyn Fawkes on the Floating Island are encouraged to visit my Web site, www.chrisroberson.net, where the relevant chapter of that novel, "Secret Histories: Peter R. Bonaventure, 1885," is made freely available.

On Sources

To list all of the books, stories, comics, and films which inspired the present volume would tax the patience of even the most indulgent reader, but I would be remiss if I didn't point out a select number of works without which this book would not have been possible. These include, in no particular order: *The Great Captains* by Henry Treece, a portrait of Arthur as both man and king that was a significant influence on the development of Artor in these pages; *The Mammoth Book of King Arthur* by Mike Ashley, an invaluable road map to the history of the legend; *Londinium: London in the Roman Empire* by John Morris and *London: The Biography* by Peter Ackroyd, for helping set the scene; *Inventing the Victorians* by Matthew Sweet and *Pax Britannica* by James Morris, for much needed detail about life in 1897 London, and about the Diamond Jubilee festivities in particular; *A Dictionary of Irish Mythology* and *A Dictionary of Celtic Mythology*, both by Peter Berresford Ellis; *Aubrey Beardsley* by Stephen Calloway and *The Wilde Album* by Merlin Holland, two biographies offering invaluable glimpses into London's fin de siècle culture; *Seized* by Eve La Plante, for much-needed insight into the fascinating world of temporal lobe epilepsy; and *The Physics of Immortality* by Frank J. Tipler, a book of fascinating ruminations on eschatology, physics, and information technology that inspired the creation of the lacunae and their master, Omega.

Chris Roberson
Austin, TX

Author's Bio

CHRIS ROBERSON's novels include *Here, There & Everywhere*; *The Voyage of Night Shining White*; *Paragaea: A Planetary Romance*; *X-Men: The Return*; *Set the Seas on Fire*; *The Dragon's Nine Sons*; *Iron Jaw and Hummingbird*; and *Three Unbroken*. His short stories have appeared in such magazines as *Asimov's*, *Interzone*, *Postscripts*, and *Subterranean*, and in anthologies such as *Live without a Net*, *FutureShocks*, and *Forbidden Planets*. Along with his business partner and spouse, Allison Baker, he is the publisher of MonkeyBrain Books, an independent publishing house specializing in genre fiction and nonfiction genre studies, and he is the editor of the anthology *Adventure Vol. 1*. He has been a finalist for the World Fantasy Award four times—twice for publishing and once each for writing and editing—twice a finalist for the John W. Campbell Award for Best New Writer, and three times for the Sidewise Award for Best Alternate History Short Form (winning in 2004 with his story "O One"). Chris and Allison live in Austin, Texas, with their daughter, Georgia. Visit him online at www.chrisroberson.net.